PRAISE FOR
RIDING WITH THE QUEEN

"Jennie Shortridge writes with an easy grace and a backbeat of the blues that lends a quiet authority to this novel of a woman trying to stay halfway sane in a wholly crazy world."

—Summer Wood, author of *Arroyo*

"A kick-in-the-pants read. Tallie Beck is as brassy a blues singer as you'd ever want to meet."

—Katie Schneider, author of *All We Know of Love*

"Like the novel she inhabits, Tallie Beck is funny, sexy, smart, and heartbreakingly real. A wonderful debut."

—Louis Redd, author of *Hangover Soup*

"A little bit country and a little bit rock 'n' roll, this skillfully written novel is gripping from the get-go."

—Caroline Hwang, author of *In Full Bloom*

Written by today's freshest new talents and selected by New American Library, NAL Accent novels touch on subjects close to a woman's heart, from friendship to family to finding our place in the world. The Conversation Guides included in each book are intended to enrich the individual reading experience, as well as encourage us to explore these topics together—because books, and life, are meant for sharing.

Visit us on-line at www.penguin.com.

RIDING WITH THE QUEEN

Jennie Shortridge

NAL Accent
Published by New American Library, a division of
Penguin Group (USA) Inc., 375 Hudson Street,
New York, New York 10014, U.S.A.
Penguin Books Ltd, 80 Strand,
London WC2R 0RL, England
Penguin Books Australia Ltd, 250 Camberwell Road,
Camberwell, Victoria 3124, Australia
Penguin Books Canada Ltd, 10 Alcorn Avenue,
Toronto, Ontario, Canada M4V 3B2
Penguin Books (N.Z.) Ltd, Cnr Rosedale and Airborne Roads,
Albany, Auckland 1310, New Zealand

Penguin Books Ltd, Registered Offices:
80 Strand, London WC2R 0RL, England

Published by New American Library, a division of Penguin Group (USA) Inc.

First Printing, October 2003
10 9 8 7 6 5 4 3 2 1

The author gratefully acknowledges permission to include the following copyrighted material:
"Riding with the King" by John Hiatt copyright © 1983 Careers-BMG Music Publishing,
Inc. (BMI). All rights reserved. Used by permission.
"Magic Man" copyright © 1976 Sony/ATV Tunes LLC. All rights administered by
Sony/ATV Music Publishing, 8 Music Square West, Nashville, TN 37203. All rights
reserved. Used by permission.

FICTION FOR THE WAY WE LIVE

REGISTERED TRADEMARK—MARCA REGISTRADA

Library of Congress Cataloging-in-Publication Data:
Shortridge, Jennie.
Riding with the queen / Jennie Shortridge.
p. cm.
ISBN 0-451-21027-1
1. Women rock musicians—Fiction. 2. Mothers and daughters—Fiction. 3. Failure
(Psychology)—Fiction. 4. Denver (Colo.)—Fiction. 5. Women singers—Fiction.
6. Sisters—Fiction. I. Title.

PS3619.H676R53 2003
813'.6—dc21   2003042085

Printed in the United States of America
Set in Goudy A Newstyle
Designed by Ginger Legato

For Shirley Frances,
who taught me to love books and who made me believe
I could do anything I wanted to do

ACKNOWLEDGMENTS

My heartfelt thanks to everyone who helped make this book a reality.

My family and my family of friends have been a continual well of love and support from which I dip often. My sisters and my dad also know the pain of living with a family member who has a mental illness; may we remember, too, some of the joy.

My band mates from long ago lived the life with me and gave me memories to last a lifetime. I promised them their own disclaimer: None of the characters in this book are real, except for Earache—how could I not use him? Thanks to everyone for the music, and special thanks to Mark Pray for the concept of "reltni."

I'd be nowhere without the generosity of fellow writers: the simpatico Lynne Kinghorn, Mary Bartek, Carol Bryant, Roxana Chalmers, Boni Hamilton, Lori Tobias, Mike Pikna, Sally Kurtzman, Angie Keane, Cathie Beck, and our dear departed Mary Halloran.

Good friends read early manuscripts and helped me believe it would one day be a book. Special thanks to Pam Vallone, Jeri Pushkin, Jon Pushkin, Ellen Johnson, Kari Burman, and others I fear I've forgotten. My literary angel, Sherry Brown, read and reread every word I wrote, and always found new and ingenious ways to keep me motivated. She is the heart of this book.

Julie Pysklo provided medical expertise and a literate eye, and her wonderful staff made me feel famous just rolling up my sleeve for a blood test.

My agent, Jody Rein, generously shared her expertise, guidance, friendship, and many a lunch. Her staying power and optimism kept our aim true, and sure enough, she hit a bull's-eye.

Leona Nevler, my editor, took a chance and made my dream come true. She understood the story and its characters implicitly, and her patient and meticulous attention to detail were invaluable.

Susan McCarty was always quick and friendly in responding to many questions, and I thank her for making the publishing experience a breeze.

And without my husband, Matt Gani, this book never would have been written. His love, unwavering belief, and indulgent support provided the foundation upon which this book was built. At the end of every day, I thank my lucky stars for bringing him across the ocean to me.

Tonight everybody's getting their angel wings
Don't you know we're riding with the king?

—"Riding with the King," John Hiatt

PART ONE

I'm going down this lonely road,
And where I'm bound it ain't my home.

—"Lonely Road," Big Gal Sal

1

The sun rises red-hot in the rearview mirror like an Atomic Fireball, one of those jawbreakers that always sounds like a good idea until you're halfway through it and sweating from the cinnamon burn and can't find a good place to spit it out. My eyes water at the mirror's fiery reflection, but after driving all night even a long blink could mean disaster. And, considering my destination, it feels a hell of a lot better to look back than ahead. I keep glancing up into that light, tracking the sun until it rises out of view and throws hot unforgiving light across endless rows of corn stretching in every direction.

Beneath me, the wheels beat out the rhythm of an old blues song: *I got them traveling blues, Lord. They got me down today.* The road goes on and on forever, disappearing finally at the edge of the earth into the empty morning sky. A sign flies by: GOODLAND 188, DENVER 432. I wish I was going someplace as happy-sounding as Goodland, but the plan is to arrive in Denver before nightfall.

Ahead, a band of blackbirds stands guard over a lump of roadkill, stubbornly holding ground until only a few yards remain between their prize and my wheels. When I'm close enough to see the blue sheen of their wings, they lift gracefully into the air. I become one of them, flying west over hundreds of miles of sweltering prairie, skimming low and stealthy across the earth's muggy surface. It's only a matter of hours now. I take a deep breath, shift in my seat, grip the wheel tighter. After being AWOL half my life, I'm going home.

In the distance a building floats miragelike on the flat Kansas horizon. I squint at it through the bug gut–painted windshield until it becomes a gas station. No, a truck stop. Caffeine. Thank God. I gun the hatchback I paid the drummer three hundred bucks for, almost everything I had, even though it looks like a rusty tin can. Even though what I really wanted was for him to come with me.

"What the hell is in Denver?" he said, green eyes shifting the way that lets you know this person no longer gives a damn about you, if, in fact, he ever did. He turned his lanky frame away, long blond ponytail hanging down his back, busying himself with tearing down his kit so he wouldn't have to deal with me. I could almost feel the soft hair in my grip, the snap of his head if I yanked, but I walked away, tossing the key in my hand like dice.

Granted, Denver is no musical Mecca. If I had a choice, I'd go to Memphis, or San Francisco, or even Austin, but I don't, so I concentrate on the truck stop instead, push the accelerator to the floor, the metal hot and sticky beneath my bare foot. As the speedometer needle licks seventy, the car rattles like a cheap tambourine. You'd think I'd have learned my lesson about dating musicians.

The truck stop morphs from mirage to piss yellow cinderblock with a hand-lettered sign: EAT AND GAS UP. At least they're honest. I pull off and a cloud of hot choking dust follows me across the gravel lot. Visions of home fries and runny eggs and strong smoky coffee fill me as I wind through pickups and fancy big rigs to an empty parking space near the door.

I turn the key and the engine shudders a lingering death. Two cowboys leaning against a fire red pickup turn their heads, smirks on their faces. I ignore them, take a deep breath, and pull the rearview toward me. I wipe mascara gunk from the corners of my eyes and pout like Madonna, fluff my hair into its usual curly lion's mane. Nothing helps—I look like hell.

Hoping for a miracle, I squeak open the hinged lid of the worn sky blue cosmetics case in the passenger seat. A gift from my mother for my sixteenth birthday, although she didn't pull her shit together enough to give it to me until the week after, when she finally reemerged from her bedroom, blinking and pale as a mole. I only keep the case because it's sturdy and roomy enough to hold all my trade secrets: ultra-size Aqua Net, black eyeliner, Miss Clairol Summer White, extra-coverage concealer, Secret roll-on in Shower Fresh scent, Shimmer Pink lipstick. The tubes and boxes and bottles lie jumbled in whatever order I last used them, and I dig through impatiently, my stomach twisting from not eating. What I really need is a cigarette, which I've been out of since 4 A.M., so no amount of makeup is going to make me feel better.

To hell with it, I decide, snapping the case shut. It's only a truck stop in Kansas. I reach down and pull on the strappy high-heeled sandals I wear onstage, even though they're probably too fancy for cutoffs and a jog bra. Leaning into the backseat, I rummage through one of my two battered cardboard boxes for a shirt, yellowed box-tape sticking to my arm. I pull free and a square inch of peach fuzz is liberated from my arm, so, to hell with the shirt, too, I decide, and kick my way out of the car. I hitch my bag onto my shoulder, lean over to roll up the window, and catch the cowboys staring at my chest.

"Never seen boobs before?" I call over, yanking down the stretchy fabric. "What are you, a couple of gay caballeros?"

The smirks slide from their faces and the bigger of the two turns his back. The little one hitches up his jeans, raises his chin to fix me with a tough-guy stare.

Whatever. I've got my own problems. I can't get the car to lock, no matter how I wrestle the key in the keyhole, no matter how many times I open the door, press the button, and slam the door shut. Everything I own is sitting in there: my stage clothes, my 1964 turquoise Stratocaster, my Shure SM58 microphone, bought with the first-ever real gig money I earned.

"Wanna let me have a stab at her?" a low voice says behind me, and I turn to see the big cowboy standing too close, smelling of diesel, sweat, and pomade. He's even bigger than I thought, bull-chested and a sadistic glint in his bloodshot eyes, and I wish now I hadn't egged him on.

"That's okay," I say. "It's just a piece-of-shit car and nothing works on it. No radio, no AC, and now, no locks." I laugh a little and shift from one strappy sandal to the other.

"Gimme the key." He stretches a hand toward me that looks like a slab of beef.

"No, thank you," I say, trying to sound polite. "I'll just keep an eye on it from the window." I start to squeeze by him and he snags the key from my hand and jiggles it in the lock. The button inside disappears from view.

"How'd you do that?"

"Sometimes they like to wiggle around a little, is all," he says. "Especially when they's kind of old and, uh, overly used." He throws a wink at his buddy and strides back toward the pickup.

I open my mouth to bite back, then lower my head and walk toward the door. I hate this feeling, this better-be-careful bullshit. It's the feeling I've worked my whole life to outrun.

The truck stop's dusty decor is a mixture of '50s diner and wagon-wheel chic, and half of the tables are occupied by men, young and old, in sweat-stained caps and faded brown overalls, dirty jeans and thread-worn cowboy shirts. After a quick stop at the cigarette machine, I head for the stainless steel counter, waiting for the customary feel of men's hungry eyes. It must still be too early in the morning, though, because not one greasy trucker lifts his head.

I straddle a rickety chrome stool. The cracked red vinyl seat is covered in dirty duct tape; it sticks to the underside of my thigh no matter how I reposition myself. A round, gray-headed waitress sees me, putting up a finger like she'll be with me in a sec, so I pull a laminated menu from between a napkin dispenser and a ketchup bottle and fire up a Salem. She's walking toward me with a cof-feepot and I'm pushing my cup at her when she says, "Sorry, hon."

"But it says 'smoking section' right on that little sign."

She sighs. She looks like a roly-poly bug in a pink waitress uniform. "No, I mean, sorry, we can't serve you without a . . . without proper attire."

I look down at myself, then back up. "You're kidding. Girls wear jog bras all the time these days."

She shakes her head and shrugs. "If it was up to me . . . but you know how it is. Wayne, he's the owner and he's a Christian."

"Wow, that's pretty Christian," I say, smiling, trying to win her over. I sure as hell don't want to go back outside with Buford and Bubba. "Is Wayne actually here today?" I look around but the only employees I see are a hair-netted Hispanic teenager flipping pancakes behind the window and a tired blonde working the tables. "I mean, what he doesn't know—"

"I really am sorry, hon," roly-poly bug says. "I'm not going to be able to serve you unless you put a shirt on. We've been having a lot of trouble lately with, you know . . ." She looks embarrassed. "Solicitations."

I stare at her and she sighs again. "Look, I know everybody's got to make a living, and I don't hold it against you none. We're just not that kind of place, okay?"

"You think I'm a hooker?" I say suddenly and too loud. Everyone in the place looks up. An old guy in a John Deere cap raises an eyebrow. "I'm not a prostitute," I hiss. "I'm a musician!"

"Well, then, hon, just get you a shirt and we'll be happy to serve you," she says, but I don't care anymore about food. I don't care anymore about coffee. I don't even care so much about Buford and Bubba.

Something in me wants to cry, at these clueless hicksville idiots, at the thought of getting back into that crappy tin can in this heat, at all the shit that's happened in the last twenty-four hours, but I pull it together, stub out my cigarette, stand, and clack my heels evenly across the linoleum and out into the hazy white sunlight. The cowboys' truck hasn't moved but they're nowhere to be seen, so I jump into the car like a Clyde-less Bonnie and hightail it the hell out of there, spraying gravel as I whip onto the highway.

Like some freight-train phantom from out of nowhere, a semi

whips around me, passing in a vacuum roar of wind so loud I barely hear the long horn blast. When he's pulled back into his lane in front of me, I check the rearview. There in the backseat sits a black woman wedged between my boxes. My breath catches like a plug in my throat at the sight of her, big-boned and impeccable in a red silk dress and black hat, head cocked and cherry red lips pursed in dismay. "Tallulah Jean Beck, pay attention," she says, shaking her head before she disappears.

I'd know her anywhere, but still.

2

♪ The rutted shoulder shakes the car mercilessly as I pull off the road. I need to rest and think and get a grip—I really should have gotten some sleep last night. Humid heat wraps around me like a steaming towel and I pick up an old cigarette pack, try to fan myself with it, then throw it to the floor with all the other trash. I do not look in the rearview again.

As a kid, seeing Big Gal Sal made me feel better, not worse. I don't remember a time when she wasn't in my life. In our house she was revered. I knew from birth that she was the Queen of the Delta Blues and that sometimes she was all that kept my mother from sliding into the cavernous sinkhole in her mind. Before I was even school-age, I knew Mom was happy when she'd play Sal's scratchy records on the stereo in the living room. We'd dance, doing sultry hoochie-koochie moves and singing, my baby sister, Jane, bumping along on Mom's hip. "She died the day you were born, Tallulah Jean," Mom liked to tell me in her silky Southern tenor. "She must have given you her voice to take care of for her, because I've never heard a five-year-old who can belt it out like you do."

During these bright periods I felt more love for my mother than I knew what to do with. The excess of it would make me giddy and nauseated, like being on a carnival ride. I knew even then that kind of love was dangerous—if I let my guard down too long, I wouldn't see the warning signs; I'd miss that crucial moment when she changed from light to dark and it no longer felt safe to be her daughter.

Sal was the only other grown woman in my life—even if she was dead. I'd look at her face on the album cover, big and round and dark like my snack-time Moon Pie, and I'd know she was watching over me. She died in a car crash the day Mom pushed me from her womb: April 17, 1964. Sal was on a comeback tour when she died, making her way from Memphis to Chicago, playing nights, driving days. She was sleeping in the back, they say. She never saw it coming.

I've done my share of crisscrossing the country, driving with no sleep after late-night shows, or sleeping in the back while someone else drove, but it spooks me, now, to have this connection, having to travel this far by myself across these cornfields. The car could lose its steering or the brakes could fail, leaving me twisted and bloodied in a pile of steaming wreckage. But it spooks me worse to have a ghost again as a supposed adult. What's that saying? The nut doesn't fall far from the tree.

Finally, I screw up enough courage to look into the backseat and see only my boxes, guitar case, rubber-banded sheet music and songbooks. Sweat trickles down my sides and damp heavy hair clings to my neck. I could use a dose of seventy-mile-per-hour wind coming through the windows, so I grab the steering wheel in one hand, the key in the other, and start the car. I turn my head to the left to check for oncoming traffic. "Pay attention," I remind myself, then ease out onto the blacktop.

The steering wheel is sticky beneath my fingers, which I *tap-tap* along to the song in my head: "Nowhere to Run" by Martha and the Vandellas. I look down at my hands and sigh. I started the drive with well-manicured fingernails—short on the left hand for pressing guitar strings to fretboard and long on the right for strumming. Now, they're all chewed short and I've started in on the leathery calluses on my fingertips, thick and stone-smooth from years of playing. I lift a hand from the wheel, find an edge of hard skin beneath my index fingernail, dig with my tooth, pull, spit. It hurts like hell to play guitar without them, but in Denver I'll only need to stroke smooth ivory keys.

The road clicks like a metronome, providing the downbeat as I sing. I used to make up songs while driving, wishing I had one of those mini-cassette recorders so I wouldn't forget a lyric or snippet of melody. Jedd always said the good ones stuck, not to worry about the rest. Of course, he said that back in the early days, when marrying me was the best thing he'd ever done. Before he turned on me, saying my songs sucked, my voice was all wrong, I was washed up. Before he became the big star, transforming from Jedd Maxfield into '80s icon Jett Maxx. Now look who's washed up. No one listens to metal-lite hair music anymore, not even thirteen-year-old boys.

I'm sure there's talk that I'm a has-been, too, that I've sunk to the level of human jukebox, singing only other people's songs. It's true I haven't written a new song in a while. Maybe that's why Lyle decided the band should go in a "new direction," without me. Whatever. This new gig will give me a place to settle down for a while, develop some new material. Make a demo, maybe. I still have my looks, my moves. And my voice, thanks to the Big Gal.

Yesterday, halfway through our twelve-week tour, my band, the Blue Light Specials, and I showed up for a five-night stand at the Nose Dive, a run-down blue-collar joint somewhere near St. Louis. The tour hadn't been going all that well anyway—people just weren't coming out to see us like they used to—but I knew from the moment we walked into that place that something was going seriously south.

There was the usual smoky din of locals swilling happy-hour beer and the nondescript thumpy music people listen to these days coming from the jukebox. It was a bar like any other, except no one looked up when we came in, and the bartender folded his arms at the sight of us. Where our posters should have been, hastily produced flyers read DJ KENNY TONIGHT: DANCE TO YOUR FAVORITE '80s TUNES.

"What the hell," I said to the guys, but they looked baffled, too. "Well, we have a contract, right?" I reasoned. "We should go about business as usual." After a quick powwow it was decided that the bass player would call Lyle from the pay phone, and the rest of us would set up our gear.

I ambled over to the bartender to finagle some information. That, and a drink. "Can I have my first-set drink early?" I asked, sweet as can be.

"I don't think there's going to be a first set," he said.

"You know, we do have a contract, and our bass player's on the phone right now with our agent"—after all these years I still love saying "agent"—"and I'm sure it will all be straightened out soon. So, could you make me a bloody?"

"Suit yourself. You're just going to have to tear all that stuff back down," he said, but he mixed me the drink.

When we had most of the gear up, I shielded my eyes from the overhead light cans and said into the mike: "Can somebody turn down the house music while we do a sound check?" I waited a beat or two, but the *thump thump* from the jukebox didn't stop.

"Hello?" I called out, then stepped off the stage and made my way back to the bar. The bartender stared past me.

"Could you turn off the jukebox?" I asked, leaning onto the bar to expose some cleavage. It never hurts.

His jaw worked a plug of chew. "Don't know how," he said and picked up a Bud can to spit into.

"Well, then, do you mind if I do it?" I asked, annoyed now but still playing nice.

He shrugged. "Knock yourself out."

I leaned farther onto the bar and saw his eyes dart down. "So, who's the manager around here anyway? You?"

"Kenny," he said, looking me straight in the eye again. "And your tits are getting wet."

"Shit." I straightened up, dripping beer or God knows what, grabbing cocktail napkins to blot where I'd leaned into a puddle. "You could have told me sooner."

Finally he smiled, then turned and strolled to the other end of the bar to yuck it up with a couple of construction workers who'd been watching the whole thing.

"Losers," I muttered under my breath, heading for the jukebox. I yanked the cord from the wall, relieved at the silence, and walked over to the bass player who was still on the pay phone.

He rolled his eyes at me and shook his head. "Okay, but, damn, Lyle," he said, turning his back, lowering his voice, "you have to tell her."

Whatever I'd felt when I first walked in was nothing compared to this. This was sirens and warning bells and emergency vehicles running through my blood. I thought I might hyperventilate and fall over. "Tell me what?" I asked, and the bass player handed me the phone.

I must have blanked out during the conversation, because I remember only pieces of it, but they are banner slogans printed indelibly on the inside of my forehead: musical tastes have changed, the tour's been canceled for lack of interest, the guys are going to back some new singer named Rio who's more "current" (I pictured nose rings and tattoos). I came to again when Lyle was saying he'd gotten me a steady gig in Denver. That would be good for me, right? Since I had family there and all? Since I was so low on funds?

I believe my reply was something along the lines of "Fuck you, Lyle." The next thing I remember is the guys all standing and shuffling around the reloaded van, no one saying a word, not even the drummer, and me in the shit trap of a car, pulling away and making sure I didn't cry.

I hit the road for good at seventeen, and from that first step out my mother's door I breathed easier, laughed harder. Whenever thoughts of home rushed in I'd drown them in beer, pot, whatever I could get my hands on, including a tight piece of ass, until the thoughts were faded pictures, the images rubbed away and the corners worn smooth. I've loved my life on the road, but I don't know what I'll be anymore when I arrive at the end of this stretch. Somebody's long-lost daughter, maybe. Somebody's shithead of a sister.

At the Kansas/Colorado border, I pull into a gas station to pee, grab a Diet Pepsi and some Fritos. I slide back into the car like maybe I could just keep driving forever, but then I climb back out and crunch over gravel to the grimy phone booth. I remember Jane's married name, but the husband's first name is a mystery.

"Could it be Andrew?" the operator asks. "I have a listing for Andrew and Jane Gladstone on Meadowlark Circle."

"That's it," I say, relieved and queasy at the same time. That clammy sick feeling made me hang up the few times I tried to call over the years, but now I swallow hard and say, "Could you connect me? Collect, from Tallie."

Then, there's Jane's voice, calm and deliberate, mature, but I recognize it. If I'm thirty-four, that means my little sister is thirty, something I have a hard time picturing. She was thirteen, all knobby knees and elbows the last time I saw her, but now on the phone she sounds more adult than I'll ever feel.

She accepts the charges.

"It's me," I say, hoping to start out friendly and familiar. She has to be mad at me. As far as she knows, I haven't tried to contact her once in the seventeen years since I left her alone with our mother, and here she is all grown up and married and a mother herself.

I only know this much about her because Mom tracked me down through Lyle one Christmas years ago and sent a card and letter with a photo of Jane, the husband, and a bundle of yellow blankets. I cursed myself for the one weak moment when I'd given Mom Lyle's number, and I asked him not to be so goddamned forthcoming with my whereabouts after that. Even though he lectured me about the importance of family, I never got another card or letter.

At the other end of the line, Jane sighs. After a long moment, she says, "Where are you?"

"It's called Kanorado, believe it or not," I say, trying to laugh a little, cool, casual. I pull a long drag off my Salem. "It's on the Kansas border with Colorado. Get it? Kan-o-rado."

The phone is silent. A truck roars by so I push the phone harder against my ear. "You there?"

"Yeah," she says like she wishes she wasn't.

"Anyway, our tour just ended," I continue quickly, not mentioning the canceled part, "and I've got a gig in Denver." She still doesn't reply. "A long-term gig."

Finally, she sighs again. "And you need a place to stay." Her voice is flat.

"Just for a few days, until I find my own place," I say. "I'll be making good money, my agent says. I'll be out of your hair in no time."

I'm thankful she's the one who brings it up so I don't have to ask. She was always good like that. She took care of things, especially our mother. I gave up on Mom years before I left home, but not before our father did. He hit the road so long ago I can barely remember his starched white shirts, the smell of hair tonic, a wedding band shiny gold when he'd swing me in dizzying circles out in the yard.

Without too much more prompting, Jane tells me her address. I clench my cigarette between my teeth and scramble in the bottom of my bag for a pen, then write her careful instructions in my palm, nearly drawing blood as the ink runs dry.

3

Jane's neighborhood is one of those "planned communities" they build these days in old farm fields and pastures, houses huddled together like cows in a herd. Curving streets with similar names hold rows of hulking monstrosities that are all garage and surrounded by neatly clipped green grass and gravel-lined walkways. Most of the streets end in cul-de-sacs, going nowhere.

After driving around for what feels like hours, I finally find Meadowlark Circle, and there sits Jane's house, just where she said it would be. I slow down and check the address against the smeared one in my palm. This is it.

My hands shake on the wheel, my pulse speeds up. To relax, I hum a god-awful Kenny Loggins song we covered years ago, "I'm Alright." I drive another half block and pull over between two houses so no one thinks I'm casing their place, bump the curb, kill the engine.

Leaning into the backseat, I rummage through a box until I find a T-shirt that isn't too wrinkled and pull it on. I slip my feet into the strappy sandals and notice chips in the red polish on my toenails. Lifting my arm, I sniff to see if I need more Secret, and notice someone, a kid, staring at me from across the street. It's wearing a baseball cap, T-shirt, and jeans. Shoo, I think, avoiding its gaze as I apply deodorant, fluff my hair with spritzes of Aqua Net. I dig through my cosmetics case and pull out the major artillery, making a big show of applying my makeup. If it is a girl, she'll need to know this anyway. If it's a boy, whatever. To each his own.

When I finally look presentable, I take three deep breaths, start the car, drive around the block, and pull into Jane's driveway like I knew how to find it all along. My heart is pounding like a bass drum now, but I put on my show-time face: all-knowing, amused by the world, but cool. I climb out of the tin can and fast food wrappers and pop cans follow me. I'm stuffing them back inside when I see the rug-rat kid walking toward me. I ignore him/her, kick the door shut with a solid *chunk,* and walk confidently to Jane's door. After another deep breath, I ring the bell.

The door opens with a whoosh, and a cool wave of air conditioning soothes my arms, my face. There stands a frumpy housewife with a mud-colored bob of hair and no makeup, wearing khaki shorts and a sleeveless denim blouse. Big mistake with those arms, I want to tell her, but I smile. This woman could be anyone, but I take a guess.

"Jane?"

It must be her. The serious expression is familiar, and I feel a pinch in my gut at the big cow eyes.

"Emma," she says, looking behind me, so I'm guessing she doesn't recognize me, but then she says, "Meet your aunt Tallie."

I turn and look into another pair of brown eyes, set in a pointed little face under a black baseball cap. The kid.

"Hey, wow, yeah," I stammer. Of course it would be getting big by now. "I'm your . . . yeah, I guess I'm your aunt all right." I hope the kid won't mention my primping to her mother. We all stand there in awkward silence. No one seems very glad to see me.

"Did you have any trouble finding the place?" Jane finally asks, still standing in the doorway, arms barricaded across her chest. I'm not so sure she's going to let me in.

"Oh, no. Not at all," I say, laughing, shaking my head, thinking how good a cigarette would taste. "No problemo."

"She drove by like eighty times," the kid, Emma, says and pushes past me into the house.

"Yeah, well. I found it," I say, trying not to sound irritated. Maybe I should have looked up Jedd instead. I hear he built a big house up in the foothills, Evergreen or some ritzy place like that. I hear he still lives on his royalties.

Jane sighs and backs up into the house, motions me in. "Don't you have any stuff? A suitcase? Bag?" I picture the boxes in my car, the torn sides and years of yellowing tape holding them together, and wonder how I'll get them in without her seeing me. She turns without waiting for an answer and walks up a wooden staircase, her rear end another indicator she hasn't been counting calories. Emma stands in the foyer, skinny and sullen, thumbs hooked in the front pockets of her jeans. I try a smile, but her expression doesn't change. I follow Jane up the stairs.

The house smells like a combination of potpourri and something cooking. It's not a totally unpleasant smell. "Nice place." I try to be polite, checking out all the doodads she has hanging on the walls, embroidered things, a plaster heart embedded with a small handprint, little mirrors in brass frames. It reminds me of the room we shared as kids. Her side was decorated with her drawings, awards from school, knickknacks, and neat as an old lady's. My side was perpetually messy, clothes and school papers seeming to sprout from the floor. My decorating consisted of a poster of the Jackson 5, and later, when I got cooler, Heart. Even then, I tried to be away from home as much as possible.

"Here's your room," Jane says from a doorway down the hall. A line of fluffy pink throw rugs leads to the floral-themed bedroom, small and obviously unused. Something tells me smoking here is out of the question.

"Nice," I say, sticking with polite mode, nodding at prints of young girls in old-fashioned dresses, a stiff-looking flowery bedspread and curtains, dried floral arrangements covered with a fine layer of dust. "Hey, I really appreciate it, you know?"

Jane stares at me blankly.

"Where did you say you had a job?" Her tone says she doesn't believe I actually do.

"Oh, God, thanks for reminding me. I need to call my agent, see when I start." Oozing confidence. "It's some piano bar place, downtown."

She nods and walks out.

"So can I use your phone?" She doesn't reply, even as I follow her back out into the hall, down the stairs, and into the kitchen. There she points to a phone hanging on the wall next to a neatly organized bulletin board. Everything is clean and tidy, in its place. There isn't a dirty dish on the counter, a crumb on the kitchen table. I pick up the phone and dial. Emma enters the kitchen and takes a seat at the table, still eyeing me as she takes off the hat. A wimpy mop of brown hair falls to chin length. Her hair is cut exactly like her mother's.

I smile as I wait for Lyle to answer. "So you do have hair," I try, an olive branch.

"What happened to yours?" she replies, just as Lyle picks up.

"Hey, Lyle. It's me." I ignore the kid's rude comment, thanking my lucky stars I have a paying gig so I can get the hell out of here as soon as possible. "I'm in Denver, at my sister's."

"Tallie! Good girl, you got there in plenty of time."

"Well, of course I did, Lyle. Jesus, what'd you think?" Emma's listening intently, even though she's pretending to study a hangnail, so I put on my best professional voice. "So what's the story with this gig? When do I start?"

"Tallie, honey. Slow down. Let's see, I've got the paperwork right here. Okay . . ." He pauses, reading. "The auditions are next week, Monday through—"

"Uh, excuse me, Lyle, I think you've got the wrong paperwork," I say. "You said it was a job, not an audition." I try smiling at Emma again. She ignores me.

"Tallie, honey. Remember? I said audition. I said it was as good as yours, but I said audition."

"Fuck!" I yell. Emma and Jane both jump. "Audition! What the hell are you trying to do to me, Lyle?"

Emma's eyes and mouth go round as Jane quickly ushers her into another room, scowling as she passes. I try to convey with a shrug and sign language that this is a serious problem, here, but she ignores me.

"Now, Tallie—" Lyle says.

"I am not auditioning for some stupid piano bar, Lyle. You said I had the job! You made me leave the band for"—I try not to let the waver into my voice—"for this? I mean, what the"—I decide to take pity on Jane—"what the heck have I been working for all these years? And what kind of agent are you anyway?"

"Now, Tallie, you know and I know you're not in a position to be pulling any prima donna shit here. But you're gonna get the gig, right? You just have to open your mouth and you're gonna get it. Come on, now."

"Jesus, Lyle."

"Who else has the pipes you do, the bod, right? Wear something low-cut, you got it. Right?"

"Yeah, yeah." He's almost always right. "But goddamn it, Lyle. You acted like I had the job. I mean"—I lower my voice—"I told my sister I had it and everything."

"You'll knock 'em dead, Tal." At least he always has confidence in me. I write the name of the place—Sing Out, how corny is that—and the address and the name of the person I'm supposed to see on a notepad by the phone. Audra Lyon. A woman. So much for the low-cut approach.

After I hang up, Jane stalks back into the kitchen, fuming. "I will not put up with that kind of talk in my house," she says. She is standing as far away from me as she can and still be in the same room. "You lied about having the job and you look like death warmed over." She scowls and looks me over, hand on her hip. "Are you on drugs or something?"

"God, Jane, I'm just tired. You would be too if you drove all godda—all night. Give me a break." I look at my ragged fingernails, stuff my hands into my pockets. A ripple of panic makes my head tingle—she's going to kick me out before I've even unpacked. I look into those big brown eyes, try to transmit telepathically: Please, let me stay.

"You smell awful," she finally says. "Why don't you go take a shower?" Then she turns and strides from the kitchen.

This is some homecoming.

"What were you expecting, child, the welcome wagon?"

I hear the voice, but I won't look.

"Okay, have it your way," Sal says, and, even though I don't want to, I turn my eyes in the direction of her voice, just in time to see a flash of red silk disappear.

4

I can't remember the last time I touched up my roots. It must have been in Milwaukee, in that prison green motel room that smelled like wet dog, or maybe in Cincinnati, where we shared a room in the back of the bar. Otherwise, we've been sleeping in the van, so it's been at least a couple of months. Now my long blond curls are attached to my head by a cap of muddy brown roots. Thank God I got a perm when I was still making some money.

I reach into my blue case sitting on the toilet seat in Jane's bathroom and pull out the Summer White. The audition is less than a week away, and I've never felt so unprepared. I pull on the plastic gloves, fill the applicator, clamp my finger over the top, shake. I haven't played a real piano in years, just short-keyboard synthesizers. Maybe I can go to a mall music store, say I'm looking to buy a piano so they'll let me noodle around on one. I'm squeezing the solution onto my hair when a loud knock on the door makes me jump. A splotch of bleach lands on yet another pink throw rug.

"What?" I grab a tissue to blot at the bleach. A perfect, quarter-size circle of white glows on the rug.

"Are you going to be in there forever?" Emma says in an exasperated tone from the other side of the door. Apparently she hasn't heard that children are supposed to be polite to grown-ups.

I toe the end of the rug with the spot underneath the cabinet, toss the tissue into the pink wastebasket, and pull the door open. Emma stands there with her arms crossed over her skinny chest, a miniature version of her mother.

"Do you need to pee or something?" I ask, displaying my gloved hands, the bottle of bleach solution. " 'Cause I have to get this stuff on or I'm going to end up striped. Like a skunk." I wink, trying to coax a smile out of her.

She stands and stares at me, then grimaces. "Eww, gross. That stuff smells." She pinches her nose closed with her fingers. "Whad are you doig?"

"Well, it's probably no secret, but I'm not a natural blonde. It takes work to get my hair like this." I wave a handful at her, which actually stabs outward, it's gotten so stiff and brittle. I'd forgotten how dry Denver's climate can be.

She unclamps her nose. "You're just ruining it," she says.

"Excuse me," I say, swinging the door closed. Jane and I may not have grown up in the best of circumstances, but at least we had manners.

"Mom," Emma calls as she clomps down the stairs. "She's stinking up the bathroom with hair dye. And she spilled it on the rug."

There goes a chunk of my first paycheck before I even have the damned job.

I listen for a response from Jane, but all's quiet. After I apply the bleach, I set my mental alarm for twenty minutes and sneak a couple of puffs from a cigarette with the fan on full blast. Then I fill the time repainting my toenails, filing my fingernails smooth, tweezing stray hairs from my lip, my eyebrows. The bathroom's fluorescent light is not flattering. I see every pore alongside my nose, the lines etched from each nostril to the corners of my mouth, the dark bruised look around my eyes. And a turkey gobbler is forming along the front of my neck when I look down, which I vow never to let myself do in public again. I thrust my chin forward, turn my head to a three-quarter view. It's an old trick from having promo photos taken.

The shower feels like heaven when I finally get in, luxuriously hot and steamy. I can't remember the last time I had a decent one. The shower in Milwaukee spat rusty-looking water when I turned the tap. I've learned to live on sponge baths in public restrooms and Secret.

"There ain't nothing I can do, nothing I can say," I sing as I lather my hair with Jane's shampoo, some discount store brand, working the foam through to the ends. Next to Big Gal Sal, Bessie Smith is my favorite. *"That folks won't criticize me."*

As my hair becomes saturated, it straightens to almost waist-length. When it's dry, the perm springs it up to my bra line. Something doesn't feel right, though, as I run my fingers through my hair, and I stop singing. A hunk of it comes off in my hand, and then another, and I feel like I'm in the middle of some bad dream, like where you're running around naked, or your feet are stuck in mud. I'm grasping the horror that my hair is rapidly detaching itself from my head, and I know I'm wide awake because I can feel the hot water on my neck and shoulders, I can see hair and foam swirling around my feet near the drain, I can hear myself screaming bloody murder.

Then there's banging on the door, and Jane shouting, "Are you okay?" I step from the shower, water puddling on the floor, and unlock and open the door. Jane stands there, wide-eyed, as I thrust my handfuls of hair at her and cry, "What's happening to me?"

Emma hangs gape-mouthed behind her, but Jane shoos her away, then steps into the bathroom and closes the door. She grabs a towel from the rack and wraps it around me, tucking the corner in at the top so it won't fall down. In a calm voice she says, "Shh, it's okay. Let's have a look." She moves my case from the toilet and I sit there, staring at my handfuls of hair while she inspects my head. "Major breakage," she says, pulling away a matted blond clump.

"Oh, God, no," I moan. "Not my hair. How bad is it?"

"Bad," she says, dumping the hair into the wastebasket. "I think we'd better take you to Ramon, my hairdresser."

No offense, I want to say, but look what Ramon's done to you. Realizing, however, that: a) I probably have no choice, and b) she's actually being nice, I just nod.

"You get dressed," she says, all business now, "and I'll give him a call. See if he can take you right away."

She guides me out of the bathroom, past Emma, who starts to say, "Told you s—" before her mother shushes her, and into my room. My boxes of clothes sit on the floor next to the Early American pine dresser, and in this potpourri environment even I can tell they smell like a bar, with that smoke-beer-vomit stink fouling the room.

I sit heavily on the bed in my pink towel, still dripping, wads of hair still in my hands. I'm afraid to look in the mirror. I'm afraid to even touch my head, let alone towel it off. A familiar, old feeling paralyzes me, the tingly crazy sensation that makes me think one day I'll turn out just like my mother. At times like these I try not to think about her, but I usually don't get a say in the matter, it just comes flooding back.

Mom vacuuming at two in the morning, humming, stomping around like it's two in the afternoon. Jane climbing out of bed, walking to the living room, turning off the vacuum, leading Mom to her room. Mom murmuring, "But I'm not the least bit tired," then not getting out of bed until after we get home from school the next day, her bedroom ransacked as if by an intruder, her face pale and slack.

Another late night, and Mom in our bedroom doorway, wrapped tightly in an old crocheted afghan, hair on end like the bride of Frankenstein. Mute. Wild-eyed. A steak knife protruding from the folds of the blanket. "Don't go," I whisper to Jane, and we pretend we're sleeping. The next morning we walk warily into the kitchen. Mom hums an old tune as she scrambles eggs with American cheese and chopped-up hot dogs, just the way we like them.

When I was little, I would lock myself in our bedroom when Mom became her other self. I'd listen to Big Gal Sal, tracing her face on the album cover with my fingers as the stylus traced the scratchy grooves of the record, and sing along, drowning out whatever was happening on the other side of the door. But as I got older, I got angrier. Yelling at her did no good. She'd freak out even worse, and then Jane wouldn't speak to me. I learned that the best thing was to escape, to stomp from the house, slam the door. Dredge up one of the other bad kids in the neighborhood to hang out with. Party, which, at that age, meant sneak cigarettes and beer pilfered from someone's parents. Creep back in late at night, looking for some all-clear sign, like no lights on, everyone sleeping, or Mom watching Johnny Carson, a blue glow illuminating her face in the dark living room. She was usually okay again if she was watching Johnny Carson.

It's not that Mom was crazy all the time—just sometimes. But those times came faster and got worse as Jane and I grew older, especially after Dad left. Sometimes she'd manage to hold on to whatever legal secretary job she had at the time, but sometimes she wouldn't leave her room for days. Then, of course, she'd be "let go." She never said "fired." And when she wasn't working she'd act like it was no big deal. "I can take in typing," she'd say. "There's always plenty of typing to be done."

But when she was really gone, really whacked out, there was no typing, no money coming in. There was a secret, unbreakable rule in our family that we were not to tell anyone at school, any of our friends or their parents about our predicament. We didn't have close ties to other relatives—Mom and Dad were Denver transplants, far from home. And later, without Dad, the three of us were all each other had. Even as kids, Jane and I knew better than to put our tenuous family at risk by telling anyone our mother's secrets. We would just lie low, try to eat less, making cereal for breakfast, lunch, and dinner, waiting for the magic moment when Mom would become her good self again and take over.

Ramon isn't so awful. In fact, he's kind and sympathetic. "Sorry, hon," he says. "It's got to go."

"But why?" I say, trying to keep my chin from quivering. "What happened?"

"Overprocessed. Too many chemicals for too long." He fingers my remaining hair gently. His touch is comforting. "And you just got into town? The dry air must have been the final straw."

"She bleached it," tattles Emma, sitting in the row of dryer chairs behind us, smacking purple lips as she inserts a huge grape lollipop into her face. It bulges like she has mumps.

"Mind your own business, young lady," Jane says, and Emma picks up a magazine, sulks behind it.

Ramon snips here, snips there, and my long damp tresses fall to the floor in surrender. "What, uh, style are we going for?" I ask.

"Very in, very cutting-edge, a sexy boyish crop. An Audrey Hepburn kind of look," he says, working quickly, sliding around the chair in a circle until he's in front of me and I can no longer see myself in the mirror. When he moves away and I reappear, a skinny twelve-year-old boy sits in front of me. I wish I had put on some eyeliner, some lipstick.

Jane leans in next to me, looking into the mirror. Emma steps up, pulls the sucker from her mouth, eyes wide. She's quiet, for once.

"Wow, there's quite a resemblance, once you get rid of the hair," Ramon says, standing back, scissored hand on his hip.

"Yeah," Jane says, sighing, studying the three of us. "That's the funny thing about families."

In the reflection, I see the door behind us swing closed on the ample backside of a large black woman in a red silk dress.

5

Jane shoved Emma off on me this morning when I said I had to go to the mall. She said, "I need some time to myself. Consider baby-sitting as payment toward your room and board." Then, to top it off, she said, "Oh, and if you must smoke"—big emphasis on *must*—"I'd appreciate it if you'd do it on the back porch." Like she could smell the few puffs I blew out the window last night.

"Turn left here," Emma says from the passenger seat. She has to raise her chin to see over the dash.

"How old are you anyway?" I ask. "Seven? Eight?"

She turns to fix me with a cold stare. "I just turned ten."

"But I got your baby picture, like, seven years ago."

"What was the year?" She sounds impatient.

"Year? God, I don't know." I try to remember. I was in that top-forty band with the horn section and two drummers, and we were doing Phil Collins and Mr. Mister covers. Not the best gig, but I was between bands at the time, depressed about Jedd's success and my floundering. Lyle saved my butt by having me fill in while the lead singer had a baby. "I guess it must have been about 1989-ish? Maybe 1990?"

"Do the math."

"Do you always speak to adults this way?"

Emma turns away and tugs her cap low on her brow, speaking only to give me directions.

I feel like Emma, wearing my own stupid cap, although mine is cooler than hers. It's from a tequila promotion in a bar in Oklahoma City and the front of it reads SUCK ON THIS. I think it's funny. Jane said it's appalling. Her word. She's so sheltered she didn't know about tequila hookers, how you suck a lime wedge after licking salt from the back of your hand and throwing back a burning shot of Cuervo Gold.

After meeting the husband, I understand. He's good-looking enough, blond, tall, but as boring as a box of saltines. They've been together since they met in their sophomore year at CU. Jane's probably never slept with anyone else—turns out they got married that same year, and Jane quit school to raise Emma. It doesn't require advanced math skills to figure that one out. I wonder if either of them has ever experienced any true excitement, arousal, the stuff that makes life worth living, or did, before I became a poster child for Rogaine.

I miss my hair. It still feels like a bad dream when I reach up and nothing's there. It feels like petting a dog, that inch of lifeless nothing lying flat against my head. How can I perform looking like this? I'll whip my head around and nothing will fly wild through the air. I'll have no tender curls falling into my face during ballads. I'll look small and meek on stage, with all the presence of a geeky schoolboy. I won't be "the smoking queen of blue-eyed soul" or "the red-hot lioness of the Midwestern club scene" anymore. I've memorized every good thing ever written about me in reviews, even if they were in college papers and small-town rags. What could someone possibly write now? "The bald chick who, oh, yeah, happens to sing well?" There are enough Sineads in the world.

South suburban Denver has changed. Chain restaurants and strip malls fill what used to be open fields, and acres of housing developments spread east to the horizon and west to the mountains. Off in the distance the jagged skyline of downtown is taller than I remember it, skyscrapers spiking the flat plain. When I left Denver it was still a cow town, although I didn't realize it at the time.

After doing all we could for ourselves around Colorado,

Wyoming, and Nebraska, Jedd and I had headed for Los Angeles with our band, the Holy Rollers. That was our name at first, although we changed it when we kept getting booked at church group functions and religious singles' dances. We became the Holy Smokes, and no one was confused anymore. We were young and hopeful and certain we'd be stars in no time. We'd been big in Denver, gigging at the best clubs, getting airplay on local radio, playing warm-ups for national acts coming through. When we arrived in LA, we realized what small potatoes we were.

The booking agent we found in the yellow pages sent us to small, cavelike bars that catered to bottom feeders. We'd also called a handful of other agents who mostly ignored us, but Lyle came to a dingy biker bar we were playing one night and signed us after the first set. He sent us out on tour, the Midwestern circuit. "Good place to get your feet wet," he'd said, his rings flashing as he puffed his stinky cigar. We didn't care where it was. It was the most exciting thing that had ever happened to us.

"You missed the turn," Emma's saying in that snotty tone.

"Why didn't you tell me?" I crank the wheel, pull into the next turn lane.

"I did. Hey, U-turns are illegal, you know."

"Yeah. Whatever." I whip around, then turn into the mall parking lot, navigating the confusing road system that rings the shopping center. "What the hell is this about?" I ask, trying to find a way into the parking lot.

"Traffic control. And you're not supposed to cuss in front of me. Mom said." Emma looks worried, peering up over the dash, gripping her armrest. Her nervousness satisfies me, and I finally find the correct turn and make my way to a parking space near Dillard's, a department store from the looks of it.

"What happened to Joslin's, and May D and F?" I ask, naming the department stores from my childhood.

"Never heard of them." Emma carefully unbuckles her seat belt. It's probably the first time that particular safety device has ever been used, I think with a sudden pang. I remember being in that seat in the fully reclined position, the drummer on top of me, my knees jammed against the console and the passenger door. I remember wishing we had a room of our own, a bed, hell, even a couch, but we didn't. We were just thankful he had a car.

"Hellooo." Emma is standing outside her door.

"Just let me check my face," I say, pulling the rearview toward me. I tug the cap lower on my head, glancing into the backseat. It's empty, of course. I climb out, heels banging against the door frame. Emma walks in front of me, like we're not really together. We enter the store through the glass doors farthest away from each other.

There is no piano store. Emma looks at me like I'm a moron when I ask her about it. "There used to be a piano store in every mall when I lived here," I explain, but she rolls her eyes. Mission number two is a wig store, which I'm sure as hell not going to share with her.

"Would you like to go look at toys or something? While I shop?"

"In case you haven't noticed, I don't play with toys."

"Not even Barbies?" I ask. "I played with Barbies when I was ten."

She snorts. "Figures."

"Well, look at clothes, then, or whatever it is you like." I vow not to lose control, no matter how bratty she is. "What *do* you like?"

"Not shopping," she says.

I give up. We walk along the tiled floor, my heels clicking and her sneakers squeaking, passing the men's section, the handbag section, the perfume section. Then we're out in the bustling noisy mall.

"I need to look at the directory," I say, heading for a black monolith with maps and store listings. I scan the rows of shop names. No wigs.

"What are you looking for?" she asks. "I bet I could find it."

"I thought you didn't like to shop."

"I don't. Mom does."

This I can't imagine, but then I remember the doodads, the pink rugs. Housewares. What women shop for when they've given up caring how they look.

"You know, it's kind of private," I say, deciding to level with her. "I need some space. Let's meet back here in half an hour." Neither of us has a watch, so we ask a slow-walking old man for the time. Ten thirty. "See you back here at eleven," I say and head off on my own.

I inquire at every clothing store, every accessory shop, a hair salon, but everyone says the same thing. No wigs. Who knows what people who really need them do. It's almost time to meet Emma. Then, in the back of a long, narrow, darkened shop, I see rows of Styrofoam heads and, hallelujah, wigs. The shop is strange, filled with stupid joke tricks like whoopee cushions and boob-shaped coffee cups. I head for the back, pick up a perfect replica of my old hair—blond, curly, and long—and replace my cap with it. I'm looking for a mirror when I see Emma standing next to the lava lamps, sticking something into her pocket. She looks around to see if anyone has noticed and sees me. A quick flash of panic crosses her face, but then she bursts out laughing.

"That's a joke wig!" she says, and I snatch it off my head, toss it on the shelf.

"I know. I was just goofing around." I snug my cap back on.

"Nuh-uh." She almost sings it. "You were really going to wear it."

"And what did you put in your pocket?" I say, walking toward her.

"Nothing." She quits laughing.

"Come on, hand it over or we're going to the store manager."

"You would, too, wouldn't you?" she says, but she sticks her hand in her pocket and pulls out a key chain with a glow-in-the-dark alien head attached to it.

"For this you're willing to go to jail?" I ask, grabbing the thing, holding it up. It costs $1.19.

She bites her lip. "Are you going to tell my mom?"

I wait a beat, just to worry her.

"Tell you what. I won't tell her about you, if you don't tell her about the wig." The more I look at it, the more I know she's right. It was sitting between a hot pink Mohawk wig and a rainbow-striped clown's wig. "But you have to promise: no more stealing."

She rolls her eyes, fidgets back and forth from one foot to the other, but she nods. "Okay."

"Say it."

"God! Okay, I promise not to steal. You'd think you were, like, in charge or something," she says, but her tone is softer than before.

"From now on, Miss Thing, you treat me like I am, because I'm older than you, and I'm your aunt, for crying out loud. Treat me with some respect."

I head up the aisle, not looking to see if she's behind me, but when I get out to the mall, she is. We walk back toward Dillard's, not close exactly, but closer. When we pass a toy store, she sneaks a peek at the window display. I look, too, and two capped heads look back from the reflection. Emma sees me and quickly turns her eyes forward.

6

♪ *Jedd Maxfield called.* Those three words and a phone number are written in Jane's careful hand on a pink sticky note stuck to my bedroom door. Jedd called.

It could mean anything, but my heart races ahead of my brain. Lyle must have told him I was back—who else would know? No one's left from the old days. The Holy Smokes flamed out. Marco and Billy crashed and burned in separate drunken car wrecks. Our own Jimi Hendrix, Randy "Gitar" Handelman, OD'd in a motel room in Austin, less than a year after he left us to try to make it big. Pat, the keyboard player, became some computer genius out in Palo Alto. Left music totally. I hear he's rich now.

After all this time, Jedd wants to talk to me. The last time I saw him was right after he'd made it as Jett Maxx. His record had gone platinum and he'd graduated to doing stadium shows. It was like a miracle, after all the years of trying, only we weren't together anymore. I wasn't too gracious when I saw him backstage after the Pittsburgh show, the first time I'd seen him since he dumped me. In fact, I was drunk and plenty pissed off, especially when I saw the gaggle of underage groupies hanging out in his dressing room. I'd suspected he'd been messing around the whole time we were married. Fucking pig. I think that's what I called him when he looked up to find me in the doorway. Someone pulled me away, down a narrow corridor, and I screamed like a mental case. The thing I remember most clearly is Jedd looking at me with that curl in his lip.

It's stupid, but my heart flutters at the thought that he called, like butterflies trapped under my rib cage. I am a sucker for a pretty face. And long gentle fingers that can slide up and down a guitar neck like it's made of silk. And, at that time anyway, hair almost as big as mine, but a soft ebony. He'd wear those skinny black leather pants that laced up the side and I'd be gone. I loved to lay my cheek against his smooth chest after we'd make love, listening to the wild thumping of his heart slow back to normal. He loved me, I know he did. Soul mates, he said, sliding a long finger along my spine.

I go to the kitchen, make sure no one's around, dial his number. After three rings, a machine picks up.

"Hey, bad timing. Leave a message." Jedd's voice.

I hang up.

After a deep breath, I pick up the receiver again and redial, listen to the message, then say, "Oh, hey. Jedd. It's me, Tallie. Heard you were looking for me. Give me a call sometime." Breezy, light, no neediness implied.

I set the phone back in its cradle and it rings almost immediately. "Well, if it isn't Tallulah Jean Beck Maxfield," Jedd says when I answer, his honey voice giving me shivers.

Asshole. He was screening, but I play it cool. "One and the same. Long time no hear from, Jeddo."

"No kidding. It's been too long. Too damn long. How're you doing anyway?" He sounds caring, familiar, like we never stopped talking.

"Good, good. Got a gig here in the old cow town. I'm sure you heard."

"Yeah, Lyle was telling me. Said your band had a major blowout. Bad luck, Tal." Good. Lyle didn't tell him he pulled me off the tour.

"Yeah, that's rock and roll for you. So, what are you up to these days?" I don't say I haven't heard his name in eight years, except for in-jokes about over-the-hill rockers.

"Well, that's why I'm calling. I'm working on a new project, and I thought you might like to be involved since you're back in town. I've got a studio up here at the house, a nice one. You'll love it."

A wave of something, nostalgia, joy, gratitude, I don't know what, washes over me, and I can't speak for a moment.

"Tal?"

"Oh, Jedd. That is so great. A new record. Wow." And you want me on it, I don't say. Everything is turning out perfectly. This must be why the fates landed me back in Denver. Jedd and I will finally do something great together, and with his past fame, the radio stations might actually play it, the newspapers might actually review it, people might actually buy it. My life is starting again, right this very moment.

"Are Saturdays good for you?" he asks. "How about we start tomorrow?"

"Hmm, let me check my social calendar. Hell, yes."

He gives me complicated directions to his place in Evergreen. "Right across from Willie Nelson's old pad," he says, and I try not to gasp. Someone is looking out for me after all.

"It ain't me, honey," I hear a familiar voice say, and I squeeze my eyes shut.

For a long while after I hang up, I sit at the kitchen table, drumming my fingers over and over, humming the first song Jedd and I wrote together. We'd drunk a couple of bottles of Riunite at the time, and I seem to remember lots of fooling around between verses. We called it "Liquid Kiss," and it was something of a hit on KROK, Denver's hippest station in those days. *In your arms I'm melting, falling. Come on and give me that liquid kiss.* It sounds lame now, but in the '80s it seemed so cutting-edge.

"Liquid kiss," I'm singing as Jane and Emma bustle in through the back door.

"You're in a good mood," Jane says. Her hands are full of zucchinis, onions, tomatoes. Emma's knees are caked with dirt, and she's swiped a muddy streak across her forehead.

"You garden, too? Wow, how domestic."

"Gardening relaxes her," Emma says, helping her mother wash the vegetables in the sink.

"So, you got your message?" Jane looks at me over her shoulder.

"Yeah. Guess what. We're going to make a new record together." I like saying it out loud.

"Really," she says.

"Yeah. I might not need that stupid piano bar job after all." I wonder what it would be like to live up in the mountains with Jedd, go out on real concert tours, not sleazy club tours. Maybe we could even get married again.

"But you're going to the audition, right?" Jane has turned to me now, her mouth a thin straight line.

"We'll see. I'm going up to Jedd's studio tomorrow for our first session."

"Okay," Jane says, voice shaking. "First of all, you're going to the audition, or you're moving out. Second of all, Mom called and we're having a family dinner at her place tomorrow. In your honor. Meaning, you need to be there."

"Mom?" Spoken aloud, it's like summoning evil spirits, like waking the dead. What's that saying? Speak of the devil.

"Remember her, Tallie? The woman who gave birth to you?" Her face has gone purple. I don't remember her being so touchy about everything.

"Of course I remember her. God, what do you think? I just didn't know how she ... or what she ..." I fumble helplessly. Then I get pissed off, too. "I didn't even know if she was alive or dead, or in some goddamned loony bin or what."

Jane tells Emma to go clean her room.

"But I don't want to," Emma whines until Jane gives her a look, then Emma trudges off. I vow to remember that look.

"How can you say that?" Jane hisses when Emma's safely upstairs.

"Oh, let's see. I don't know. I just seem to recall the last couple of years I was home, our after-school routine. Remember? You and me checking her pulse after she'd choke down all those pills? And calling the drug overdose hotline so often they practically recognized our voices. How about the stints with the ambulances, the emergency rooms? Those nosy social workers? Remember?"

"That was years ago, for God's sake, Tallie," she says. "You'd know how much better she was if you'd bothered to stay in touch. If you'd called even one time in all those years. You haven't even asked about her in the two days you've been here."

I just couldn't, I want to say, but I don't. What's the use? I'm a horrible daughter; Jane's the good one. "I . . . you know, I didn't call because I was always traveling," I say, but it sounds hollow. "I wanted to," I try again, but she shakes her head, turns back to the sink, furiously scrubs at her vegetables, spraying water haphazardly across the counter onto the cabinets.

"Anyway, I promised Jedd, so tell Mom I'm sorry I couldn't make it," I say, and leave her there, a madwoman with a scrub brush.

A soft *plink, plink* wafts from my room. I tiptoe to the door, peek inside. Emma is sitting on the floor in front of my open guitar case, picking at the strings with her grubby hands.

"I thought you were supposed to be cleaning your room."

She turns in surprise and draws her hands into her lap. "No. She just says that when I'm supposed to leave the room. My room's always clean."

"Oh. Well, I'm not going to get mad about you being in here, but you could at least wash your hands before you touch my stuff. Especially my Strat. It's expensive, you know."

She thrusts her hands deeper between her legs, and looks down. "Sorry," she says in a small voice.

"It's okay. No big deal. Do you like my guitar?"

She looks up and nods, wiping her nose with the back of her hand. "Why did you think Grammy would be dead?"

"Why did I . . . ?" I try to think how to put it. "Well, Emma," I finally say, hoping I sound like a responsible adult, "when I was young, my mother was very, very . . . sick."

"You mean her bipolar disorder?" She says this as if it were the most normal thing in the world.

"Is that what they're calling it now?" We heard everything back then: an overactive imagination, female troubles, allergies, drinking, depression, agoraphobia, a nervous constitution. One shrink said she was schizophrenic. It was something new every time she changed doctors, which was often, and some new treatment to go with it. None of them worked.

"Yeah. If she didn't take her medicine, she'd be sick, and she'd have to live in the hospital." Emma doesn't bat an eye. She looks almost bored by the topic.

"Have you ever seen her when she's"—I search for words—"sick?"

She shakes her head and leans back on her palms. "No. Mom says my being born helped her get better."

"Cool." I give her a little smile, but I could almost throw up that my being born didn't have the same effect. "You know, Emma, I need to do some stuff. Alone."

She nods and stands, giving the guitar a wistful look.

"You can play it sometimes, with clean hands," I say, and for the first time, she gives me an honest-to-God smile.

"Will you teach me?"

"Oh, well, I don't really think I'll be here that long."

Her face falls back into its usual shrouded expression. "Figures," she says and scuffs her way across the floor and out the door. Her bedroom door slams.

"It's *your* mother who wants me out of here," I mumble, kicking the guitar case closed. Not that I'd stay any longer than I have to, not in this house, not in this crummy town. But the bed is soft and comfortable, not at all like motel beds. I pull the door closed, then curl up on top of the covers and think about my new life with Jedd. No one's ever come close to making love to me the way he could; thinking about it now draws my hands to my breasts. I play with them the way he used to, imagining him in the corner watching me. *"Come on and give me that liquid kiss,"* I whisper-sing.

When I was a little younger than Emma, I woke up one morning and dressed carefully in my Brownie uniform. Jane and I were used to getting up by ourselves, fixing cereal, and getting ready for school. Mom didn't usually rise until long after we'd gone.

It was Brownie meeting day, which meant I got to wear my uniform at school all day before going to Mrs. Halloran's house afterward. There we'd do an art project, or sew or have a nature talk, then eat oatmeal cookies and see who'd earned what badges. It was my favorite day, a day I didn't have to come home until nearly dinnertime.

After I'd knotted my orange tie I trotted out to the one bathroom in our house. The door was closed. "Jane?" I called through the door, then knocked. "Hurry up. I gotta pee."

No answer.

"Janie? Come on." I locked my knees together.

Jane walked down the hall from the kitchen in her nightgown, her hair still tousled from sleep. "Mom's in there." She rubbed her eyes with her fists. "She was up all night because she thought there was a cat trapped in a tree outside."

"Was there?" I asked.

"I don't think so." She yawned.

"How long has she been in there?"

"Since before it got light outside. If you have to pee, use the kitchen sink."

"What? No way," I said. "Did you?"

"I had to go." She shrugged.

I was filled with horror at the thought of attempting it myself. What if I got pee on my uniform? What if a neighbor saw me through the window? "Well, I'm not going to. We have to wake her up." I banged on the door, hard. "Mom? Wake up. I have to go to the bathroom."

"Go 'way," came a drowsy voice from the other side, then the telltale *clank* of a bottle.

"Mom, come on! I really, really—" At that moment, my body betrayed me, and warm urine dribbled into my underpants. I squeezed my legs tighter, screaming, "Mom!"

I couldn't hold it. I couldn't get to the kitchen. I stood there screaming and peeing all over my prized brown kneesocks, into my brown penny loafers with shiny 1972 pennies in the slots. I felt the back of my dress dampen, then cling to one thigh.

I hated my mother so much at that moment that I imagined her staying in that bathroom forever, dying from starvation and her own stupidity. I knew right then that I was smarter than she'd ever be. I'd never be like her.

I wake suddenly, terrified. I can't breathe. I look around the room, panting, wondering where the hell I am until it hits me. Denver. Jane's house. Cutesy bedroom. In the flat colorless dark I can just make out the fuzzy gray shapes of the dresser, my boxes. Even after sitting up I can't catch a full breath, so I scoot toward the end of the bed, reach for the window. It's already open, but I push it higher, press my face against the screen, sucking up oxygen the way I would have a line of coke years ago.

I have to get out of here.

The clock on the nightstand says 12:18. It's early. I pull on the shorts and T-shirt thrown to the floor a couple of hours ago and grab my sandals and bag. Then I creak open the bedroom door, peer into the hall. Jane and Andrew's door is ajar and someone is snoring with the steady drone of a low-flying plane. I creep past and peek in: Two lumps lie at either edge of the king-size mattress, the space between them as vast and flat as the landscape outside. Emma's door is wide open and I move quickly, lightly, past it. A floorboard squeaks and I stop, my heart racing, until I realize I'm an adult, for God's sake. I can do whatever I want to. I walk normally the rest of the way to the stairs, down and out the front door, which I don't lock since I don't have a key.

I let the car roll down the incline of the driveway and out onto the street before I start it, and leave the headlights off until a few houses away. As I drive through the dark empty streets, the cool wind gradually soothes my breathing back to normal. I've had these breathing attacks before, starting when I was a kid. They scare the hell out of me because I can only imagine they mean I've inherited more from my mother than I would like, but usually, if I wait long enough, or do something to distract myself, they go away.

We used to play at a bar in a Podunk town called Parker, which must be only a few miles south of here. It was way out in the sticks in those days, a dive with killer margaritas, cockroaches dancing on the bar, and live music every night. Diablo's, it was called.

At the highway I head south, then turn off a mile or so down the road at a sign that reads PARKER/LINCOLN STREET. None of this looks familiar, but I drive along an empty four-lane street walled in by huge suburban houses until I reach Parker Road. There I turn right, toward town from memory, and find what I think is the place. It's no longer called Diablo's, but it looks similar, like it might have been refurbished and a row of dark storefronts attached to either side of it. A worn, hand-painted, peach-and-turquoise sign over the door says PEDRO'S—FINE MEXICAN DINING, COCKTAILS, ENTERTAINMENT. It has a howling coyote in the lower right-hand corner.

It looks more like a restaurant than a bar, but the parking lot is crowded, even after the witching hour in what is apparently now suburbia, so I decide to check it out. I'm mortified to discover that I've forgotten my hat, but as I walk toward the door, the unmistakable thumping of live bass and drums is like sweet medicine.

I throw open the door and there sit my comrades, my muchachos. No one I actually know, but the kind of people who make me feel at home. Guys in leathers, black T-shirts, facial hair. Not a pair of Dockers in sight. And women with some sex appeal, women who know how to dress to turn a male head—women who know that wild hair, low-cut blouses, and high heels are the keys to never being lonely again. I reach into the bottom of my bag, pull out my Shimmer Pink, and slick some on before anyone can see me, then torch up a Salem.

A power trio is banging out an Aerosmith song from a small stage in the corner. They're not very good. I slink along the wall to an empty seat near them, and a cocktail waitress appears almost immediately. She looks like the guitar-playing sister from Heart.

"What are you having?" she yells over the music, giving my head a double take.

"Triple vodka rocks with a twist," I yell back, holding up three fingers so she gets it right. She nods and gives my head one last look before strutting her tight-jeaned ass back through the crowd, carrying a tray on one slim arm above her spiral-permed hair. I try to shrink into my seat, smooth the wrinkles from my T-shirt. Tonight, the strappy sandals are the best thing I have going for me, so I cross my legs like a Playboy bunny, wiggle my foot suggestively in time to the music.

After a couple of drinks, I don't worry so much about how I look. The band plays a ZZ Top medley and they finally sound pretty good, so I make my way to the empty dance floor, dance-stepping right up to the stage. "Why aren't any of these losers dancing?" I ask the bass player, commiserating, one muso to another.

He looks young and scared, greasy long hair hanging in his pimply face, and he keeps plucking his thick strings without making eye contact.

"Hey," I say louder, moving so that I'm right in front of him. "You aren't ignoring me, are you?" I move my hips in time with the music, rub my hands on my stomach, reaching one up under my shirt. "Bet you can't ignore this, huh, greaseball?"

Someone is grabbing me from behind, rough-arming me through the crowd. "No harassing the band," a deep tired voice says as I'm shoved toward the door.

"I'm not harassing anybody, goddamn it!" I argue, but I'm on my way out, no matter what I say. I try to turn to see the gorilla who's manhandling me, but he's got a tight grip on both my shoulders, so I yell, "I need my purse, asshole!" Then we're at the door and I'm through it, standing alone on the sidewalk as it swings closed. A few seconds later my bag comes flying out, landing with a *whump* beside me, the contents scattering like scurrying mice.

7

♪ I had the rotten luck of being named when my mother was
newly parted from her Southern heritage. Dad took a job in
Denver shortly after they married, and Mom hated the dry air and
dull flat earth. She'd imagined living in the mountains, how it
would be like the rolling hills of Georgia. Instead she found herself
in a tiny box of a brand-new suburban house surrounded by nothing but prairie grass and howling winds. During her pregnancy
with me, she ate boiled peanuts and dreamed of her favorite old
movie, *Stage Door Canteen* featuring Miss Tallulah Bankhead,
who was Mom's idea of the true Southern belle—a little spice
thrown in with the sugar, she'd say. Like you, honey.

Jane, on the other hand, must have been named in a better state
of mind, or a moment of penance for overdoing it on me, escaping the Scarlett or Annabelle that could have tainted her for life.
Her name suits her, plain and simple. Maybe Mom knew how we
would turn out, even when we were just red wrinkly things.
Maybe we turned out the way we did according to her mental
state, her lunar orbit at the time of our births. Whatever. I hated
my name as a kid, longing to change it to Kim or Tracy, but as an
adult I've come to appreciate it. Having a dramatic name in my line
of work is a plus. People remember it. Jedd always loved it.

I wake with a start, remembering that I'll be seeing him today.
I try to sit up, then flop back down with a startling headache and

a hazy guilty memory of getting kicked out of the bar. I slide carefully from the bed and realize I'm still wearing my clothes, which
have a long dark grease stain down one side. It takes a second to
remember I had to crawl under a car to retrieve my rolling lipstick.
The inside of my mouth feels like I've been licking an ashtray, and
if I don't pee soon I'll burst.

I'm relieved to see that the other bedrooms are empty. I'm almost safely inside the bathroom when Jane calls from the bottom
of the stairs, "Tallie? I need to talk to you." She sounds annoyed.

"Okay," I call back, head throbbing at each syllable. "In a minute."
As I close the door, I hear her climb the stairs. I turn on the fan to
cover the sound of my peeing and sit gratefully on the toilet, the
blasting release almost as satisfying as an orgasm. Then I splash
cold water on my face and take a long hungry drink at the faucet.
Although I don't hear her, I can just imagine Jane waiting outside.
Ignoring the conga rhythms in my head, I try to put on a bright
face and open the door.

By some miracle, she's not there. I pad quickly back to my room
and find her sitting on my disheveled bed. She does not look
pleased.

"What's going on, Tallie," she says, an accusation, not a question.

"What do you mean?" She's looking at the road grime on my
shirt, and I wrap my arms around my middle. "Okay, I went out last
night."

"And?"

"And I came home," I say, shrugging. "I didn't think I needed
anyone's permission." I shift to my other foot, force a laugh. "Surely
you're not mad at me for going to see some music. I'm an adult.
And it's my job, practically."

She stands, looks at my boxes, then at me. Her face is stern, un-
changing. "Pack your stuff."

"What? Oh, come on, Jane. Why?"

"You went out drinking and came home blind drunk. You
think we couldn't hear you stumbling in at two in the morning?
For God's sake, Tallie, you expect me to subject my daughter
to . . . to you?"

I disgust her.

It hits me with such painful clarity that I reach out for her, try to make her see I'm the same old Tallie, the big sister she used to look up to, but she pushes past me. Since I've come back, it's more like she's the older sister.

"You smell like a saloon, and you look like you've been rolling in the gutter. I want you out of here." She's almost reached the door when she stops. "Why did you even come back?" She slumps against the wall, looking like a bewildered defenseless kid. Finally, she looks the way I remember her.

"Jane, come on," I say, wanting to go over to her but pretty sure it's the last thing she wants, so I stay put, talking softly, soothingly, I hope. "I'm sorry. I had to get out last night. I was going crazy. I'm just homesick for the road." I guess it's true, because I feel like I could cry. "Don't kick me out, please. I don't have . . . I don't . . ."

Jane's eyes widen. She's cracking, so I keep babbling. "I want to do better, really. What do you want me to do? I'll do it. Just tell me."

She sighs and shakes her head. "God." She takes a deep breath like she's going to say something, then blows it out, shakes her head again. "Okay," she finally says. "One more chance. But while you're under my roof, no drinking, no drugs, no smoking in the house, no 'going out,' no profanity, no craziness. Got it?" Without even waiting for my reply, she yanks open the door and storms away.

Realizing that everyone in the house is probably just as disgusted with me, I close the door and hide out in my room for most of the day. I listen as they move around the house: someone is vacuuming, someone is running water, someone—Emma, probably—is watching a noisy television show. Muffled voices across the hall rise in anger, then someone slams a door.

I hear them go out around noon and I run down to the kitchen to grab a Coke and some Oreos, greedily stuffing them into my mouth. I find a note on the kitchen table from Emma:

Dear Aunt Tallie,
Mom really wants you to come to Grammy's tonight. Here's a map Daddy drew.

At the bottom is a grid of streets and written instructions. I crumple it to throw in the trash, grab a banana from the fruit bowl on the counter, and head back up to my room.

There, I sift through piles of accessories from my box of stage clothes, looking for something to wear on my head when I go to Jedd's. I try tying a fringy purple scarf, à la Stevie Nicks, around my head. Too gypsy. A gold-sequined baseball cap that looked great on top of my wild-woman hair looks lonely on top of my bald head. Everything I try makes me look like a kid playing dress-up.

In the end, I settle for my SUCK ON THIS cap, extra mascara, and a tight T-shirt, knowing Jedd's eyes won't be on my head. Remembering what a leg man he always was, I finish with a black denim miniskirt, the strappy sandals.

Downstairs, I hear the happy family bustling through the door, Emma jabbering, Jane laughing. Pretty soon I hear a lawn mower outside. A curious mixture of comfort and melancholy wells in me for a moment. I haven't heard that sound in so long.

I still have a few minutes, so I polish my Strat with an old pair of underwear until it gleams and try playing a riff or two, but the strings feel like cheese slicers. Why did I chew off my calluses? It's been less than a week since I played it, but I'd swear I've already lost some of my chops. Figuring it's nerves, I return the Strat to the case, give her one last wipe, and snap the latches closed.

As I head out of my room, Emma beckons from her bedroom doorway with a twiglike finger. "Come here, Aunt Tallie."

"I'm kind of in a hurry," I say, but she strikes an adamant pose, so I set the guitar case in the hallway and slip into her room. She presses the door closed behind me.

"This is Grammy." She pulls me to a framed picture on her pink-and-white dresser. A younger Emma sits snuggled into the lap of a smiling kind-looking grandmother.

"That's *my* mother?" My mother has brown hair, not gray, and is thin, not plump. But the dark eyes look right, and the curve of the mouth.

"You don't recognize her?" Emma is about to launch into her exasperated routine, so I say of course I do, and pick up the picture to look closer. It's my mom all right, but something beyond her physical traits has changed. She's not the mom I remember. I set the picture down. Then Emma points to a painting over her bed, one of those wild colorful ones that aren't really of anything but look nice.

"She made me that." She looks from me to the painting and back.

"She paints, huh? Wow."

Emma falls dramatically to her bed and looks at me.

"What?" I say. "I need to get going."

"Are you sure you can't come? Not even after?"

Her puppy eyes almost make me say maybe, but I think better of it. "We'll be pretty late," I say, hoping it's true. Hoping I'll just stay, spend the night, the rest of my life. "I don't think so."

"Mom's right." She's gone all pissy again. "You only care about yourself."

"Let me tell you something, Miss Thing," I say. "If you don't look out for yourself, you're screwed, because no one else is going to. It's a fact of life."

I turn and open the door, pick up my guitar, stride quickly from the house before anyone else can lay a guilt trip on me. Just like leaving the first time, almost. Everyone's mad at me, but I'm heading for something better.

I get lost several times on Upper Bear Creek Road, a winding dirt road on the outskirts of Evergreen. Passing through the small rustic town brings back memories of happy times, playing the Little Bear, Evergreen's rowdy mountain bar. Evergreen hasn't changed much, not the town itself. What has changed is the number of sprawling log mansions and upscale housing developments surrounding it. I remember modest cabins and alpine chalets. The town lake has some fancy-looking clubhouse now and a golf course surrounding it. Of course, they could have always been there and I'm misremembering. We consumed a lot of substances in those days.

I finally find what I think is Jedd's house, a rambling Southwestern adobe complex with a satellite dish on one end. An army green Range Rover sits at the end of the dirt drive next to a silver BMW, a Harley-Davidson, and a red Jeep Cherokee. How many vehicles does one person need, I wonder, pulling in next to them. My tin can looks pretty scrappy next to this fleet.

I pull the Strat from the hatch, wobble over the rocky, rutted drive to the front door and push the doorbell. I could get used to this, the towering pine trees, the wildflowers everywhere. The air smells sweet and woodsy.

A man opens the door, says, "Yeah?" He has a slight paunch and his hairline is in full retreat. Definitely not Jedd, no matter how much he might have changed.

"Oh. Maybe I have the wrong house. I'm looking for Jedd Maxfie—"

"Jedd!" he calls out, then walks away. I feel like the Avon lady.

I shift the guitar from one hand to the other, looking into the open doorway. Jedd's house is gorgeous inside, terra-cotta-colored walls and wood floors, leather furniture, Indian artifacts. A man's house. I could live here, I'm thinking, just as Jedd appears and sends my heart thumping. He's as tall and lean as ever, wearing tight jeans and a cowboy hat and nothing else. His face is slightly more rugged than when I last saw him, but his eyes are penetrating and appreciative, the way I remember them.

"My, my, my," he says, smiling his foxlike smile, running his tongue over his bottom lip as he reaches a turquoise-braceleted arm out to me. I'm about to hug him, in fact I can almost feel his smooth chest hard against me, when he says, "Let me take that old guitar, Tallie. A little thing like you shouldn't be straining herself." I fumble with the case, like I knew he was reaching for it all along, not me. I smooth my hat down over my skull, a stupid move.

"What's this?" He snatches my hat off my head before I can stop him. He laughs and I almost turn and run, but he takes off his cowboy hat with a flourish. His hair looks exactly like mine, cut close to the head, smooth and dark. "I guess we really are soul mates after all, huh, Tallulah?"

God, it's good to see him.

*   *   *

The studio is awesome. It's been a few years since I've been inside one, and I know technology changes quicker than you can make the first payment on your already-obsolete equipment, but Jedd's place is futuristic. There isn't even a tape machine. When I ask where it is, he smiles his slow easy grin. "Digital, babe. No tape."

The man who answered the door is Jedd's engineer, Buddy. He doesn't talk much, just sits in the control room at the console twiddling the knobs, looking like a sullen Buddha. I get the feeling he doesn't like me already. Jedd seems to think he's great, cuffing him on the arm, saying how he makes magic.

I should have known better than to bring my Strat. Jedd has always owned a ridiculous number of guitars, even in leaner times. The studio is lined with gleaming showroom models on stands. Three Stratocasters—one red, one blond, and one almost like mine but with a nicer neck—a couple of Telecasters, a vintage sunburst Gibson Les Paul with mother-of-pearl inlays, a cherry wood SG with Humbucker pickups, and those are just the ones I recognize. Then there's a whole row of acoustic guitars, including Martins, Gibsons, an Ovation or two, and a Taylor that must have set him back thousands. A banjo, a mandolin, a National. My guitar sits in its case like a wallflower at a high school dance.

The studio is decorated in a Southwestern style—heavy wood beams cross the ceiling and Indian rugs cover large squares of earthen tile. Tall sun-filled windows line one side of the room, overlooking a stream and waterfall and more wildflowers. Jedd says deer and elk gather there at dusk.

My favorite part is the isolation booth, where I'll be singing. It's roomy but cozy, and dusky-colored Indian blankets cover the soundproofing material. Jedd shows me the dimmer switch, adjusting the light inside. He knows I always loved singing in near darkness, hiding in it so I could really let go. An industrial-size microphone hangs in the middle, and a plush high-backed leather stool looks like it's just waiting for me to hop up and settle in. There's even a stand for holding a water glass, headphones, tissues, cough drops, all the things a singer needs when she's working her butt off in that little room. I sit on the stool, place the headphones over my ears, touch the cold metal of the mike with my lips. I feel at home.

"So," Jedd says after showing off all his stuff, "want to hear what we're working on?"

I nod, feeling a familiar rush of anticipation, and follow him back to the control room. There, we settle into deep corduroy couches along the back wall. I consider asking if it's okay to smoke, then change my mind. I don't see any ashtrays, any crumpled packs lying around. Nobody smokes anymore, and Jedd has that reformed look about him, that smug I'm-so-damned-healthy glow.

"Beer?" he asks and I nod, feeling better. At least he still drinks.

Jedd reaches into a small refrigerator next to the couch and pulls out a bottle of Fat Tire, hands it to me, then grabs one for himself. I don't say it, but I remember when he used to scoff at anything but Coors. Said if you were from Colorado, you damned well should support its businesses. He catches me looking at the label and smiles. "Brewed up in Fort Collins. I know what you're thinking."

Then he gives Buddy a nod, and Buddy punches up a song on playback.

"Now this first one doesn't have a vocal track yet." Jedd leans forward, elbows on knees, beer bottle dangling from his right hand. I smile and nod and try to keep my eyes off the satiny olive skin stretched over his lean frame, the long expanse of back, the beautiful hands. He brings the beer bottle to his mouth and I remember his velvet kisses, the hard flesh of his lips and the shiny clashing of our teeth before our kissing became a well-choreographed dance. I haven't been kissed like that in way too long.

A soft drumbeat fills the room, but not a regular trap-set kind of sound. It's more a soft rhythmic thud, and then a flute plays over it, a silky fluid line of melody. It sounds almost tribal, or New Age, not at all like Jedd's old music. It's okay, but I'm not sure what I can sing over it. I'm more of a belter, really. A bluesy rock and roller. But I keep listening, thinking, I could change. I could sing softly. Prettily.

Layers of instruments keep building: soft guitar strumming, maybe a bass, but I can't be sure. There are other sounds, from a synthesizer perhaps, thunder, water. I turn to look at Jedd and he's lost in the music, the way he used to be when we'd get something really good going.

"Okay, I think you get the idea." He tries to sound cool, but there's unmistakable excitement in his voice. "Buddy, punch up the next one, with the vocal."

"So, you're thinking, what, vocal duets?" I venture, since he must already have some of his vocal parts laid down.

"No, just one main vocalist." He holds up a finger, like *Listen*.

Again, the drum thing starts. I'm feeling impatient, nodding along to hurry it up, when a sudden harsh caterwauling pours from the speakers. I look at Jedd, wondering if it's a mistake.

He smiles. "Little White Deer."

"I don't get it."

"This is Little White Deer singing. I met her at a healing cere- mony in Jackson Hole last summer. Isn't she fantastic?"

Uh, no, I want to say. She sounds like both sides in a cat fight. Something sinks inside me. "Healing ceremony? Like, Indian stuff?" There is an awful lot of it around the place.

"Yeah. It's a mind-blowing experience, the sweat lodge, the vi- sion quest. You should try it sometime, but you're supposed to have Indian blood. At least up in Jackson." His eyes are shining; his face has that look of wonder I used to love in him.

"How'd you get in?" I ask, wondering more about the Little White Deer part. Her wailing is getting on my nerves. Buddy could at least turn it down.

"I'm one-sixteenth Oglala Sioux. Just found out last year when my grandfather died. He never wanted anyone to know because there used to be so much discrimination." He swigs his beer, wipes his lip with the back of his hand, smiles that delicious smile I'm re- alizing is not for me. "But it's opening up whole new worlds for me, Tallie. I've found my calling, my spirit, my . . . oh, I don't know." He grins shyly. "I guess I'm babbling."

"And Little White Deer is . . ."

"Oh, baby, she is the best thing that ever happened to me." He looks dreamy and lost and in love. He fishes in his back pocket, pulls out his wallet. "Here's a picture," he says, carefully extracting it by its edges.

I take the small rectangle of glossy paper, smudge it with my thumb. She looks all of twenty-three, long black hair, chiseled dark face. Caught midlaugh in the photo, her eyes are bright, her mouth luscious. Her hair flows over her shoulders like a silky blanket. I touch my head and pull my fingers back quickly. I blink hard a couple of times and lay the photo on the couch between us.

"So, what exactly did you want me for, Jedd?" My voice is ugly, raw with jagged edges from this familiar turn of events.

"Well, you know, Lyle said you were down on your luck and all . . ." Then he seems to get it. He picks up the picture, puts it away. A pitying look softens his eyes.

"What did you want me for?" I demand again. Goddamn that Lyle.

"I thought you could do some background vocals, you know, maybe some choral-effect layering stuff."

"Background vocals?"

Buddy looks at Jedd, then stands and leaves the room.

"I'm going to be way too busy with my new gig to drive all the way up here just to lay down some goddamned background vocals. Jesus, Jedd, anyone could do that." Now I'm standing, although I don't remember willing my muscles to move.

"Excuse me for trying to help." Jedd empties his beer bottle, clinking the glass against his teeth, then tosses it to the carpet with a soft thud. He leans back into the sofa, lays his arms along the back of the couch. The old curl has returned to his lip. "God, Tallie, why are you always so hell-bent on being a bitch?"

"I don't need your help," I say, and then I'm moving away from him. I'm picking up my guitar, walking back out over the smooth tiles, past the paintings and the rugs that are all inspired by her. Out the door. I step on a rock, twist my ankle and pain shoots up my leg like a rocket, but I keep walking, hobbling to my car.

Buddy is leaning against the Jeep, smoking a cigarette. He

watches me throw the hatch open. "Jedd was right," he says, flicking a gray cylinder of ash to the ground.

"What? What's Jedd so right about?" I don't look at him, just wrestle my guitar into the back of the car.

"You *are* a goddamn prima donna."

8

♪ I am driving like a madwoman, flying down the mountain, taking curves too fast, squealing through hairpins, and accelerating even more on the straights. The hatch rattles loudly. I slammed it hard after Buddy's remark and it must not have latched. My left ankle is throbbing and I can barely push the clutch, but pain is the last thing I'm upset about.

"Honey, he was just trying to help, although I'll grant you he's trouble in tight pants."

"I'm not listening," I say. A series of hairpin curves appears out of nowhere and all of a sudden I'm skidding sideways, then bumping along the dirt shoulder before I can bring the car to a complete stop, two feet from the edge of the shoulder, which drops to the rushing Bear Creek below.

"You're driving like a maniac, girl. You're going to get yourself killed."

"Please don't," I say, a death grip on the steering wheel, and then I'm sobbing, choking, gulping big breaths of air.

"Honey, I tried to leave you alone, but look at you. What kind of a state have you gotten yourself into?" The scent of honeysuckle fills the car. "Go on, you just cry," Big Gal Sal says, and while it feels crazy, it feels good to have her on my side again. To have someone, *anyone* on my side again. I look into the rearview. Sure as hell, there she is, red dress, black hat and all.

"Why am I doing this to myself?" My hands tremble on the wheel.

"Got me. I was wondering the same thing. You could have crashed right into the creek." She shudders as she cranes her head toward the window to look.

"No. You." I turn around. "Why am I imagining you?"

"Oh, my," she says, raising an eyebrow. "Now you're calling me your imagination."

"Holy fucking shit." I lower my forehead against the headrest. Maybe I should check myself into the loony bin right now.

"That's just stupid talk. You're no more crazy than I am."

"What, you read minds, too?"

"Don't you remember anything? Tallulah Jean Beck, your memory can't be that bad."

She's right. This is all so familiar, but distant, like remembering some old black-and-white movie, and the more you think about it, the more it comes back, piece by piece. Bit by scary bit.

"You weren't scared of me back then." She leans forward. "Why are you now?"

You've gotten a little pushier, I think, forgetting about her mind-reading abilities. She draws back, manicured nails pressed daintily to her considerable chest, and mouths, "Me?"

I laugh, turn back around to sink deep into the seat, and put my palms to my face. "I'm scared of everything." As I say it, I realize it's true. "Couldn't you just go away?"

"Not likely, honey. Not until you're ready to fly solo."

"Like I haven't been on my own my whole life," I snort, but, really, I'm not minding her being here half as much as a sane person should.

"Child, climb down off that pity pony of yours and go see your mother," she says. When I turn around to protest, I see only the torn empty seat.

Mom thought of Sal as a kindred spirit because they were from the same small Appalachian town in Georgia—Cheluga, a small spray of wooden shotgun houses and a general store along the banks of Poplar Creek. Mom always told us stories about growing up there, about playing in the woods, catching toads and crawdads in the creek, and stealing Popsicles from the store's outdoor icebox on steamy summer afternoons.

When she was thirteen her mother died and her father moved the family to Atlanta. She never saw Cheluga again until she married Dad. She wanted one last look so she could remember it before they moved to Denver.

She cried for days at what had happened to her hometown. It had never been more than a backwoods country settlement, but in the days since she'd left, the old folks had passed on in one way or another, if not to the cemetery then to the nursing home in Marietta, and the young had moved away. The buildings were in shambles and tall grass and weeds grew up through the porches; only vermin lived inside. She ripped a piece of floorboard from her old house to take with her. She kept it in the drawer of her nightstand.

Sal had left Cheluga before Mom was born to make her fame and fortune in Memphis. She was discovered, the legend goes, while she was mopping the kitchen floor in the Blue Bell Diner just off Beale Street. It was late at night, near closing time, and Sal was singing to herself, keeping time with her mopping, her mournful low wailing wrapped around an old gospel tune. Mr. Walter O'Connor—well-respected agent to the white singing sensation of the time, Darlene Sugarman—was sipping the last of his coffee and paying the bill when he heard her through the swinging doors. The rest is history, as they say.

I need an agent like that.

The crumpled map Andrew drew lies spread out on the seat beside me. Something had made me fish it out of the trash before I left Jane's. The sun is hovering just above the mountains behind me. It must be close to dinnertime. I speed down the highway toward town, with the eerie feeling that I am hurtling toward the inevitable, just like when I was driving across Kansas.

*   *   *

Mom lives right in the middle of the city, a surprise. She was always a country girl at heart, she liked to say. Now she lives in something called the Milk Wagon Stable Lofts, which sounds like she lives in a barn. The address is vaguely familiar—1739 Wyanee Street—and as I drive along rows of old brick buildings I realize why. On the corner of Seventeenth and Wyanee, a red neon circle of sign reads SING OUT! Somewhere in the back of my mind, Sal snickers.

Mom's building is just two doors up, a redbrick structure about ten stories high with garage-size wooden doors at street level. The words MILK WAGON STABLES span the top rows of brick, old-fashioned lettering in faded blue and pink. It looks like it's from Denver's pioneer days, but the rows of windows are sparkling new, and a set of glass doors have been awkwardly inserted into a space between the old wooden doors. A fancy brass sign above those doors says MILK WAGON STABLE LOFTS, and neighboring buildings have similar signs: GRANARY LOFTS and STREET CAR LOFTS. That's a hoot. This end of downtown used to be solely the domain of drunks and bums, but now it looks like an invasion has taken place, the well-to-do ousting the down-and-out.

I drive around the block a few times, looking for a parking space on the street, damned if I'll pay ten bucks to park in a lot. I haven't told Jane, but I only have twenty-six dollars left in cash, an overdrawn checking account, and a credit card Lyle finagled for me, which I had to stop using because it got so far over the limit. I finally find a space a couple blocks away and walk toward Mom's building, wincing with every step. My left ankle has puffed around the strap of my sandal, so I stop and kick them both off, then resume walking, limping, swinging the shoes in my hands.

When I pass Sing Out! the familiar bar smell reaches out to me through the propped-open door. That smell means home more than any house I remember. In that smell, that murky, smoky embrace, I have been happy, content, revered. What I really need is a spotlight fix, the thrill of being singled out onstage, the hot light blinding but like a blessing from above.

I step toward the door and peer inside. It's a nice place, classy.

On a high stage in back sit two black baby grand pianos, facing each other like ships about to collide. The performers are either on break or they haven't started yet—an old Bob Seger song blares over the PA. Customers cluster in groups around the room, all talking in that louder-than-need-be bar volume. It doesn't look too happening, but who knows. It's early. I've seen even the scummiest dives become the coolest places late at night, standing room only and everyone straining to see over the top of everyone else.

Content in this reverie, I continue walking, almost passing Mom's building. Then, with a sick feeling, I remember what I'm doing here. Since no one's expecting me, I could turn around and hightail it back to my car, drive back to Jane's, and sneak back up to my room. I'll certainly make an interesting first impression on my mother: tight T-shirt, no bra, stupid hat, dirty bare feet, and I probably have mascara smeared all over my face from crying in the car.

I search the directory but there are no Becks on the list. Then I see JACKSON—801. Mom must have gone back to her maiden name. I push the button and a sharp *buzz* sounds, so I swing the door open, enter a small lobby with plank wood floors, high ceilings, and an old-fashioned elevator that looks like a cage. I punch the UP button and wait. The elevator grinds and screeches from somewhere above, and the lights on the panel in front of me count down so slowly I could have climbed the stairs twice, with a good ankle.

The elevator finally arrives, doors whining open, and I step in, push number 8. My palms are sweaty, and I keep wiping them on my skirt. I'm glad Emma showed me the picture of Mom or I don't think I would recognize her. She might not recognize me, I realize, and my heart goes into overdrive as the elevator cage door finally opens. There are two doors. One is unmarked and the other says 801.

I can still turn back, I tell myself, but even as I think it, my feet are moving forward, my hand is forming a fist, my knuckles are rapping on the door. My mind has frozen, as thick and slow as a 7-Eleven Slurpee, and I even feel the pinpricks of an ice cream headache coming on. And then the door swings open, revealing warm soft light, splashes of color bouncing off the walls, and my mother in a loose flowing dress, hair long and brownish-gray, tears springing to her eyes and hands flying to her mouth. "Oh, honey, you came," she says and reaches across the space between us to pull me toward her.

I hug her back, but it feels like I'm hugging a stranger. She keeps holding and rocking me even though I go stiff, and sniffling and saying, "Oh, Tallie, honey." For seventeen years I've rehearsed excuses, reasons I left, reasons I never called. Reasons I'd never come back. Useless words that have been riding high in my throat since I began this journey, just days ago. Now my excuses flitter away like leaves in a soft wind. Here I am, in Denver, Colorado, my mother holding me and rocking me like I'm still a little girl, like I'm not the biggest fuckup on the planet. Like I never left her and my sister behind.

Like she might not hate me after all.

9

♪ No one else has arrived yet. Mom leads me into her living room, notices I'm limping, and makes me sit in a plump white chair the consistency of Wonder bread. She frets and clucks around me, propping my leg up on a large matching ottoman, inspecting my ankle, making sure I can still move it. "Ice," she says and heads toward a door. When she pushes through, a stainless steel kitchen gleams behind it, like in a restaurant. The door swings closed behind her.

I sit and look around the place, shifting my leg to try to stop the throbbing. The ceilings are higher than in most houses, and every wall displays a gargantuan, brightly painted canvas like the one in Emma's room. The furniture is all big and overstuffed, in varying degrees of white. The floors are bare wood, scattered with woven straw mats, and translucent sheers flutter over the windows. It's beautiful, tasteful. Expensive, maybe, but the word "austere" occurs to me. I feel dirty, sitting here in this white oasis, like I don't match the decor. Like I'll sully the atmosphere just by existing in it.

"So, what, you paint for a living?" I call out. It's a sure bet she'd never afford all this on a secretary's salary.

Mom walks back into the living room and toward me with a Baggie of ice and a hand towel. "Yes, actually. I've been very fortunate," she says, smiling. "Certain people"—here she shakes her head—"certain very *rich* people, anyway, seem to love my work." She kneels down and covers my ankle with the towel, then arranges the ice over it. "Is that okay?" She looks up at me, something pleading, needy in her eyes. I nod and she pats my knee, going back to the kitchen "to fetch us some wine." Her accent has softened, but she still has that mouthful-of-honey sound.

I don't know this person at all. She's obviously changed over the years, transformed into someone she was probably always meant to be if she hadn't been crazy. She's not the mother I remember, the only mother I know how to have. She's neither the scary depressed Mom I'd do anything to escape nor the high-on-something, way-too-happy Mom I dearly loved, even though that Mom could scare me, too. She's even-keeled now, or so she seems by her unhurried movements, the steady look in her eyes. In my memories of her, her eyes are either darting about, like she's looking for something she can't find, or they have that dull look of depression or booze or too many pills. I could ask her questions, find out what's happened to her since I left, but I like it better this way. It's like meeting someone else's mom, or watching a TV-show mom. She could just be a new acquaintance, if I didn't think about it too hard.

She backs through the kitchen door into the living room, full wineglass in each hand. I'm wondering how I'll answer her questions about me when there's a knock at the door.

"Coming," she says, bringing me the wine. Rather than spoil the mood by telling her Jane won't let me drink, I set the glass on the table beside me.

And then there's the chaos of Jane and Andrew and Emma arriving, Mom kissing and hugging everyone, Emma chattering like a happy little bird. She clearly loves her grandmother. She looks at her with starry eyes, the way I've looked at lovers.

Andrew saunters over in that easy way tall men have. His Dockers are impeccably pressed, with creases in the middle of each leg. "What happened to you?" he asks, smiling sympathetically, the crinkles at the corners of his eyes almost attractive. He doesn't seem angry with me, so maybe Jane covered for me. Or maybe he's not as pussy-whipped as I thought.

Before I can answer, Emma sees me, and I swear that starry look transfers to me. "That's Aunt Tallie," she whispers loudly to her grandmother, then looks shy. She pulls on her hand and they all walk over to stand around me like I'm lying in a hospital bed.

"Jesus, I just twisted my ankle," I say.

"I take it things didn't work out so well with Jedd." Jane wears a poker face, but there is unmistakable gloating in her voice.

"Well, no. Not really. I told him to find another singer." In a way, that was what I had said. "Told him I'd be too busy to drive all the way up there."

Jane glances at Mom. She thinks I don't notice.

"I have to pee," I say, which is partly true, but mostly I want to escape the inquisition. Andrew helps me to my feet, keeping an arm tightly around my ribs as I grab my bag and he guides me to the bathroom.

"Thanks, bro," I say as I close the bathroom door, a reminder that I'm his sister-in-law. He may be nice and kind of a dork, but he's still a guy.

The bathroom is as sterile white as the rest of the place, from the tile floor to the cabinets to the towels. Nothing looks like it's ever been used, not even the soap. I groan when I look in the mirror. I have dark mascara circles under my red puffy eyes—a Patti Smith look. Definitely not the look I'm going for.

Quietly, I open drawers and cabinets, looking for makeup. Mom was definitely wearing some, so where is it? After a thorough search in which I find only bars of soap, rolls of toilet paper, a few home decor magazines, and a toilet brush, I give up. I sure as hell can't wipe my face on the pristine white towels. I pull wads of toilet paper from the roll, wet them, wipe my face, then try to wipe away the rolled bits of paper stuck to my cheeks. In less than a minute, I've made a mess of the bathroom without even trying. I pull more paper from the roll, wipe the counter, the sink, sweep the rolled bits into my palm and flush them.

Looking back into the mirror, I pull off my cap, rake my fingers through my hair. Jedd's looked great. Modern. I take a step back and survey myself. My head isn't such a bad shape, and my face is pretty enough, with makeup anyway, that I could pull off this—what did that hairdresser call it?—this boyish thing. Very in, he said, very sexy. I pout at myself, and I can see it. I cram the cap into my bag and rummage for a lipstick. I'm relieved to feel a plastic cylinder at the bottom of my bag, down among the pennies and dirt. I pull out the tube, expecting Shimmer Pink, but it's my old color, Raisinette. I uncap it and wipe the grainy surface with a tissue. Leaning into the mirror, I apply a neat thick coat to compensate for no mascara, then press my lips together with a smack. The purple-brown color looks good with my dark eyes. I straighten up, turn my head just so, smile at my reflection. I am reinvented.

At dinnertime we sit around a long wooden table in Mom's kitchen. "Everyone want wine with dinner?" Mom asks, holding up a bottle.

I meet Jane's eyes across the table as she says, "Yes, please."

"Just a little to be sociable," I say to Mom, holding my glass up for her, my eyes never leaving Jane's until she shrugs.

Everyone seems happy together, talking, joking around. I don't get half of what they're saying, all the references to things that have happened while I've been gone, things I don't know about, but it's nice to sit back and listen, feel the buzz of them around me, the buzz of the wine working its way into my head, my arms and legs, dulling the throb of my ankle.

Mom dishes up ham hocks and green beans with cornbread, my favorite meal from when I was a kid. She makes it differently now, though, more gourmet. She's replaced the ham hocks with chunks of real ham, no gristle or bone, and the cornbread is laced with cheese and green peppers and kernels of corn. It's delicious and I stuff three pieces of it into my mouth before anyone's even touched their forks. I've gotten used to road food—grease in a variety of forms. Greasy hamburgers, greasy grilled cheese sandwiches, greasy French fries, greasy doughnuts. Somehow, through it all, I've kept my figure. I look at Mom and Jane. It seems some women in our family go soft as they get older. I wonder who skinny Emma will take after, them or me.

"So, Tallie," Andrew says, and suddenly I am the focus of everyone's attention. "Tell us what you've been up to for the last few years."

"Seventeen," Jane says. "To be exact."

"Me?" I wade through a mouthful of cornbread as a flush works its way up my face. "Oh, nothing. Well, you know. Singing, working. A lot. Every night." I swallow the dry lump and gulp some wine to wash it down. "That's pretty much it. The glamorous life of rock and roll," I say, laughing a little, shrugging.

"Do you have a CD?" Emma asks. "Or a video?"

"Not yet," I tell her, ignoring Jane's snort, "but someday."

"Cool." She nods like she believes it.

After dinner, Andrew does the dishes while we "girls" go back to the living room. It's like we're a family you'd read about somewhere. It's all so unreal.

"You haven't seen the rest of the place, have you?" Mom says, and Emma immediately volunteers to give me a tour. "Well, just a quick one, Emma. Aunt Tallie shouldn't be walking on that foot."

Emma comes over and puts her arm around my waist, like she's going to help me walk, all fifty or sixty pounds of her. Dumb little rug-rat, but it's kind of sweet. I place my hand on her knob of a shoulder.

Mom and Jane settle into opposite ends of the couch, and as Emma guides me down the hall, I can hear Jane speaking in a low voice, no doubt complaining about what a pain in the ass I am. I hope she doesn't bring up last night.

"It's not really a loft," Emma's explaining, so I give up trying to hear Jane's fading voice. "Lofts don't have walls, like in real houses. Grammy says it's just a condo with a fancy name so they can charge more." She stops and points me toward the bathroom, which I've already seen. "Bathroom." She announces it like a conductor on a train. Then she spins me around, wraps her arm back around my waist and walks me to another door. "My room," she says. It's a bedroom with high windows and an old iron bed, a familiar-looking quilt and simple unpainted pine furniture. Another straw mat lies on the bare wood floor. It looks like a nun's room. I like it.

"What do you mean, your room?"

"Well, it's my room when I sleep over." She's already pulling me toward another door at the end of the hall.

Behind it is a combination bedroom and sitting room, with a bathroom off to one side. Another simple iron bed, an oak antique dresser and nightstands, straw mats, the high, sheer-covered windows. Stacks of canvases lean against the walls on the sitting room side, with more hanging above them. There are two easels and a rolling table full of tubes and brushes and other mysterious items. "Grammy's room," Emma says.

"This is where she paints?"

Emma nods, using her free hand to rub her nose.

The paintings here are like the paintings in the living room and the one in Emma's bedroom. Vibrant. Flowing. Wild, almost. It's like all the craziness that has been medicated out of my mother flows onto these canvases, but here it looks beautiful. Safe. Confined to these surfaces where it can do no harm.

My ankle is pounding now, so I let Emma guide me back out to the living room, where Jane sits with her arms folded across her chest, her mouth that straight line she seems to have acquired.

Mom smiles at Emma and me, hobbling along. "Thank you, Emma, for being such a good tour guide," she says. Then to me, "More wine, dear?"

Music is playing in the background now, and I recognize it immediately. *Don't you do wrong, baby. Don't you do wrong now . . .* The Big Gal. I hope this doesn't mean she'll make an appearance. I look cautiously around the room, but, thankfully, no red dress appears. "Yeah, sure," I say without thinking. "I'd love some more vino."

Jane looks outraged, as if I've just agreed to shoot up heroin.

"Oh, come on," I say to her. "It's only a little wine."

"Fine," she says, standing. "Emma, go tell Daddy we're leaving."

Mom looks disappointed. "Honey, don't leave yet. I've barely talked to Tallie all night," she says.

"Actually," I say, a wave of heat rushing through me, "I don't think I'm going anywhere." Jane's silence confirms this. She follows Emma toward the kitchen, where she has a muffled but firm-sounding conversation with Andrew.

Mom looks at me and I shrug, toeing the edge of the straw mat on the floor. My heart is pounding. I consider asking if I can stay in her extra room, but I have nothing with me, no toiletries, no clean clothes.

"What's going on?" Mom asks as Jane, Andrew, and Emma walk back into the living room.

"Ask Tallie," Jane says, and Andrew looks away. Emma tucks herself in next to him, grabbing his hand with both of hers.

"Let's all settle down," Andrew says, nervously poking his polo shirt into his waistband with his free hand. Jane gives him a look that, by all rights, should incinerate him on the spot.

"Whose side are you on, exactly?" she demands, and his face goes blank, a storefront closing up for the night.

"Will someone please tell me—" Mom tries again, and Jane loses it.

"Your precious little Tallie hasn't changed one iota since she left. She lies, she manipulates, and she has no respect for anyone, not even herself."

"Why, Jane!" Mom says in surprise. "She's only been home a few days. Why on earth would you—"

"She's a mess, Mom. Look at her. She's a drunk."

Emma looks at me, eyes wide, and I wish I could figure out how to make Jane shut up, to defend myself, but Mom beats me to the punch. "Oh, come on, honey. She's only had a little wine. We all have."

"Okay, you think she's so great, you take her. Let her use you for a while. I've had it." Jane heads for the door. Andrew gives Mom a sheepish peck on the cheek, and Emma hides her face in his side. They turn and follow Jane, who is already out in the hall, tapping her foot in a quick staccato as she waits for the elevator. Andrew pulls Mom's door closed as Emma leans away from him to give us a wave of her birdlike hand.

Mom and I stand speechless and awkward. It hits me that she has not yet invited me to stay. "So," I say, shifting to my good foot.

"Why would your sister think you're an alcoholic?" she asks. Her voice is flat, making her sound stupid, her eyes glassy. She, herself, has consumed quite a few glasses of wine in the last couple of hours, far more than I have. I remember this look on her face, this slight sway in her stance, from long ago, whether it was from her nightly cocktails to "unwind" or, later, from her pills.

In some deep dark place, I know her so well, yet I don't really know her at all. We haven't seen each other in seventeen years, and boom, here we are, alone together. I realize how much easier it would be to be sucking up to Jane right now than explaining anything to my mother, or worse, attempting polite small talk without the safety net of the family.

"I'm going to go talk to Jane," I say, picking up my bag, and Mom nods. I feel immediate relief until I step into the empty hall. I've missed them. I take the next elevator down, limp an excruciating couple of blocks to my car, and head south to the suburbs.

I imagine what Jane would say if she were sitting in this shitty car, noticing the slipping gears, the brake pedal with no pad, the smell. When did my life become so pathetic? I wonder. There had to have been a turning point I missed, some warning sign that it was all about to implode. Was it when Mom asked me if I wanted more wine? Or earlier, when Jedd asked me to be a backup singer out of pity? Or was it Lyle on the phone last week, telling me as I stood in that dingy hellhole bar in Missouri that I was washed up?

I've never been fired before. Lyle said, in an earnest careful voice, that no one liked the band's "sound," even though he immediately hooked the rest of the guys up with that new singer. I still don't get it. In the old days, that sound made us one of the most popular bands on the circuit. Club owners begged for us. They knew we'd pack their crummy bars to the rafters. They knew they'd sell plenty of drinks. We were a party band, a let's-get-drunk-and-stupid band, encouraging the patrons to buy the special shot of the night, to tip their bartenders and waitresses. We played music with a groove. Fast or slow, it was music for dancing, from full-tilt boogying to slow sweaty grinding. I loved watching those love-clutched couples on the dance floor, eyes closed, hands traveling, hips locked together and moving in unison. I was creating that energy, that aura of pure hot sexuality in the air—me and the band, of course. But it was my singing, the way I would moan or growl or plead, that made people snap together like magnets. Those moments always gave me a twinge, a quickening in my bloodstream, a need to find the closest good-looking guy available after the show. A "wonder-surge" the guys in the band called that feeling, when you get so horny so fast you almost vapor-lock. I haven't had a good wonder-surge in a while. And now, that's the least of my troubles.

I pull up to Jane's house, feeling light-headed and nervous, and limp up the drive. The upstairs bedroom lights are on. I press the doorbell, and after a long uncomfortable moment, Jane grudgingly pulls open the door.

"You shouldn't have come all the way out here," she says, sounding more tired now than angry.

"Jane," I say, groveling, "I'm sorry. I thought it was okay to have wine tonight. But I know, I shouldn't have, right? After I promised you."

"It's not just that." She softens her stance, leans into the door frame, but she doesn't ask me in. "Andrew says I overreacted, but the point is I don't want you living here. I have my family to think of."

"But I'm fam—"

"No," she says. "You're not. You made that clear a long time ago."

Fuck, I think. Fuck, fuck. "So what am I supposed to do? Beg Mom to take me in?"

"Oh, that would be perfect," Jane says, angry again. "Why not? She feels guilty for ruining your life. You have her so manipulated with your sorry-looking self, your stupid twisted ankle, your messed-up life . . ." She looks at me through narrowed eyes and says, "She's been fine for ten years, Tallie. Don't you dare make her sick again." A whip of air hits me as she slams the door.

I feel sick to my stomach. Three days back in town and it's happening all over again. This is why I didn't want to ever come back:

this feeling that something's wrong with me, that all I know how to do is fuck up. I stand there for a while, until all the lights in the house blink out, one by one, until it's clear that Jane is not going to take pity on me. I limp back to the car and slide into the driver's seat, light a cig.

I recline the seat to the drummer's favorite position, close my eyes. I've slept in cars before. It's not the most comfortable place, but at least it's not the street. I'll catch a few hours, then I can figure out what to do in the morning. Morning's always a better time for thinking anyway. If I let myself think at night I end up panicked and sweaty, every little problem churning and swirling into a nightmare. I stub out my cigarette in the ashtray and settle in, practice piano chord changes on my thighs until I get sleepy.

Somewhere during the night, a tap on the window makes me jump, my heart slamming into my throat. Jane is standing outside, wrapped in a ratty pink chenille robe. I sit up and roll down the window.

"Come on," she says. "I don't have it in me to let you sleep out here." She's already walking away. "God! You drive me so damned crazy."

10

♪ People always look surprised when they hear me sing for the first time, craning their necks to see around me, to find out who's really singing. It couldn't be that scrawny little white girl; she couldn't have such a big voice.

Now, as I sit high on the stage at Sing Out!, shiny piano bench smooth beneath my bare legs, keys willing and supple under my fingers, I close my eyes and pound out chords, wailing my favorite Bobby "Blue" Bland tune, "(If Loving You Is Wrong), I Don't Want to Be Right." The sound fills my chest, vibrates my head, and I am filled with sensation. I feel Big Gal Sal's presence—I feel the spirit of all the music women who have gone before me, from the mothers who first crooned to their newborns or yodeled delight into their lovers' ears to those who took their first step onto a honkytonk stage before women did that, scared and nervous, but needing it, too.

I open my eyes and return to the room. The bartender stands motionless at the beer taps, grinning. The cleaning lady leans against the back wall, tapping her foot, mop held off to the side like an afterthought. The other auditioners sit at the tables, looking nervous but swaying or nodding in time. Best of all, the big red-haired woman named Audra Lyon, the boss lady, is holding her pen over her pad but not writing. She stares at me with her chin hanging slack.

By the second verse, I know I have the job.

When I first walked into the bar, refusing to limp even though my ankle ached, she looked bored when I told her I was there to audition. She perked up when I gave her my promo kit and she saw my name. She nodded, like she knew who I was, or at least like she was expecting me. As she turned my 8x10 glossy over in her hands, she kept looking from me to it. My signature blond hair, my perfect curly mane, stared back from the picture. I was afraid she'd think I was too plain now, not glamorous enough, but she said, "Out-of-date picture, huh?"

After a few perfunctory questions about music-reading skills and years of experience, I hit the stage. I love the feeling of climbing stage steps, looking out over the room, even when it's almost empty, like now. Everyone always looks up at the stage, no matter who's on it. It could be roadies or technicians or some drunken idiot, but you're always in the limelight as soon as you reach that top step.

As I go for the big dramatic moment near the end of the song, there isn't a soul out there I don't have complete control over. After the last note echoes off the walls and dies, they clap madly, all eight or twelve of them. The sound is paltry in the big room, but the drug of applause is fulfilling just the same.

Audra does not clap, however, just makes a few marks on her pad. She says the usual thing, "You'll hear from me in a few days," but I know she's just going through the motions now with the others. I saw her face when I was singing, that amazed, greedy, she's-all-mine look I've seen on others who thought they could make a buck off me: Lyle, club owners, new bands.

I gather my things to leave, say a humble, "Hey, thanks," as I'm congratulated by the other poor fools who have to go on now. The cleaning lady has tears in her eyes and says I'm the best damned singer, dead or alive, she's ever heard, and I let her hug me. She smells like Clorox and sour milk. I escape her clutches only when the bartender waves me over.

He's cute, in a Gen-X kind of way, his head growing out a shave and one ear peppered with metal studs. It makes me wonder what else he has pierced. I gear up for the inevitable gushing, the almost-certain come-on.

"Jason," he says, extending his hand. "Congratulations on the new job." No gushing, and I don't sense imminent flirtation, a shame because he's even better-looking up close. His olive eyes are flecked with brown, his cheekbones hard and square.

I shake his hand across the bar. "Tallie. And I don't think the results are in yet."

"Maybe not." He goes back to wiping the taps. "But you know you got it."

I shrug. "Maybe."

"Yeah, you got it. We've never had anyone who could sing like you do. We get lots of namby-pamby, Celine Dion, Michael Bolton wanna-bes." His eyes scan the room, filled with contempt for the others waiting to audition. I decide I like him even more.

"You," he looks at me, "you've got something real." He shakes a cigarette from a crumpled pack and offers me one. I say no thanks, even though there's nothing I'd like more right now than a smoke to calm the aftershocks of the audition. If I held a cigarette now, though, my trembling hand would be a dead giveaway that I'm not as cool as I look.

"So, you like working here?" I ask.

"It's okay," he says and lights his cigarette, cheeks sinking deeper as he sucks it to life. He exhales a thin blue stream; it smells like heaven. "But it doesn't seem right for someone like you."

I take a step back, hitch my bag up on my shoulder, strike a sultry pose. "Well, Jason, was it? Even someone like me needs a job." I turn to go.

"Cool hair," he says. It's all I can do to keep from turning around and hugging him, but I just throw an extra dose of bump and grind into my stroll as I cross the floor.

I step from the darkened bar into hot bright daylight and suddenly feel conspicuous. Businesspeople wheel by in pairs and small groups, heading for power lunches and meetings. Suits everywhere, and I'm in a clingy black minidress with rhinestone bobby pins in my hair. Emma loaned them to me, showing me pictures of short messy hairstyles in a *Cosmo* magazine she had hidden under her mattress. She made me take off most of the jewelry I'd put on, and dug the bobby pins out of her jewelry box. Even though I barely have enough hair to make them stay in place, they looked kind of cute when she was done anchoring them to my scalp.

"At least you look like you're from this decade," she'd said, which I decided to take as a compliment.

Now, standing out in the brilliant noonday sun, I want to celebrate. Against my better judgment, I head down the block to Mom's place, moving toward the memory of her happiness to see me the other night. I push the buzzer labeled JACKSON. Lee Jackson does have a nice ring to it, a comforting Southern sound. I can't blame her for wanting to rid herself of all remnants of my father. He never called after he left. It was easier for all of us to write him off, pretend he didn't exist, than to think about him.

"Yes?" Mom sounds businesslike over the intercom.

"It's me," I say, then add, "Tallie," in case she doesn't recognize my voice. I almost say, "Your daughter," but she cuts in.

"Oh, good! Come up!" The door buzzes and I push through.

Another long elevator ride, and then she is standing in her doorway, dressed in a denim smock splattered with a kaleidoscope of paint colors. Her hands and bare feet are dotted, too, and a few specks cling to her cheek. Wisps of hair fall haphazardly into her face from a loose ponytail. Somewhere along the line, my mother has turned into a hippie—all these flowing natural fabrics, the long hair—but it's not a bad look on her. It's artistic.

"How'd the audition go?" she asks. I notice again that her accent has softened, and her words are slow, leisurely in a way that could just be her Southern cadence, but it's something more than that. She speaks differently than I remember. "You look fabulous. That dress is so sexy." She motions me inside, toward the couch. "I need to cap some paint tubes, dear, and I'll be right back. I wasn't getting anywhere today, anyway." Then she glides down the hall. She seems to be buzzing along in her own little atmosphere, but she's coherent, she looks happy. She's fine, I tell myself. This is the way she is now, on medication. I just have to get used to her.

"I think I got the job," I call out. I can't believe I'm this stoked about a stupid piano bar gig. I won't even be able to do any of my own songs. Audra alluded to a playlist. I can only imagine what will be on it—I pray there's no Barry Manilow. But, it's money, and good money for a musician. Four hundred a week, plus tips. And no equipment needed, no technicians. All I have to do is show up.

"Of course you have the job," Mom says as she comes back down the hall. "Audra would be crazy not to hire you." She's taken off the smock, revealing a peach-colored sundress, and slipped sandals onto her paint-splotched feet.

"You know Audra?"

"Sure. We're neighbors." She smooths back loose strands of her hair, smiles. "Now, how would you like to try some sushi for lunch?"

"Um, okay." I feel seasick at the thought.

Mom smiles. "Never mind. I know a great Italian place, right up the street. You still like lasagna, don't you?"

I remember Jane's accusations of manipulation. "No, that's okay. I just came to say hi, and tell you about the audition."

"I insist, Tallie. Come on. I want to celebrate."

"Well, okay," I say, feeling shy but pleasantly doted upon.

"She had it all planned," I tell Jane. "I didn't even ask. Besides, I'm going to pay rent. She *wants* me to live there." Unlike some people, I don't say, but even I'm surprised at Mom's insistence that I come stay with her. It's like ollie-ollie-in-come-free time. Amnesty for the rogue daughter. And from the look of things, she's put her craziness behind her, left it in our past lives. I get to start over with a brand-new mother.

"And when I've saved enough, I'll get my own place," I tell Jane, feeling more optimistic all the time.

"If you got a real job, you could get your own place now."

"It is a real job," I argue, but it's useless.

The problem is that Mom needs a day or so to "get ready" for me to move in, whatever that means. "Just some personal things I need to attend to," she said mysteriously, so in the meantime I'm stuck under house arrest at Jane's, which I'm sure thrills Jane about as much as it does me.

Good-bye, pink rugs, I think, ignoring Jane's warnings that I'd better not drive my sane mother stark raving mad. Good-bye, dusty old knickknacks. Good-bye, rug-rat. But that one, to my surprise, doesn't conjure up quite the same thrill.

11

Audra Lyon calls Jane's house the next afternoon and asks me to come in for a follow-up interview. You'd think she was hiring a CEO with all the rigmarole she's going through. Hey, it's singing, not rocket surgery, I want to tell her, but four hundred bucks a week is four hundred bucks a week. I agree to come right down.

When I arrive the place is bustling, waitrons wiping tables, organizing chairs, bartenders replacing kegs, refilling bar stock. Unfortunately, it must be Jason's day off. He's nowhere to be seen. Audra sees me walk in and crosses the room, shakes my hand, points to a two-top. "Have a seat," she says, taking one herself, and spreads a file folder in front of her.

"Miss Beck—"

"Tallie," I say.

"Fine, Tallie. I'd like to go the next step with you in the hiring process, but first we need to discuss a few things. For example, there's the matter of the contract." She pulls a legal-size form from her folder.

I shrug, lean back in my chair. I'm a professional. I've signed plenty of contracts. "So I've got the job?" I ask.

"Not so fast. Let's do this my way, all right?" She's gruff, so I decide to change my tack, sitting straighter in the chair, folding my hands in my lap. I can usually weasel my way around club owners, but Audra Lyon makes me nervous. It's more like Audra *the* Lyon. She has a fuzzy red hairdo and short crimson fingernails, and I'll bet she'd bite if provoked.

"Our contract states that performers agree to at least one year of employment—"

I draw a breath so quickly that I suck spit into my windpipe, causing an abrupt fit of loud coughing.

"You all right?"

I cover my mouth, try to swallow back the cough. Contracts were made to be broken. I nod at her to continue.

"And this clause states that performers will not perform in any competitive venues," she says, looking up at me like she's expecting another coughing fit.

"Meaning?" I cough lightly once, twice.

"Meaning you won't perform in any competitive venues."

"I can't sing anywhere else?" I feel any graciousness fall from my face. There goes my career.

She looks around, then lowers her voice. "Well, it mostly means you can't sing over at Coyote Cry, our main competition. You know, another participation piano bar."

I nod, relieved. Like I'd want to sing there, anyway.

The rest of the contract is mumbo jumbo, and I say I'll have my agent look it over.

"Fine," she says, extracting another piece of paper from her folder. "And here are the training and rehearsal schedules. Mandatory for all performers."

The paper is a complex grid of days, times, and names. A *schedule* for God's sake. "You have sheet music, set lists, right? What do we need training for?"

"It's a performance we're putting on, Tallie, almost like a play." She squints at me. "Haven't you been down to see a show yet?"

"I haven't had time," I mumble. It's just a bar—I know what goes on in bars—but I know what side my bread's buttered on and who's holding the knife. I promise to come to a "show" soon. I resist making the quotation marks with my fingers.

Next she holds up a teal-colored polo shirt with a white Sing

Out! logo over the left breast, saying, "Of course, there are other colors and sizes in back." It takes me a moment, but then I notice everyone here, excluding her, is wearing one of these god-awful things.

"So, what? The bartenders and waitresses . . . ?"

"And performers," she says forcefully enough that I know there's no negotiating. The prospect of people seeing me dressed like that is horrifying. With no hair to speak of, I'd been counting on wearing sexy girl stuff on stage—dresses, high heels, jewelry.

Then she whips out one more piece of paper, the performance schedule, and drops the final bomb. "Here are the open slots I need to fill: six to ten on weeknights and two in the afternoon till eight on Saturdays. Okay?" She gathers her things and stands.

"Warm-up slots?" I ask, heart sinking, and she nods. I stand only because I know I should, and take her hand when she offers it.

"Think it over, Tallie, and come check out the show. I know you're just coming off the road and this is different, but it's not all bad." She smiles at me and I look away. "Some people even say it feels like family, working here." And then she strides off, yelling at a bartender to check his wineglasses—they sure as hell don't look clean to her.

My past life is fading fast. Moving from town to town, bar to bar, being the star for a few hours a night, singing whatever you have a mind to. I try to remember the line from "Me and Bobby McGee," the one about freedom, but I come up blank. Whatever freedom is, it isn't mine anymore.

I head for Mom's. She doesn't answer the buzzer, so I let myself in with the key she gave me and call Lyle. "What the hell have you gotten me into?" I demand as soon as he answers.

He sighs and takes his sweet time replying. Then he says softly, "You gotta start somewhere when you're starting over, Tallie, honey."

"Excuse the fuck out of me," I say, trying not to let on I'm about to cry. "I didn't realize I was starting over." I slam Mom's phone so hard the mouthpiece cracks. Just one more thing I need to buy with my first measly paycheck.

*   *   *

Two days later, way out in suburbia, I pack my stuff into my car, remembering the glimmer of hope I had before reality struck. I had it all pictured, the beginning of something new and glamorous. Moving into town, into the middle of that spiky outline on the horizon, going where all the action is, and making a big splash. Now I picture myself dressed like a parking attendant and warbling smarmy cover songs to the few nerdy customers who arrive early to get a good seat for the headliners. My splash will be more of a drip.

Emma helps lug my stuff down the stairs and outside. She wants to carry my guitar, but I don't let her. "I never even got to play it," she says, head lowered, voice pouty.

"You still can," I say, squeezing her weedy shoulder. "When you come to visit Grammy and me."

She looks more cheerful and waves as I drive away, flapping her little hand until I'm out of sight. I decide to teach her some chords when she comes over. At least I can pass my legacy on to her, if nothing else.

Sal's low chuckle comes from the backseat. "Oh, my," she says. "Aren't we the queen of high drama."

I can't believe I have a bedroom, a closet, a door that locks. Nothing has been mine in so long, nothing but cardboard boxes, a guitar, and the hot circle of a spotlight for four hours a night. I like having a void that I can fill with anything I want to, or with nothing. Jane's place was jam-packed with crap, no room for anything or anyone else.

I like having a window that faces the street, where I can hear cars honking and people yelling and buses rumbling by. I even like the late-night sirens, the inevitable brawls that tumble outside from the bars after they close. I'm used to sleeping in the middle of everything. For half of my life I've slept in vans parked in alleys, in thin-walled motel rooms, in the backs of bars. The noise is a comfort.

Living with my mother, however, will take some getting used to.

We move around the house carefully, say hello in the corridor like we're surprised someone else is there. Did we ever feel like a real mother and daughter? I wonder. Maybe when I was too young to know better. As a teenager I only remember hating her, brushing off her weepy apologies when she felt guilty for being such a mental case, screaming the word "fuck" enough to make her leave me alone. Escaping every chance I got.

But she's better now. Never mind that I can't shake the old creepy feeling, the concrete molded into the bottom of my gut. It's a proven fact that she's fine, and I should get used to it.

On moving day, I nearly tripped over a cardboard box sitting by the door as I hauled my things in, but when I went to move it Mom almost had a heart attack. "I'll do it," she said quickly and slid the box out into the hall. "It's just some stuff for a friend to pick up."

It registered then. A friend. One who must have been accustomed to spending the night. Like I care she has a boyfriend. Maybe that's all it is, a mother embarrassed by her private meanderings, readjusting to this new twist in life just like I am.

I miss being with a band, how easy that was. Life was all about the joy of playing music together, and joking and partying when we weren't, and I was always the only female except for the occasional groupie flitting around. I had special status, especially with the guys who had crushes on me, or whoever I was sleeping with. I had brothers, lovers, friends, the occasional father figure. I got back rubs, attention, and there was always someone to hang with. Nothing too serious. Nothing too real.

Here at Mom's, I don't know how to get comfortable. Everything is clean and white. I'm like a smudge on a piece of paper, a fly in a bowl of milk. Luckily, she's usually either behind her closed bedroom door, which I gather means she's painting, or she's at one of her meetings or hanging out with her strange artist friends. Everyone knows her. The first time I went for a cup of java at the techno-cool coffeehouse on the corner, St. Beelzebub's, I noticed one of her canvases on the concrete wall.

"That's my mom's," I told the guy at the counter, an anemic scraggly hipster with a tiny silver nose ring between his nostrils.

"You're Lee Jackson's daughter?" He pulled his lips tight in a smile, flipping the nose ring up in the process.

I nodded, trying not to gag at the nose ring. "Tallie," I said, eyeing the raspberry scones instead. Jesus. Two dollars and fifty cents.

"Damian," he said and shoved a scone at me. "My treat."

According to Damian, Mom is the center around which the downtown art scene revolves. Lower downtown, to be accurate, although everyone says "LoDo" like they live in New York or San Francisco. Skid Row, I'd like to tell them, would be its historically accurate name, but who am I to burst anyone's bubble? This place does have a lot of galleries mixed among martini bars and chichi shops, Starbucks and nightclubs, and Damian looked hopeful when he said it's known for "a very supportive base of collectors." Mom's president of this alliance and involved in that organization, and she has weekly get-togethers of artists—"gatherings," she calls them. Apparently, everyone who is anyone attends.

"She's like our patron saint." Damian beamed idiotically, handing me a blistering hot paper cup of Colombian. If you only knew her when, I felt like saying, but I've never told anyone my mother's secrets.

Friday night at Sing Out! is just as I'd hoped it would be: jumping. I'm checking it out, like I promised, sitting at the old wooden bar nursing a beer. Jason's working the other end of the bar, the noisy end near the stage, where the seats are full and everyone looks like they're having a hell of a time.

This end is quiet, and the bartender is named Eileen. She looks wholesome, like a college girl. She has no piercings or tattoos that I can see, and she frequently tucks her putty-colored hair behind her ears in a nervous gesture, fingers splayed and ears red from all the handling. It's the way my life is going lately, sitting at the loser end of the bar with this girl-next-door bartender.

When I tell her I might be singing there, though, she looks impressed.

"That's my dream," she says, smiling as she shoots herself a soda from the bar gun. "I'd love to hear you sing sometime."

"Shouldn't be too long," I tell her. "Just the paperwork to wrap up." Then I kick back to watch the action on stage.

When I first walked in, there was only one performer on stage, a big guy cracking jokes and shouting at people in the audience between songs like "Old Time Rock & Roll" and "Born in the U.S.A." Now he's been joined, with much fanfare and applause, by someone named Rebecca, who is tall and, I have to admit, stunning, with long white-blond hair. My old color, but her hair is straight and gleaming against her shoulders. She's wearing the polo shirt, but it's cropped at the ribs, and her jeans ride way below her tiny pucker of a belly button. The denim looks almost painted on her just-curvy-enough ass and long legs.

But can she sing?

The big guy introduces "Somewhere Over the Rainbow" as Rebecca's "spotlight song," and I snort. Everybody thinks they're Judy Garland. Two notes into the song, though, I'm dumbfounded at the obvious skill in her voice. I sit back like everyone else to watch her. It's as if we've all stopped breathing.

Jason was wrong. This girl may not have a big gutsy voice, but she has a satiny quality, with that half-sob emotional catch in just the right places, and she can handle the soft pretty parts like nobody's business. And she's got me on range. She's got me on height, hair, age, and God knows what else.

"Rebecca's great, huh," Eileen says, wiping the bar in front of me. "Chuck, too, but Rebecca's our star. The paper did a write-up on her."

I nod but don't look at her. There's no way I can work up a fake smile just now.

"You know that place, Coyote Cry?" Eileen continues, and again I nod. "They're always trying to get her to go sing over there. And agents and stuff? Someone's always trying to steal her from us."

I feel sick. Eileen wanders away, wiping as she goes.

"Shit," I say under my breath.

"Jealousy is vain, and besides, it's a road to nowhere," comes a voice from the seat behind me. To most eyes, the empty seat.

"I know, I know," I say, keeping my eyes riveted to the stage.

Just what I need, to be seen talking to an invisible dead woman at my new gig. Audra is hanging out by the door. She can probably see every move I make.

"You're as good as her, and you know it," Sal says. "Better, as a matter of fact. You have a gift."

"Please shut up," I whisper, trying not to move my lips. "I'm trying to get a job here."

"What, and I'm standing in your way by giving you encouragement? Well, excuse me, princess. Nobody talks to me that way."

"Come on, Sal, don't be pissed," I say, turning to her seat. No one's there, of course, and I act like I was just turning to look around the place, scope it out. Audra isn't by the door anymore, thank God. I blow a sigh of relief.

"So what do you think?" Audra asks from behind the bar.

"Shit!" I say before I can stop myself. "I mean . . . sorry. You scared me."

She smiles and places one stubby red fingernail on her bottom lip and nods toward the stage. "So? What do you think?"

Both Chuck and Rebecca are talking now, swapping insults, making jokes with the audience. They have some poor sap singled out, a heckler probably. "Well, it's . . . chatty," I say, trying to make that sound like a good thing. "I don't usually do a lot of jokes, but I have good patter, good audience rapport."

"Scripted. It's all scripted." She watches for a few seconds more, then turns to me. "Come back to my office. Let's talk."

Her "office" is a converted broom closet, through a door at the end of the long bar. Inside the cramped room an old metal desk fills the majority of floor space, along with a rusty file cabinet and two folding chairs. The fluorescent fixture overhead turns Audra into a green-skinned zombie, but I'm sure I don't look much better. Everything vibrates with the music from outside the door.

"Sit," Audra says loudly, indicating a chair piled with paper towel dispenser refills. "Just put those on the floor."

I try to stack them neatly, but they tumble into a heap, some escaping their brown wrappers. I start to gather them up, but then I decide I'm not being hired as a janitor, so the hell with it. We both sit down.

"What do you think of Rebecca?" She yells to be heard over the music.

"She's pretty good," I yell back. "If you like that kind of stuff."

Audra leans back in her chair, balancing on the rear two legs. She's a large woman, and I worry that she'll topple backward, knock herself out on the filing cabinet behind her. I'm not big on blood and guts, and there's no way I'm giving her mouth-to-mouth, so I wish she'd stop. She's obviously studying me, considering me, and it's getting on my nerves.

"What?" I finally yell, trying to make it sound like a sincere question, which isn't easy when you have to shout it.

She smiles. "Your agent said you could be a handful."

Goddamn Lyle. I don't know how to reply, so I just sit there. It's true, I guess, but still.

"I don't think that's necessarily a bad thing," she says, "but I won't put up with prima donnas. Just so you know."

I nod. Yeah, yeah, everybody hates prima donnas.

"I want to give you a try in the warm-up slot," she says, like it's a big deal. She leans forward, bringing her chair back to earth and lowering her voice to within the normal volume range. "Rebecca isn't going to last forever. She's got agents and managers and scouts sniffing around her like she's a bitch in heat."

I like that she uses the word "bitch" in reference to that Amazonian Judy Garland out there. I get her drift—take the warm-up as a temporary thing. Something else, something bigger is sure to develop.

"I hear Coyote Cry is trying to steal her from you," I say, hoping to fan the fumes of Rebecca's demise.

"I think Rebecca has bigger fish to fry than rinky-dink piano bars," Audra says, searching the papers on her desk until she finds a blank contract and pushes it at me. I don't know if she's saying this place is rinky-dink, or if she's saying Rebecca thinks so, but either way, it makes me think twice about taking the gig. It is rinky-dink and I know it. It's nowheresville for someone like me, let alone Miss Star out there on the stage, who couldn't possibly be more than twenty-five—what could she have done that I haven't?— but then I hear her launch into "Lover Man" through the thin walls. She's a white girl, but when she digs deep enough, she's got soul.

"Billie Holiday is on the playlist?" I ask Audra.

"That's one of Rebecca's spotlight songs. We usually give each performer one an hour, but she gets two. You get to pick your own spotlight songs, with my approval, of course." She hands me a pen, looking impatient. "So? Do you want the job or not?"

I rub my head, the soft scrubby feel now familiar. "Can I have two spotlight songs?"

"Don't push your luck," she says, but she's smiling.

It's something, I guess. Better than nothing, and hell, maybe I can sneak in an original tune here and there. "Yeah," I say and pick up the pen. "I'm in."

12

The next morning as I'm coming out of the bathroom, my mother's door is ajar. I tiptoe down the hall, stop so she won't see me, and listen. I don't know what I expect to hear—painting is a fairly noiseless operation—but I feel like a detective or something, searching for clues about this mysterious person who used to be my mother.

At first I don't hear anything, but then I do—an odd low moan, a groan maybe. I flash back to the times Jane and I stood outside our mother's closed bedroom door, the noises we heard, the things we imagined happening in that room. Or the silences, which seemed even worse.

"Uhnf," my mother grunts again, then mutters, "Dear God."

"Mom?" I call out against my better judgment. We never bothered her when she was having what we called "a bad day." I step closer to the door. "Are you okay?" I peer in, and she's standing at her easel, brush in hand. She turns and looks at me, blankly, like she's forgotten I live here.

"Oh. Tallie," she says. "I'm fine, just painting. Or trying to anyway." She dumps her paintbrush in a jar. "Where are my manners? Come in, see my studio."

"No, that's okay. I didn't want to disturb you. It's just, you were making . . . you made a noise." I step back but she motions me inside.

"Did I? Oh, dear. I get so out of it when I work. I'm so . . . I don't know. Consumed by it or something. It's like therapy, or like madness—I can't decide which." She laughs at this, like it's something a normal person would say, and turns back to her canvas, picks up her brush. The back of my neck prickles at the mention of her illness.

"Sometimes I think madness might even be preferable, but these days I'm as even as a long straight stretch of road, going for miles and miles." She dabs at a blue splotch. "Going nowhere, I think sometimes," she says, swiping a diagonal stroke across the painting. I'm no expert, but I'd say she ruined it.

"God, Mom."

"It's okay, Tallie," she says, turning to me, calm and smiling. "This painting was going nowhere. I try and try to attain that state of grace I used to, when I first started painting, but it's not always forthcoming." She shrugs, surveying the canvas. "I can just paint over this. No big deal. Wait for another inspiration to strike."

My diaphragm tightens against my will, that muscle I usually have such control over from singing my whole life, but I try to sound casual when I ask, "So everything's okay, then? This is just, what, normal?"

She laughs the pretty laugh I always loved. "You're not worried about me, are you?"

"No. Of course not." I try to breathe evenly, relax. Maybe I should change the subject. "So when did you start doing this? Painting, I mean."

She shakes her head, folds her arms across her chest, paintbrush and hand resting over her heart. "Lord, a long time ago, when I first started experiencing my manias, back before you were born." She smiles, like she's remembering an old friend. "I used to love painting during those high times. I had such vision, such energy. I stopped after I saw my first doctor, started my first round of medication."

We aren't supposed to talk about this; I feel as though I could be struck by lightning any moment, swallowed in a flood. I edge toward the door, say, "Well, I'd better get going," even though I have nothing to do and nowhere to go until my training begins on Monday. I leave her there, staring at her spoiled canvas, reminiscing about what apparently were her good old days.

It's Sunday, the day the artists gather at my mother's, every week, rain or shine, not to mention the day before my first rehearsal at Sing Out! I hide out in my room after the first guests start arriving, but pretty soon Mom knocks at my door. "Come on, honey. I want you to meet my friends," she says, and I tell her I'll be out in a while. I hide out another half hour until she knocks again, and then I let myself be pulled out into the fray.

These people are funky-looking, almost like musicians. Mom introduces me to a handsome black man with mini-dreadlocks and eyes like melted Hershey's. His name is Shanti, "My spiritual moniker," he says. I nod. I have no idea what he's talking about, but the way his mouth moves when he talks, like he's sucking ripe peaches, makes me want to know him better. Unfortunately, he seems to travel inside a cloud of rich white women who hang on his every word while ogling his biceps.

I find Damian nearby with his artist girlfriend, Mia. The female version of Damian, she has a nose ring more tastefully anchored to the side of a nostril, so at least it doesn't move when she talks. I focus on her instead of him as we chat about my job at Sing Out!

"It's so cool that you'll be infiltrating that yuppie-establishment perversity," she says. "You can be a force of change, a radical in the lion's den."

"You got that right," I say, thinking of Audra's playlists and polo shirts and schedules. We all nod, then fall silent until Mom sweeps by with another of her friends.

"Tallie Beck! I'm so excited to meet you," says a rabbity bald man named Arnie, pumping my hand like he's trying to get water out of me. I have a hard time imagining him as an artist, but it turns out he's an art dealer. "I used to come see you and the Holy Rollers all the time," he says, "at the Eagle Bar on Broadway, and at Eddie's on Colfax." He looks way too old to have been interested in us then, but apparently he's still only in his thirties, because he asks if we could regroup to perform at his fortieth birthday party in the fall. Uh, no, I politely decline. It's cool to be recognized, though, especially in a roomful of people I don't know.

"So," bald man says, "whatever became of Jett? Do you see him anymore? You guys were the coolest couple."

"No, I don't see *Jedd*," I say. "I don't know what happened to him." Then I mumble something about needing a drink and escape to the kitchen, where rows of open wine bottles are calling to me.

Wine's not my drink, but I could use a little something. I grab a wineglass and study the bottles, some green, some brown, some blue even, wondering what the difference is between all of them.

Then, something across the room catches my eye, a breeze lifting a curtain, and next to it a man who does not fit with Mom's crowd, as strange as it is. He looks homeless, like a street person, a wino maybe, and it startles and frightens me that he's just standing there, that he's slipped in unnoticed and I'm alone with him. I gasp and the wineglass slips in my hand; I catch it as it shatters against the counter. The sharp pain in my palm gives me a good excuse to scream, and people rush in as the warm puddling of blood fills my hand.

The homeless man, rather than running out the door to escape, grabs a dish towel from the sink and walks quickly over to me. "We need to put pressure on it," he says in a quiet and efficient way, taking my hand and wrapping it mummy-style in the towel. Then he presses it between his two hands and lifts it between us. "Keep it above heart level," he says, still pressing, looking at me with eyes so translucent I feel dizzy looking into them.

No one finds it strange that this intruder is playing doctor. They act as though he belongs here.

His dark hair is shaggy, but not in the cool, deliberately unkempt way that Damian's is. And his clothes are clearly not his own. They're at least one size too large and look like they've had more lives than a curious cat. At first I hold my breath against the odor I imagine he must have, but then I breathe normally, smelling only a hint of something recently cooked. I must be going into shock, because I start to enjoy the feeling of him squeezing my hand, particularly so close to my breasts.

Mom bursts in then, saying, "Tallie, what happened?" She is trailed by a small strange entourage: a tiny old woman in a purple turban, a transvestite with facial hair, a man with tattoos covering his bald head.

Patches of light and dark flash before my eyes. "I think I'm going to faint," I hear a voice say, and it's mine. The next thing I know, I'm sitting on the hard tile floor and everyone is looking at me from on high, eyes wide.

"Honey, are you all right?" Mom kneels down and touches my forehead as if I might have a fever. "Let's take a look, see if you need stitches."

The rest of the onlookers get bored that I'm not dying and filter out of the kitchen, all but the homeless man and the turban lady. She stands behind my mother, who inspects my hand—the hand that needs to be able to play piano tomorrow. The old woman's raisin face is painted dramatically with turquoise eye shadow and orange lipstick, which has clumped like neon cottage cheese in the corners of her mouth. In a cigarette voice she says, "So this is your daughter, Lee?"

"What?" Mom sounds flustered, but she quickly regains her Southern civility. "Oh, yes. This is Tallie. Tallie, Miranda is a renowned sculptor."

"We've heard so much about you, dear," the raisin says, bending down to offer a knobby, vein-mapped hand with long curving magenta fingernails. "Welcome home." She apparently hasn't noticed that my right hand is out of commission, so I reach up with my left one. She doesn't actually grasp my hand, just lets her own hover there for a moment, so I quickly clutch it and then pull my hand back into my lap, resisting the urge to wipe it on my leg.

"And, Tallie," Mom continues, "your knight in shining armor here is my friend Perry."

"And Perry is . . ."

"One of your mother's projects," he says. He smiles, a small, almost secret smile. I want to smile back but I get a grip. The guy's a bum, for God's sake.

"Oh, Perry," Mom says, tsking him. "You most certainly are not a project." Then to me, "He has the potential to be a wonderful artist."

The raisin pipes in, "He's a bit shy, aren't you, dear? You should come out and be with us, participate in the sharing of ideas, the camaraderie of other artists, not hide in the kitchen."

I get the feeling that the whole point of our being gathered here has gone by the wayside. "So is anybody going to tell me what the hell is going on with my hand?" I'm finally feeling more like myself.

"Well, dear, the cut's not too deep and the bleeding has already stopped." Mom stands and pulls me to my feet. "We just need to clean it up and get a bandage on it."

After my hand is cleaned, dosed with antibiotic ointment, and bandaged, I decide to call it a night. I thought I'd be lying low for a while at my mother's, no major dramas. Instead, I'm living in the middle of a three-ring freak show.

I push through the crowd in that way I've always done in bars, gently but firmly, smiling, nodding, "Yes, I'm the singer, but I have to go on now," acknowledging compliments and deflecting groping hands. I have to admit, groping hands are not a problem at this party, but this is an unusual crowd, after all.

An unmistakable head of red hair comes through the door. Audra the Lyon. Mom sees her, too, and waves. They may be buddies, but I find the woman pushy and loud. I thread through the crowd, escape to my room.

I can't stop thinking about Mom's homeless "friend." He must be a wino, hanging out in there with all those bottles, but there appears to be something more to him. Mom seems to think so, but she's naive when it comes to people, letting all those strange creative types lounge all over her white furniture, scuff their Doc Martens soles on her nice wood floors.

I leave the lights off as I undress, then open the window to let the night air fill the room. The moon beams down and I lie in the pool of its light on my bed, sinking into the bed's embrace. I keep my bandaged hand on my chest, above my heart, flexing my fingers into C chords, G-minor sevenths. Relieved that my hand is, indeed, operable, I relax and drift away, up into the moon's brilliance, her white-chocolate Moon Pie face smiling and kind and familiar.

PART TWO

Pig's wallowed in the mud long enough.
Time to pick his self up and strut his stuff

—"Pig in a Pen," Big Gal Sal

13

Some days creep by so slowly you'd swear the clock was broken, while certain indelible moments last forever—whether pleasant or horrifying—but in general, time is this crazy rushing river that flows swiftly around all sides of you. Say you want to stand still, just until you get your bearings, figure things out. Too bad, because the bottom's slippery as snot and the force of all that water from upstream carries you somewhere new and different, whether you're ready or not.

Sal says, "Don't fight the river, child. Flow with it."

I wish that was as easy as it sounds.

At my second gathering, I'm determined to spend some time with the sexy black man, Shanti. So is every other female in the room. I find him in the overstuffed chair I first sat in at Mom's place, surrounded by women, some sitting on the ottoman, some on the wide arms of the chair, one leaning annoyingly close to him and laughing prettily into his ear.

I walk up and he stands immediately, causing his groupies to splutter and give me the evil eye. "I've been wanting to talk with you," he says, and my erogenous zones prick to attention. My visions of the two of us, intertwined, mingling sweat and saliva, fizzle when he says, "We need your mother for this."

He pulls me by my hand through the crowd. I enjoy his tight

grip and sense of urgency until we come upon Mom in the hall-way. She is surrounded by a band of powdered, black-haired, counterculture types who look like Boy George's love children with Johnny Rotten.

"Lee," Shanti says with an odd authority in his voice, "it's time to talk."

Mom flutters a little, hand rising to her heart the way it does when she's nervous, but she apologizes to her pale friends and follows us into the kitchen. I look around for the homeless guy, but the three of us are the only ones in the room.

"What's going on?" I ask as we settle around the table, the two of them on one side, me on the other. With the bright light overhead, it feels like an interrogation.

"Your mother has something to explain to you," Shanti says.

Mom gives him a pleading look, then sighs and turns to me. "Yes, dear. I do."

I wish I were in my room or anywhere else but here. I wish I were in Kansas.

"There's a reason you're back in Denver," she starts.

"Yeah, I got this job."

"Well, yes." She nods, looks at her hands, then at me. "Actually, I found you the job, through my . . . through Audra."

"No," I say slowly, "my agent, Lyle, arranged it."

"Well, yes, we asked for Lyle's help, that's true."

"But, I *told* Lyle . . ." It's out of my mouth too fast to think about it, and Mom nods.

"I know. You told him not to let us know where you were, and he never did. Not in the ten years I've been trying to get him to." She shakes her head and sighs. "But when Shanti said you were in trouble . . ." She looks away for a moment, then back. "Please, honey, don't be upset with me. Even Lyle knew it was time for you to come home."

"Hang on." I put up my hands like a traffic cop. "What the hell does Shanti"—I look at him apologetically, not wanting to blow my chances with him—"know about me? About anything? He just met me, for crying out loud."

He nods, seeming to accept this, and says, "I'm a spiritual advisor, Tallie, a clairvoyant. I was born with a gift, like you were. Yours is singing, your mother tells me. Mine happens to be knowing things, seeing things that others can't."

Like that explains it. I turn to Mom, exasperated. "What are you saying?"

She looks at Shanti, then me, twisting her fingers together on the table. "Shanti did a reading for me and got a message from the spirit world, from a singing female spirit—"

I sit straighter in my chair.

"—who said you were in trouble and you needed to come home. I tracked down Lyle and, sure enough, he said you were about to lose your job." She gestures and raises her eyebrows, like "See?" then reaches across the table. "I asked him to send you home. I've messed up your whole life, Tallie. I wanted to make things right."

She lays her hand on my arm, but I don't react. One thing is for sure: I'm firing Lyle's ass tomorrow. Goddamn him. Goddamn her, for that matter. My life is not that messed up. "So it's all been bullshit? This is all charity for the loser daughter? The audition was a sham?"

"Oh, no," she says, pulling back. "Audra insisted on a regular audition."

Three of Shanti's admirers break noisily through the kitchen door, empty wineglasses pointed like compass needles toward the bottles on the counter. They see us, though, and retreat quickly into the living room without refills.

We sit silently for a long moment. Mom looks like she might cry, but I could give a shit. What if she wouldn't have "rescued" me, what would have happened then? Surely Lyle would have gotten me a gig with another band. He always found me something fairly decent, when he could. I'll bet he'd have never thought of Denver or this piano bar thing on his own, without her input. I remember my last conversation with him: "You gotta start somewhere when you're starting over." Maybe he didn't mean starting my career over. Maybe he meant starting over back at home. He always did like to lecture me about how wonderful family is.

I stand, look hard at my mother. "Well, thanks for ruining my fucking career," I say and slam back out into the thick boozy crowd. I have to figure out how to fix this disaster, somehow, but first I'm going to get good and drunk.

Later, Audra arrives in the melee of the party and quickly attaches herself to my mother's side. Mom kisses her cheek, looking relieved with her arrival. I feel sick, knowing I'll feel even more awkward around Audra now, knowing she thinks I'm some pathetic loser. Knowing she's thought that the whole damned time. To my credit, however, I have kept Shanti's full attention since he chased after me when I left the kitchen.

"Does it bother you?" he asks now, looking at me carefully, then at Mom and Audra.

I'm thickheaded from wine—it never was my drink. Is he asking about the job thing? Of course it bothers me. Or does he mean that my mother is friends with my new boss, and that the two of them conspired in all this? I mean, look at them together, all hands like junior high school girls, like fruitcakes, actually. Then I realize with blinding clarity what he means. Suddenly I am off-kilter, light-headed, the world turning sideways, and I take a step back to regain my balance. I shake it off, turn my back to them. I work to steer the conversation back to safer ground, touching Shanti's arm in a way that I hope will seduce him into forgetting he ever asked me that question.

We'd been talking about Jedd and me, about reincarnation and coming back lifetime after lifetime to work through certain problems. I'm stymied by this notion, by the thought of another lifetime spent in the spin cycle of pain with Jedd, but I want Shanti to continue, to keep talking to me in his melodic voice. I want to hear that voice in some dark steamy place, where it's just the two of us.

He says, "The whole point is to work out the problems now, in this lifetime, to find eternal peace." I don't ask what happens when you work it all out. Does that mean you never get to come back, and if so, isn't that more of a punishment than a reward? I mostly try not to think about it, or Jedd, which works about as well as trying not to think about Mom and Audra.

Thank God bad news can only come in threes. The final blow of the night comes when Shanti casually mentions that he's celibate, "for spiritual reasons." I maintain my composure, nod politely like this is not the most idiotic thing I've ever heard, but I feel like a balloon pissing air. I can barely stand the thought of not having him. Then it occurs to me—Jason, the bartender. He can't be celibate. My thoughts continue, though, past Jason, careening down another path, toward a shaggy head of hair, a pair of electric blue eyes. It scares me so much I shut down the old lust generators for the night.

When I first memorized Lyle's phone number so many years ago, it was like a magical string of digits, their order perfect and satisfying to tap into a phone. *Deet do deet, do deet do, do deetle deet.* A melody that meant I was somebody important, somebody with an agent. I've waited all morning for Mom to go to her Artists as Advocates meeting. Finally I'm alone, nursing my thumping head and flip-flopping stomach with a tall glass of Alka-Seltzer. I *knew* wine wasn't my drink. With little of my old enthusiasm, I pick up the phone and punch in the numbers.

One ring, another. I'm waiting for his machine to come on, rehearsing how to ask whether or not he really thinks I'm washed up, when he answers, "Lyle Owens."

"Hey, Lyle. It's me."

"Oh," he says. He's still pissed at me for hanging up on him.

"Listen, I'm sorry I've been so emotional lately, but you have to admit, life hasn't exactly been going my way."

"Yeah," he says. "Life's a bitch. What can I do for you?" I've never heard his voice sound so cold before. Lyle has always loved me; the thought that he might not now makes me swallow hard, close my eyes.

"Hell, Lyle, I don't know exactly why I'm calling you, except that you've always been the one person on my side, no matter what. Remember when I got stuck in Madison that winter? When those stupid Flock of Seagulls clones left me high and dry because I wouldn't cut my hair? You saved my ass. You've always been there for me."

"Yeah, well, that's my job." I hear him sigh, then his tone softens when he says, "So, what's up? How's Denver?"

"My mom told me about her arranging for me to come home."

"She's a good lady."

"But, why did you do it? Why didn't you find me something else, like before? Something out *there*"—I'm about to cry, damn it, snot and all, and there's no pretending I'm not—"not *here*? Something *better* than this, anything but this . . ."

"Come on, Tallie girl. Calm down." I can picture him rubbing his brow, cigar smoldering between his stubby fingers. "It was the best option there was. If it hadn't been for your mother calling, right at that moment, I don't know what I would've done."

"But, Jesus, Lyle. You have a million connections. You know you only did this to please my mother, to satisfy your warped desire for me to get back with my family."

"As strange as that logic is, honey, I wish it was true." He sighs again. "I truly wish it was."

It sinks in finally, and it's like getting fired all over again. Not fired from some stupid bar, or a twelve-week tour, but fired from the only thing I want to do. Hell, know *how* to do. I'm doubled over with it, crying from a place so lost in me that I can't talk anymore, not even to can Lyle's ass. I drop the phone and sob into my hands, bawling uncontrollably until I worry Mom will come home and find me like this. I jam the heels of my hands against my eye sockets, force myself to stop, then sit quietly for a while, trying not to hiccup. Pretty soon the sound of Sal's voice, singing low and sweet, fills me like it always used to.

"Okay," I whisper, hugging my knees to my chest, fingers laced in prayer around them. "Whatever." I feel like I'm giving up, like I'm giving in to something strange and powerful and beyond my comprehension. But, hell, I don't know what else to do.

Soon after my father left us, Mom went through the first of many religious phases. I didn't mind too much that first time, because when I arrived in the Sunday school classroom, there in the corner stood a gleaming black upright piano. I was drawn to it, like a nun to holy water, and it took everything in me to wait until class was over to check it out.

As soon as the lady in the pink suit dismissed us to run upstairs and find our parents, I strode toward that shiny blackness, hopped onto the bench, and pressed middle C. *Doe,* from the song I called "Doe, a Deer." I knew the next note was higher, and the next higher, and I sat there and picked out the tune, never hitting a bad note, according to my mother.

She and the Sunday school teacher stood behind me in the doorway, chatting at first, then stopping when they realized I was playing a song.

"Your daughter takes lessons?"

"Why, no," Mom said. I remember the pleasant surprise in her voice. "I don't believe she's ever even seen a real piano before."

They clapped when I finished, so I played it again, singing along this time, and they stood wordlessly.

"You have a talented girl there, Mrs. Beck," the Sunday school teacher said when I was done.

Mom said, "I guess I do," hand on her cheek, giving me a look that made me run and throw my arms around her waist. "Well, my little star," she said, smoothing my hair. "You're full of surprises. Let's go get Janie."

I have never felt more famous.

I certainly don't feel famous now, walking into Sing Out! for my first performance. I used to love arriving at whatever club we were playing, entering the supercharged atmosphere, everyone whispering and smiling as I'd carry my guitar case through the crowd. Now, as I walk into Sing Out!, I'm empty-handed and no one recognizes me. The few patrons who have arrived early mill around restlessly, there either to get a good seat for a long night of partying or to have a quick drink before moving on to one of LoDo's countless restaurants, bars, clubs, and coffeehouses.

Audra meets me next to the stage. "You've got your set list? Sheet music?" She acts more nervous than I am, which is saying something since I really am nervous, a condition I barely remember from my early days with the Holy Rollers.

I nod, and she continues her checklist. "You remember the segues, the routines? Just don't wing it, okay? Not your first night, please, Tallie. Leave it up to Domingo if you forget."

Domingo's my dueling-piano partner, like Rebecca's Chuck. We've been rehearsing together all week. He's not date material—he's a flaming preener, with a wild flip of hair and such long skinny legs that I secretly call him the Flamingo—but he's kind and funny, and so far he makes life at Sing Out! bearable. And he's good at this piano bar thing. I've watched him a few times. No matter what insult he hurls at the audience, no matter how prancy he gets, he always wins them over. Even the burly macho men end up laughing and applauding. He says we're going to be great together because we have a Sonny and Cher energy, like yin and yang, black and white, perfect balance.

With no introduction, we climb the stage steps. A few patrons glance up, then go back to their drinks, their conversations. I take a seat at the piano I've been practicing on, stage right. It's the nicest piano I've ever touched, a Steinway baby grand, and I already think of it as my compadre.

Domingo raises his eyebrows at me from across our two pianos and I nod, lick my papery lips. We've decided to start with something he sings, which I'd originally bristled at, but now I'm relieved. He plays the opening chords to "Yesterday." I launch in a half bar late, then realize I'm in the wrong key. From across the room, I can almost hear Audra's sharp intake of breath, feel her stingray eyes. I correct quickly, no big deal, but it's a lousy start. Not that the audience cares. Some of them nod along a little, but no one bothers to quit yapping or sucking down their beers.

At the end of the song, three people clap, but Domingo nods politely. "Ladies and gentlemen, boys and girls," he says. "Welcome to the best little sing-along joint in Denver. My name is Domingo, and joining me tonight for the first time ever on the Sing Out! stage, just back from her national tour"—here he winks at me—"Denver's own Miss Tallie Beck!"

This time two people clap and I hear a girl in back say, "Who?"

"Ready, Tallie?" he says, not quite far enough from the mike, and

I feel myself flush, knowing that now everyone will think I'm an amateur.

"You bet your sweet ass I'm ready," I say fully into the microphone. This time I don't just feel Audra react. I see her head snap around, the frown on her face, and not one bone in my body cares. "Come on, everybody, it's 'Mustang Sally' in the alley, time to get on up and boogie down." As I say it, I realize this is not a dance bar. Of course no one is going to boogie down, and I'm sure I'll receive extra demerits for straying from the script. But as I belt out the first verse, mustering up every ounce of attitude I've got, heads swivel, chairs scrape, and I seal the deal with the only people who really matter in this business.

Despite the fact that I sing at a freaking piano bar, the actual routine isn't too bad. I lounge around during the day, watch VH1 and E!, read the entertainment section of the *Denver News Daily*, the horoscopes. Go for coffee. I usually manage to avoid Mom. It's uncomfortable, but there are pluses to this arrangement. I never have to lug heavy equipment through narrow doors or up rickety steps, and I never have to travel six hundred miles in a crowded stinky van to the next gig. I get ready for work at about four or five, go do the show, and get home early enough to lounge around some more before bedtime. I never used to come offstage before two A.M. If I hadn't gotten lucky that night, I would lie wide awake wherever I was supposed to be sleeping and listen to the loud ringing in my ears, an occupational hazard.

As I get ready for work now, it hits me how living here has already changed me. I've always had to be a chameleon, creating the right look for whatever band I was in, and now I'm beginning to look like the other performers at the bar, even the funky artists at Mom's parties. I broke down and got clodhopper shoes like everyone wears since wearing heels with a polo shirt is about like drinking champagne with pork rinds. Fortunately, like Rebecca, I know a thing or two about looking sexy no matter what the obstacle. I slide a tight miniskirt up my hips and wiggle into a black size XS Sing Out! polo shirt. It fits me like snake skin and rides in a come-hither way up my stomach. I've kept the buzz hairdo and I splurged on an updated makeup palette for my new persona: smoky, smudgy eye colors, shiny dark lips. Shimmer Pink is history.

I spray my new unisex perfume, YX, down my top and up my skirt, a good luck ritual for attracting male company. I haven't gotten anywhere with Jason. It's hard to get near him; girls flock around like he's the second coming of Elvis. He's probably too young for me, but that could be a good thing. I stare into the mirror, thinking about his nubby head sandpapery against my neck, the metallic clink of ear studs against my teeth. Once again, though, my thoughts zing out of control, sliding past Jason to Perry, the homeless man. My thoughts drift to him too often for comfort, but there's something fascinating about him, like watching a bug on its back with its legs waggling in the air, waiting to see if it will roll itself over.

Maybe that's Mom's fascination, too. When I asked her about him, I saw it in her eyes as she talked about him—that moist, sorrowful look she fixes on me, too, since I've been back. She says Perry lived on the streets up until a couple of months ago and now he stays at the Denver Homeless Shelter a few blocks away. He recently started to work there. She met him at one of the freebie art classes she teaches to the perpetually down-on-their-luck at churches and schools and shelters.

Maybe she's out to fix her past mistakes by rescuing the poor homeless-artist wanna-be. Maybe she's trying to reinvent herself as a good parent by taking in the wayward daughter. Whatever. All it means to me is I have a place to stay and a steady job until I can pull myself out of this hellhole.

I'm taking one last look in the mirror to touch up my lipstick when the phone rings. It's Jane.

"Oh . . . hi," she says, like she's surprised I answered. "I was calling to talk to Mom."

No shit, I want to say. We haven't talked to each other since the day I moved out of her house. "Well, you missed her," I say tersely, so she'll know I'm in a hurry. "I'll leave her a note." And birds fly south in the summer.

"Um, okay," she says, and I hear something in her voice. "So how's it going over there? You settling in?"

"Yeah, sure. Nice place. Easy commute anyway." I humor her, curious. She sounds friendly, but it's more likely she's checking up on me.

"Have you gone to one of her parties yet?" she asks.

"Unfortunately. What a trip. How do you get out of it?"

"She's never invited me," she says. "I'm not . . . I don't know." That thing in her voice again. "The right kind of person, I guess."

"Really?" I ask. And I am?

"So anyway," she says, all business again. "Guess I'd better get dinner started."

After we hang up, I rummage through a drawer until I find a pen and some scratch paper, then write: *Call Jane.*

14

♪ "R-E-S-P-E-C-T," Sal's singing, dressed in a tubular little '60s number with her hair teased to kingdom come. I'm boogying along, when I realize I'm asleep and dreaming. Otis Redding wrote and recorded "Respect" in 1965, two years before Aretha made it a hit and a year after the Big Gal died. There's no way she could be singing it. And there's no way she'd wear that dress.

I struggle to open my eyes, see it's barely daylight, and crawl out of bed. I stumble into the kitchen all foggy and sleep-wrinkled, and Mom's making breakfast. "We haven't exactly gotten off to the best start, so I thought I'd make you some pancakes," she says, sliding another onto a plateful on the counter, "like the old days."

The pancakes are in animal shapes—a mouse, an elephant, something else I can't quite make out. I'd forgotten this about her. On her good days, the days after bad days, she'd make us special food—grilled cheese sandwiches in cookie-cutter shapes, pigs-in-a-blanket, and once she even made cherries jubilee, flames and all. As kids, Jane and I loved these peace offerings, but the sight of her there in her bathrobe, spatula in hand and a shy expectant smile on her face, causes my stomach to churn. This isn't supposed to be like back then. Everything is supposed to be different now.

"Oh, wow," I say, hands going clammy. "Actually, I really don't eat much in the morning." I grab a coffee mug from the cupboard. "I mean, thanks and everything, but you shouldn't go out of your way."

Her brows gather and she looks like she might say something, but she turns the stove off, sets the spatula gently on the counter, and leaves the room.

I knew Sing Out! was a "participation-style" piano bar, but the reality of it didn't hit me until the first night I sang on that stage. When everyone—every obnoxious drunk, every ham, Dick, and Harry—sings, it pretty much drowns me out. Even on my spotlight songs, people chime in instead of just listening like they're supposed to. Tonight I pick the most obscure song I can think of to throw them off, an old Rod Stewart ballad from before his disco days. The audience comes in on the chorus anyway, even though they don't know the words, mouthing along like guppies.

I turn my attention toward Domingo, who is listening with his eyes closed, an appropriately reverential look on his pretty, dark face. "This is the way it's done," I'd like to tell the audience. "This is listening, folks." But I concentrate on the smoke curling behind him in the pink spotlight, the way he sways just slightly in time to the music. I sing the song for him, rooting out every tender emotion I can find.

Audra corners me as soon as I walk offstage.

"Tallie? I need to see you in my office, please." She walks away briskly and I follow, feeling busted. The waitstaff watches us pass.

"What's up?" I ask as she settles behind her desk. She reminds me of every principal I ever had to talk to in school.

"I think you know," she says, and my mind spools through the last couple of weeks. What have I done? Was it that extra comp drink I finagled out of Eileen last night? That extra cigarette I smoked before going on last Saturday, which made Domingo so anxious I thought he was going to hyperventilate? Or was it a few nights ago when that cute Wall Street-looking guy sent up a napkin with his phone number? I mean, they fling insults to customers around here all the time. All I did was broadcast his number for any single females in the audience who might like to call him. Okay, and I made him stand and turn around, so everyone could see how cute his butt looked in his chinos, but it was all harmless fun. And besides, I thought Audra was in her office.

"I honestly don't know what you're talking about," I say, rubbing the back of my neck and finding a pimple, volcanic and about to blow.

"It's so many things, Tallie. Where do I start?" She looks tired. "It's not that difficult to work here. You show up on time, you do your set—as written, thank you very much. Then you go home after having one complimentary drink at the bar. You sing one spotlight song, approved by me, per set. You wear a polo shirt that fits." She sighs, leans back. "Got it?"

If I wasn't related to my mother, something tells me I'd be out of here already.

"Yeah, sure." I shift to my other foot, then back, and say, "But you know, the spotlight songs are the only variety I get around here. And the audience. Don't you think they want a little something different every once in a while? I mean, I'm pretty good at judging what they're in the mood for, usually . . ." I trail off as her eyes narrow. "But yeah, I've got it. No problem."

I'm almost through the door when she says, "And Tallie—"

I turn, hand on the doorknob.

"You might want to reconsider your attitude at home, too. Your mother is doing the best she can."

This morning, like more and more mornings, I wake up as soon as the sun lights the window. It's not that I haven't been awake at six a.m. before, but usually only when I haven't been to sleep yet. This is new and strange. Who would have guessed I was a morning person?

I avoid the kitchen, opting instead to throw on a pair of cutoffs and a T-shirt and slip quietly out the front door. I take a long walk around LoDo, smoke a few Salems. Shuttle buses rumble in place at the Market Street Station and businesspeople hurry by even at this ungodly hour. Winos sleep on bus benches, in doorways. A group of them sit on a small patch of neat grass in front of the

Westin hotel, shooting the shit, passing a brown bag. I avoid the alleys—where the Dumpsters smell worse than anything I could imagine, like large, long-dead things are in them—and stick to the nicer streets, the ones with shops and restaurants and offices. After I've made my rounds, I head for home, taking a detour to the bar, another morning habit I've developed.

In case of emergency, Audra hides a key outside, behind a removable brick. She told me this as part of my "orientation," and she even told me the security code, made me write it on a piece of paper to keep in my wallet. All the employees have this information, but I'm the only one who seems to take advantage of it. No one's ever here before noon, not even the cleaning lady, so I figure, why not make use of those nice pianos? Hell, if I practiced the playlist, that would make it almost legal.

It's spooky-quiet inside, and dark. I don't open the blinds or turn on the lights, just find my way through the maze of tables and chairs by the cracks of light filtering through the uneven blinds, knocked about by unsteady patrons last night. The stale bar smell fills my lungs like a tonic. I grab a mineral water from the fridge, twist the top off, and pull a long fizzy swig from the bottle. Jedd always liked to watch me drink beer from the bottle, said it was sexy. As hard as I try not to think that particular thought, it dizzies me enough that I have to grab the counter. Then I shake it off and head for my piano.

Sometimes I do practice the playlist, but more often I end up singing my favorite blues tunes, or cover songs from eons ago. "Don't You Want Me," an '80s synth-pop song sung flatly by British art students posing as musicians, becomes a scorching ballad when I slow it down and pour emotion into the simple lyrics. And the mindless Van Halen anthem "Dance the Night Away," where David Lee Roth screeches and howls through the whole thing, becomes gospel rock and roll when I give it a rollicking, old-time feel.

I keep hoping if I just let go, sing whatever comes to mind, I'll find the inspiration to write again. It's like I'm a plugged-up pipe— it's all there inside me, from the fresh clear stuff to the slimy hairballs, but I can't find the damned Drano.

Today I'm in the mood for the Delta blues. I start with "Walkin' Blues," by the master, Robert Johnson. It's always been my traveling song, running through my mind in time with the road clicking under the wheels. As I sing it today, though, I remember the stories about Robert Johnson selling his soul to the devil, how he gave up everything for some hot guitar licks and the tiny bit of fame he got while he was still alive.

I remember how lonely it could be on the road, even when I was surrounded by people. I've always wondered about that feeling—how the hell could it be?—but it dawns on me now that most of those people probably never really gave a damn about me, except as their meal ticket or their sure-thing lay. It feels so painfully true that I laugh out loud to chase it away, then stand and stretch. I can't shake it, though, so I go to grab a breath of fresh air out the back door.

I click open the dead bolt, but the door won't push out. I lean harder and someone says, "Ow!" from the other side. Homeless people sleep everywhere, even in these smelly alleys. I push the door just enough to peer out and see Perry standing in the middle of the dirt alley among broken beer bottles and yellowed newspapers, rubbing his shoulder.

"I was just listening to you sing. I didn't scare you, did I?" He looks scared himself, like he thinks I'm going to yell at him, or call the police.

I shake my head no, smooth my hair back, wishing I'd put on some lipstick. I'm worried what I look like to a homeless man. When I first saw him in Mom's kitchen he was a mystery, and today I'm even more confused. His black hair is combed neatly and his shirt is pressed, though his pants are too big and torn at the bottom from dragging. It's like he's a reverse Hulk, going from ogre to human, from torn clothes to neat, and I've caught him in the middle of his transition.

"Your voice is really amazing," he says. "I mean, *really.*"

"Thanks," I say, fighting the urge to invite him in. Audra would kill me.

He nods, looks around. "Well, anyway."

He's about to leave and I can't think of anything to say, so I blurt, "Guess what—I have a ghost." I'm immediately mortified. I've never told anyone this.

He cocks his head, squints a smile. "Yeah?"

"Well, kind of a guardian angel ghost."

"What's this ghost's name?"

I hesitate, study him to make sure he's not making fun of me. "I'm not sure I'm supposed to talk about her."

"Yet you brought it up." Not mean, just stating the facts, ma'am, and I like it that he's busted me like this.

"It's just that, you know, in the movies the person with the ghost usually never talks about it to anyone, because then everyone will think she's crazy, and when she does talk about it, the ghost goes away."

"You don't want her to go away." Something in the back of his eyes, something old and aching and familiar, makes me realize why I can't stop thinking about the guy.

I rub the back of my neck. "You think I'm crazy?"

"I'm not one to judge," he says, thrusting his hands into his torn pants pockets, "but, no. I don't think you're crazy."

I look down to hide the smile that has involuntarily spread into a grin. I haven't felt this awkward since junior high.

"Well, then," he says and turns to walk away. His shoes have no laces, causing him to shuffle-step, shuffle-step in the dirt.

"Perry," I say quietly, so he won't hear me.

He stops and turns and looks at me, eyes like searchlights as they travel up and down my body, not stopping at the obvious parts, just seeming to take me all in. I should say something to stop him, but I don't. I let him look at me like that, like a lover. I'm repulsed and excited at the same time. I should go back inside, quit leading the poor guy on, but I close my eyes, feel his eyes turn into sensitive hands, gliding over me gently. Oh, what the hell, I decide, and open my eyes.

Perry is nowhere in sight.

15

♪ My family is coming to see me sing today, a pleasant little outing on a Saturday afternoon, after which we'll have another "family dinner" at Mom's. Jane, Andrew, and Emma have come over a couple of times since I've been living there, but I lied each time and said I had to cover for Rebecca, who I claimed was late one time and sick the next. I switched to "sick" when I realized the "late" excuse didn't get me out of the entire evening. Mom made everyone wait for dessert until I came home.

At least I don't mind hanging out with Emma, who has taken to playing guitar like Eric Clapton Junior. I've only shown her a few easy chords and strums, but she practices at home on a student guitar and Jane signed her up for private lessons. The other thing she gets from me is her rebel soul. What I'd thought was just brattiness seems more complicated. It's like she's fighting against something that's horrible but invisible and she keeps swinging to make it stay away.

When the four of them walk into Sing Out!, the place is half empty. I'm singing the Top 40 ballad du jour and the women in the audience are emoting with me. I hate this song, so hearing all these off-key choir girls ruining it is like sweet justice.

Mom stops and puts her hand to her face, beaming that proud mother smile at me before she finds Audra at the bar. They settle onto bar stools, chatting like they haven't just seen each other the day before. Jane probably knows less about them than I do. Other than at Mom's parties, where alternative lifestyles are a given, they seem pretty secretive about the whole thing.

Jane and Andrew look around nervously for a table in the back, but Emma sprints to the front, pulls up a seat at a table in the front row. Her parents look wary, but they join her.

Emma's face shines up at me. She's never seen me perform. No one in my family has, for that matter. Andrew leans toward Jane, says something to her, then nods at me and smiles. She shrugs and nods halfheartedly. He ignores her and sings along, bumbling the words and nudging Emma. He seems like a fun guy—I wonder what he sees in my sister. Jane gives one of the PA speakers a dirty look. It's too loud for her. The waitress brings their drinks: a draft beer for Andrew and Cokes for Jane and Emma.

Unfortunately for my sister, they've arrived at the point in the show where the Flamingo goes in search of the most uptight woman in the audience to bring up onstage for a rousing rendition of "Why Don't We Get Drunk (and Screw)." I know who he'll choose, and I can't think of a way to tell him it's not a good idea. We've worked out some signals, but we need a new one: hands-to-throat, a choking motion, meaning "She'll kill me if you pick her!"

Even though Jane avoids eye contact with him as he sashays across the stage, the Flamingo stops right in front of her and holds out his hand. When she ignores him, he incites a near riot in the rest of the audience, until finally Jane has no choice but to stand to boisterous applause and take her place on the stage.

I look over toward the bar and my mother is laughing and shaking her head. Emma is so excited that she giggles uncontrollably into her hands and shimmies in her seat like she has to pee. Andrew tries to hide a smile, but he's obviously enjoying it, too. Jane looks terrified, sitting next to the Flamingo on his piano bench. He gives her a handheld mike to use, and she keeps pointing it at the floor, right into a monitor. Screeching feedback results, making everyone in the audience laugh. The Flamingo reaches over and shows her how to hold it and I cover his piano part while he's convincing her to sing. Luckily for me, I play no part in this little scenario other than playing and singing harmony on the choruses.

Finally, Jane sings along, although at an inaudible decibel level. She coughs away from the mike and shifts nervously in her seat, but she keeps singing about getting drunk and screwing.

These lyrics, of course, send Emma into shrieking peals of laughter. Jane makes a face at her daughter, and by the second chorus she turns up the volume. By the end of the song, I'd swear she was enjoying herself. When she finally climbs down to her seat, Emma looks at her with renewed respect. Mom and Audra have joined them at their table and they all have a good laugh together. I'd say it was a successful family outing, and I'm surprised how relieved I feel.

When it's time for my spotlight song, I play an old favorite, "Guilty" by Randy Newman. My palms go sweaty as I vamp on the intro, playing it several times around before I start the vocals. I realize I haven't run this song by Audra, and I look up at her. She's sitting back in her chair, arms crossed, but I can't read her face. I shrug at her, trying to convey an innocent whoops, but her expression doesn't change. I look down at my hands working the keys and keep singing. This is a damned fine song; if I play it well enough, she'll have to love it as much as I do.

Toward the end of the second verse I catch Jane watching me intently, her face relaxed, her mouth slightly open. I sing the chorus, closing my eyes and losing myself to the powerful words of guilt and regret.

When I finish and look back at Jane, she quickly turns her face away.

"I'm worried about Perry," Mom says. It's the morning after he hasn't shown up at a gathering for the second week in a row—ever since I found him in the alley behind Sing Out!—and Mom's sitting at the table eating toast while I lean against the counter, sipping coffee. It's as close as we've gotten to actually having breakfast together.

"He wasn't even at art class this week," she says.

"So he's not a project, huh?"

Mom finishes her toast in silence. She stands and puts her dishes in the sink, then says, "I know you hold a lot of things against me, but my trying to help people shouldn't be one of them."

I try to protest but she shakes her head, holds up a hand. "I want this to work out, your living here, but you need to think about giving a little, too. I can't be the only one trying." Then she walks out, beating her usual retreat to her room for the day.

I mutter under my breath as I rinse my cup in the sink, mumbling about how some people can't be trying too hard themselves if they're always hiding out behind closed doors. Then again, I guess I'm lucky. It's not like I want to sit around all the time having meaningful mother-daughter chats.

The day stretches ahead endlessly, and I wonder if I should get another job somewhere, but I have no skills, other than musical. I sigh and take my usual position on the couch, pick up a book I'm trying to read about men being from a different planet. If only they knew Perry.

I want a real boyfriend. I want someone who will take me driving in a convertible on hot summer nights, the wind washing me clean, stripping away years of road grime and frustration and never quite getting what I want. I want someone who writes me poetry and whispers it in my ear when I'm scared, someone who makes me want to write a love song. I want someone who has a tight enough grip to hold me when I want to run away and a soft enough touch to make me glad I stayed.

I don't want some homeless drifter, no matter how nice he is.

"You got yourself quite a shopping list there," Sal says. From out of nowhere, she's sitting at the far end of the couch, picking something from between her teeth with her long red pinkie nail. "Why don't you just graciously receive the gifts already being offered to you, child?"

"If I saw something good being offered me," I say, "believe me, I'd grab it in a heartbeat."

"Oh, you would?" Sal says, looking at me sideways. "Then be good to your mother and go down to the shelter and look for Perry."

"You know, Sal, I think you're a little out of touch with reality. Why the hell would I want to do that?" No doubt the shelter is a scary musty place, filled with old drunks, criminal types, crazy people. "You go."

"We'll both go," Sal decides, smoothing her dress over her knees before standing.

I called my mother twice from the road. The first time was on my twenty-first birthday when I made the mistake of giving her Lyle's number. The second was right after Jedd dumped me and went solo. That time, I was lying low in the suburbs of Chicago, in the basement apartment of a friend of our bass player, Billy. Jedd had left us all, not just me, but I was taking it the worst. I hadn't lost just a guitar player.

I wouldn't drag my ass off the beer-scented sofa bed, not even for our nightly gig, not for two weeks. The guys had drummed up a local guitarist who sang some to cover for Jedd, so they just played without me, too. Realizing: a) they could do this, and b) no one knew the difference, sent me over the edge. If Billy's friends had kept guns in the house, or a good stash of downers, I might have been history.

At my lowest point on a Friday night when everyone was at the club, I crawled from the grungy mattress across gritty gold-and-beige linoleum to a phone sitting on a small table. I put it beside me on the floor, staring at it for the longest time before I picked up the receiver and dialed the number. My heart quickened as the earpiece trilled once, then twice. When my mother finally said hello, I gasped at the sound of her voice, so foreign and so familiar. I wanted to wrap that voice around me like an old lady's shawl, to crawl back into bed with it and sleep for days, but I just sat there, trying not to breathe, hoping she'd say something else.

After a moment, the phone clicked dead in my ear. "Bitch," I said, and never called her again.

It's only three and a half blocks from the lofts and restaurants and coffeehouses, but the Denver Shelter could be in another world. The block is "in transition," as they say around here, with vacant warehouses getting snatched up by developers but still graffitied and broken down. The shelter is a long low brick building that fills half the north side of the street, and has only small glass cubes for windows. It was probably some kind of modern architecture at one time, but now it looks like a prison.

Small knots of men stand around outside, smoking, leaning against the wall, and staring at me as I walk toward the entrance. "Honey, if they could see me, believe me, they wouldn't be watching you," Sal says, daintily moving her large frame across the pavement in four-inch heels. I laugh and tell her she ought to look into these clunker shoes. I haven't twisted my ankle or had sore feet in weeks. The homeless men look away when they see me talking to Sal, like I'm crazier than they are. They're filthy and have that too-tanned look of those who live every day, all day, out in the sun. I scan them for a familiar face, but they're scruffy, rough-looking—a different breed of bum altogether from Perry.

Inside, the shelter has the antiseptic smell and fluorescent glow of a hospital, but shabbier. A big open room is visible through a set of double glass doors, with rows of institutional tables and chairs, like a school cafeteria. The small reception area in front looks like those in run-down motels, with a high counter, an oscillating fan blowing papers thumbtacked to the walls, and a grubby old-fashioned dial phone and typewriter on a metal desk. The only things missing are the rows of keys motel clerks give out. A big hand-lettered sign reads NO ALCOHOL, NO DRUGS, NO WEAPONS, NO HATS. What's wrong with hats? I wonder. A smaller sign below it politely asks that everyone sign in. There's no one around, and it seems odd that all those men are standing outside.

"Hello?" I call out. "Anybody home?"

Up pops a head from behind the counter, like in a puppet show. Perry. Once again, he's wearing a clean shirt and his hair is combed. He's recently shaved and a plug of tissue sticks to a red dot on his neck. He looks as surprised to see me as I am to see him. A slow flush works its way up from his collar.

"Oh, hey, Perry," I say, looking around for Big Gal Sal, hoping for a little guidance, a little support. Wouldn't you know it? Right at the moment of truth, she's popped herself out of this space-time continuum.

Perry nods a greeting and grips the countertop a little too tightly with both hands. Even his fingernails are clean. "Wow," he says. "What a surprise, your coming here. I didn't know you knew I . . ."

He seems embarrassed, so I decide to make a joke. "Yeah, well, two can play this let's-spy-on-people-at-work game."

"That's not why I—"

"I know, Perry, I know," I say, laughing, "I'm just giving you shit. I came by because Mom's worried about you."

He loosens his grip on the counter, blood pinkening his white fingernails. "Oh. Of course." He swallows against the top button of his shirt, and I fight an urge to reach over and undo it. "Yeah, so tell her I'm okay. I've just been pretty busy here."

I nod, and he nods, and we pretty much stand there nodding for a too-long moment until he says, "I really did love listening to you sing." He smiles and shrugs, then says in a rush, "It made me feel better. I mean good. You know. Just good."

"Well, why don't you come in during a show, then, instead of hanging out in that dirty old alley?" I laugh—in a friendly way, I hope—until his smile withers. The cover charge. It didn't occur to me that someone this down on his luck couldn't cough up a few bucks just to listen to someone sing. He probably makes next to nothing here. "Nah, on second thought, you're better off staying away during the shows," I say. "They're all scripted and corny, and everybody sings off-key, and half the people are just there to party anyway. They talk so loud you can't hear yourself think sometimes."

Again, the mutual nodding, then we fall silent. Finally, Perry says, "Want a tour?"

"Sure. I've never seen a homeless shelter." I immediately worry that I sound like a snob. "But I *have* been in more run-down juke joints and motel rooms than you can shake a stick at." Now I just sound like an old hooker, but he smiles and steps around the counter and holds the glass door to the cafeteria open for me.

Somewhere inside lunch is being prepared and it smells delicious. I inhale deeply.

"Spaghetti," Perry says, raising his eyebrows like Groucho Marx, and I laugh. He has the manners of someone with a good family, and he reminds me of an old-time movie star, although it might just be the Salvation Army retro clothes. I try not to let on how much I'm checking him out, but he's watching me closely, too. I'm glad I put on a tank top this morning, not one of the T-shirts I usually wear.

According to Perry, the men are standing outside because they're not allowed inside during the day, except for lunch. Then they have to leave again until dinnertime. After that they can sign in for the night, but not all of them do. "Some people just take their meals here," Perry says, showing me the activities room, where there is an ancient television with an upside-down coat hanger for an antenna and assorted couches and chairs that have seen better days.

"But where do they sleep?"

"Wherever they want to. Some people need more freedom than they get here." He coughs into his fist and turns away.

When he shows me the dorms, one for men and one for women and children, I get it. Cotlike beds form row after regimented row, and each contains a folded pile of gray-white sheets and an army blanket. The beds are so close together you could touch the person sleeping next to you. I've slept in some skanky places, but never anything like this. I look around for wood to knock on.

Perry catches me shaking my head. "It's hard to imagine living like this," he says.

I nod, say nothing.

"But it's a place to go, and sometimes that's all that matters." He looks hard into my eyes and I feel myself blush. "Do you know what that's like?"

"Yeah," I try to say, but it comes out strangled, a whispered croak.

We walk back toward the entrance and Perry says, "Tell your mother not to worry about me."

"Yeah, well, you know her," I say, backing out the door. "She can't help herself."

"Me either," I think he says as the door swings closed, but I definitely could be mistaken.

16

Tonight I'm being a good daughter, attending Mom's little party at Audra's request. Between the two of them, they're keeping me housed and employed, and while I don't exactly have a reputation for kissing ass, I'm no fool.

I wish Mom kept beer around, or hard liquor, but it's always just wine, so here I am with a glass of something pink. It's mostly for the security of being able to look busy, holding it and sipping alone in the middle of babbling strangers. But, I'll admit, I do love the initial warm feeling after the first fumy mouthfuls, the tingly weakness in my arms and legs, the pleasant hum in my head. At times in the past I've drunk more than I should have, like when Jedd got famous and I didn't. But since I've been at Sing Out! I rarely drink while I'm working and I have only one nightcap (two if I can swing it) after my shift ends. No problemo.

I usually avoid Mom's parties, staying in my room or slipping out into the dark open city. Sunday nights are quiet in LoDo, and I walk the long blocks, checking out the bums and the tourists and other city dwellers like me, out walking their dogs or swinging hands with companions of the opposite, or sometimes same, sex. I nod at the pedal-cab drivers, the waiters smoking outside the restaurants during their breaks. The carriage drivers let me pet the bored-looking horses that lug out-of-towners and young lovers up and down the streets.

Now I wander through the artists instead until I find Shanti talking with an older couple dressed in matching tweeds. I don't understand what they're saying, so I stand quietly, holding my third glass of wine, sipping it occasionally, and when I feel brave, nodding at something one of them says. Pretty soon my glass is empty. I excuse myself and head for the kitchen. *"My, I am such a good daughter,"* I sing to the tune of "Oh, What a Beautiful Morning."

I'm pouring myself another half glass when Sal clears her throat behind me. I turn and she gives me a look but says nothing. I ignore her, fill my wineglass the rest of the way, and head back into the fray.

Mom, Audra, Miranda the turban lady, and a group of younger women are engrossed in a conversation about famous women artists: Frida, Artemisia, Georgia, names all ending in "uh" sounds. I walk past instead of joining them—just one more conversation that's over my head—but I stop within listening distance. Maybe Mom should change her name to Le*ah*, I think, feeling a little high, and maybe I could be Tal*ia*.

There's no place to sit because the furniture is draped in starving artists. They dress like they're starving anyway, in dingy dark colors, nothing ever ironed or neat. And baggy is a big deal—younger men wear baggy pants falling off their backsides, older men wear baggy pants cinched tight around their waists, and the women come in either the granola, loose-dress variety or the shapeless, neopolyester, messy-hair category. Like my entire life, I don't fit anywhere.

"But they didn't medicate their art out of their grasp," I hear Mom say. Her voice has risen in volume and pitch. It frightens and attracts me at the same time. I edge over, keeping my back to them.

Audra's talking now. "You have to find a balance, Lee. Yes, you have to be able to create, but you can't just take it into your own hands, for God's sake." There's something in that big bossy voice I haven't heard before. She sounds scared.

"Oh, leave her be," an older voice says. Miranda. "She wants to find the muse, yes? She doesn't believe in mediocrity. Who can blame her?"

Just as Mom starts to say something, the obnoxious little bald man swoops in on me, talking a mile a minute.

"Hey, Tallie, remember me? Arnie. Hey, I swear I'm gonna catch your show soon. You doing any of the old songs? How about 'Little Girl Lost' or 'Liquid Kiss?' " He doesn't breathe or wait for an answer; he just keeps going like a wind-up toy on speed. "You writing anything these days? I bet it's hard without Jett. Have you heard from him since you've been back in town? Did you hear his new song on the radio? That weird-ass New Age thing with that Indian chick singing? What's he thinking anyway?"

Fuck. I gulp the rest of my wine. "Here, hold this." I hand him my glass, then whip around and invade Mom's little group, heart pounding. I push into the circle and Mom gives me a curious smile.

"Honey? Are you all right?"

Audra moves closer to her, hulking and, now that I think about it, downright dykish as she assumes the role of protector.

"I was going to ask you the same thing."

"Well, I'm fine. Whatever do you mean?" She's holding wine in one hand, swaying slightly, and her other hand flutters about until it lands on her hip. The Southern belle in distress.

"I know you better than anyone here, right?" I demand, looking from her to Audra, to the raisin and back. "Yeah, I'd say I know a hell of a lot more about you than these people, and I know what you're up to."

"Tallie." Audra's voice is a sharp warning. "I think you've had too much to drink."

"Mother, please tell your friend here to mind her own business. Besides, who the hell in this place hasn't had too much to drink?" My voice is too loud. Everyone looks at me like I'm crazy. The raisin's eyebrows arch so high they almost touch the bottom of her turban.

I turn, brush by the little bald man who's still holding my glass, and escape through the front door.

If I had some money on me, I could stop in somewhere, find a vacant stool at a bar, strike up a totally normal conversation with someone I don't know. I wish I'd at least brought my cigarettes. As it is, I wander aimlessly down the street, looking into windows, trying to breathe and think and get a grip.

My mother's losing it and Jedd's fucking song is on the radio. Fucking asshole motherfuckers, I chant in my head. All of a sudden I can't stand it anymore and I kick a newspaper box. It feels so good I do it again, and again, bashing the flimsy metal until several large dents appear. Thank God for industrial-strength shoes.

"Excuse me," a voice says from above. Great, now I'm hearing God, but I look up and it's a policeman sitting on a horse, Denver's citified version of a Mountie.

"Sorry," I say, trying to appear repentant. "My boyfriend just broke up with me."

"Have you been drinking, miss?" He shines his flashlight into my eyes.

"No. Not really." I squint, hold my hand against the light. "Is that really, uh, necessary? To blind me? I can walk a straight line if you want."

"Do you have some identification?"

"Nope. Just taking a walk. Not driving. Didn't think I'd need any." I'm trying to sound polite, but I'm not entirely successful.

He unclips a handheld radio from his belt and speaks gibberish into it. I have no idea if he's talking about me or ordering a pizza. Then he lowers the radio and says, "You know, I could charge you with vandalism, destruction of property, even malicious mischief, miss. Where do you live?"

"Just up the street," I say, pointing.

"Why don't you head on home, then? I'll be watching."

"Thank you," I say, even though I want to tell him it's a free country, damn it, and I can walk anywhere I want to. Instead, I walk toward the Milk Wagon Stables. True to his word, he sits and watches me every step of the way. As I cross the street, I turn into the doorway of Sing Out! on a whim. It's closed on Sundays, so I'll have the place to myself.

I pull out the removable brick, feel for the key, and slide it into the lock. When it clicks open, I scoot inside the door and pocket the key. As an afterthought, and almost too late, I punch in the security code. Leaving the lights off, I feel my way through the darkness to the bar, knocking my shins and elbows on tables and chairs. At last I grab the smooth wood of the bar top and slide around until I've found the swinging gate where the bartenders walk through. I trip on a rubber floor mat and catch myself with one arm, nearly wrenching it from its socket. "Goddamn it," I cry out, and the sobbing sound echoes back to me. My arm hurts, my shins hurt, and my toes hurt from kicking that stupid box.

I could really use a drink, a real drink. Fortunately, I'm staring at rows and rows of bottles, all faintly illuminated from the streetlight creeping in through the blinds. They look so pretty I run my fingers over them, feeling the shiny glass, letting the murky shadows dance across my hands.

I took my first drink when I was almost twelve. That's not so young, really. I've met plenty of people on the road who started drinking earlier. Ten. Nine, even. Younger than Emma.

I took my first drink because no one was looking, and because I knew from watching Mom's after-work routine that it would make life easier to take, and because it had been a bad day.

Early on a Saturday afternoon, Mom had gone to the grocery store. She'd asked what we wanted for dinner that night, and if we felt like making brownies for dessert. She left in a good mood; she returned home hysterical and desperate. "Agoraphobia," the latest doctor called it. In those days she was always having appointments with new doctors, who gave her new diagnoses and prescribed new pills to treat them. That afternoon, she hurriedly gulped down her medication—"Just a mild sedative," she said—and went to her room to lie down. We had no idea then that she was in the early stages of a doomed love affair with bulldozer-strength tranquilizers and sleeping pills.

An hour later she emerged from behind her closed door, glassy-eyed, stumbling, slurring her words. Jane helped her to her favorite chair in the living room, holding Mom's flailing arm with her own skinny ones. When Mom tried to shake a cigarette from the pack, they scattered everywhere, like an all-white version of our pick-up stix game. Jane plucked a cigarette from Mom's lap, placed it between her slack lips, then tore a match free from a matchbook and struck it across the sandpaper strip. As she held it to the wobbling cigarette, trying to find its end long enough for Mom to suck it lit, I wondered how on earth Jane knew how to do this. I'd never seen her do it before, but they obviously had the routine down. Mom sat there trying to smoke. She'd struggle to get the cigarette to her lips, knocking embers and ashes onto her blouse and the arm of the chair, which Jane would quickly brush away.

It wasn't the worst thing that had ever happened in our house. But that was the first day I sneaked into the kitchen, dragged a chair across the floor, and climbed onto the counter. I reached high above the refrigerator into the cabinet that held my mother's liquor and grabbed the bottle closest to the front. Then I hightailed it to the bathroom, locking the door behind me. The bottle was mostly full of a clear liquid and had a blue and red label. It was probably vodka. The smell of it reminded me of the swab I'd get before a shot. Just one medicinal taste and my world softened, so I had another. Then I opened the cabinet beneath the sink and pushed the bottle behind the Comet and extra toilet paper for safekeeping. I knew I'd be back.

I don't know if it's a dream or if it's real or if I've lost my mind, but I'm on the floor in a darkened nightclub, sitting between two leggy bar stools, leaning up against the vertical surface of the bar. A bottle of something sits hard and reassuring between my legs and I grasp its neck lightly, caressing it. Far away and floating high above the tables in front of me, a single spotlight shines down on the stage, and standing in its glow is Big Gal Sal. She's stunning, wearing a blue strapless evening gown, and she has a white flower in her hair, like Lady Day. She cups the microphone in both hands, crooning into it, and while I can't see any musicians, there must be a band behind her in the shadows. The words aren't clear to me, but the way she moans and shakes her head, I know it's a sad song and I know it's for me. Her pain filters across the room, seeping into me, and I cry and cry, then pick the bottle up and fling it as hard as I can, the sharp crash of glass satisfying.

The next thing I know, there's no more music and I'm being dragged across the floor, out into daylight and the gravel of the alley. I try to struggle free, pretty sure I'm about to be raped or beaten or worse.

"Calm down," I hear Perry's voice say behind me. "I'm just trying to get you out of there before someone finds you."

17

I tiptoe into the loft, slip into my room without waking Mom. After the adrenaline of being scared shitless wears off, the hangover kicks in. My head feels like it's been clanged between two cymbals, my mouth is sour with prevomit bile. I can't shake the feeling that I've done something despicable, that I've committed some heinous crime, which I don't think I have, but the empty blackness of not remembering leaves an ugly raw stain of a question.

All of this is too familiar. I couldn't have stopped drinking last night even if someone had offered me a recording contract, a national bus tour. I would have found a way to sneak another. It's always the same: I start out thinking I'm in control, I am the master of my drinking fate, but then I end up here, in this cesspool. And I always say it's for the last time.

I consider calling Jane to tell her I'm *really* going to quit drinking now, but I snap out of it in two seconds flat.

Late in the morning when I'm beginning to feel halfway human, I hear Audra in the kitchen with Mom. As much as I'd like to blow them off, too, I know this particular music has to be faced.

I slink past their too-close, too-big bodies at the kitchen table, grab a cup, pour coffee. Then I turn and lean against the counter. "Hey, sorry about last night," I say, breezy. "You were right, Audra.

I just had a little too much to drink. I don't even know what I was rattling off about." I sip my coffee, trying to look sincere.

Audra looks at me, like "Yeah, right," but she waves me off. "We've got bigger problems, Tallie. Someone broke into the bar last night."

Mom nods, forgetting herself and holding Audra's hand in front of me.

"What?" I set my cup hard on the counter, switching from sincere to aghast. "Did they take anything? Is everything okay?"

"Well, that's the weird thing. They didn't take a thing, just broke a bottle of tequila," Audra says, shaking her head, "although it was a damned good bottle of tequila. Anyway, I won't be hiding a key anymore. That must have been how they got in—it's missing. So now everything has to be rekeyed. And I'm changing god-damned security companies. Useless sons of bitches. They didn't even notice!"

She doesn't suspect me. I breathe out slowly, off most of the hooks I thought I was on. As Audra rattles on, I think about Perry. After he pulled me out of there, he left without bothering to explain why he was following me, watching me. I don't know whether to feel creeped out or flattered.

Audra is not having a good week. Coyote Cry is stealing our thunder, stealing our audience, even though they've had no luck stealing our performers. Our attendance is down—way down if you believe the rumors—and the worker bees are restless.

Especially Rebecca.

"I don't want to work at the number-two piano bar in town," she complains to anyone who will listen. "And it's not like I haven't had offers."

The other rumor is that Audra checked out the show at Coyote Cry. Something's up, because today at three-thirty, we have an all-employee meeting.

I get to the bar a few minutes late and slouch into a seat in the back. Everyone is talking at once and Audra has to clap her hands to get their attention. "Okay, people," she says. "I think we all know why we're here. It's become obvious we're not getting as many bodies through the door as we should, and we need to take corrective action."

Rebecca pipes up. "You know, I've heard Coyote Cry has double the performers we do. That might be one reason I lose my voice so often."

Audra gives her a look. "We're not here to talk about your voice."

"Well, it's hard singing for hours in all the smoke," Rebecca says defensively. Thank God I have vocal cords of steel.

Eileen, the bartender, shoots her hand in the air, says the waitstaff and bartenders want to be more involved in the show like at Coyote Cry, where they get up on stage every so often and perform stupid dance numbers, like the chicken dance or a '60s medley. "They even get to stand on the pianos," she says. I don't say anything, but there's no way someone's dancing on my piano.

"Yes, yes," Audra says. "I'm well aware of what happens at Coyote Cry. So, step one in the action plan: new routines." She hands out stapled pieces of paper to everyone, both performers and waitstaff. "And performers need to sign up for our new themed medleys. First come, first served."

I amble over and take a peek at the list. I know immediately what I want: the Motown set, the Janis set, and, of course, the blues medley. Everyone else is into the corny stuff: the '50s doowop set, the psychedelic '60s set, the disco '70s set. Then there's the *Grease* revival, with plenty of dancing opportunities for the waitstaff (Eileen's eyes light up like bulbs on a Broadway marquee) and the country medley, including the ever-popular "Lucille," during which the audience gets to scream at the top of their lungs, *"You bitch, you slut, you whore!"* every time the chorus comes around.

Audra's final step in her new action plan is the worst, though. She placed an ad in the paper for more performers. That just about tears it for me, and I follow her to the office after the meeting.

"Yes?" she says, taking her seat without looking up.

"Why are you hiring more performers?"

"Well, I hate to say it, but Rebecca's right. That damned dog-howl place is a chain and they have corporate money to burn. They have nearly twice as many performers as we do."

"So? Why should that affect us?"

"Variety. People want variety. That means I need more performers." She shakes her head, then says under her breath, "I wish I knew how the hell to pay them."

"All I know is this whole thing stinks. I liked it the way it was." Well, not really, but this is even worse.

She looks at me, sighs. "It's not about you, Tallie, believe it or not. I have eighteen people to think of here."

"Hmm," I say, thinking fast. This problem seems relatively easy to solve without doing anything rash. If Audra hires more performers, there might be someone better, prettier, younger than me, and I'll lose my next-in-line status once Rebecca splits. "How about if we handle this without hiring anyone? We could swap shorter shifts between us. That would shake things up."

"I appreciate your concern, Tallie, but I think I'll handle this my way." Her fingernails click an edgy rhythm against the desktop. Suddenly they stop and she says, "Well, I guess that could work. But we still need more faces up there."

"Have you ever considered promoting from within?"

"Like who?" She looks at me doubtfully. "Besides, say we did do this. Then a four-hour shift becomes an eight-hour shift, and I don't know what to do about the longer shifts on Saturdays. I'd be paying everyone twice as much."

"You'd have to pay new performers."

She looks at me for a long time, like that first night I sat here. Finally she asks, "What exactly are you proposing?"

"I'm not sure," I say, "but let me talk to the piano players. I have an idea."

"You want to talk to them?" She leans her head to one side, narrows her eyes. "Why would I let you do that?"

"I've been working with musicians my whole life. I know how to deal with them." It's true. Bands are worse than dysfunctional families. They're like multiple-person marriages—partnership and devotion become polluted with shifting alliances, jealousies, and enough egos to inflate the Goodyear blimp. And the musicians here are no different than any others. You just have to know which buttons to push to get the right result.

"I have a feeling I can work something out," I tell Audra. "Let me try."

She holds up her hands in defeat. "Give it your best shot," she says, shaking her head. "But don't imply that anything you come up with is endorsed by me. And I'm going ahead with the ad."

I gather Chuck, Rebecca, and the Flamingo in a quick huddle as we're making our shift change, and everyone agrees to meet at Beelzebub's after closing. Earlier I called one of the substitute performers who fills in when someone's sick. Bob's a good guy, and I heard he recently lost his techno-geek day job, so I wasn't too surprised when he promised to meet us there. I tell Eileen to come, too. And I keep thinking, my brain whirring like a machine, creating timetables and charts in my head like a corporate bean counter.

Just after two a.m., we gather in the almost-empty coffeeshop. After we've gotten coffee and pulled a couple of chrome four-tops together, I tell everybody about my conversation with Audra. "We just might be able to head this thing off at the pass if we come up with our own plan," I say.

"Like, what kind of plan?" Rebecca asks, doubtful.

"What if," I say, still working it out in my head, "what if we swapped shifts every hour?"

"That won't work," Rebecca says. "We'd all be there all night, with nothing to do half the time."

Everyone nods in agreement. "I think Rebecca's right, Tal," Chuck says.

"It would work if we had more people," I say. "And we have a star in the making in our midst." I look at Eileen, who up until this point must have been wondering why the other bartenders and waitstaff aren't here. She looks up, excitement in her eyes. "How about if she and Bob teamed up?" Bob nods thoughtfully. "Then there'd be three teams to cover all the slots."

Rebecca shakes her head. "Coyote Cry has twice as many performers as we do, for God's sake. How can two more people make a difference?"

"Look," I say, scrounging a pen from my bag, writing on a napkin. "Eileen and Bob play the first hour, then Domingo and me, swapping until it's time for your set."

Everyone leans in to watch as I draw a chart. "Then we can trade with you for the second half of the night."

"Sorry," Domingo says. "I can't work that late. I pick my kids up at the baby-sitter after my shift." We all look at him in surprise—kids?—but Chuck comes to the rescue.

"I'll partner up with you, Tal, for the second set. At least we'll still be changing chicks."

Rebecca still looks doubtful. "I don't know. It just looks like my stage time gets cut down."

"Think of it this way," I tell her, knowing just where to press. "You're still the headliner. You still get all the glory, but you only have to sing half as long each night. You won't lose your voice. You'll always be at your best."

"Well," she says, "I am usually hoarse by the end of the night. I mean, I hardly even talk during the day to conserve my voice. I'm pitching songs lower and doing everything I can think of, but I'm not willing to sacrifice my vocal cords for that lousy place."

We all know her mantra: She's moving on to somewhere better. I wish she'd get her ass in gear and go. What she doesn't yet realize is that with my little plan, I'll be closing the show every night.

"Interesting," Audra says the next day. "And everyone agreed to this?"

"Yup," I say, feeling cocky. "You'll be paying your current performers the same money and hiring only two more. That has to be about the cheapest option you've got."

"But you say you're going to play through both shifts. That means you double your money."

"Nope," I say. "I'll do it for the same money."

"Why on earth? You'll be here twice as long. That means you're making half your current wages."

"I don't care so much about the money," I say. "I like the playing time." And being away from Mom's, and inching my way into the headliner slot, I don't say. "Somewhere down the road you can make it up to me."

She shakes her head. "If that's what you want to do, Tallie, I won't say no. So, do we know Eileen can actually sing and play the piano proficiently?"

Shit. We don't. "She says she can. I guess you could audition her."

Audra sighs. "I'll give it a try. But I hope I don't hear two weeks from now that it's not working out." She looks me dead in the eye. "And you're not monkeying with the new material, no matter how much you don't want people dancing on the stage."

"Yeah, yeah. I guess I have to live with that."

"You do," she says, sounding huffy, "or you'll be looking for a job."

The words "prima donna" are imminent, ready with the least provocation to slide from between her scarlet lips, so I nod.

Then she pulls her desk drawer open, extracts a shiny new key and holds it up between a red fingernail and thumbnail. "It's not like I don't know you come in here to practice," she says. "Don't you dare tell anyone else about this." She hands me the key, which, for being so small, feels awfully heavy in my hand.

Eileen's due in at four and I watch the clock, tapping my foot. As soon as she breezes in the back door, letting in hot afternoon light and sour alley smells, I steer her to the bathroom, checking under stall doors for feet. We're alone.

"I think Audra's going to go for our plan," I say in a low voice. "Do you really sing and play well enough to pull it off?"

"Well, I was in *West Side Story* in college," she says, not sounding all that confident, "and I took eight years of piano lessons."

"That means nothing here. Can you boogie-woogie, do ballads, rock out when the songs call for it? Can you wing it, change keys without thinking, make up words on the spot? And how about the patter thing? Do you have the attitude for that?"

"I don't know. I think so," she says. "I watch you guys every night."

Jesus, what have I gotten myself into? Even though Audra's going to audition her, I want the first crack at it. "Meet me here tomorrow at eleven," I say.

"But tomorrow's Sunday. We're closed."

"Just knock on the back door. And don't tell a soul, okay?" The key in my pocket feels like a lump of lead against my thigh.

18

♪ I've forgotten about family dinner night. I walk in late and Emma springs from the couch, running over to hop around me like a yipping puppy.

"We waited for you to eat," she says, yanking on my hand and pulling me into the living room.

"Oh, goody," I say.

Mom looks up from her chair. "Was Rebecca late again?"

Andrew stands and nods a greeting at me. He's careful never to look too long, even when I'm in my skintight stage clothes. Jane would kill him. She says a halfhearted hello, then complains. "We should have snacked. I'm starving."

What you should do is lay off the snacks, I want to tell her and her ever-expanding behind. Instead I say, "You could've eaten without me."

"Then it wouldn't be a family dinner, dear," Mom says. "We want you to be here with us."

"Yeah," says Emma.

"Yeah," says Jane, not quite quick enough with the subtle roll of her eyes.

Andrew notices I've seen and gives her a look, then smiles at me apologetically. He drapes a friendly arm around my shoulders as we head for the kitchen. I'm afraid to even look at Jane.

We all sit in the places that have become ours—Mom at one end of the table, Andrew at the other. Me on one side, Jane and Emma on the other. I fill my wineglass with water so no one else will pour wine into it. Jane acts as if she doesn't notice.

Mom has made Mexican food tonight: steak fajitas, guacamole, homemade pico de gallo, black beans, and white rice with flecks of something green. Apparently, they've been discussing Jane's getting a job.

"You'd love it if I stayed barefoot and pregnant the rest of my life," Jane says to Andrew.

"No, I wouldn't," he argues. "I'm just suggesting that you might miss being around for Emma's activities, or when she comes home after school." He looks frustrated with her, but he sounds sincere.

"She's had a full-time mother for ten years," Jane says. "Surely that's plenty. You don't care if Mommy gets a job, do you, Emma?"

Emma looks at her plate, scooting a mound of black beans from one end to the other with her fork. She shrugs but doesn't speak.

"Give the kid a break," I say. "Don't ask her that. It's not exactly fair."

"Yeah, well, you know all about fairness, don't you, Tallie," Jane says. It has a nasty sting, like an angry wasp on a hot car seat.

"Stop it!" Mom's sharp tone shocks all of us. "All of you. Just stop!" She seems as surprised as we are at her outburst, and softens the rest of it. "I worked too damned hard in the kitchen all day for you to ruin my plans for a nice dinner together."

I sneak a look at Jane. She looks back at me, like in the old days, scared and unsure how to proceed. We barely breathe, waiting for the next thing to happen, waiting for that final blow that will send everything off-kilter, that will make the situation irretrievable, the moment when our lives go from normal-looking on the surface to the dark murky way things really are. All of this passes between Jane and me in that split second, and neither of us moves until Emma says, "Yeah, she worked too damned hard."

Mom looks relieved and laughs, and Andrew cuffs his daughter on the shoulder. "Language, young lady," he says, trying to look serious. Emma grins like nothing was ever wrong. Jane and I force ourselves to breathe, to laugh along, to lift forkfuls of food to our mouths and pretend that we weren't scared shitless a moment ago.

About the same time I got breasts, I realized my mother was insane. I'm not sure what exactly lit the bulb over my head. Maybe it was the years of experiencing her sharp baffling changes of mood, her long sabbaticals behind closed doors, the occasional zombie-with-a-knife presence in our bedroom doorway. Or maybe it was just part of growing up. By then I'd had repeated exposure to other, normal mothers. Whatever the case, I realized, finally, that she couldn't possibly be *trying* to act so nuts.

The three of us were sitting in the living room one evening watching Elvis in concert on TV, drinking Cokes. Mom had a long pour of whiskey in hers. It had been a normal day, a normal week, maybe even a normal month. However long we'd gone without a problem, I was lulled into my preferred state of thinking that we were just the average family.

During a commercial, I brought up a well-worn subject—my getting a bra. "You promised last week we'd go get one," I complained to Mom. She sat glassy-eyed, staring at the tube. Figuring it was the booze, I snapped my fingers. "Hello? Mom?"

"It's always about you, isn't it?" she said in a feral nasty tone, turning to cast a look over me that, even now, makes me shudder. "You spoiled fucking brat!" This was not the booze talking. This was the old familiar monster that had been lying dormant in my mother.

Jane grabbed my arm. "She didn't mean anything bad, Mom," my sister said. If anyone could talk Mom out of such moments, it was Jane, but this one was already well past that point. If our mother said "fuck," things were not going to go well.

"And you! You always take her side!" my mother wailed, like someone being tortured. She picked up her glass and sent it sailing toward the television. Elvis had come back on the screen, and we watched as glass shattered against the upper edge of the set and caramel-colored rivers cascaded over his sweaty bloated face.

She never physically hurt us. She never struck us or threw

things in our direction. Chalk it up to motherly love—maybe she did have some control over herself. But we didn't trust that things might not degenerate that far, so we took cover, escaped to our room. Then, like every other time, we heard our mother storm to her own room and slam her door. We knew we were in for a long siege.

"She didn't mean it, Tallie," Jane said as we sat together on the edge of her bed. I could feel her trembling. "She's just having a bad day."

If she hadn't still been a kid, I might have told her right then and there: "No, she's not having a bad day. She's just plain crazy." It was a revelation for me, a clear new understanding of the situation that somehow made me feel better and worse at the same time. But I didn't want to smudge Jane's hopeful image of our mother, the image I was only beginning to let go of myself. I reached over and put my arm around her small shoulders. "I know," I said.

After dinner, Jane, Emma, and I leave Andrew and Mom to do the dishes. Emma grabs my guitar from my room to show me a song she's trying to learn on guitar. "Blackbird" by the Beatles. It's a difficult finger-picking technique, but she's actually getting pieces of it right.

"Well, well, Miss Thing," I say. "I could never have done that at your age. I'm not sure I could now."

"Here," she says, handing me my Strat. "Try."

I take the guitar into my arms; it's been a long time since I've held its sleekness against me. Emma slides her sheet music over and I strain to see the strange tablature of numbers instead of notes. Instead of trying to follow it, I let my eyes go soft, think about the song, play it the way it sounds in my head.

"Wow," Emma says. "That's not what it says in the book. Teach me that way instead."

"I don't know how to teach you that, Emma," I say. "It's in my head or something. I just do it." She gives me a look, so I say, "You'll have your own music in your head, once you've got the basics down. Just keep practicing. After a while, you won't need to look at the sheet music anymore. You'll just play what comes out, your own special music."

She looks skeptical, but pleased. "Really? I'll be able to do that?"

"You will if you practice enough."

She takes the guitar back and wraps her arm around it, clutching the fretboard with renewed enthusiasm, and plays the rising intro: *plink, plink, plink, plink.*

Jane watches from across the room, sitting quietly in one of Mom's overstuffed chairs. I leave Emma struggling with the song, humming to herself, and walk over to my sour little sister. She looks miserable, and I don't think it has everything to do with me.

"She thinks you're very cool," she says.

"Yeah, well, it's easy when you're the black sheep aunt." I take a seat next to her on the ottoman.

"I wish I could do something with her that excites her that much." Jane gazes at Emma. "Something that would make her admire me that much."

"You do."

"What?" She looks at me, challenging me with that bossy tone she gets.

"You're her mom. She can't even tell you not to go back to work because she knows it would be selfish, but she just wants you around."

Her face softens. "Well . . ."

"You've got that whole family thing we never had—a mom, a dad, like Ozzie and Harriet."

Jane snorts and looks away, and I wish I could push a REWIND button on my mouth. It's not like I haven't noticed the chill between her and Andrew.

"Anyway," I say, "being a healthy, sane mother"—I look around to make sure Mom isn't in earshot—"is an amazing thing in my book."

"I don't know." She sighs, settles back in her chair. "I always thought I'd be something more."

"I know the feeling," I say, thinking about my dwindling chances of ever getting discovered. Especially in Denver, in a freaking piano bar.

"Oh, please." Jane sits up, surly again. Emma glances over and Jane lowers her voice. "Like you haven't always been able to go out and do whatever you wanted."

"It's not that easy," I whisper, aware that Emma is now fake-strumming my guitar, trying to look uninterested in our conversation. "You don't just go out there and get everything handed to you, you know? Nobody's saying, hey, you, you want to be a star? You're talented, you've worked your ass off. You've given up your whole life for this one impossible thing. Here you go. Have a recording contract, a concert tour. Shit." I lean away from her, rest my elbows on my knees, and study the straw rug.

"It wasn't so easy here either, you know."

I turn my head to look at her, but she's staring straight ahead.

"I've spent my whole life doing this, being here. Taking care of Mom my entire childhood, then finally getting to go off to college and having to quit."

She's not whispering anymore. She seems to have forgotten Emma's in the same room and I'm afraid she'll slip and mention her daughter's name, but Jane shakes her head. "I'm the one whose life is so boring she just puts it aside for everyone else." She looks at me, eyes so soft and liquid I look away. "You're the special one," she says, "the talented one. The one Mom wanted to die without."

"What?" I say loudly, and then Jane's crying, and Emma drops my guitar on the floor and runs over, kneels in front of her mother looking scared and on the verge of tears herself. Jane gathers her against her, rocking and saying, "It's okay, honey, you didn't do anything. I'm just a little sad lately."

I walk over to pick up my guitar, search it for dings.

"Did I break it?" Emma asks in a small voice, peering out from Jane's embrace.

I smile, shake my head no. She holds up her left hand. "Look at my calluses, Aunt Tallie."

She's been getting her hair cut shorter lately, more pixie than bob, making her look more like my daughter than Jane's. "Don't let them get too hard," I tell her, all too aware of my own fingertips against the strings, soft and exposed as flower petals.

*   *   *

Mom's trying to get ready for a solo exhibit at the biggest gallery in town—Mudwren, or some equally ugly name, considering it's a place that sells art. I hear her on the phone as I pretend to read my new *Musician* magazine. She says to someone at the other end, "We can't postpone? I'm just afraid I won't have anything to show."

Something in her voice makes me peek around the magazine. She's standing at the hall table, dressed in the suit she wears to meetings, saying, "Mm hmm, mm hmm. Well, I suppose." Her hand fidgets at her shirt collar. Her speech is faster, not as evenly paced as it has been.

She hangs up and I put down the magazine. "Everything okay?" I ask, knowing damn well it isn't.

"Oh, it's probably fine." She laughs shakily, and her eyes dart past me and back. "Just the jitters. Do you get nervous when you sing? Oh, I bet you don't. You were always such a wonderful performer, even when you were just a little thing. You'd open up your mouth and sing your little heart out—"

"No," I interrupt. She's talking too much, too quickly. "I do. Get nervous sometimes, I mean." Shit, I'm thinking. Shit, shit.

"Really?" She smiles gratefully. "Yes, I'm sure it's just nerves. I still have a couple of weeks to pull some work together, to get cracking."

"But, you must have enough paintings for an exhibit. You work all the time. There's all those paintings in your room."

"Tallie, the last thing I need—"

"I'm just trying—"

"Well, don't!" she says sharply.

I draw a deep breath, feeling as betrayed as I always used to.

"I mean, honey, don't worry about it. I've got it under control, okay? I'm fine." She fumbles in her purse for a lipstick and turns to the hall mirror. "I just have to buckle down"—she smooths a rosy arc over her upper lip—"and get serious about this show." She swipes her bottom lip unevenly, and when she turns to face me, she looks like a boxer after a fight.

"How do I look?" she says, smoothing her hair. "Presentable?"

"Perfect," I say, and turn back to my magazine.

After she leaves for her meeting, I decide to sneak into her room.

Her door is locked. Why would she lock her bedroom door? It's not like I'm going to steal anything or snoop through her stuff. I just want to see what she's been working on. Fortunately, I still have those bobby pins of Emma's. She let me keep them after they gave me good luck at the audition. I grab one from my dresser and bend it open as I walk back toward Mom's door. I poke it into the hole in the doorknob, feel for the catch, and the door swings open.

Everything looks pretty much the same as it did the last time I was in here. A stack of canvases leans against the wall, one sits on the easel. All neat. Too neat. I walk over to the easel and see that the canvas has been painted over with a thin coat of white, not quite concealing a few bold squiggles and slashing lines, like the one she painted the day I knocked on her door. The stacked canvases are the same, all glazed in a film of white. It's like looking through gauzy window sheers into someone else's window.

I walk over to her table of paints and brushes and see that everything is clean and put away—there isn't even a dab of paint on the white ceramic tray that she uses for mixing colors. Come to think of it, Mom hasn't had that paint-splattered look lately; her smock hangs clean and unused on a hook by the closet.

All this white, all this neatness and cleanliness where there should be color and form and artistic chaos makes the back of my neck tense. I turn to leave and kick the leg of the table, knock over a jar of brushes. As I right them, a familiar feeling of doom settles around me. Something is going wrong here, and somehow it's going to be my fault.

19

On my way to the bar to meet Eileen, I swing by Beelze-bub's for a latte. I've discovered they have twice the kick of regular coffee. Mia says they're a yuppie drug. Whatever. They wake me up. As Damian steams the milk for my coffee, I blur my eyes and look at the painting Mom has hanging here, the swirling wildness of yellows and purples and greens. Why can't she just keep doing this? I wonder. It doesn't look that hard.

At the door to the bar, I look around to see if anyone's watch-ing, pull the key from my pocket, and twist it in the lock. Inside, I walk first to the rows of bottles behind the bar, studying them, then to Audra's office. Inside her desk drawer I find a file labeled LIQUOR—PAID BILLS and thumb through the papers inside. Finally, on a bill dated more than a year ago, I find what must be the ex-pensive tequila: SPECIALTY TOP SHELF ITEM: TEQUILA DE ORO, ANEJO ESPECIAL, $78.95.

I always did have good taste.

Inside my wallet I have a crunched ten-dollar bill, seven ones, and change until payday. I slide the ten into a register drawer. It's the best I can do for now. Then I make my way to my piano.

It's still only ten o'clock, early enough to bang out some tunes before Eileen shows up at eleven. That, and try to make up with Sal. She hasn't appeared since my drunken crime spree, and I'm not all that sure I really saw her then. "Come sing with me," I say aloud, sitting on stage in the half-light coming through the blinds. "You got your way. I've gone straight." Nothing. I try again. "No more drinking. I promise." I wait for a moment longer, then spread my hands above the keys, let them hover until a song comes to me.

"*I'm sorry, dear, that I could never be,*" I start, one of Sal's old songs, "*the woman that you wanted me to be, but, honey, believe me, I'm trying.*" I keep my eyes on the keys, but every once in a while I glance into the darkened bar as I sing, looking for a flash of red. "*So now I hear that you are saying we are through, believe me, darling, when I say that I am blue, 'cause, honey, believe me, I am trying.*"

Sal wrote her own songs, unusual for a woman in her day, and "Believe Me" is one of her best. I've never been to a shrink, but it must be like singing this kind of song. I almost always feel better afterward.

I come to the end of the song and look up. No Big Gal. I play another one of hers, then another. Pretty soon I've exhausted my Big Gal Sal repertoire, to no avail. A loud knock at the back door makes me jump until I remember. Eileen. An hour couldn't possibly have passed, but I look at the time clock as I head for the door. Sure enough, it's almost eleven.

"How'd you get in here?" Eileen asks when I let her in.

"It's a secret," I say. "Remember, no telling."

"Why's it so dark?" She flips the row of light switches, buzzing the room into momentary brightness before I switch them back off.

"Jesus, Eileen, do you know what secret means?"

"Sorry. I guess I'm nervous. I can't believe I'm going to play in front of you."

"Great. How are you going to be with a roomful of drunks?"

"That seems easier, somehow," she says, smiling shyly. "You're just so . . ." She shakes her head. "You know, talented and all."

"Yeah, well, you'd better be, too, missy," I say, walking toward the stage, climbing up. "You take Domingo's piano." I show her where we tape the set lists out of view, which you eventually memorize anyway, and how the sheet music is filed by set in a small case on the floor, in case you need it. It's not like I need to show her all this, not right now. I'm just letting her get used to being up here, looking out at all those chairs and tables. It's a big room.

"You know how the requests work, right?" I ask, and she nods at the slips of paper littering the piano top. "We like to work them in if we can because it means bigger tips. Hell, they're usually songs we're going to do anyway, so we just rearrange the set a little." She nods, tucking her hair behind her ears nervously. "And you always have one of the guys looking out for you, so don't worry if some drunk climbs the stage." The male waitstaff take turns playing bouncer. They love it.

"So," I say, "ready to try something?"

She nods, her ears burning red.

"Want me to play along?"

She nods again.

"Well, then, you pick it."

"How about," she clears her throat, "how about 'Suspicious Minds'? In G."

"Ooh, Elvis. Good choice." I smile encouragement at her. "G it is."

She botches the first few notes and looks at me apologetically, but I cover for her like I would in a performance. She smiles and keeps playing, letting the progression go around an extra time before starting the words, which she sings breathily. The PA isn't turned on, so I motion for her to sing up. She tries, but it's still not loud enough to hear. This is what I was afraid of.

And then, from out of the blue, there's Big Gal Sal, standing behind Eileen like Our Lady of Auditions. She rests her hands on Eileen's tense shoulders, winks at me, and opens her mouth to sing. Eileen closes her eyes and leans her pale head back into Sal's red silk bosom, wailing out the lyrics like a juke-joint siren.

"Woo-hoo!" I yell, and Eileen opens her eyes, surprised by the awesome sound she is making. I smile, shake my head, and marvel at Eileen, at Sal, at this goddamned great Elvis song we are pounding out together, all three of us. It is a joyful noise.

* * *

Audra auditions Eileen—and only Eileen, apparently—on Monday, and the deal is done. As I'm warming up my voice in the back room that evening, Audra pulls me aside. "Would you mind giving the kid a few pointers on putting together a stage look?" she asks. "Nothing slutty. Just a little more, you know . . . Well, you know."

"I'm honored," I say. I don't ask about the slutty remark.

It only takes two seconds to decide what to do with Eileen. She has great bazoombas that she keeps hidden under her XL polo shirt, but not any longer, if I can help it. A little eye pencil, lipstick, some contouring to give her cheekbones, and she's going to be a knockout, the girl next door with an edge.

Later that night when I come off the stage, Eileen motions me over to the bar, looking as excited as Emma sometimes gets.

"I'm in!" she says.

"I know." I smile and high-five her.

"Let me buy you a drink," she says. "Anything."

"Okay," I say, scanning the bottles. It's been a shitty week and I would so love a little something right about now. It's only one drink. "How about—"

Sal appears on the bar stool to my right, brows arched in expectation.

"—a soda with bitters, extra lime. Then let's go in back and try on some polo shirts."

"Why? I've got plenty of these horrid things at home," Eileen says, plucking at her baggy shirt.

"Yeah, just not the right size," I say, winking at Sal. The guy in the next seat winks back at me, a surprised hopeful look on his face.

Just before one a.m., Rebecca checks her watch, then holds her hand over her eyes like an Eagle Scout, looks around the room, and says, "Tallie?" into the microphone. Her voice is strained. Hurray for wimpy vocal cords, I think as I stub out my Salem and make my way to the stage for the fourth time tonight. All of a sudden Rebecca realizes I'll be closing the show, not her, and for a moment it seems she's not going to vacate her bench. "Wait a sec," she croaks, looking at her watch again. "This isn't right."

"We can work out the kinks later, Bec," I say soothingly. "Go give your cords a rest." She nods, grabs her honey and lemon water, and parade-waves at the audience as she glides down the steps.

It's different playing with Chuck. He's the anti-Flamingo, and I realized during our earlier set that we'd need a different dynamic. I back off the sarcasm and go for beguiling. "Hey, Chucky," I say flirtatiously into the microphone as I settle into Rebecca's warm spot, flex my fingers. The crowd eats it up, hooting and wolf-whistling.

Chuck looks surprised, and I shake my head at him, like "Hey, buster, this is just showbiz," even while I'm saying, "What's a big handsome hunk of a guy like you doing in a joint like this?"

"Gee, Tallie," he says with a confused squint. I'm not going by the script—which calls for a rousing rendition of "I Love Rock 'n' Roll" à la Joan Jett—but Audra's in her office and Chuck's just quick enough to follow my lead. "I guess I'm just, like, working, baby." He raises his eyebrows. "What do you think I should be doing?"

Catcalls and obscene suggestions fly from the audience.

"Well, honey, I don't know about you, but I don't want to work," I say.

"You don't? Well, tell me, baby, what do you want to do?" He rises off his seat in anticipation, like he might leap over the two pianos in a single bound.

And then it's my moment. I launch right into "Bang on the Drum All Day." He joins in, smiling and shaking his head like he wasn't sure I could pull it off. The crowd jumps to its feet, dancing and singing, especially on the "bang" part. Halfway through the first verse, Audra comes flying out of her office. She glares at me, then watches the audience gyrating. The chorus comes around and everyone sings loudly, thrusting their pelvises forward. It's goofy and depraved and stupid, but damn, for a Monday night, it's about as fun as you can get. Audra shakes her head and walks back into her office.

I don't know if it's the high of the response from the crowd tonight, or teasing Chuck, or that I haven't been with someone in months, but I can't stand not being with a man for one more second. I barely remember what it feels like to be kissed, touched, to have someone lying the length of me, face-to-face, belly to belly, knee to knee. I miss the sounds and smells and tastes of it, the urgency of it. I need that energy, that appreciation, that feeling of someone worshipping me and my womanly charms.

At closing time, Jason is wiping down the long stretch of wooden bar, no pretty young things in sight. He's grown a goatee, and tonight it frames a serious expression on his face. This is a man who could use some fun, too, I decide, and take a seat at the bar near him.

"Hey," he says. "Good show tonight."

"Thanks. Where's all your girlfriends?"

He laughs. "Fickle. There's a new bartender up the street at Cosmic Hell, that dance club."

"Women," I say and shake my head.

"No, *girls*," he says, wiping, wiping, but I'm catching a definite vibe.

"I thought all men wanted girls," I say, the feeling of easy seduction coming back in a rush. I forgot I was good at this.

"Not me."

"What do you want?"

He stops and looks at me, finally, a slow sexy smile spreading across his face. "What are you offering?"

"Let's get out of here," I say and hop off the stool, walking away to gather my things. I feel his eyes on my ass all the way across the room.

Oh, Lord, those months off were way too long. Jason kneels over me on his futon, naked in a pool of moonlight. He is gorgeous, his skin pale and blue in the light, his body smooth and hard beneath my palms. His lips and teeth and tongue explore me from any number of angles you can imagine. He is young, so damned young, that I felt embarrassed at first when he tugged at my clothes. But he murmurs little comments of appreciation every time he samples some new part of me, and I'm about to explode with the desire-frustration-tension of waiting for him to hit pay dirt. Please, please, please, I want to scream, but I just moan in a voice I know sounds pretty. I don't want to sound demanding or out of control or needy. Not the first time. I want him to want to do this again.

I try moving my hips at the speed it would take to make things happen, but he gets the wrong message and straddles me with a moan. My turn, unsatisfying as it was, is apparently over.

"Oh, no," he says, "I don't have any condoms. Do you?"

"Fresh out," I say, although I haven't needed any in so long it's pathetic. "Guess we'll have to be creative." I roll him over and climb on top of him.

"Okay," he says, dreamily. "This is good, too."

I slide back and forth slowly, not taking him inside me, and cup my breasts in my hands. Men love this kind of performance. Jason stares in awe, looking like he could cry at the sight. It's that worship thing, and I know exactly how to play him to make him want me the rest of his life. I move at just the right speed to keep him from coming too soon, and I throw my head back, make a pouty O shape with my mouth, let out those pretty moans. I am better than Emmanuelle or Debbie Does Whoever, I am the queen of desire. And then, when he looks about to lose it, I lift slightly, hear him groan, feel his hands on my hips, pulling me down tight against him. He calls out in a husky voice, nothing in particular, just a lowing sound, and his eyes roll back before he closes them tight.

When his spasms subside, I roll off him, avoiding the mess on his stomach and thinking maybe I'll get another shot at it now, but he lies as still as a corpse. After a few minutes his breathing thickens and slows. So much for younger men, I think, sighing. I tuck myself against him, carefully so I won't wake him, and listen to his rhythmic breathing until light creeps like a soft murmur into the room. We can try again, I tell myself. I'll take the lead, show him how to make love to a real woman. As I finally drift off, it's to the singsong cadence of a nursery rhyme: I've got a new boyfriend.

20

♪ For my Audra-approved spotlight song, I sing "At Last," hoping Jason likes Etta James as much as I do. It's only been a few days since our big night together, but we've gone backward to that flirty stage that usually precedes consummation. A teenage game of hide-and-seek, cat-and-mouse, me hinting I'd like to get together again, him being coy and playful. His groupies are back and he looks flustered every time I walk by the bar. "Don't sweat it," I want to say. "I know you prefer women."

It's Friday, our busiest night, and the joint is jumping. When I first started here, I wouldn't have thought it possible that I'd come to enjoy the rhythm of this place. It's not just that it keeps me away from my mother. It's the camaraderie of the staff, the in-jokes and signals between the Flamingo and me, and now between Chuck and me. The buildup through the week toward the weekend and then the almost-magical release on Friday nights. Everyone in the audience is so fired up and ready to cut loose after working all week that I don't really mind the singing along so much anymore.

Tonight is even more electrically charged than the usual Friday—the air buzzes and crackles. Even during the quiet parts of the show, you feel it: Something's going to happen.

And then it does.

At a quarter to ten—fashionably late for a place that fills to bursting by eight o'clock—in walks Jedd Maxfield and his entourage.

The first thing I see is an old Jett Maxx T-shirt stretched tightly across the Buddha-belly of that asshole Buddy. Two or three guys in leather coats and expensive haircuts look around, check out the joint to see if it's worthy—Jedd's stab at creating his own musician mafia. Next the willowy dark figure of what must certainly be Little Bitch Face comes through the door. She is gorgeous, all right, with hair to her waist and cheekbones so defined they look drawn on. And then I see Jedd. He and the girlfriend are stuck together, side by side, like two peas in a pod if they weren't both so tall and skinny.

I go blank, forget the words to the song we've just started, the lamest song we do. The Flamingo picked it when we added the medleys: "Greased Lightning." I sing only alternating lines, but I can't remember the words, so Domingo takes over, giving me a concerned look. I mouth, "Sorry" and keep playing, mortified that not only am I sitting here playing a stupid *Grease* song, but a dozen or so gyrating waitrons and bartenders have jumped to the stage and a few are climbing onto the pianos. Fortunately, they do provide good cover. I peek through their wriggling bodies to see Jedd taut on his haunches, hunting for a glimpse of me up here in this chaos. I consider slinking off the back of the stage and hiding in the bathroom for the rest of the evening. Then I get a better idea.

I've been working up my own medley. Domingo loves the idea almost as much as I do, but I've been too gutless to approach Audra with it. It's a Prince medley: It ramps up with "1999," then slithers into a raunchy rendition of "Little Red Corvette," the ultimate sex song. It finishes with "The Beautiful Ones," a torchy screaming ballad.

I signal Domingo with a flip-flop of my left hand, so he knows, I'm changing something. He looks at me like "now?" We're almost at the end of our set. I nod and mouth, "Prince." His eyebrows arch and he glances toward the door, where Audra is hanging out with one of the local cops. He looks back at me, his eyes pleading: Don't do anything stupid. All I know is I can't sit here and perform this insipid shit while Jedd and his girlfriend are out there. I don't even have a chance at a spotlight song. I sneaked in two already this hour. I wink at the Flamingo, yell, "Come on!" to the side of the mike, and we wrap the *Grease* song a verse early. The dancers look confused, and I yell, "Sorry! Change of plans!" and launch into "1999." They and the crowd recognize it immediately from the distinctive intro and everyone roars with approval. Whoever wasn't already on their feet is now, and I can no longer see Jedd and company. Audra couldn't possibly complain. She knows what's good for business.

When we segue into "Little Red Corvette," the dancers jump down. It's way past time to take more drink orders, clear away empties. To my delight, Jason stays. When he hears what song it is, he crawls onto my piano, like Michelle Pfeiffer in *The Fabulous Baker Boys*. He gives me his sexy grin and I could just die on the spot. He has no idea that he is making this even better than I'd hoped; he is answering my prayer for a miracle.

As I sing to him he rolls around on the piano top like he's consumed by lust, as though my very voice is touching him, caressing him, arousing him. It's scary, amazing, this side of him, this public sexual squirming, but I don't mind at all, especially when I glance into the audience and everyone but Jedd is eating it up. Little Bird Brain seems to love it; she's smiling and boogying in her seat. Now, *this* is singing, girlfriend, I want to tell her. Not that caterwauling you do.

When I get to the ballad, Jason winks at me and jumps off the stage. Even another man would have to see what a fine specimen he is as he runs through the crowd and vaults over the bar. I sing Prince's lyrics of longing to him across the room, but he turns away to fill orders. I torch it up extra hot, even though I'm going to be hoarse by the end of it from all the growls and screams. The crowd has gone reverently quiet, with a bridal-shower group standing and waving back and forth. Someone hands one of them a cigarette lighter, and she flicks it on, holding it above her head like she's the Statue of Liberty. It becomes a trend, these swaying young women and their torches. Even Little Whatever pulls herself up, though Jedd tries to hold her down.

It may be just a piano bar, but, tonight, inside these walls, I am

a star. As we approach the big ending, I pour it on, rocking back
and forth, pounding the keys, sweating and emoting with every
last ounce of my soul. I look toward Jason, but he has his back to
me, wiping glasses and, in the process, flexing his muscles for the
girls. He turns his head for a moment and that sexy grin shoots
across the bar. I almost return it, until I realize his intended target
is a half-dressed blonde perched seductively on a bar stool between us.

Chuck and Rebecca take over, Chuck high-fiving me, Rebecca
bumping hips with the Flamingo as they pass on the stairs. Avoiding Audra, who's giving me one of her famous principal scowls, I
head straight to the bathroom to wipe the sweat from my face and
fix my melting makeup. I grab a few quick puffs of a cigarette,
then push back out the door and thread through the tightly packed
crowd. The unwritten musician's code says you must visit the table
of anyone you know in the audience. Even if you don't want to,
you're obliged. It's like karma-clapping: Musicians always applaud
other musicians, even if they hate them.

As I approach Jedd's table, it's apparent several people have recognized him. Even without the hair. I wonder how much he pays
Buddy to wear that shirt.

Jedd sits smugly in his chair like royalty, like the rock star he
isn't anymore, surrounded by his "people" and a handful of gawk-
ing, gushing fans saying things like "Jett, are you gonna get up
and play one?" and "Jett, sign my cocktail napkin," and my favorite,
"Jett, when are you going to make a comeback?"

Buddy sees me first and nudges Jedd, who looks up with that
pantherlike smile. "Tallulah Jean," he says, but he doesn't get up,
just sits there like maybe I should bow down and kiss his ring with
the other toadies.

"Jedd," I reply. Cool. Easy. I nod at Buddy, then at Little Robbed
from Cradle.

She beams at me, gushing, "Oh, I've heard so much about you,
Tallie, and I love your singing. So powerful! Did you write those
songs?"

I look from her to Jedd, back to her. "Are you kidding? You don't know Prince?"

"Oh, you mean that artist guy with no name? I haven't really heard any of his songs, I guess. Maybe that one about a strawberry beret." Still with the big, toothpaste-commercial smile.

"Raspberry," I say. His worst song ever. "Where were you in the eighties?"

"In grade school," Jedd answers for her, wrapping a turquoise-braceleted arm around her shoulders. "No, darlin'," he says to her, but looking at me, "Tallulah most certainly did not write those songs. Tallulah doesn't write songs anymore."

"Of course I do."

"Now, now," he says, stroking the girlfriend's arm with his long fingers. "I didn't come here to squabble. Tallie, I'd like you to meet my fiancée, Little White Deer."

The floor rushes up at me, but I take a deep breath, extend my hand. "Good to meet you, Little . . ."

"White Deer," she says, taking my hand in her own slim dark one. "Little White Deer, but I really go by Loretta. Jedd likes my Indian name."

"He is a sucker for exotic names." I feel the color rise in Jedd's face as if it were my own.

She laughs, takes no offense. "Yeah, he's into exotic." Goddamn it, I like her.

"So, fiancée, huh?" I say, nodding. "You pinned the old Jedd-meister down. Well, good for you, Loretta. I tried once, but it didn't take." My voice is about to give, and I don't like the way it's making me sound, all weak and wispy. "Listen, I gotta get ready for the next set, so . . ."

"Well, that's too bad, Tal," Jedd says. "We were thinking of catching this hot new band Lyle's managing, the Twang Gods. Thought you might like to come. They're playing just up the street at the Neptune. Heard of 'em?"

"Can't say I have, but then, I'm usually pretty busy." Jedd has always fancied himself on the cutting edge. The Twang Gods, for crying out loud. "What do they play?"

"Roots, baby, roots-rock music," he says. "It's making a come-back. I'm thinking of going in that direction myself, you know, stripping it down, going back to the roots of rock and roll." Loretta sits silently. Ain't no room in a roots-rock band for a magpie, I think, feeling sorry for her. Jedd continues, oblivious. "I'm writing some great stuff, getting a real organic sound."

"What about that, uh, *sound* you already have going?" I ask on her behalf. She looks sideways at Jedd.

"Oh, well, yeah, that's good, too. We're doing the Native Amer-ican thing, too, aren't we, honey?" he says, giving her shoulder an-other squeeze. "But, the roots thing, that's where it's really at. That'll be the big moneymaker." He takes his arm from around her, runs his hand over his sleek, close-cropped head, like he used to when he had his shiny black mane.

In that one gesture, it all becomes clear to me. He's always wait-ing for that next opportunity he can climb on and ride till it goes cold, like my songs and voice in the '80s until he thought metal-lite was the next big thing, and there was no room for girl singers.

"Then, you're selling out?" I ask, and Buddy spits a mouthful of beer onto the table. Loretta suppresses a laugh.

"No more than you, sweetheart," he says coolly, looking around the place. "You make your, what, your piddling five hundred a week to sit up there and play other people's songs?"

I don't bite. I used to think I had to fight him back all the time, win the argument, prove I really was someone. Even though I'm pissed off, even though he's managed to claw my heart out once again, I'm clearheaded at the same time. "Well, Jedd," I say care-fully, "it may not be glamorous, but it's a living for now. I never got royalties to live on, like you did. I can't take the big chances. But good for you. And good luck to you," I say, smiling at the girl-friend. She's going to need it.

What the hell kind of charity just came over me? I wonder as I walk away. Then I realize Big Gal Sal is holding my hand, leading the way.

In the safety of the bathroom, I lock myself in a stall. The lump I've been choking back since Jedd walked in works its way up and becomes a wail. "Asshole," I cry, spinning toilet paper from the roll to blow my nose on. " *'Fiancée.'* Fucker. *'Roots music,'* " I say between sobs. " *'She doesn't write songs anymore.'* Motherfucker."

Sal stands on the other side of the stall door, saying things like "Mm hmm," and "You got that right."

Three or four women who were primping when I burst in ask if I'm okay.

"Yeah," I say, sniffling. "I just saw my ex."

"You poor thing," one commiserates.

Another says, "Men are such bastards."

"I'm no man-hater," Sal says, "but in this case, honey, you might want to listen."

When I've put my face mostly back together, I take a seat at the far end of the bar, away from Jason. I can only play the pursuer so long. Then, miracle number two of the night, he walks over and slides me a glass of water. I take a sip and discover it's a triple vodka, my drink of choice. I look around for Sal, then nod gratefully at Jason.

"Who was that guy?" he asks. I'm surprised he noticed.

"Just some has-been old rocker," I say and take a long pull, the burn a balm on my sore throat. "Jett Maxx, king of the fucking world."

"That was Jett Maxx?" Jason laughs. "God, I remember his records from, like, junior high. That was really him?"

I nod, feeling older every second.

"And you know him?"

I drop my face into my hands, speak into my palms. "I was married to him."

"Wow" is all Jason can manage to say before he backs away, acting like he has a customer to attend to.

"Tallie," Audra's voice says behind me. "We have to talk. Tomorrow. Be here early."

21

♪ I've been around long enough to know there's no sense in waiting around until closing time to see if Jason will take pity on me and invite me home. I heard the shock in his voice as it registered just how old I really am. I see the leggy, longhaired, barely legal females flashing their tattooed midriffs and Wonderbra cleavage at him.

I leave work right after my last set, which is no longer the closing set, since Rebecca wised up. I'm back to second string.

At home, I twist my key in the front-door lock and push softly into the dark apartment, trying to be quiet. I unlace and slip off my clunker shoes, hold them in my hand so I can glide silently to my room.

Then I hear it, a raspy sound, breathing maybe.

"Mom?" I say, hoping like hell it is. Something moves, a silhouette in front of the window, a head of wild hair, a body turning to face me.

"You have nerve." It is Mom, but not really. It's Mom from long ago. That low flat voice. Possessed. Mean. I haven't heard it in years, but I could never forget it.

"What's wrong?" I say, suddenly shaking, nine years old again. I knew it was only a matter of time.

I stay near the door, wishing I'd kept on my shoes, and flip the light switch. At least I can see her coming that way. Standing across the room she looks disheveled and disoriented, shielding her eyes from the sudden brightness with her hand, her bathrobe askew and her hair frazzled.

"What's wrong?" I ask again, this time more authoritative. That's one thing I learned from Jane in the old days. Get the upper hand right away. "Mom?"

She doesn't say anything, just stands there, hand on her face, but then I see she's trembling.

"Are you okay?" I take a step toward her.

"Why?" she cries, whipping her hand from her face to reveal red swollen eyes, a twisted frown. "Why are you doing this to me?"

"Wha—"

"You've been in my room, you've been through my paintings," she howls, clawing her arms hard enough to leave red welt stripes. "Why are you spying on me? What do you want from me?"

Okay, I decide, fuck authoritative, fuck trying to settle her down. I switch into the old gears and reach behind me, pull the door open, and run into the foyer where I punch, punch, punch the elevator's DOWN button. That'll take all night, so I bolt through the door to the stairwell, run down three flights before I remember I'm holding my shoes and jam my feet into them when I come to a landing, not even tying the laces until I'm down the rest of the way and back out on the street.

I breathe, in, out, keeping a wary eye on the front door as I squat down to tie my shoes. Then I take off running again. Audra's leaning in the doorway at Sing Out!, smoking a cig. She looks alarmed when she sees me.

"What's wrong?" She throws down her cigarette and reaches out to grab my arm.

"Something's up with Mom," I pant. "I'm not going back there."

"Sweet Jesus," Audra mumbles, looking inside the bar. "I'm short a closer. Tell you what," she says, looking like she has a plan. "Can you take over here? Close out the registers, make sure everyone punches out? Lock up?"

I nod.

"You know the safe combo?" She hands me a set of keys. "S.O.S.:

Sing out, sister. Got it? Just put everything in the safe. I'll deal with it tomorrow." She strides down the block, yanking the Milk Wagon Stables door open with enough power to tame even the wildest force of nature.

I bend down and pick up Audra's still-smoldering cigarette butt, then lean against the brick wall, take a long pull of nicotine. The tops of my feet throb from how tightly I tied my shoes.

Why did I go into her room?

Jane was right. She's always right. My mom's sane for ten years and I fuck it all up.

I stand there, paralyzed, until Rebecca shouts, "Thank you and good night!" from the stage inside. People stream from the bar, brushing past me in loud laughing groups, singing, shouting, making plans where to meet for breakfast. No one recognizes me. I feel like a small invisible child, and I wait for an opening, then edge my way into the bar. Chuck and Rebecca are gathering up their sheet music, laughing, Rebecca tossing her hair like she always does. Eileen's counting out her drawer, the waitstaff are clearing tables, glasses and bottles clinking like strange music.

I head for the office, open the door, bump into something, someone, in the dark, and scream louder than I realized I could.

Amid much scrambling and giggling, I see the backs of two people, one male, one female, fleeing through the door, tugging clothes back into their proper places. I know without seeing his face which particular scumbag bartender it is. I stand in the dark a moment before switching on the light, closing the door against him, against the sudden barrage of indicators that my life hasn't changed at all, really.

After I've given Jason enough time to disappear, I peek through the door. All clear. I empty the register drawers and lock the money away, shoo the last gabbing waitron out, and shut down the PA system, then pour myself another triple vodka. Before locking up, I stand in the back doorway for a while, looking up and down the alley, sipping my drink. The night air is cool; it's almost fall. Soon the Colorado winter will be here, and I find myself wondering what all those people who like to sleep out in the open will do.

Hell, what will I do, for that matter. I am just as surely homeless now as they are.

I could go to the shelter, a thought that surprises me. It's not like I'm broke anymore. I could spend a few bucks on a motel room, stay a few days until I found an apartment. It's not that I'm totally out of options. The shelter occurs to me more because in spite of how weird that damned Perry is, I feel safe around him, which makes no sense at all.

I push the heavy door closed, turn the locks, shut down all but one bank of lights near the bathrooms, secure the front door, and switch on the alarm system. After poking around in the storage room, I arrange a makeshift bed up on the stage with clean bar towels and polo shirts. Like a cat, I feel best up high, so I can see what's coming. Like a scared kid, I feel best protected by something large and sturdy over me—my piano. Then I fall into a murky state of semiconsciousness, hearing every creak inside, every shuffle and bump outside, reminding myself I've locked both doors, set the alarm. I'm safe. But I don't feel that way. I feel the way I did when I was a kid, curled up tight in my bed, making myself as small as I could. Then I remember something I'd forgotten: that's when Sal first started singing to me, but not songs from her records. Other songs, songs Mom sang sometimes. "Swing Low, Sweet Chariot" or "You'll Never Walk Alone." I loved those songs. I start to hum, low and easy. Then I hear a louder humming, coming from above, and I see sturdy brown legs swinging from the piano bench, pumps kicked off to reveal bright red toenails on surprisingly small feet. Sal's throaty humming turns to soft crooning and I fall asleep like a baby.

"Tallie," someone is saying, shaking my shoulder. I jump into action and my head hits the underside of the piano with a sharp nauseating crack.

It's Audra, and it's daylight.

"Oh God," I moan, rubbing the knot already rising under my fingers. I look around at the mess I've made, illuminated now. "Sorry I messed up all these shirts," I say in an unsteady voice.

"Jesus, Tallie, I don't give a damn about those shirts," she says. "Come on. Get up. When you didn't come home last night, I figured you'd stayed here. I brought you some coffee."

I roll out from under the piano, trying to ward off the throbbing in my head by moving carefully. I follow Audra to the nearest table, where she's set two Beelzebub's lattes in paper cups and two lumpy bran muffins. She's even brought packets of sugar, napkins, stir sticks. This unexpected gesture of kindness sends me over the edge. I take a seat and begin to sob, face hidden in my hands as Audra sits silently.

"Sorry," I finally say, sniffling and wiping my nose with a napkin. "I don't know what's gotten into me. I'm a basket case."

"Of course you are," she says. "Who wouldn't be? Your mother was in quite a state last night."

"Yeah, well. You'd think I'd be used to it." After a quivery sigh, I take a sip of thick milky coffee.

"Honey, was your mother like that a lot when you were a kid?" This is a new side to Audra. She's never been this personal, and, hell, she's never called me honey. Last night I was pretty sure she was going to fire me.

"Yeah," I say. "She had her moments."

She shakes her head, bites her lower lip. "Well, Tallie, I'm sorry for that. I truly am."

I don't know how to respond. No one's ever been sorry about it before, or told me so anyway.

"You know, at least I think you know, that I love your mother," she continues, looking straight at me.

Yeah, yeah, I nod, looking away.

"It's not that we're ashamed or anything, but your mother's not comfortable with you girls knowing, so keep it to yourself." Like I want to broadcast it, but I keep my mouth shut. She says, "The other thing we don't talk about is this." She leans onto her elbow, sighs. "We've been through these episodes before. A couple of times."

"What?" I slam my cup on the table. "I thought she'd been better for ten years."

"Well, the thing is, Tallie, your mother is mostly better. Truly, she is." Audra tries to look convincing, but she just looks tired. I wonder how long she sat up with Mom last night. "She's almost always fine, except . . ."

"Except when her evil long-lost daughter returns?"

"Now, you know that big exhibit was eating at her."

"She's had exhibits before, right? Even big ones? I think we all know what set her off." I look away to keep my chin from trembling.

"Look, Tallie. I've done a lot of research into this disease, and this is not an unusual occurrence. It goes with bipolar territory. But it embarrasses the hell out of your mother. She wants you girls to think she's doing okay now, after all she's put you through." Audra looks uncomfortable and glances down at her shirtfront, wiping away nonexistent muffin crumbs before she looks back up. "Now, I'm going to do what I can to get her through it. And you, too, kiddo. We'll get through this."

From out of nowhere, I'm sobbing again, the onset so fast I choke and splutter, and Audra's handing me napkins and saying, "Together, okay? It'll be all right." She stops short of hugging me, which I'm thankful for, but it's probably the nicest thing that's ever happened in my life, and all I can do is bawl and wipe endless rivers of snot on the napkins Audra keeps handing me.

Audra and I sit and talk, smoking her Kent cigarettes. She tells me she sat up with Mom most of the night, calming her down. She finally got Mom to admit she'd skipped about four or five days of medication in her desperation to regain her ability to paint.

"I called that damned gallery and told them your mother was going to hang a retrospective, 'The Best of Lee Jackson,'" says Audra. "Put an end to that nonsense."

Then, she called Mom's shrink, made her an appointment for later today, even though it's Saturday, and got a prescription for some tranquilizers to ease Mom through the transition back onto her medication. After taking them, Mom fell asleep in Audra's apartment.

"Did she tell you about me going into her room?" I ask. "That's what set her off."

"Honey, you could have danced a minuet on the kitchen table, or you could have done nothing, and she would have gone off," Audra says. "It's a chemical imbalance we're talking here, not what anybody does or doesn't do to your mother."

"I wish Jane knew that," I say through a mouthful of muffin.

"My God, Tallie. She must. She's been through this more than anyone else. But she doesn't know it still happens, and your mother would like to keep it that way, got it?"

Fine with me, because I don't think Jane would see it quite the same way Audra does. It's not so easy when it's your own blood involved, your family. Your crazy mother. Your no-good sister.

Audra says Mom's going to stay with her for a while until she gets evened out again. It's like we have our own family social worker. Where the hell were you twenty-five years ago, I want to ask, but at least she's here now. She doesn't even bring up the Prince medley.

While I was on the road, it was like my childhood never happened. I was an orphan child with a blank-slate past. I'd spent my life building a wall inside me, and I learned to never let anything through it.

Since I've been home, though, a crack has formed, leaking things I thought I'd never have to think about again, widening now to reveal this ugly part of my life, my family, me. I can't *stop* remembering now, and each new realization sends me spiraling downward, feeling just as loony as my mother.

I remember the terror of her closed door. Sometimes Jane and I could hear banging, moaning, entire one-sided conversations. But worse was when there was only silence. That felt more ominous, as if we were waiting for the inevitable end, because we knew if her life ended, ours would, too. We'd reason that she might just be sleeping, but the surer bet was that she'd taken something or done something really bad to herself, and it would be all our fault. She had that thing for knives, after all.

The knives are the worst part. I can't look at a kitchen knife, a pair of scissors, anything sharp without shuddering now. I remember that feeling from long ago. After all these years, they scare me again, the sight of them a sensation in my chest, in my back, in my legs and arms. She never did anything but carry them around in her paranoia, but how were we to know she wouldn't? Jane and I made elaborate shelters on "bad" nights when we went to bed. We'd pile pillows, stuffed animals, extra blankets around us, deep enough so a knife couldn't get through. We figured the mattress beneath us was enough protection from the underside.

One morning after a bad night, Mom had turned sunny again and stood smoking a cigarette in our doorway as we woke, surveying our handiwork. "Nice fort, girls," she said before turning away and going to wash the cold cream off her face.

It was an up-and-down world. We were an up-and-down family. And now, I guess, we still are.

Even though I know Mom is under Audra's watchful eye next door, when I go to bed in the empty apartment late Saturday night, I lock my bedroom door. I pull the covers to my chin and consider gathering all the pillows in the place. For the second night in a row, I finally fall asleep to a calm and loving humming and dream of strangely peaceful things: a porch swing, a pitcher of sweet iced tea on a small white table, the smell of honeysuckle.

PART THREE

I don't need no man to love me,
But your good love makes me weep.

—"Good Loving Man," Big Gal Sal

22

♪ Like clockwork, like the phases of the moon, Saturday is family dinner night once again. Mom is pretty much Mom again, slow-talking and placid from the medication, and full of those creepy apologies that still piss me off. She must sense it, now, though, because we never get to the point where I scream at her just to make her back off.

Tonight she's cooking some exotic Vietnamese meal, teaching Emma how to roll noodles and vegetables in rice paper. I watch Jane laughing at her daughter's ripped and baggy results, and wonder how she could not know what transpired in this house a week ago, how she could not feel the energy of that ghost from our childhood still haunting the place. I feel like a traitor, not telling her, and lonelier than ever. At least when we were kids, we shared the ugliness, diluting it so it didn't seem quite so bad. But this problem is all mine now. Just like when I was a kid, I'm keeping my mother's secrets, only this time, even Jane can't know.

Jane is happy tonight. Jane is happier lately, having found a part-time job at the local library. I don't say a word about how at least she has the look down pat. "It's really not much of a job," she says as we sit down for dinner, "just shelving books and helping people," but her face is animated as she talks about it, her eyes bright.

The more she talks about it, the quieter Andrew gets. Mom tries to engage him in the conversation, saying, "So, Andrew, are you proud of your career-woman wife?"

He nods without enthusiasm, then shovels a forkful of lemongrass chicken into his mouth. Jane looks at him and sighs. "No," she says flatly. "He's not."

Mom changes the subject, asking Emma if she's ready for fifth grade. Emma shrugs, like it's no big deal, but from the way she was showing off her new school clothes earlier, my guess is she's pretty excited to be queen of the heap in elementary school. She's grown at least a couple of inches this summer without gaining an ounce of weight, her knees and elbows Tinkertoy connectors between sticks. Tonight she's spiked her pixie haircut with mousse. She picks at her rice noodles and tells us the pros and cons of nose rings and tongue piercings, both of which her friend Nikki's sister has. "Not while we're eating, Emma," Jane reprimands, flashing me an incredulous roll of her eyes when Emma's not looking, like "Can you believe this is coming from the mouth of my ten-year-old child?"

Andrew is passing Mom the peanut sauce, and Emma is pouting, and Jane and I are acting almost like sisters. We look like a normal family.

Still, I lock my bedroom door at night.

After dinner, I catch Jane alone in the living room. She seems to be feeling chummy, so I ask, "Have you noticed anything, um, unusual about Mom lately?"

"No," she says. "Like what?"

"Just different from however she's been. I don't know. You know her better than I do."

She frowns. "What's going on?"

"Nothing," I say. "It's just weird, you know, getting to know each other again. That's all."

Jane gives me a long look, but I smile, shrug.

"Tallie . . ."

"No, really. I swear." I hold up three fingers. "Scout's honor."

"You never made it out of Brownies," she says, still giving me that look, but she lets it drop.

On Sunday the artists' party goes on as it does every week except last week, when somehow Audra got out the word that Mom was too sick. "That Asian flu," she said, and like magic, no one came.

I was sure someone would still show, so I dressed nice and sat in the living room, picking up my book, putting it down, switching on the television, clicking it off. I tried to convince myself it wasn't Perry I was expecting.

Tonight I feel the same, wearing a new red sweater and hanging out near the doorway. My heart does a little cha-cha every time the door opens, cool night air ushering in everyone but him.

Mom is solidly back in her role as art diva. I hear her saying, "Yes, I decided on a retrospective. After all, my career does span quite some time, as much as I hate to admit it." Her smooth Southern drawl is used to particularly good effect on such occasions, charming everyone within her enchanted circle of listeners. I can hardly listen to her without shuddering, so I move away.

Shanti is sitting by himself on a windowsill at the back of the room, and I decide he needs company. His dreads have grown, dangling now rather than stabbing out, and he's wearing a snug-fitting undershirt that defines his smooth hard chest and tight belly, tucked like a lucky lover into his low-riding baggy pants. It's unbelievable that he has no female company tonight. Most likely, word has gotten around about the celibate thing.

He looks up at me with a somber expression.

"Hey," I say and squeeze in beside him on the windowsill. His thigh is warm against mine and he scoots over only slightly, leaving our legs touching. "Why're you sitting here by yourself?" I ask. Up close, his eyes are red-rimmed, wet. "Are you okay?"

He takes my hand, nodding, trying to smile. He turns toward me then, bumping knees, our joined hands brushing my hip.

"What?" I ask. His hand is hot, pliant, and I immediately want to touch more of him.

"I got some bad news today," he says. He squeezes his eyes shut for a moment, pinches the bridge of his nose. A thin transparent line of tears rolls down one cheek and I wipe it with my thumb, wishing I could taste it, but I let my hand settle in my lap, wait for him to talk. He breaks down and cries in earnest then, hiding his face in the crook of his arm.

"Come on," I say, standing. "Let's go somewhere quiet." He nods and lets me lead him through the maze of people. No one notices us as they chatter and laugh. I pull him into my bedroom, close the door against the noise.

"It's more private in here," I say, feeling awkward now that we're alone. "Do you need a tissue?"

He nods and sits heavily on my bed, leans over with his face in his hands. His sobbing has a strange sound, like a rare birdcall, like nothing I'm used to. I don't believe I've ever heard a man cry. I squeeze back out the door, make my way through the crowd to the bathroom, which is occupied, then to the kitchen to grab some paper towels. When I get back to my room, Shanti has composed himself and looks embarrassed.

"I'm sorry," he says, taking the paper towels and wiping his face. "My mother's in the hospital, back home in Chicago. I'm flying out in the morning. They said to expect to stay a while. She has cancer, advanced. Bones, liver . . ."

"Oh, Jesus," I say, sitting next to him on the bed, instinctively putting an arm around his shoulder. He begins to cry again and turns toward me.

"Why didn't I know this?" he sobs. "I see things, I should have seen this. I could have—"

"Shh," I whisper, stroking his back, his neck, his shoulders. "Come on, Shanti, it's not your fault." I rock him a little, trying to be a good friend, but I'm ashamed at the tug between my legs. This guy has been nothing but nice to me and now when he needs comforting I get the wonder-surge of all wonder-surges.

His arm is wrapped nearly all the way around me, his warm hand wedged beneath my arm, so close to my breast he must feel the rise of it beneath his fingertips. Beside my ear, his breathing grows steadier, the jerky hiccups smoothing out. We're still rocking, slightly, but then gradually more deliberately, and my nipples harden against his chest. I try to pull away a little, create some space there so he doesn't feel it, but he pulls me into him and I feel his face turn against my neck, his lips moving, whispering maybe, then kissing me. I pull myself against him with my palms, then stop.

"Are you sure about this?" I ask, drawing back, hoping, praying he'll say yes. I could back off, could say You're just upset, let me give you some time alone, but I don't. I want to give him comfort, solace, and I want him to comfort me, give me something that somehow can only be gotten this way, in this intertwining and stroking and rocking. "Are you sure?" I whisper, kissing his wet cheek lightly, tasting the salt, the tip of my tongue against his skin, just ever so lightly, really, but my breathing is coming harder now, and I can't help it, I'm pulling him against me, whispering, "Are you sure? Do you want this?"

I think he's nodding, but he's sure not saying no, he's pulling my sweater up, he's pushing me down against the bed, and I can feel him hard as a brick through his pants as he lies on top of me, rubbing against my thighs, my pelvis. Then we are fumbling with zippers and buttons, pulling clothing up over torsos and heads, down over hips and legs, stroking and kissing each new thing revealed, moaning, each of us, like something wounded or wild, both on the verge of tears. I've never felt this when making love, this deep sad place inside me, an empty place that needs something, although I don't know what, just *needs,* and I cling to Shanti like a child who has been lost. I can't fathom it—I'm here with this gorgeous man, halfway to coming each time he touches me or flicks at my skin with his tongue, but tears are rolling down my face and I am gulping air with that unmistakable sound of crying.

He stops, pulls back, and rolls off me. "What are we doing?" he says, and I know from the shamed sound in his voice that we are not doing it anymore.

"I'm sorry," he says and stands, his body a mahogany sculpture in the moonlight.

"No, it's okay," I say, wiping my eyes. "I don't know why I'm crying. It's not because of you. I want to do this with you, to be with you." I'm teetering on the brink of explosion, or implosion, maybe, like those buildings on TV, and I don't like the feeling. I've lost every scrap of control and I feel stupid and exposed, lying across my bed with no clothes on, and I sit up and grab a pillow to cover myself.

"This isn't right," he says, stepping into his pants, pulling them around his waist. "I shouldn't have taken advantage of you. I shouldn't have been weak."

"You're not weak," I try. "You're in pain. People help each other in time of need, right?" That's what he said when I first came home, when I first met him.

"I've dishonored myself, my beliefs," he says, pulling his shirt over his head, tucking it into his pants. "I've dishonored you. You're my friend." He kneels on the floor in front of the bed, hands on either side of me. "I hope you'll still be my friend," he says, looking sad, looking delicious, actually, but I know that ship has definitely left the building.

"Yeah, yeah, of course you're my friend," I say, and reach out to hug him with forced casualness.

As he pulls the door open to leave, a ribbon of light pours over me, the pillow, the rumpled bed behind me. In that instant before the door closes again, I see Perry leaning against the opposite wall, eyes wide as he looks from Shanti to me. I jump up and pull a T-shirt over my head, open the door a crack to peek out. Both Shanti and Perry have disappeared into the crowd.

I have never felt so guilty, so sad, and so horny all at the same time. At least I can do something about that last one, I think, settling back into bed and staring out at the moonless sky, feeling where Shanti's hands and mouth have been.

23

After work, I decide to make peanut butter toast for a late dinner. I search the refrigerator for my jar of Skippy, finding it deep in the back of the bottom shelf, surrounded by Mom's weird stuff—tandoori paste, kalamata olives, some Oriental-looking bottle labeled "fish sauce." When the phone rings I don't answer it. Mom's at a meeting, so it's probably just her telling me she'll be late. At the last minute, though, I change my mind and grab the sleek black cordless from the countertop, the replacement for the one I broke, and say, "Yo."

"Oh, good," Jane says on the other end. "It's you."

That's a first, but the late hour and the edge in her voice keep me from dispensing the usual comments. I close the fridge. "Are you okay? Is Emma okay?"

"God," Jane says with a laugh, "do I sound that bad? Yes, we're fine. Mostly." She pauses, then says, "Andrew and I are separating."

"Whoa." I fumble for a response. "I mean, you know, I'm surprised. You two seem so . . . normal." I'd started to say "happy."

"Looks can be deceiving, I guess."

My toast pops up looking more stale than browned and I push the plunger back down. "What happened?" I ask, although I can imagine. "The old wandering-eye syndrome? The old let's-bag-a-teenager-before-we're-too-old-to-get-it-up story?"

"If you're asking if he cheated on me, he didn't."

"Then, what?"

"Actually, I'm the one who cheated." She sounds more proud than ashamed. "I don't know why exactly. It's not like I fell in love or anything. I didn't even like the guy that much. But he liked me. I guess that was enough."

I can't imagine Jane appealing to anyone in that way, with her housewife hairdo and clothes, her hell-in-a-handbasket shape, but she's trying to explain it to me, so I concentrate on her deliberate voice, rising and falling as methodically as when she's telling Mom how to make pasta in her new machine, or when she's telling Emma how to solve a math problem. Only now she's telling me her marriage is over and that she—my goody-two-shoes sister—is the reason.

"I just decided to do something for me," she says. "My whole life has been for other people—Mom, Emma, Andrew." I cringe, waiting for her to say something about my skipping out, but she doesn't. "I kept thinking, Tallie doesn't take care of anyone but herself and she gets along fine. Why should I?"

There it is—the sucker punch.

"See, the thing is"—she hesitates—"the thing is I can say it's because of you, but really, I realized I didn't like this life he, we, created. It just happened over the years. I always thought I was happy, but, I don't know. I guess I wasn't. I was . . ."

"Wild guess. Bored?"

"God, I'm such a stereotype. Yes, goddamn it. I am so bored!" She yells this, then whispers, "Shit, I probably woke Emma."

I try not to laugh; she sounds ridiculous cussing. "So," I say, "how'd Andrew find out?"

"I told him."

"Oh, my God, Janie," I say instinctively. I'd forgotten I called her that when we were kids. "Why would you do that?"

"He's my husband. He should know." The way she says it, so simple and matter-of-fact, I can't even figure out how to argue with her. "So, he's been working late a lot, sleeping in the den, and he's moving out on Saturday, which is why I'm calling. Could you and Mom take Emma for the weekend?" Finally, I hear a wet catch in her voice. "We don't want her to be here when he packs up and goes."

"Sure, of course. Does she know?"

"I think so. You know her, she knows everything." She sighs. "I told her Daddy was sleeping in the den because he was angry with me. She didn't ask why, which she usually would, so she must know something's up."

"Well, when are you going to tell her?" It sounds too much like when our father left; he was there one day and gone the next. Vaporized. We never talked about him after that. Mom was always one step from the edge as it was.

"I know. I have to talk to her. I just can't believe this is me, this is happening to me." Her voice thickens, wobbles, but she regains control. "I can't believe I did this."

"I can't believe you told your husband you did it. Now, the *doing* it, well, hell. You are human. We make mistakes." For instance, I don't tell her, I mistake sex for love all the time, even when the man du jour has no interest in anything but sex, like Jason. Poor Shanti just wanted a connection, a lifeline, and I pushed it too far. And I keep seeing Perry's face in that ribbon of light, that look of confused betrayal. I feel guilty even though there's nothing between us, like I cheated on him somehow, just as Jane cheated on Andrew.

"So she'd love it if you picked her up from school on Friday," Jane's saying. "She can show you off to all her friends, her glamorous rock-star aunt."

I jot down the address, the directions to Emma's school, paying extra attention to Jane's careful details. "What time?"

"She gets out at three fifteen, but she gets really upset if you're late, so why don't you aim for three?" Jane's casual way of telling me I'm likely to be late. But something else is going on between us, something new and fragile. I don't want to break it, so I don't argue.

A key turns in the front-door lock, and I say, "Mom's just walking in. Do you want to talk to her?"

"I guess I'd better." Jane sighs, and I hand the phone to Mom as she breezes into the kitchen.

"Oh, dear," Mom says as the news is relayed to her, and I decide to head for bed. There's no way I'm in the mood for a heart-to-heart with her, too. I notice a smoky quality to the air—my toast. I turn to see it sitting black and dejected in the toaster.

I always lie when people ask if I remember my father. "Not really," I say. "I was just a baby when he split." Actually, he left when I was seven going on eight, two weeks, in fact, before my birthday. I always figured he just forgot. I don't think he would have done it on purpose. I don't think he would have left if he didn't feel he had to.

I remember a lot about my father. He had strong, smooth hands. He always wore a fresh-smelling, white button-down shirt and combed pink tonic through his hair, slicking it into even rows of waves over his forehead. He was the only one in the family with blue eyes and he had a tiny scar that nicked the outside corner of the left one. His teeth were a shiny pearl color and long and straight, all except two on the bottom that crisscrossed each other like fingers wrapped together against a promise.

He taught me to ride a neighbor's red bicycle we borrowed one cold winter afternoon. He'd play outside with me on summer nights, letting me catch him when we played tag, and swinging me in dizzy circles. He'd get up early on Saturday mornings and watch cartoons with Jane and me, chain-smoking Camels and drinking black coffee. And he was just as hopeless around Mom as I was. When she'd start up, he'd get a lost look on his face, his hands slack and useless in his lap. He'd sit there and stare after she'd storm from the room.

Jane was too young to remember him, but, unlike me, she has always pretended she does. "He didn't care about us," she'd whisper knowingly in the night when we bundled ourselves together in one of our twin beds, insulating ourselves against the dark. "He didn't want to have children anymore," she'd say, or "He was mad at us, he was mad at Mom," trying out different reasons for his departure.

"Who knows why he left," I'd always say. "I don't even remember him anymore." Then I would roll over and pretend to sleep.

*　　*　　*

I don't drive my car that often lately, and as I buzz south along the highway, I wonder if it's safe to take Emma anywhere in it. It rattles and thunks like a one-man band with no rhythm. I've tried to clean it up, but it's always going to be a piece of crap, with its rust and primer patches, its torn upholstery and missing knobs. It's a big metal version of my life, everything half-assed held together just long enough to get to the next stop and then the next, always arriving on a hope or a dare. Always wondering if this will be the time when it all falls apart, or if I'll keep cruising indefinitely.

I drive to Emma's school and park in the sea of black asphalt that surrounds it. I glance at the watch I'm wearing, a cheap plastic number I picked up at the drugstore. Three-o-five, it says. I'm early. I wish I had a cell phone, so I could call Jane. "See?" I'd say. "I'm reliable."

I light a cig and sit in the car, listening to the motor tick and cursing its radioless status for the millionth time. I don't even have a song in my head, which scares me. "Mm mm mmm," I hum, searching for a melody.

"Be quiet with yourself," Big Gal Sal says, suddenly filling the passenger seat. "What's that thing they do nowadays, meditation? Just meditate, honey. Find some peace." She closes her eyes and leans her head against the seat, looking calm and serene. I relax just looking at her.

After a few moments, she opens one eye, looks at me. "Why're you looking at me, child? You have to do this for yourself."

"I don't want to."

"You don't?"

"I don't like too much quiet: no noise, no distraction, no nothing. Just me. I hate that."

She raises an eyebrow.

"It makes me feel . . . I don't know. Crazy."

"Are you still thinking you're going to turn out like your mother, honey? Is that what all this is about?" She half turns in the seat, searches my face. "You are not your mother, you know, and you will never be your mother. As crazy as you drive me sometimes, you, yourself, Tallulah Jean Beck, will never be crazy. I guarantee it."

"But how can you know that?" I argue, although I want it to be true so badly I'd do anything—I'd even sell my soul, pull a Robert Johnson, if that was an option.

"You take it from me, Tallulah Jean. I've got connections." She winks and leans back into her seat to meditate. I study her face, the high smooth forehead, shiny eyelids fringed with curly dark lashes, round burnished cheeks, plump rose-petal lips. I close my eyes and my thoughts settle in place, not swirling as they usually do, and for just a moment, I feel peaceful.

The school bell sounds and I jump, startled. I gather my bag on my shoulder, pull the keys from the ignition. As I climb out, I turn to thank Sal, but there's just the empty seat. Not even an impression from her womanly derriere remains.

On the drive back toward town, Emma is quiet. She sits in the seat next to me, filling very little of it compared to the Big Gal, fingering the zipper on her hot pink backpack.

"So, what do you want to do this weekend?" I ask, like this is nothing more than the usual sleepover she has with us every once in a while.

She shrugs, eyes focused on the road, chin jutting forward, meaning she's angry or hurt. I know her expressions now almost as well as I knew Jane's when we were kids; they're pretty much the same, anyway. Back then, I had a knack for softening that look in Jane, making her crack an unwilling smile, or at least getting her to roll her eyes.

"Wanna play Barbies?" I ask, always guaranteed to get a rise out of Emma.

She shakes her head.

"How about ride the elevator up and down all day?" She loves doing that, but she still doesn't answer.

"Emma," I say, reaching over to squeeze her knee. "Do you want to talk?"

She shakes her head again and looks away.

"Okay, then. Maybe later. We're almost home." I flick the turn signal and downshift, exit the highway and head into the city.

After dinner, Mom fusses relentlessly over Emma. "I made your favorite dessert, sweetie," she says, sliding a gargantuan square of chocolate and caramel onto a plate and placing it in front of her. "Marble brownies."

Emma picks at the brownie with little enthusiasm, but she eats it nonetheless. Mom's trying too hard. I feel almost queasy watching her cluck around Emma like a mother hen. Even though it's still early, I decide to get ready for work.

I've been experimenting with my look, trying to develop something showier than a stupid polo shirt. Using Mom's old sewing machine, last week I modified one of the large shirts, taking in the sides, cutting off the sleeves, and trimming under the back of the collar, down the sides, and across the back. After getting rid of about half the fabric, I've created a skintight, halter-top minidress. Until tonight, I haven't had the guts to wear it. "I'm wearing the shirt," I keep rehearsing for when Audra sees me the first time. "Technically, I'm legal." My final crowning glory is slipping into my long-neglected strappy sandals.

As I'm putting on my makeup in the bathroom, Emma comes in, sits on the toilet, and watches me. She's changed since that first time she watched me in my car outside Jane's house. She watches with interest now, and I can see her cataloging the how-tos and techniques for a couple of years from now. I brush her cheeks with a dab of blush and she smiles for the first time all day, leans over to see herself in the mirror.

"Do you think Daddy will still come see me?" her reflected face asks.

"Oh, God, Emma. Yeah. Of course." I could strangle Jane. She should be the one talking to her daughter about this.

"Did your dad, after he left?"

"Well, no. But your dad will. He loves you a lot."

"Didn't your dad love you?"

I stare into the mirror, not sure how to answer.

Mom calls out, "Emma? Where have you gotten to? I thought we were going to play old maid."

Emma runs out and after a moment I hear her giggles and Mom's easy low laugh. Then they're quieter, and it's mostly Mom doing the talking. I walk out to the living room when I'm ready for work and find Mom holding Emma almost like a baby, sitting on the couch and rocking her, Emma's face hidden in Mom's shoulder.

I am so glad that Emma has you for a grandmother, I want to say, but where the fuck were you when I needed someone to comfort me?

"Come sit with us, Tallie," Mom says, rearranging Emma to make a place for me on the couch. "You don't have to be to work for a while yet. Let's all just sit together."

"I need to talk to Domingo about . . . stuff," I lie. "I think I'll get in early."

"Honey, please. For Emma," Mom says. Of course. For Emma— never for me.

Tears well in my eyes and I look away quickly, trying to wipe them before they ruin my mascara. "No, really, I promised."

"It's okay, Aunt Tallie," Emma says, her voice nasal and ragged from crying. "You don't have to." She says it without a trace of manipulation. She doesn't expect anything from me. You'd think that would be a refreshing change, considering the rest of my family, but it breaks my heart.

"Well, I guess I have a minute," I say, trying to give Mom a dirty look, but her eyes won't meet mine. Reluctantly, I fit myself in next to them, holding myself centimeters from the warmth of Mom's arm.

Mom whispers to Emma, "See? We're all in this together, sweetie."

24

♪ When I walk into the bar, Eileen's eyes go as round as yo-yos. "Oh, my God, Tallie. You look fantastic." She shakes her head. "I can't wait until Audra gets a load of you."

"She can't complain," I say, "it's one of her god-awful shirts," but my palms are sweaty. Hopefully I'll be on stage before she makes an appearance.

No such luck. We nearly collide as I head for the back and she walks from her office. "Oh, no," she says. "No, you don't." She backs up and looks me over more thoroughly than any guy ever has.

"What?" I ask. "It's a shirt. It fits. What's the problem?"

"You cannot be serious. This is a joke, right?" She squints at me, frowns, then shakes her head. "No, Tallie. Absolutely not."

"Listen, Audra. The music business is all about sex appeal. Look at any CD cover, any video, any *anything* associated with music. It's sex. Period."

"Not in my bar, it isn't." She folds her arms, four crimson fingernails tapping her ample upper arm impatiently.

Obviously, I'd like to say, but I'm not stupid. I go for reason.

"Aren't we trying to set ourselves apart from the competition? I don't think making us all look like clones provides the best entertainment value for our customers, do you? They want performers to look—God, I don't know—special, exciting. Different from everyone else."

She keeps tapping, but she's not talking, which I've learned means she's thinking. "Well," she finally says, "it's not like you have time to change now. It's almost time for your set."

I feel a smile inch its way onto my face.

"But I'm not giving in here, Tallie," she says. "We'll see about this later." She walks off, shaking her head. Eileen's been watching from behind the bar and I give her a thumbs-up.

As I step on the stage, I feel the thrill of appreciative eyes on me. A bachelor party lets out a round of wolf whistles. I bend over to talk into the mike, revealing more cleavage: "Shouldn't you boys be at a strip joint?"

Audra is apparently used to my ad-libs; she doesn't react. In fact, the Prince medley is on the playlist now, and a request for it comes flying up first thing on a cocktail napkin. When we launch into "1999," Jason doesn't come to dance on the stage with all the other waitstaff. He's going steady with one of those young tattooed twigs he's always attracting. The audience leaps up at the sound of it, though, and the whole place jumps and vibrates to the methodic punch of chord changes.

My favorite part of the medley is the ending ballad. As I sing it tonight, I keep my eyes on the crowd, scanning just over the tops of their heads, making everyone think I'm looking straight at them while in reality, I'm looking at no one at all. It's an old performer's trick, like when I grab the mike and walk to the edge of the stage, lean down, and grab a few hands. They all think we're making this big connection, but I'm probably just gauging the mood of the audience, thinking about what song to do next, or wondering how I can, without anyone noticing, extract the wedgie I've acquired from sitting so damned long.

I don't even look for the best-looking guy in the crowd anymore, like I used to. I'd make a game of it, try to make him think I had a thing for him by singing some sexy lyric right at him, see the surprise in his expression change to expectation. In the old days, I'd occasionally let the guy find me after the show, and if I still liked him, we'd end up in the van, or in the dressing room, or at his place.

But not in a long time and certainly not anymore. Let them look at me all they want, but I will not succumb to another pretty face, another tight belly, another pair of broad shoulders. I haven't had a good boyfriend since, well, never, and I'm finally wising up. I'm not saying I'm going to the other side, like my mother, but, for now, I'm giving men a rest.

Mom never liked my boyfriends, not the ones I let her meet anyway, which amounts to a small percentage. To be fair, she loved my kindergarten boyfriend, Bobby McMaster, who I now realize was probably a rip-roaring homosexual, but back then I considered it a plus that he liked to play dress-up.

From seventh grade on, I had boyfriends she never knew about. We'd meet in the park, or at someone's house whose parents both worked, neck breathlessly for hours. I didn't let anyone touch me below the waist until I was fourteen, though, and I didn't let any-one poke me until I was almost sixteen. I figured I had almost nun-nish restraint, considering what other girls were doing.

My mother had romantic ideas about boyfriends, unrealistic sce-narios that she loved to tell us like fairy tales. In her stories, we'd always fall in love at first sight with the man we were going to marry. We'd mate for life, if you believed her, and live happily ever after. I knew she was full of shit, even then. She couldn't even keep Dad around and she'd never had another man since, as far as we knew. But I nodded along, mostly for Jane's sake.

Mom had such hopeful dreams for us in which our lives were special, blessed. I would be a famous star, she thought, with all my natural talent, and Jane would do something really smart, like be a lawyer, or a doctor. We would marry and have children, live satis-fying lives that dreams were made of.

I knew what she meant was that we'd have lives that were nothing like hers. That part I wanted badly to believe.

I decide to sign up to volunteer at the shelter to help serve the upcoming annual Thanksgiving dinner for the poor and home-less—and not just because I want to see Perry. I truly want to help out. That, and I have no doubt it will be easier than spending the day with my family.

After my orientation meeting and official tour, I'm loitering in the cafeteria, hoping Perry will show up. Another volunteer, a husky tattooed guy named Carlos, is working back in the kitchen, scrubbing an enormous stack of industrial-size pots and pans.

"Want a hand?" I say, walking toward the kitchen and pushing up my sleeves. It gives me a good excuse to hang out longer.

He flashes a gold-toothed smile and hands me an apron. "I never say no to a pretty lady," he says. "You one of Perry's new recruits?"

I shrug, wrapping the white apron ties around my waist.

"Yeah, Perry found me a month ago," he says, and I realize he thinks I've been homeless. "I was living in a box, man." He shakes his head, using his ragged fingernails to pick stuck-on bits of food from the large square pan he's cleaning. "Perry told me I could make a choice about my life, but I thought he was full of shit, like all those other street preachers and do-gooders always coming around the bridges."

"What made you change your mind?" I ask, spray-rinsing the pans he's finished.

"Because, Perry, man, Perry has been there. He's been on the streets and he's been as sick as anyone can be, and he's made himself a better person. He told me if he could do it, anyone could."

Sick. I shiver at the word, the image of Perry lying in the gutter, drunk, stoned. Or worse. It's too much to contemplate, so I keep quiet, rinsing pans and stacking them on the counter. Carlos glances at me sideways.

"What?" I ask.

"Are you the one Perry's always talking about?"

"Depends. What's he say?"

"He thinks you're an angel." Carlos finishes with the last pan and bangs it into my side of the sink.

I can't think of one smart-ass thing to say.

Since we started swapping shifts at the bar, our family dinners are early in the evening, before I go to work. Lucky me. Now I never have to miss one.

Tonight Jane has to work late (which naturally makes me wonder who she's "working" with), and we're having dinner without her for the first time. Andrew volunteered to bring Emma. When they arrive, Emma is clearly upset, face sulky and arms wrapped tight across her chest as they walk through the door.

"Emma," Andrew pleads, "let's try to make it a good night, okay? Even without Mom?"

"Hey, Miss Thing," I say, catching her as she tries to stalk by me. She stops and lets me hug her from above, dropping her arms to hang as limp as banana peels, but I don't let go. I rub her tense shoulders and she finally wraps her arms around my waist and lays her head against me.

I look at Andrew and the hurt in his eyes surprises me, but it's so familiar, too, that look of having been dumped like yesterday's garbage. He shakes his head and walks into the kitchen to find Mom.

"What's up?" I ask Emma.

"Nothing."

"Did you know it's normal to think your parents suck sometimes?" I ask, then whisper, "It's safe to talk, he's in the kitchen."

She shakes her head against my torso, but doesn't let go. We stand like that until Mom and Andrew come back into the living room, Mom noisy and laughing like she's trying to cheer everyone up. She's giddy, in fact. She must have hit the sauce early.

"Sweetie pie," Mom says to Emma. "Where's my sugar?"

Emma lets go of me and dutifully walks to Mom, plants a kiss on the cheek Mom stoops to offer. "Hi, Grammy," she says in a dull voice.

"Oh, my poor baby," Mom says, gathering Emma to her, smothering her against her bosom.

"Jesus, give the kid breathing room," I say. "She's fine, and she's not a baby."

Mom releases Emma and looks at me dumbfounded. "Why, Tallie. What on earth is the matter with you? Is everyone in a bad mood tonight?" She shakes her head, makes a little sound of exasperation that boils my blood.

"Why do you always act so goddamned high and mighty, like everyone else has the problems?" It's out of my mouth before I know it.

Mom's hand flies to her throat. "May we talk about this in private, please? In the kitchen? Andrew, perhaps you and Emma would like to watch some television."

I follow her through the kitchen door and she wheels around. "What is wrong with you, embarrassing me like that? I was simply giving my granddaughter affection, for goodness' sake."

"How wonderful of you," I say. "I'm glad you're a good grandmother, at least."

"Oh, Tallie. That isn't fair!" she exclaims, then lowers her voice, tears in her eyes. "I loved you and Jane to the best of my—"

"Yeah, yeah, it wasn't your fault. Nothing's ever your fault."

"I'm not saying I was a perfect mother—"

I bark a laugh and roll my eyes.

"—but can't you give me credit for getting better? For the way I am now?"

"Don't you mean the way you are *sometimes* now?"

Mom looks like she's been hit, and I feel the old shame. It doesn't matter that I'm an adult, that she is, in fact, fucked-up. For my entire life it has been ingrained in me: I am never, *never* to mention it.

"How could I have raised such a cruel daughter?" She turns away.

It's so butt-ugly pitiful, the way she says it, so goddamned self-absorbed, that I just shake my head for a minute. Then I say quietly, "Do you remember *any* of my childhood?"

"Don't do this to me, Tallie," she warns.

"Yeah, okay," I say. "Whatever. Can we eat now? I have to get to work."

Thank God Jane isn't coming tonight, so I can have a goddamned drink.

After an uncomfortable dinner during which Emma and I are silent and Andrew and Mom force conversation, I escape to my room to get ready for work. I'm still shaky from the argument, so I do my warm-up exercises while looking in the mirror, taking deep expansive breaths, trying to prepare for the night ahead.

Audra hasn't said another word about the dress, but she hasn't exactly endorsed it. Eileen asked me how I made it and Rebecca mentioned it might make a nice halter top, so I guess there'll be more showdowns soon. I'm shimmying the thing over my head and down my torso when someone knocks lightly at my door. Figuring it's Emma looking for a place to hide out, I say, "Come on in."

Andrew steps in just as I pull the fabric over my hips. "Oh, God. Sorry," he says and ducks back outside.

"No, it's okay. I'm decent now." I smooth the dress down over my thighs. Good thing I wear underwear these days. "You can come in. I thought you were Emma."

He comes in, but stands just inside the door, keeping one hand on the knob. "I wanted to thank you for all you've done for Emma," he says, trying not to look directly at me. "This has all been pretty hard on her." There's something about him that's sweet and gawky, and I realize I've never noticed how strong his jawline is.

"No problem," I say, aware of my breasts against the tight cotton jersey fabric, and my hip bones jutting forward in direct alignment below. I shift my weight from one bare foot to the other, feeling my hips rotate, seeing them through Andrew's eyes, which are, for just a second, drawn there before they move away again.

"She thinks the world of you," he says, digging a hand into his pocket to jingle coins. He wants so badly to look at me I can feel the heat across the room, but he keeps his eyes lowered.

I step forward, reacting to the prey. I feel the look form on my face, the soft eyes, the parted lips. I don't put it there on purpose; it just wills itself there like it always does in this situation. I'm not even thinking, because if I were, surely I would not be doing this, walking toward my brother-in-law—who isn't really my brother-in-law anymore, is he?—and smiling seductively and rubbing a hand across my stomach, a feature he has to love in me, seeing as he hasn't touched one this flat in so long.

"In fact," he says, "she had to write an essay at school about her hero, and it was you."

I stop cold. What the hell am I doing?

I use the hand on my stomach to scratch an itch that isn't there. My heart is beating way too fast, and I try to act casual. Sisterly. "She's . . . God"—I laugh nervously—"she's something, isn't she?"

He turns to me, smiles. "Yeah, she is. I'm glad she has you in her life, especially now."

I nod, out of words, and he shrugs, embarrassed at all the sentimental talk, it seems. When he's gone, I walk to the mirror, look at myself hard. I can see now how my mother could scratch her arms to bits.

I step onstage still shaky, upset, even after the quick drink Eileen sneaked me. What the hell is wrong with me? Am I a sex addict, or what? Why the hell would I put the moves on my nerd of a brother-in-law? I can't bring myself to make eye contact with the crowd or Domingo as we launch into our set opener, "Saturday Night's Alright for Fighting" by Elton John. Domingo sings it, so at least I can sit here and try to pull myself together.

Midway through the set it's still not happening. Domingo keeps giving me concerned looks, and he mouths, "Are you okay?"

I nod, but I'm not. My chest won't stop banging, and I can't pull a decent breath. When I sing, my voice is thin, and my banter is unsure, phony-sounding. This is worse than any breathing attack I've ever had, and I've never had one onstage before. I don't know what to do.

The audience, already primed by several rounds of drinks, is clueless, but I can't handle it any longer. When the song ends, I say, "Eileen?" into the mike, and like magic she walks up, smiling and ready to cover for me. Domingo looks worried, but smiles broadly at Eileen and the crowd, ever the professional.

I climb down the steps and push through the crowd. I can't see; everything blurs around a small circle in front of me. I don't know where to go. I need a drink, but I don't want to go to the bar. The bathroom isn't private. Audra's in her office doing paperwork. I am percolating to the point of explosion, heart thunking even louder than the music now. Blood thrums so thickly in my head that I'm sure I'm about to die.

I head toward the front door and out into the cold dark quiet. The pulse of the bar retreats behind me as I walk faster and faster away from it. I have no idea where I'm going, but I want to outrun this feeling. The frigid air snaps me to life, clears my vision, and all I want is to walk and walk forever.

The *clop-clop* of horse hooves comes up behind me and when I turn, there's Sal, riding like the Queen of Sheba high in the back-seat of a tourist carriage.

I have never been so glad to see anyone in my life.

"Come on, honey, take a ride with me," she says, waving me up.

I look at the driver, a friendly older woman I recognize from my walks, and she says, "Jump in. I'm just cruising, looking for a fare." I look from her to Sal and back again, and the driver says, "It's okay. It's on me."

I climb the steps and sit next to Sal, who draws a comforter over our knees.

"It's getting damned chilly at night," she says. "I miss the South. It never got this cold in October."

"What are we doing?" I ask, looking at the driver, but she's plugged a set of headphones into her ears. Tinny country music leaks out.

"Distraction," Sal says.

"What?"

"You're feeling better, aren't you?"

As a matter of fact, I am. My heart has stopped slam-dancing and I can breathe. I pull a cold sharp breath through my nose and lean back, smelling wood smoke and horse. For the first time, I notice how pretty the old-fashioned lights lining Wyanee Street are, and the old stone building fronts. The comforter is heavy and warm on my legs and the night air refreshing on my face and arms.

"What the hell was that all about?" I ask.

"We used to call them nerve attacks, in my day." She studies her nails, holds them up toward a streetlight to check their shine. "You got yourself worked up is all."

"Worked up? I'd call it insane."

She drops her hand, turns to look at me. "I know, honey. I used to think that, too, back when I had them."

I look at her, her dark eyes glittering and moist.

She says, "It's not crazy to be scared."

I consider this, pull the comforter to my chest. We ride silently for a while until she says, "You know, you and me? We're a lot alike when it comes to sex and men and love. Always looking to get a little love, a warm feeling that everything's okay. That we're okay." The steady rhythm of horse hooves accompanies her like a metronome, and I lay my head back against the seat, look up at the scattering of stars against the purple-black sky. "A man's attention," she says, "is like a drug for us, like one of those happy pills your mama takes. We call it love and we believe in it with all our hearts until we're proven wrong. Until we discover it was just sex after all."

We're quiet for a moment. I don't tell her I've figured that out already—she must be losing her edge. Then Sal reaches over and takes my hand. "But it's not wrong to seek love, child. You're not bad for trying. You just gotta know where to find it, because it's waiting patiently until you're ready, until you can accept it as it is."

I swallow back a salty taste, wipe my nose with the back of my hand, then sit up straight. The buildings here are vacant, boarded up; we're no longer in the familiar confines of LoDo. "God," I say, "where are we?"

Sal shrugs.

I lean over the front of the carriage and tap the driver on the shoulder. She pulls one side of her headphones away from her ear and a whine of sad-sack lyrics pours out. "Yeah?" she says.

"Where're we heading?" I rub my arms, suddenly cold.

"Nowhere in particular. Just following my nose, or rather, Old Bony's nose there." She chuckles, nodding at the horse plodding in front of us. She lets the headphone snap back to her ear and gently slaps the reins on Old Bony's backside.

Up ahead a figure is walking toward us with a purposeful stride, carrying something bulky under one arm. "Shit," I say, sure we're about to be mugged, or worse. The man walks into a pink-orange pool of light beneath a street lamp and looks up. It's Perry.

I turn to Sal. "Did you plan this?" She tilts her head and shrugs, palms splayed open to the sky, then does her usual disappearing act. "Can you pull over?" I ask the driver, and she nods slowly in three-quarter time with some aching country ballad.

Perry looks as astonished to see me in a carriage, in this neighborhood, as I am to see him there in that pool of light, holding a newspaper-wrapped bouquet of roses and dressed to beat the band, sporting a 1940s-vintage striped suit, two-tone shoes, and slicked-back hair.

"I was just coming to see you," he says as he climbs into the carriage.

The driver turns around and smiles. "Where to, folks?"

"Seventeenth and Wyanee, please," Perry says, handing me the flowers. "That piano bar on the corner."

"Oh, yeah, Sing Up or something," says the driver, turning around to nudge Old Bony back into motion.

"Sing Out, sister. Sing Out," Perry says, leaning back and settling in for the ride. He doesn't look directly at me, but smiles and folds his hands over his wallet, gazing out into the dark like this is all completely normal.

I cradle the bloodred roses like I've seen beauty pageant winners do, the petals smooth as silk on my arms, the fragrance drifting upward sweet and satisfying. Perry's body is warm against my side and he pulls the old high school trick of yawning an arm overhead so it can settle comfortably behind me.

For once I feel like a real person, someone who dates and gets flowers and gets married eventually and maybe has some kids.

Just like my mother always said.

25

When we arrive at the bar, we waltz in like royalty, me in my sexy dress, Perry in his old suit. Audra scowls at me for being gone so long, but when she sees the flowers, she fights a smile. "Get your ass back up on stage," she says. "And this is the last night you're wearing that damned dress."

I find a spare chair for Perry and squeeze it in up front. He doesn't sing along or do any of the corny hand motions or dance steps, but his eyes never leave me. And when I dedicate the blues medley to "my friend Perry," he presses his hand to his heart and smiles.

At the end of my last set, I pick up the flowers placed carefully beside me on the bench, climb down from the stage, and grab a chair for myself. He reaches clumsily for my hand and lifts it, pressing his lips into my knuckles. The smell of roses wafts all around us. We sit and watch Rebecca and Chuck do their thing like we're taking in a first-date movie. Before you know it, the night's over.

"Thank you for a wonderful evening," he says, rising as the lights come up.

I can't think of what to say, so I mumble, "Mm hmm," like I'm a waitress and he's thanking me for a coffee refill. He leans over as if he might kiss me, but then he smiles and turns to walk out with the rest of the crowd.

* * *

On Sunday morning, Mom's door is open and the smell of oil paint and turpentine wafts into the hallway. I hear her humming inside. It reminds me of everything I used to love about her: her sweetly melancholy voice, the hymns and songs of her girlhood, the times when she felt good enough to hum.

I lean against the wall, try to make out the tune, then sing softly along to "Rock My Soul," the original, not the Elvis version.

"Honey?" Mom pokes her head out the door, smiles tentatively, paintbrush in her hand.

"Guess what," I say. "Perry and I are dating. I think."

"That's lovely, dear." She smiles, then returns to her painting.

I stand there a moment longer, trying out the words I'd say if she were still listening.

Perry calls later in the morning and asks if I'd like to have lunch with him today. Sure, I say, casual, cool, not knowing what to expect. Probably not a restaurant, hopefully not the shelter. He gives me directions to a park I never knew existed just blocks away and we plan to meet at noon.

It's a sunny but cool fall day, so I slip a sweater over my T-shirt and find some socks to wear with my clunky shoes. As I look in the mirror, debating whether or not to wear lipstick—does Perry like lipstick? will he try to kiss me?—I notice that I look like a school-girl, like Emma, with the demure little sweater and knobby knees poking out from my short skirt. I'm nervous about what I look like, going out on a date with a homeless man.

I get to the park early and there's Perry, nervous and fidgety in a too-tight orange sweater and army pants. He leans against a tree capped by a brilliant dome of autumn leaves, not seeming to notice as bright ovals float down to rest on his shoulders and the brown carpet of dead leaves and grass below.

"Hi," he says. He's holding a paper bag. I check out its shape and size, then feel mean that I could even think it would be booze.

"Hi yourself." Who knows what he's checking out about me.

He points to a nearby bench and we cross a semicircle of con-crete path to sit on it. The wood slats give slightly beneath our weight, and he unpacks cheese sandwiches and a thermos of hot tea. He offers me the first drink from the plastic cup on top; it smells like incense and tastes like oranges. We sit quietly, sipping tea, eating, and watching eddies of leaves swirl in the sharp sunlight, wisps of wind rattling the empty paper bag.

"I like your skirt," he finally says. "You remind me of girls I used to go to school with."

"Great," I say. "That's the look I'm going for—prepubescent."

He doesn't reply. I take a big bite of sandwich, the soft white bread and American cheese adhering to the roof of my mouth so that I can't speak. When I've swallowed, the moment for any kind of retrieval is long gone.

He finishes his sandwich and neatly balls the plastic wrap to place in the bag.

"I like your . . . sweater," I try, afraid the date is about to end.

He laughs. "No, you don't."

"Well, kind of." I sigh. "God. I used to be good at this, this dating thing."

"What happened?" His smile reveals a neat little nick of a dimple beside his mouth I've never noticed before.

"Hell, I don't know. Too many assholes. Something."

"I was *never* good at this," he says. "You had me fooled. I thought you were pretty good."

"Right," I say. "You're just trying to make me feel better."

"Maybe," he says and slides closer, kicking cracked brown Oxfords out in front of him. At least they fit, and they're laced and tied. "Let's start over. What should we talk about? The weather? You?"

"You," I say, turning to face him on the bench. "Let's talk about you."

Perry tells me about his job at the shelter, how he started as a night clerk but now there's talk about making him a manager. He likes taking care of people, he says. Even on the streets, he'd try to scrounge up enough food to share, find a cop when someone wasn't moving. He met my mom at an art class she teaches at the

Opportunity School near the shelter, which he signed up for because he'd been an art major during the one year he tried college. He'd never stopped drawing, it was just the surfaces that changed, from paper to brick walls and sidewalks. "But I'm no tagger," he says. "I just like to draw."

I ask about his family and he tells me he grew up on the western slope near Grand Junction; his dad was a mining engineer, his mom a housewife. Like me, he has a kid sister named Jane and we go through that "Oh, my God, what are the chances" thing that people do when they're looking for some kind of connection, but it's nice. His Jane sounds friendlier than mine. She has three young sons, and Perry looks happy when he talks about them.

I can't bring myself to ask the questions I really want to—why was he out on the streets if he comes from a nice family, is he a drunk, an addict? And why does he always appear out of the blue, like some kind of benevolent stalker? Is it out of craziness, or obsession, or is it just a unique but disturbing way of showing affection? Instead I ask him the easy questions: his nephews' names and ages, how often he sees them. What brought him to Denver, the answer to which surprises me: There's more opportunity here.

When he asks about me, I shake my head and laugh. "Let's not go there. This date's finally going okay."

"Well, then, how's your ghost?"

"Sal's great," I say. "Sometimes she's all that keeps me sane."

His eyes widen ever so slightly. He thinks I'm as loony as my mother.

"God, you take me so seriously!" I say, laughing, then stand and stretch. "Don't you have to get back to work soon?"

I walk back with him, leaves crackling underfoot and a pleasant wet dirt smell all around us. Every time our hands brush together I feel a buzz—not quite a wonder-surge, but definitely a tingle of things to come.

The next day, I arrange our third date: coffee at Beelzebub's. We decide to meet there, and I find him in back, surveying a row of dimly lit photographs on the far wall. His hands are clasped tightly behind his back, and when I say his name, he turns quickly, flushes.

"Maybe you don't want to look at these," he says.

I move to get a closer look, then laugh. Genitalia. At least I think it is. The photographer has a thing for zoom lenses and whipped cream. "Charming," I say, settling my bag on a rickety chair at the nearest table, but I find it sweet that he'd worry about it. If he only knew. He takes a seat across from me as I fish money from my bag.

"What'll it be? My treat."

"Whatever you're having." He shifts on the metal seat, like he can't find the right way to sit on it.

"Latte?"

He nods.

"Double? Single?"

He looks at me helplessly. Of course. He doesn't know this language; I've only just learned it myself. I smile. "I'll surprise you."

I return with two grande caramel lattes and set one in front of him. He removes the plastic top and downs it inside a minute.

"The shelter coffee isn't very good," he explains, looking up from his cup with a foamy mustache. I blot at it with my napkin and he grasps my hand before I can pull it away. "Are you afraid of me, Tallie?" he asks.

"I don't know," I say, my knuckles nestled in his palm like chicks in a nest. They feel safe there and I make no move to pull away. "Should I be?"

He stares at me for a moment, considering, then leans over the table to kiss me. I close my eyes, feeling his breath before his lips. It's over way too fast.

I wake up the next morning humming the screaming guitar intro to "Magic Man," and then the lyrics:

> "Cold late night so long ago,
> when I was not so strong, you know,
> a pretty man came to me,
> I never seen eyes so blue."

I lie in bed, startled. Jesus. Did I concoct this guy from an old Heart song? Have I created an imaginary dream date from a hobo? Am I so pathetic that I have to scrape the bottom of the human gene pool for a boyfriend?

Maybe. But I've known enough guys with money and homes and cars who were truly bottom-feeders, and not one of them was half as kind as Perry.

Today is our fourth date. Perry and I decide to take my car and head west toward the mountains, with no particular plan in mind. A Sunday drive. He says his family did that when he was growing up, and he and his sister would sit in back playing I spy and twenty questions.

"Your childhood sounds like Richie Cunningham's," I say once we're under way, keeping my eyes on the road as I rattle across three lanes to exit westward on I-70. I don't tell him that mine was more like the Fonz's.

"Maybe when I was younger," he says. "My parents gave up on me after a while. I was a handful."

"Really?" I turn to look at him. "You don't seem like a handful. You're pretty mellow."

"Yeah," he laughs. "I'm great on meds."

The world stops. I feel the jolt as if it were a ball stopped in its tracks by a brick wall.

"Meds?"

"Your mother didn't tell you?" He turns his head toward the window and we're quiet for a moment. Then he looks at me and says, "Tallie, I'd never have thought of seeing you without you knowing about my . . . about me." His voice shakes, his cheeks flush.

"Mom and I don't chat much," I say calmly, but my stomach is flopping like a dying fish.

"Well, there's a reason your mother and I connect," he says. "We have the same, you know . . ." He expels a long sigh. "I guess I thought she'd told you."

"Yeah, well, she didn't," I say, the words snapping out of my mouth like the crack of a whip. "But, then again, neither did you."

He nods, turns to stare out the window again. After a few uneasy minutes of silence, he says, "Do you want to go home?"

"Not just yet." I'm feeling better for some reason. Maybe because I've never been just plain mad about this before. With my mother, there's always some gunked-up mixture of guilt, worry, and fear mixed in. Pure anger is refreshing. Invigorating.

The exit for Indian Hot Springs lies just ahead, and I ease into the turn lane. "Let's go swimming."

"Uh, but we don't have suits, or . . . or anything," he says, tightening his grip on the armrest.

"True."

He's quiet as I find my way from the highway along crumbling roads to a cluster of rustic buildings alongside a river.

"We're here." My voice is psycho-cheerful.

"You're serious?"

"As a heart attack. Are you coming?" I climb out, then lean in to look at his bewildered face.

I don't know what I'm doing exactly, but I feel righteous, empowered. Angry and not willing to put up with any more shit from anybody, crazy or not. He's still sitting there looking dazed, so I swing my door closed with a satisfying *chunk* and walk across the dirt parking lot toward the entrance. I've gotten most of the way there when I hear a car door open and close behind me. I stop in my tracks, so flooded with relief that my knees almost buckle.

"Wait up," he calls, and the crunch of running footsteps coming toward me is sweeter, I think, than any sound I've ever heard.

26

♪ We sit silently at first, immersed in hot bubbling water up to our necks, breathing sulfur and gazing at pine-tree tops and clear blue sky. Between us we scrounged the twelve bucks for an outdoor hot tub tucked inside a cedar-fenced enclosure, and we managed to avoid actually seeing much of each other as we quickly undressed and slipped into the water.

Finally, I can't stand the quiet any longer. "So, just how crazy are you anyway?" I blurt, then try to soften it. "I mean—"

"No, that's okay," Perry says firmly, eyes the color of the sky behind him and dark stubble peppering his cheeks. Stripped of his cast-off wardrobe, I realize how handsome he is. I almost lose my resolve, watching him.

"I was diagnosed with manic depression when I was seventeen." He stops and swallows hard, Adam's apple rising and falling, then starts again. "I wasn't always that way. I remember being happy as a kid. I used to draw comic books about all my friends and our adventures. We liked to go camping up on the monument, exploring and pretending we were the only humans left on earth. Goofy stuff, kid stuff."

I smile, picturing him as a boy, running around the woods, hanging with his buddies, until I see the grief in his eyes. This is tearing him apart, remembering.

"When I was fifteen or so, something started to change. I mean,

I could actually feel it, like the wiring in my brain going haywire or something, but it wasn't like I was going to tell anyone. I was moody, and I was a teenager; people thought it was normal. But I started doing too many hard-core drugs, taking too many stupid risks, blowing off my friends, my schoolwork." He stops, thinking, it seems. I watch him and wait, and he sighs and begins to speak again.

"Finally, I wrecked my mom's Jeep at three in the morning, not out with friends partying, just all by myself. On purpose, and I hurt my leg pretty bad. My parents took me to a shrink. I had him convinced for the longest time that I was just another rebellious teenager, but then I tried to drink a bottle of paint thinner my dad had in the garage."

I flinch, hoping he doesn't notice. I am hungry for this, these details, even though I feel dizzy, nauseated by the swirling heat and the ugliness of the truth.

"I decided to trust this guy, this doctor, so I 'fessed up, told him something was really wrong with me. I told him I always felt like I was either balancing on the edge of a cliff or trapped in a deep dark hole full of poison. Nothing ever felt good anymore, not even the highs. What would it matter if I died? I just needed some relief."

My mother must have felt this way, too, I realize, when she pulled her suicidal stunts. I never thought about what she might be experiencing, what horror might be unraveling in her mind. I only thought about how it affected us.

Even after telling the doctor everything, Perry tells me, he was misdiagnosed. "He thought I was just depressed, so he put me on some antidepressant. It made it worse. I felt like I was burning alive. I started punching walls, breaking doors, and it got to the point that my mother was afraid to have me living there. She thought I might hurt her, or my sister. She didn't realize that the only person I'd even think about hurting was myself." He works his jaw back and forth, staring dully at the water. Three months before Perry turned eighteen, he says, his parents sent him to live in an institution for disturbed youth. A warehouse. He split. That was the first time Perry lived on the street.

The years that followed became a circular nightmare: repeated hospitalizations, medications, shrinks, halfway houses, home, then back. And always back to the street eventually, where he'd let his meds lapse and fall into his old patterns. I nod. This cycle is completely familiar to me, just not from the other side.

Finally, even though I'm afraid to ask, I say, "But what about now? What about when I first met you?"

"That night in your mother's kitchen, I'd been on my meds for a couple of months but I still felt so alienated from . . . I don't know. Everything. But I was trying to do what they say: Get out there and join the human race."

We're silent for a moment. I know this is hard for him, but I need to know everything now, so I work up the nerve to say, "You've followed me."

He looks startled at first, then nods. "I didn't mean to scare you."

"It's a little creepy," I say.

"Yeah, I'm sorry." He looks flustered, his cheeks going crimson. "I just felt comforted, seeing you. Being near you, from that first night." He groans and looks up into the sky. "God, I don't know how to explain it."

"Try."

He looks back at me, rubs his chin. I imagine the stubble against my own fingers, feel it brush my face.

"Okay," he says, then pauses. "See, meeting your mother is one of the best things that ever happened to me. My own parents never tried to help me as much as she does. She knows exactly what I'm going through. I think of her as my savior."

I nod, trying to imagine my mother in this holy light.

"But then I met you"—his voice wavers—"and you made me want to *stay* better." He looks so deeply into my eyes that I pretend to have an itch on my foot that requires my complete concentration, but he continues anyway. "And that's never happened before."

"Why me?" I ask, not looking up.

"I wish I could explain it. I just feel it."

I let go of my foot, float my hands on top of the bubbling water,

watching them bob and bounce like sailboats in a storm before I
swim them around to grab the sides of the tub and look at him again.
He copies my arm movements, drawing himself up higher in the tub
to grab the sides, and his shoulders tense into well-defined globes,
the top of his chest glistens with beads of water. Dark hair lies flat
in the triangle between his collarbones. I feel an odd twinge in my
chest. I could love this person way too much.

He lets go of the edge and skims his hands across the water
until they're floating in front of me. I let go, too, and slowly drift
my hands toward his, bob and bounce, fingertips bumping finally
together. I lace my fingers through his and his face relaxes. I am
sinking, going too deep into this, I know, but every cell and fiber
that makes me who I am propels me farther into the crazy idea that
I should be with him, be with this man, who, for all I know, is
going to freak out just like my mother always has and grind my
heart into tiny bits.

We aren't so shy when we emerge from the water. You'd think
discovering these things about Perry would send me screaming
down the mountain, but it has the opposite effect. I want to hang
out with him some more, talk about things, all kinds of things. I
want to know everything about him, and I want him to know
everything about me.

We towel off casually, not hiding or looking away. The weird
part is that seeing me in the altogether doesn't seem to arouse him,
and I check the obvious indicators. Nothing. I feel a stirring, but
it's more the anticipation of his seeing me, and when that doesn't
create the big bang I expected, my own spark fizzles.

But we smile like goofy kids as we yank clothes over damp skin.
It's the right feeling, that first-glimmer-of-love feeling, but without the usual accompanying lust. Even stranger is that we're ex-
posing our sordid histories before we even hit the sack. An
alternative universe, just like everything is with Perry.

We get home in time for Mom's party, which Perry says he
would really like to attend, so I say sure, okay. Why not. It won't

be so bad together. We make our way through the crowd to an empty corner. He leans against the wall, pulling me against him, my back to his front. Having him here, having someone to be with and not feel like such an outsider, is so comforting that I don't even think about having a glass of wine until Mom comes over and offers me one.

I watch the two of them talking and think about what they have in common, the faulty wiring, the inner workings that drive them to do almost anything to escape their own thoughts. Except the one thing that really helps, of course. I'll never understand why it's such a problem to take a little pill every day.

Can Perry do this? I wonder. Can he keep his shit together? I close my eyes, lean my head into his shoulder, willing one thought into him: please, please, please.

"Are you all right, honey?" my mother asks, and I straighten up, nod.

"Just tired. Perry and I had a big day."

After the party, Mom and Audra clean up around us, giving each other smirky looks as we try to say good night. They finally go into the kitchen and leave us alone, and Perry kisses me at the front door. It's a real, solid kiss, with tongues and teeth and lips mashing together in a slippery dance.

He's a good kisser, a fact that makes me want to jump up and down and yell "hallelujah" to the heavens.

As we pull apart, I whisper, "So, why didn't we do it when we had the chance today?"

He just breathes heavy and pulls me back against him.

The sound of clattering dishes comes from the kitchen. Without another word, I lead him back to my room.

This time we undress each other, slowly, painstakingly. By the time we're both naked, standing inches apart in the pale glow from the window, it's all I can do not to force his hands onto me. For once in my life, though, I wait.

We stand looking into each other's eyes for a long moment. Perry smiles, a new sexy smile I haven't seen yet, then takes a step back. He's looking at me like he did that day in the alley, just look-ing, eyes moving from my face to my neck, my breasts, my stom-ach, my pelvis, my legs. I feel nervous, not at all sure of anything, and my leg muscles jump and quiver, my heart pounds.

He sighs and looks at my face with a dreamy expression. "How can this be happening? How did this finally happen?"

I raise my shoulders in a small shrug, because I can't speak. My throat is choked with sounds I don't want to escape, not just yet, not before he's even touched me. He sees my legs quaking and asks, "Are you cold? Should we get into bed?"

I nod even though cold has nothing to do with it, and Perry guides me to the bed, lays me down on my back, hovering over me. I open my legs—it seems the obvious thing to do—but Perry just strokes and kisses me.

"There's plenty of time for that," he says. "Let's get to know each other first."

Sal hangs out with me in the bathroom the next day as I'm get-ting ready for work. She sits on the edge of the tub, leaning against the white tile. With her red dress and dark skin, she's the most colorful thing in the room.

"So, how come I can see you in the mirror?" I ask as I apply eye pencil. "I thought ghosts didn't have reflections."

"That's vampires, honey," she says, "and that's only in the movies."

"Yeah, I guess." She hasn't said a word about Perry. "So, you know everything, right?"

She shrugs.

"Oh, come on, Sal." I mess up with the eye pencil and draw a Cleopatra line across my lid. "Shit," I mutter, wetting a Q-Tip with spit to wipe it off, then I turn to face her. "What's the deal with Perry?"

"Oh, you don't know?" She pulls her chin in, looks at me doubt-fully.

"I know that I like him and that he likes me. That we're all gaga like thirteen-year-olds and that he's a great kisser, among other things. That's what I know."

"Ain't that sweet?" she says.

"It's what you've been pushing for, isn't it? And now it's happened, so tell me the rest." I turn back around, pick up the mascara. "Do we live happily ever after? Or," I ask, my heart quickening, "does he go nuts again and find a nice box to live in?"

"I'm not a fortune-teller," she says, folding her hands in her wide lap. "Some of this stuff you've got to figure out for yourself."

"But you wouldn't encourage me to get together with a—a potentially insane person, would you, if you knew he wouldn't be able to hang in there? Right?"

"I encouraged you to be open to love, Tallulah Jean, that's all. It's never wrong to love someone." Her voice fades as she does, and the room, once again, becomes stark and white and sterile.

27

♪ It's a slow Monday night and I'm back in my XS polo shirt and jeans. Chuck and I toss around halfhearted banter. Apparently, with all our changes, Coyote Cry is eating our dust again, but you couldn't tell it tonight. The place is less than half full and the customers seem content to just hang out, drink, talk to one another. They don't pay much attention to us.

It's time for the '80s party medley, starting with "Love Shack" by the B-52's. Chuck looks at me. "Ready?"

I cover the mike with my hand, lean over. "I'm not in the mood, and I don't think they are either," I say, nodding toward the audience. "How about the blues medley?" Sure, he indicates with a nod of his head. Audra's been giving us more leeway in our sets—we can mix stuff up now, as long as we still play our approved songs.

The blues medley is my baby; I sing all the songs. It's not obvious to most people, not even old eagle-ears Audra, but I don't always sing the same ones. Hell, it's just a 1-4-5 progression, over and over, the twelve-bar blues. Only the keys change, and Chuck's always quick to follow. I decide to do a Big Gal Sal classic.

"Well, I've been looking for a man to love me, I've been looking all night and day." I rock slightly on the bench, feeling good. Out in the audience, people sway with me, their focus turning to the stage. *"Said I've been looking for a fine man, one who will make me kneel and pray,"* I sing, working my way to the punch

line. *"If I don't find someone real soon, darlin', then I might ask you in to play."* A group of gray-suited businesswomen pump their fists in the air. "You tell 'em, honey!" one shouts.

"Yo, Tallie!" someone else yells, and I look over to see Arnie, the bald guy from Mom's parties, sitting at a two-top with another chrome-dome. Arnie waves frantically and I wink, just to calm him down.

"Said a fine man could make me holler," I sing, my favorite verse. *"A fine man could make me jump and moan."* The crowd goes wild, all thirty or so of them, and one couple stands to do an improvisational gyrating dance. *"A real good man could love me without trying to call me his own,"* I tease Arnie and his friend. *"But if he don't come along, sugar, well then I might just take you home."*

After the set, I make the usual courtesy visit to Arnie's table.

"Great show, Tal," he says, standing and reaching across the table to hug me. Like we're old friends or something.

"Yeah, not too bad for a Monday."

His friend has a much cooler look, up close, than Arnie. He's wearing the requisite black jeans and leather jacket that music-industry people wear. He can't help the shiny head. In fact, he's shaved what remains so he looks more hip than old.

"Tony Vega. *Denver News.*" He stands and shakes my hand. "Arnie's told me a lot about you."

I pull up a chair. "I would have sworn you were in the music business."

"He is, Tallie," Arnie says, squirming with excitement. "Don't you know who this is?" Without waiting for an answer, he blurts, "Tony's the entertainment editor, and he's here to write about you!"

"For real?" I say, looking at Tony, then Arnie, then Tony.

Tony nods, pulls out a small notebook. "Mind if I ask a few questions?"

An interview. I've been waiting for this all my life. I've been reviewed before but never interviewed. For as long as I can remember, I've rehearsed *Rolling Stone* interviews while waiting to fall asleep at night, practiced witty, cool answers, dreamed up meaningful insights, and imagined my picture spread across glossy magazine pages.

"Oh, God. Do you need a photo?" All I have is my big-hair shot.

Tony shakes his head. "If we decide to run this, we'll send someone over. We're thinking of using it for a Sunday entertainment feature."

"That means you'd be on the cover, Tallie," Arnie says, looking like he could burst with the excitement of it all. "Is this cool or what?"

For once, I have to agree with the guy.

I'm trying to seduce Perry for at least the tenth time. We're alone at Mom's, locked in my bedroom. It's a gorgeous twilight outside and I've had a half bottle of wine while he's been sipping tea all afternoon. I started kissing the back of his neck when he was sitting on the living room couch looking through one of my mother's art books, and he reached over and squeezed my arm. Okay, this is good, I thought, and worked my way between him and the book, and again, he responded positively, so I pulled him to his feet. "Let's go where it's more comfortable," I said and led him to my room.

It's become obvious that he's shy about this stuff, so I've bagged the whole Debbie Does Denver act. "Don't you want to make love?" I ask, using his terminology, half undressed and full of desire.

"We are making love," he says, kissing me and stroking my stomach.

"You know what I mean."

He rolls onto his back, removes his hands from me, clasps them beneath his head. "I've told you. I just need to take this slowly."

I try not to sound as desperate as I feel. "I thought we *were* taking it slowly. Extremely slowly. Don't we ever get to speed it up? Not warp speed, or anything, but just . . . normal speed?"

He rolls away from me. I've pushed it too far again, but I've never known a man who didn't want to do the horizontal boogie, given half a chance. It's not that Perry doesn't satisfy me. He'd spend hours bringing me to orgasm after orgasm if I let him, a wonderful thing, a stupendous thing I've never experienced before. Most women would thank their lucky stars, but I've become obsessed by the fact that he doesn't want to fuck me.

I study his back, the low sloping curve from shoulders to hips, the three dark freckles that form a triangle on his left shoulder blade. I reach over and trace lines between them. "Don't you like me?"

"This isn't about you. I've told you that."

I laugh. "Yeah, it is. Who else would it be about?"

"It's about me and the stupid drugs I have to take just to be a halfway normal person." His back rounds as he draws his knees higher. "My medication makes it hard to . . . you know."

"Oh, Perry. God," I say, turning to lie alongside him. "I am such an idiot. Please don't hate me. I didn't know, or I wouldn't have—"

"I know," he says. His voice is quiet and faraway.

Mom comes home from a meeting looking harried and disheveled. Her suit jacket is twisted toward one shoulder and large sections of her hair have worked loose from a messy bun high on her head. Worse, she has a worried nervous look that verges on frantic.

"Mom?" I say as she unbuttons her jacket in the front hall. "What's up?"

She looks up at me with tears in her eyes. "Oh, Tallie, I'm ashamed to call myself part of the human race."

Goddamn it, here we go again. "Did you take your meds this morning?" I say like Nurse Ratched, breaking the rules and not caring.

"Tallie!" She sounds pissed, but she just straightens her jacket, smooths her hair. "I am allowed a human emotion or two, am I not? If you knew what happened at some of these damned things. Jesus. All we're trying to do is support fellow artists, human beings . . ." She trails off, shakes her head.

"What human beings?"

"The Gay and Lesbian Art Teachers Association."

"The Gay and Les—"

She sighs impatiently. "We just want to support their efforts in the schools, for God's sake, try to ensure this city's children receive an art education, and now we're being lambasted with protestors at our meetings, with ugly, horrible hate mail. You'd think we were all ax murderers."

She picks through the mail on the hall table, calmer it seems, and then she whacks a magazine against the table edge. She holds up an envelope for me to see. "Addressed to 'Faggot Child Molesters,'" she says. "How on earth did this get through the U.S. mail? It drives me insane."

God, I hope not, I think, and head for my room.

Perry meets me after work most nights. He likes to joke that he's there to walk me home, all twenty or so steps from door to door. Some nights he does just that, kisses me good night at Mom's door, gives me a smile that melts my skeletal system, then leaves. Other nights I convince him to come in and we slip silently into my room where he makes his unique style of one-sided love to me until I am so electrically charged I can't stand to be touched anymore. Tonight he's leaning against a lamppost when I walk from the bar, hunkered against the cold. He smiles at the first sight of me.

"How was your night?" He kisses me with cold lips.

"Not too bad. Rebecca completely fucked up the words to 'Piece of My Heart.' Serves her right for even attempting Janis." I slide my arm through his. "Hey, you're shivering. How long have you been out here?"

"Just a little while," he says. "I wanted to hear that last song you always do, about the arms of the angel."

I look into his face. He is exactly the right height for me, just slightly taller, not so tall I can't easily kiss him, not so short I can't wear heels. "Sarah McLachlan," I say. "Good taste."

We walk toward the lofts. At the door, I turn toward him. "I don't feel like going in yet. Want to go for a walk?"

He nods and we pull together against the cold, our breath mingling smoky white in the thin dark air.

We walk quietly for a couple of blocks as I try to pull my thoughts together. I want to talk to him about my mother. As I get to know him better, I learn more and more about bipolar disorder and what it takes to deal with it. He sees a volunteer therapist at the city clinic, goes to support groups, takes his medicine whether he feels like it or not, and keeps busy finding new ways to help out at the shelter. I don't know if my mother has it in her to work that hard.

We round the corner from Fifteenth Street to Larimer, the prettiest block downtown. Multicolored banners hang from wires stretched across the narrow street, old stone buildings line the sidewalks, storefronts lit like Christmas. People mill about in front of a coffeehouse called the Market and, farther down, Shooting Star, a noisy dance club.

"I need your opinion," I finally say. "You're my new crazy expert."

He stops, grabs his heart. "God, you're brutal," he says, but then he makes that funny little smile I first saw in Mom's kitchen and keeps walking. "Okay, shoot."

I tell him about Mom's little episode, how it apparently still happens sometimes and nobody knows but Audra, and now me.

He shakes his head. "Man. I can't believe it." I've just crucified his role model.

"I'm sorry, Perry. I wouldn't have told you, but I'm worried about her. She's so damned wacky sometimes. I can't tell if she's acting crazy or if I'm just paranoid now. How the hell do I tell the difference?"

"You talk to her about it," Perry says.

"No way. Aren't there just, like, signs or something? Symptoms?"

"Well, sure. If she's going into a manic episode, it's all the stuff you already know: rapid speech, being hyper or agitated, delusions of grandeur, feelings of persecution."

"See. That's what I think. This gay art teacher thing. I don't know if it's for real, or as serious as she's making it, or what."

"You need to talk to her."

"I can't," I say. "We don't do that in my family."

"Maybe it's time you should."

"I'm not that brave."

He laughs, stops, and turns me toward him. "You are one of the most courageous people I know." His breath turns into vapor, then disappears.

"No way." I shake my head. "I'm a coward. I'm a ninny, a scaredy-cat. I'm a big fat baby when it comes to this particular shit, this crazy mother shit."

He smiles. "Well, I'm here to tell you you're courageous. You climb onstage every night and face a roomful of people—"

"Big deal. Monkeys in the circus do that."

"Don't interrupt. You don't take grief from anyone. You saved yourself when you were just a kid and went out in the world to live on your own."

"That wasn't brave. That was scared."

"Courage isn't about not being scared," he says. "It's about being scared and doing something anyway."

"Running away?" I snort.

"Surviving." He links his arm through mine and we walk silently through the sounds of the city—cars cruising, people laughing, a siren in the distance.

More and more lately, Mom paints with her door open. If I'm passing by, she waves me in and we talk for a few minutes while she's mixing colors or treating virgin canvases with milky primer. It feels like practice to me, like if I keep doing this, talking about trivial stuff, I might eventually find a way to talk about more important things. At least I can keep an eye on her this way, check her mental condition from time to time. I haven't asked her again about her medication, that's for sure.

Mom gets a nostalgic look on her face when we talk, a shy smile, that needy look in her eyes. She asks me how it's going at the bar, or how I'm adjusting to life here, but what she really likes is to hear about the years I was away, my life on the road. I tell her lies. It was a glamorous life, full of excitement, I say. I always had the luxury of motel rooms to myself, and we were a big hit everywhere we went. I had a steady boyfriend (a real nice guy, I say) for the last few years. I even named him—Steve—and I went ahead and made him a drummer. Apparently we were heartbroken at parting there in Missouri, but he understood that I needed to come off the road and make a new start. I, being the saint I am, understood his need to move on to the next gig without me. The look on her face makes me almost believe it myself.

The upside to these chats is that I find out interesting things about life around here. Like Audra bought the first painting Mom sold seven years ago when Mom was still struggling as a legal secretary. Turns out Audra is something of a tycoon. She owns this building we live in—she owns most of the block, in fact. I have a feeling Mom gets a break on the rent.

I know that Audra is good for her—it's obvious not only from Mom's cushy circumstances but also from their goofy lovesick glances when they think no one's looking. Okay, okay, I want to tell her sometimes. I get it. You're gay. Just don't do anything gross in front of me.

I tiptoed closer to more serious territory the other day and asked her about the gay art teacher thing. She shook her head. "We've threatened those lunatics with legal action, so they've backed off a bit," she said, then smiled at me gratefully. "It's nice that you care about it, dear."

This morning when I set out for my walk, the bone-numbing chill in the air sends me straight to Beelzebub's instead for a triple latte. When I push back out through the door into the cold, the air smells wet and musty, like a storm's coming, and the clouds color the sky a heavy gray. I decide to skip the walk entirely, seeing as I'm itching to play the piano anyway. I use the paper coffee cup to warm my fingers as I head for the bar.

Inside, I climb the stage steps, set my cup on a cocktail napkin with "Freebird" written on it. A three-screaming-guitar Lynyrd Skynyrd song and some nut wants us to play it in a piano bar. It doesn't matter where you go, or how many years it's been since that unfortunate day the band's plane was plucked from the sky, if you are a musician playing in any public venue, someone will always ask for "Freebird."

I settle in at the piano and zone out, letting my fingers move around on the keys, trying different chords together until I have a soulful-sounding progression that reminds me of Bill Withers' version of "Lean on Me." I change it around a little, still doing the ascending pattern, but adding a cool harmony and syncopating it. Now words come and I start to hum, then sing: *"It's almost daylight, almost daylight again."* The melody is nice and it has a gospel feel, so I sing it over and over until more words come and soon I have a good workable chorus. Just like in the old days, a song filters in as if by magic, like someone is whispering it to me, handing me a gift. It takes a minute to sink in, but when I realize I'm writing a song, after being dry for so many years, I look around for the Big Gal. Surely she's here somewhere, but, no.

It's just me.

It's a raging Friday night when Tony and the *Denver News* photographer finally come to the bar. Luckily, I got a heads-up from bald Arnie and I'm wearing the dress. To hell with Audra.

As soon as I see the two of them milling around the bar, I make a beeline to the bathroom to make sure I look all right. I'm fighting a cold that's going around, so my throat's scratchy, but it shouldn't matter. Tony's heard me singing at my best; tonight's only a visual thing. I freshen my lipstick, tug the front of my shirt-dress down, and lean forward, doing what I can to create some cleavage.

Eileen and Bob's final song is winding up, so I push through the bathroom door, ready to hit the stage. They stand at their pianos, still playing. This is the Flamingo's and my cue to head up there and slide in next to them, so the music never stops. My idea, and one even Audra loves.

"Ladies and gentlemen," Bob leans over and announces into his mike, "please welcome to the stage, Domingo Marquez and the suh-moking Tallie Beck!"

The crowd is fired up and noisy, better than I could hope for, and I see a few tables of regulars near the front, people who come almost every weekend and know our show by heart. "Go, Tallie! Go, Tallie!" a tableful of women chant. Domingo has his own groupie table on his side of the stage, men dressed in expensive, tight polyester, cheering him on. We grin across the pianos at each other, high-fiving Eileen and Bob like tag-team wrestlers. Out of the corner of my eye, I see the photographer fighting through the crowd, angling for a good viewpoint. It's never going to happen. The place is jammed, a firefighter's nightmare.

Domingo howls his way through "Good Golly, Miss Molly" with more passion than Little Richard himself, and I play along, thinking, thinking. When the song ends, I say, "Damn, Domingo, you are one hot mama."

"Takes one to know one, Tal," he replies, and the audience hoots and whistles. My, they are in a good mood.

"We have a couple of Denver celebrities with us tonight," I say, "and we all know what that means, right?"

The crowd goes wild. Whenever a local sports star or TV personality is in the audience, we call them up onstage to embarrass the hell out of them with a particularly raw version of "You Can Leave Your Hat On."

"Ladies and gentlemen, boys and girls," I say, "please put your hands together for Tony Vega of the *Denver News* and Photographer Guy, right over there!" I point toward the two of them, huddled near the bar. Much applause ensues and they look around, confused. "Okay, you two, get your butts up here!" I call out, and the crowd roars encouragement. Finally, they make their way to the stage and climb the steps behind me, the photographer clicking away at every opportunity. I make sure I give him all my best angles and I rake my dress up higher on my thigh. There's more than one way to get a good close-up.

"'In the rowdy party atmosphere of Sing Out!, Denver's premiere piano bar,'" Eileen reads from the paper, "'songstress Tallie Beck rules her subjects with a commanding presence and a whiskey voice.'"

We're sipping java at Beelzebub's late on Sunday morning and

I'm looking across the table at the cover of *On Stage,* the full-color Sunday paper pull-out in her hands. There I am, pumping the piano, veins and muscles bulging from my neck and arms, my face contorted in a wail. I look like I could be giving birth, or like I'm getting stuck in the ass with a hypodermic.

"What does he mean, 'whiskey voice'?" I ask. I had a damned cold. He could have remembered the first night he saw me when my voice was perfect.

Eileen ignores me and keeps reading. "'As a seasoned veteran of the music business'—"

"Old!" I interrupt. "He might as well have said old."

"—'Beck's high-energy performances have increased business in recent months, according to club owner Audra Lyon.'"

"Holy shit. Audra said that?"

Eileen nods and keeps reading. I relax a little, listening to words like "chanteuse" and "diva" being applied to me, knowing there are thousands of people out there, right now, reading the very same things, thinking I'm a big shot. Jedd, maybe. I think I'll send a copy to good old Lyle—make him sorry he ever canned my ass back in Missouri.

When she's done reading, Eileen hands me the section. Inside is a smaller picture of me, smiling slyly into the camera, beckoning the photographer up on stage. So what if it's only from the shoulders up, no cleavage, no thigh? I look hot. If I was a guy, I'd hit on me.

28

♪ "So, who is this guy?" Jane asks as she fills small bowls with odd things: raisins, cashews, shredded coconut. We're helping Mom fix dinner, an Indian feast she calls it, and the whole place smells of spices. I'm rolling dough into balls, then palming them flat according to Mom's instructions. Whatever happened to meat loaf, spaghetti, I'm thinking, wondering if this meal would qualify as a delusion of grandeur.

"His name is Perry," I say, hoping she'll leave it at that. Even though we're getting along better, this is Jane. I'm sure homeless guys don't rate big in her book.

Mom fills in the details, in her vague flowery way. For once, I appreciate her style. "Perry is a charming wonderful man. He has a very creative spirit, an artist's soul."

"Well, what does he do? Where does he live?" Jane looks doubtful as she spoons something sticky out of a jar. Chutney, it says on the label. I dip my pinkie in it and taste. It's sweet and hot, and I go for seconds, stalling, until Jane gives me a look. "Well?" she says.

"He's a manager and he lives nearby," I say, then decide to get it over with. "He just got promoted to day-shift manager at the Denver Homeless Shelter, and he has a new apartment in the projects. Subsidized housing. It's a hell of a lot better than where he used to live, which, before the shelter, was nowhere."

"Oh." Jane nods and presses her lips together. After a beat she says, "And how did you two meet?"

"Mom set us up."

"Tallulah Jean, I did not," Mom protests. She turns to Jane. "He's an art student of mine and he comes to the gatherings."

"Oh." Jane nods again. "I see." She's silent for a moment, surveying her bowls like she's wondering if she's forgotten something. She folds her arms, rests her chin against her fist. "Your little parties. Me, I've never been invited, but I suppose I'm not 'artistic' enough."

"Now, Jane, you know you're welcome anytime." Mom dons floral oven mitts, wrestles a large casserole dish from the oven. "You don't need an invitation. Besides, I didn't think you were interested. It is mostly artists, after all, and artist talk. It gets a little flaky sometimes, even for me."

The doorbell sounds and we hear Emma run to the door, followed by polite conversation then Emma running toward the kitchen.

"Oh, Aunt Tallie," she singsongs, pushing the door open enough to peek in. "Your date is here."

"Thank you, Emma," I sing back. "I'll be right the-ere." She snickers and runs away again.

"Come on, Janie," I say, running my hands under water, wiping them on my jeans. "You get to meet your first homeless man."

"Lovely," Jane says and follows me into the living room.

Perry and Emma have their backs to us as they study a drawing Emma's been working on. Perry compliments Emma on her shading. She grins up at him, wrinkling her nose, like "Really?"

"Hey, Perry," I say, and he turns.

He's dressed up in baggy slacks that are belted to fit his waist, a starched shirt, and some kind of crazy tie from an era long ago. He holds a bouquet of yellow flowers. "For your mom," he says, looking nervous.

I walk over and take his arm. "Perry, meet my sister, Jane."

He steps forward and shakes her hand.

Her lips pull into an artificial smile, but at least she's trying. "Nice to meet you, Perry. I see you've met my daughter."

"She's quite the artist. Takes after her grandmother."

"Mmm." Jane raises her eyebrows, pretends again to smile, but I'm sure she's thinking, God, I hope not.

We've about worn out the pleasantries when Mom breezes in, all Southern hospitality and charm. She fusses to get everyone provided with drinks, takes the flowers, thanks Perry for his thoughtfulness, and generally puts everyone at ease. It's the thing about her I'd most like to have inherited, her easy gracious way with people.

Something tells me I'm more like my father.

We've almost gotten through the entire meal with no calamities when Mom starts talking about Thanksgiving. "It's almost here," she says, looking worried, "and we haven't made any plans yet."

"Well, actually," I say, "I have. I'll be volunteering at the shelter."

"But—" Mom starts, interrupted by Jane.

"And Andrew's taking Emma to his parents' for Thanksgiving. I don't think I'll feel like doing much."

Emma steals a glance at her mother. "I don't have to go."

"Yes, you do, young lady. It's part of the deal. I get you for Christmas."

Emma slumps in her chair.

"God, Jane," I say, "she's a person, not a thing. You can't play Let's Make a Deal with her."

"Actually, Tallie, I can do any damned thing I want with her. She's my daughter, remember?"

"Enough!" Mom says loudly, then sinks her face into her palms. I get that scared feeling, but when I look at Jane, she's avoiding eye contact, trying not to let on that she's blinking back tears. I glance over at Perry to see if he's alarmed at Mom's outburst, but he's staring politely at his plate.

Mom takes a deep breath, then folds her hands on the table in front of her, speaking slowly as if to young children. "I would just like for us to be together on Thanksgiving, that's all. Now, Tallie, when will you and Perry be through at the shelter? And Jane, can you pick Emma up after dinner at her grandparents' and come over later? Certainly we can make this work, even if it's a late supper. It's been seventeen years since we've celebrated Thanksgiving together, and it's important to me that we find a way to do it. Okay?"

We sit silently, nod like obedient children, but there is nothing I want less than to spend a holiday with my family. Volunteering was my way of avoiding the whole mess, and now, not even being a do-gooder will save me.

In our family, holidays were not exactly joyous occasions. The three worst were Thanksgiving, Christmas, and Mother's Day, but even birthdays could throw my mother into one of her manias to try to outdo every occasion ever celebrated. The buildup to a holiday was usually a wary but hopeful time for Jane and me, watching Mom and her plans escalate. Decorations were hung, parties planned, groceries and gifts bought. The actual day, say Thanksgiving, could start out fine, Mom happy and buzzing around, taste-testing the stuffing, laying out the good silver. But the day never ended well. It was as if my mother had a biological holiday timer inside her, and at some point during any special day, it went off like a bomb that had been ticking.

I was seventeen years old the last time I spent Thanksgiving with my mother and sister. By then I was hardly ever at home. I had an exciting new life away from them, away from the calamitous feeling that nothing would ever be all right, no matter what some new doctor had to say, no matter what new miracle drug or herb or vitamin or alternative treatment or church my mother was trying. Jane didn't need me anymore, I reasoned. She could take care of herself. Hell, she was already more mature than I'd ever be.

I'd joined a garage band and fallen in love with the lanky guitar player. Jedd. We were the cool couple in our counterculture clique at school, the batch of longhaired, cigarette-smoking, drug-taking kids that didn't fit anywhere else. It didn't hurt that I could party with the best of them—hell, I'd been practicing since I was a kid. Jedd loved that I could drink so much, do so many drugs, and still stand. Still worship his teenage self, which I now know was just skinny and pimply and pathetic. At that age, it's astonishing what's attractive.

Jedd had invited me to Thanksgiving at his parents' house. They lived in a nicer neighborhood than we did and the view of life inside that olive-green tri-level from the outside looked like heaven to me: a rock-solid dad who always told corny jokes and called me Miss Bankhead; a plump motherly mother who scurried around trying to please everyone; a friendly little sister who looked up to me like I was a grown-up. I mean, it's still obvious why I would choose to spend a holiday there, rather than at the nuthouse where I lived, where my mother was guaranteed to lose it and Jane and I would have to deal with a half-baked turkey and mashed potatoes flung against the wall. We didn't even want to celebrate holidays, Jane and I, but Mom always insisted. We were family. It would be better this time, she'd say.

Mom threw a fit when I said I was going to Jedd's house for Thanksgiving, but a sane fit. A normal, motherly fit. She wanted me home for the holiday; she wanted us to be a real family. Her new doctor's theory was that if she just quit taking all the drugs she'd been prescribed over the years, she'd be fine. Yet another miracle cure. She made me promise to come home by six, since Jedd's mother was serving at three, so we could have our own dinner together afterward. "Bring your boyfriend," she said. "I'd like to meet him."

Even at that late stage of life with a crazy mother, I hooked in to her logic. After all, the doctor said she'd be okay and she said she'd stopped all the drugs. "Okay," I agreed. "I'll ask Jedd to come."

Jedd's mother hurried the meal along on our behalf. At five fifteen, when dessert was delayed because her first pumpkin pies hadn't set up right, I fought off the familiar panic feeling, said it was no problem. I even called to tell Mom we'd be a little late, but the phone was busy. We were leaving soon, anyway. I didn't try again.

Jedd had taken care to dress up in a button-down shirt and corduroy pants, a far cry from the holey jeans and black T-shirts he usually wore. I'd never let him meet my mother before, although he knew she had problems. I always said it would be best if he dropped me off in front of the house; you never knew what you were walking into. But everything seemed okay, so far, and I thought maybe my mother would try extra hard since we were having a guest.

It was black outside when we climbed into his rusty Ford Fairlane. His parents stood under the porch light, waving good-bye as the engine sputtered for a few moments, then thundered into motion. We sped away down that pristine block of well-manicured lawns and happy families, and I turned and watched them wave until they were out of sight.

I should have known by then never to enter our house when it looked so dark. But, I rationalized, maybe Mom was working by the light of the tiny bulb over the stove. I could almost see her there, wearing her brown-and-yellow apron over her dress, reading a cookbook and stirring a pot at the same time.

And Jane would be holed up in her room at the back of the house, reading like she always did by the light of her bedside lamp. That light wouldn't travel to the front of the house, where you could see it from the street.

So we climbed from the Ford, held hands as we walked up the concrete steps and into the front door. I wanted it to be like Mom had said, a nice family holiday dinner together, a chance to show off my new boyfriend. I wanted it so much I ignored the dank chill feel to the air inside the house when we entered. I called out, "Where is everybody?" with an exasperated tone, like I was in some stupid TV sitcom or something.

And then I flipped the light switch.

At first I thought a tornado must have blown through our neighborhood; everything was that torn apart. Of course, I knew the tornado was confined to our house, and that it was in fact my mother, but I was always surprised at the force and strength of her rampages. The couch had been flung into the center of the living room and teetered upside down on its broken arm. A vase of flowers Jane and I had gone in on for the special occasion was smashed against one wall, the flowers still fresh-looking despite the broken stems and shards of glass lying in a puddle around them. I knew the kitchen would be worse. I didn't go there.

"Oh, my God," Jedd said. "What happened?"

"Go wait in the car," I said, begging more than ordering, but he wouldn't. He followed me as I tiptoed up the stairs. "Janie?" I whisper-called, poking my head into her room. It looked fine, but Jane was nowhere to be found. My room was untouched, and my mother's bedroom door was open, meaning that it was all clear.

"Shit," I said, heading back down the stairs. Where the hell were they?

The doorbell rang and I rushed to answer it. Mrs. Stephens, our neighbor, stood there with a worried look on her face.

"I saw the light on," she said, "and I knew it must be you. Can I come in, dear?"

I looked behind me at the chaos and edged out the door onto the porch, pulling Jedd with me. "What's going on?" I asked, breath turning to mist in the cool night air. "What happened?"

"Your mother and sister were taken to the hospital in an ambulance, that's all I know," she said, biting her lip, looking like she could cry. "I don't know what exactly happened, but your mother was on a gurney. Jane looked okay. She walked to the back and climbed in with your mother. I told the driver that there was another daughter, so he told me where they were taking them. Swedish Hospital." She reached out and squeezed my arm. "Do you want me to drive you there, dear?"

"No, we can manage," I said, nodding at Jedd's car. I didn't want her help. I didn't want her to know the intimate details of my family's inner workings. We'd come this far without anyone knowing about Mom, and I was old enough now to take care of things. "Thank you, Mrs. Stephens," I said, trying to sound gracious like Mom would have in such a situation.

She looked unsure but smiled grimly and walked away, turning once to say, "If I can do anything at all, Tallie," and I nodded, waved.

We drove to the hospital in silence, except for when Jedd said,

"Whoa, this is pretty intense." I gave him a look that made him stay quiet the rest of the way.

I'd been to this hospital before and knew my way around the emergency room and the system. I walked quickly through the maze of people sitting in the waiting room, trying not to look at bloodied heads or twisted appendages. "My mother and sister are here somewhere," I told the woman at the check-in desk. "Lee and Jane Beck."

"And you are?" She flipped through her logbook.

"Tallie Beck. It's my mother and sister," I repeated. I knew I had to be firm with these people or they'd push me all over the place. "I want to see them."

"We're going to need insurance information. Your mother wasn't exactly—"

"I want to see them now," I said, even more firmly.

She sighed, closed the book. "Down the hall, third curtain on the right. But we'll need someone to fill out these forms tonight." She said "tonight" like an ultimatum, like I'd care about her stupid forms.

Jedd followed me down the hall. I could tell the place gave him the creeps, but I knew better than to even suggest he stay in the waiting room. He seemed determined to do this with me.

I pulled the third curtain aside, peeked in, and saw Mom lying high in a bed looking pale and wrung out. Jane sat beside her on a red plastic chair, tapping her feet. She looked glad to see me. Mom did not. I held the curtain tight against the side of my face so Jedd couldn't see in.

"Where the hell were you?" Mom said in a voice that started as a moan and ended in a caterwaul. "Janie and I waited and waited, and I cooked all day, and you were off with your new boyfriend, weren't you? You ungrateful bitch!" She struggled into a half-sitting position, which appeared to pain her, because she gasped and moaned, but she didn't lie back down. Her face had gone from white to red, and her gown slid down one shoulder to reveal the top half of her left breast. Spit formed in the corners of her mouth as she spoke and mascara stained her cheeks. Her arms were mottled with bruises, her fingertips bloodied.

"Mom, we weren't that late," I tried to explain, and Jedd nudged in beside me, nodding like maybe he could convince her.

"You whore! Were you fucking like mad dogs, you and this ugly kid? Didn't I teach you to have better taste, Tallulah Jean? Where the hell did you find this piece of shit? In the toilet?" She seemed spent then, because she moaned again and fell back against the pillows. I couldn't even look at Jedd, but I could hear how his breathing had gone fast and shallow.

Jane stood and pulled Mom's gown back up on her shoulder. "I told her it was only five o'clock," she said, shrugging. Jane was dressed in her good plaid jumper for Thanksgiving, and she still had the slight body of a child, even though she was officially a teenager.

"Come on, Janie," I said. I had to get her away from Mom. "Jedd and I will take you home." One glance at him confirmed this. He was more than ready to blow this place.

Jane looked uncertain, and Mom roared into action once again. "No, you don't, you fucking bastards! You're not taking my only daughter away from me!" she screeched, reaching for Jane as if she were a lifeline, a valued perfect treasure.

A door closed inside me then, with a final sense of relief. She'd said it: She was not my mother anymore.

A nurse and two orderlies rushed in, shooing Jane away from the bed and holding my mother down while they injected her with something that quickly stilled her thrashing. "Motherfuckers. Get the hell away from me," she moaned, then passed out.

I had a fake ID for playing in bars that said I was twenty-one. The hospital staff let Jedd and me take Jane home. In the past, they'd threatened us with foster homes when Mom was hospitalized, but somehow Mom would pull her shit together enough to save the day, convince them she was fine. She was in a psychiatrist's care; why didn't they call him? And they needn't worry about her daughters, she'd say in velvety tones. They would be just fine as soon as she was allowed to leave and take them home with her. She would never take her medication incorrectly again, she'd promise. Send the social workers by the house to see, she'd say. We have nothing to hide.

That night, I knew I, at least, would never have to witness it again. And while it bugged me that Jane would, I knew she'd be fine. Mom depended on her, so she'd surely never hurt her. And as much as Janie had been through, she loved our mother with the devotion of a saint.

Like I always said, she was the good one.

29

♪ I haven't slept well since all the talk of Thanksgiving. I can't get excited about playing or even about seeing Perry at the moment. He asks if I'm okay and I say, "Sure," but we both know I'm lying. I feel like a cardboard cutout, like I'm going through the motions. I watch myself from afar—see Tallie chain-smoke through the day, see Tallie get ready for work, see Tallie sing—and the only thing that takes the edge off is a couple of stiff drinks, but even then I don't sleep. I hold my pillow against my stomach, watching the door.

Near daylight, I drift into sketchy dreams. This morning Sal is singing in my dream, a slow shuffling blues I've never heard before: *"Don't you let nobody tell you that it ain't so. I'm here to tell you, child, that you're the one who'd know. So don't you let nobody try to tell you what you don't know."* The music stops suddenly, jarring me awake. I feel like I was never asleep.

I get up and brew a strong pot of coffee, then stand near the window with the phone in my hands. It's only six o'clock and still dark out, but Jane will be up, getting Emma ready for school. I punch in her phone number. When she answers, her voice is cheerfully curious at who could be calling this early. Emma is singing some little ditty in the background.

"It's me," I say.

"Are you okay?"

After pondering the question too long, I say, "Can we get together sometime and talk?"

"Sure, Tallie, of course," she says in a tone she uses when Emma stubs her toe or has a fight with a friend. "Why don't you come down here today? It's my day off."

I remember her sounding this way with me before, when I first arrived at her house and obliterated my hair with bleach, when I was screaming as it fell off in my hands. She took care of me then, only it didn't occur to me at the time how nice she was about the whole thing.

I hang up feeling better. Jane's seen the shit I've seen, she knows what I know about Mom. She gets it. I thought we'd lost the you-and-me-against-the-world thing we had as kids, but I realize now that we've had it all along, the glances and nods, mutual sighs and nervous laughs. My sister may act disapproving of me, and she has reasons by the bucketful to resent me, but when I've really needed her, she's been there. In light of my disappearing act seventeen years ago, this hits me with fresh guilt, or maybe old guilt recycled as something new and surprising.

It's still dark outside, but a rosy glow seeps through the windows. I can almost feel the rays of the sun tracing up my back, over my head, making me a promise. It's almost daylight.

"I barely remember Mom's bad days anymore," Jane says as she flips a grilled cheese in the skillet. "That first year, right after Emma was born, when she was still getting used to the medication . . . well, she was up and down. You know. Mostly better, but she had her lapses." She looks at me and shrugs, then says, "But she hasn't had any in years."

I came here to tell her the truth. I came here to tell her what's really going on with Mom, how Audra just takes care of the problem, and since Jane's all the way down here in suburbia-land, she's never the wiser. That it's not my fault, or hers. It never was. I look her in the eyes, searching for a way to say it, and she smiles.

"What? You don't believe me?"

"And she's been fine every Thanksgiving?"

"Yes, and every Christmas, every Easter."

"Mother's Day?"

"Believe it or not, yes." She lifts a sandwich from the pan to look at it, then puts it back, turns to me. "It must be hard to get used to, the fact that she's healthy now. But you can relax, Tallie, really. I know I was pretty hard on you at first, but, actually, I think it's been good for Mom, having you there."

"You really thought I was going to send her over the edge, huh?" I try to make it sound light.

She smiles, shrugs, then says, "Let's eat." She sets a plate on the table in front of me, gooey orange cheese dripping down the sides of toasted bread, and pulls condiments from the fridge. "You still like ketchup and mayo on your grilled cheese, don't you?"

I nod, breathe in, out. I have to let it go. Jane will never see things any differently, no matter what I tell her. It seems Audra's always able to corral Mom back into sanity without Jane's knowing, so why should I mess up the system? Jane likes me now, and I don't half mind it.

She reaches into a high cabinet for glasses, lifting her new sage-colored sweater and revealing a Calvin Klein label on crisp new jeans. She turns back around, looking happy, flushed, and I notice the green of the sweater influences little green flecks in her brown eyes. "You've lost weight," I say as she settles in across the table.

"You think?" She crosses her arms over her middle self-consciously. "I know I'll never be as thin as you—"

"No, you look great. Really."

She smiles, wrinkles her nose like Emma. I was always the pretty one, she the smart one, but lately it seems like we might be swapping places.

As we eat sandwiches and drink Cokes, Jane tells me about her new single life. The good parts: buying Frosted Flakes (Andrew always insisted on healthy cereal) and reading in bed until one in the morning. The bad parts: Emma's late-night crying jags and Andrew's lost look whenever she drops off Emma at his apartment.

"Have I destroyed everybody else's life just to make myself happy?" she asks, eyes filling. My throat closes against any answer I might make. She shakes her head—like Who the hell am I asking anyway?—then stands to clear the table.

I nurse my pop, swirl ice cubes.

"Hey," I say, finally, and she turns from the counter.

"What was it like?" I ask, heart pounding. "After I . . . you know, split."

She looks at me for a long moment, plate dangling from one hand over the sink. "It was pretty much the same as when you were there, except I only had one person to take care of." She turns back to the dishes.

I let another beat go by, two, three. "So I take it you're still mad at me." I tap double paradiddles the drummer taught me on the table.

This time she doesn't turn, but her head drops forward, her arms go slack. "Let's not go there, okay, Tallie? Not today." She sighs, then turns on the faucet.

"That means you are."

She makes an exasperated sound. "You've never exactly apologized or anything." She picks up the next plate, rinses and places it between racks in the dishwasher. "You've never even asked about it before."

"I know," I say, craving a cigarette mightily. "But I am now."

She sighs, reaches down to dry her hands on a dish towel, then comes back to sit across from me at the table.

Jane remembers my leaving better than I do. She remembers that it was late afternoon, not morning the way I always picture it. I thought I sneaked out first thing while Mom was sleeping, but she shakes her head. "Mom *was* sleeping—it was one of her bad days—but I was watching *Gilligan's Island* after school," she says. "That means it was four or four thirty."

We both remember Jedd's car, its jackhammer idling in the street. But while I don't remember saying anything, just hoisting my duffel bag to my shoulder and slipping out the door, Jane says

I told her that everything would be okay and I'd be back for her when I made some money.

"No," I say now, a metallic taste working its way up from my throat. "I didn't say that, did I?"

She shrugs and looks away.

"I swear I don't remember that." I scan back through years of alternating haze and clarity, but come up with nothing. Why are some moments so vivid, like TV reruns, and others just gone? "Anyway, I never did make any money," I say, laughing a little. "God. Holy shit." I rest my forehead in my palm, stare at my elbow, pale and thin against the wood grain of the table. "I do remember your face in the window. You looked so . . . I don't know." I don't say "terrified." I look up at her. "I waved, but you didn't wave back."

She shakes her head. "I wasn't at the window. I never moved from the couch, just watched the rest of *Gilligan's Island*, like nothing had happened. Then, when Mom got up, I told her you'd left and all hell broke loose."

Of course it did, but I've never let myself imagine it. Once I was free I put everything about my family and my past out of my mind. "So, she took pills?"

"She actually took enough to kill herself, for once." Jane expels a dry hard laugh, runs her index finger around a knot on the table. "I called the paramedics, made sure the door was unlocked, and hid when they came, so they wouldn't put me in a foster home. Everyone assumed we'd both left, because Mom kept wailing about her babies leaving her. They kept her over a week that time." She looks up at me. "It was the only time I've ever been by myself. I loved it."

"You weren't scared?" A thirteen-year-old kid on her own like that.

"Not any more scared than I'd ever been before," she says. "When she came home she was still a mess, but she never let herself get that far down again. She didn't want to lose me, too, she kept saying, so she was more motivated. It was pretty much the same old same old, though. You know." She shrugs. "Good days, bad days. Occasional horrible days."

"How about when you went away to college?"

"Well, sure, that was a bad time. I was the only girl in the dorm getting late-night calls from her mother instead of boys. She'd do that hysterical 'I think I'm dying' thing, remember?"

How could I forget.

"She was better the second semester," she continues, "and then, when Emma came—"

"Yeah," I say sharply. "She finally got her shit together."

"Better late than never is the way I always look at it." She eyes me curiously.

"I guess." I work a smile onto my face. "Hey, I really need a cig. Mind if I step out back?"

She stares at me for a moment, then asks, "Got an extra?"

Sing Out! is breaking all records for attendance, receipts, and general popularity around town. I don't believe I'm the reason we're doing so well, as Audra told the reporter, at least not the only reason, but I do feel a part of things here. Playing on the road all those years was exciting, but we were always leaving just as we got to know people, the waitstaff and bartenders, the patrons. When we'd get back to town a few months later, there'd be new people, or the ones who'd been there before acted indifferent, like they barely knew us. Anything more than casual friendship was impossible.

Tonight I arrive at the club early to watch Eileen and Bob, finding a place at the bar where a quiet new bartender is stationed. I still can't bring myself to hang out too close to Jason. He's standing at the wash sinks, running glasses under water, wearing long loose shorts, even though it's mid-November. He's just a kid, really. Why didn't I see that before? I order a triple vodka rocks, putting a finger to my lips when the bartender raises his eyebrows. "It's just water, right?" I say, winking at him.

On stage, Eileen sings her spotlight song, a torchy version of "My Funny Valentine," Bob laying down simple accompaniment in the shadows. The audience is quiet, swaying as she croons, and at the climax when she reaches for an almost impossibly high note, chills run up my legs. The audience is on their feet, whistling, clapping, hollering.

"She's pretty good," a male voice says in my ear, and I can feel the slither and snakelike charm of Jedd Maxfield in the seat next to me.

"You bet she is," I say, clapping till my hands hurt.

"Why aren't you up there?"

I let a moment pass before I turn toward him. His hair's grown out to a short mess of curls and he's wearing a nubby cable-knit sweater. He looks good.

"I'm not the opener anymore,"

"Yeah, I read about you in the paper. You're getting to be quite the star around here." He studies me, like a specimen. It's what I've wanted all along, ever since we broke up—his approval—but somehow it doesn't thrill me as much as I would have thought. His eyes flash the way they would have in the old days when he had one of his brilliant ideas.

"Let's go somewhere we can talk," he yells and pulls me to my feet and out of the door, past Audra.

"I'll be back in time for my set," I tell her and she waves me off, swamped by the crowds waiting in the cold to get in.

"It's Tallie," people in line whisper, their breath hanging frosty in the night air. I hope like hell Jedd hears them.

"There's a coffeeshop at the end of the block," I say, extracting my hand from his. He doesn't seem to notice, just strides down the sidewalk in that long-legged familiar lope. I walk quickly to keep up, rubbing my arms against the cold.

"So, what's up?" I say when we've settled at a cozy table in the corner of Beelzebub's.

"Roots rock, baby," he says. "It's happening. We got us a tight little rhythm section, a guy who plays accordion. We're working up some great bluesy-country-zydeco-type numbers. We got Lyle behind us. He's booked a tour on the eastern seaboard, and he's got A and R guys coming to see us at the shows. It's only a matter of time before we get signed." He leans back in the small metal chair, tipping it back on two legs, and runs a hand over his head. "Roots is big, baby, I'm telling you."

"Well, hurray for you, Jedd," I say, looking at my watch. I go on in half an hour. I don't have time to sit here and listen to him brag.

"Tallulah Jean, I don't think you understand what I'm saying." He leans forward, the chair hitting the floor with a scrape, and stretches across the table, almost touching me. I can smell the woodsy, earthen scent of him. "We need you to sing," he says. "It's your time to shine, girl."

30

♪ I'm explaining it to Perry, taking his hand as we sit at
Beelzebub's, at the same table that Jedd and I shared the
night before. Perry's retro, Salvation Army style appears to be giving way to the suburban yupster school of dress. Today he's wearing khaki slacks and a light blue shirt with a button-down collar.
Unlike most of his other clothes, these actually fit and they look
new. His hair has been recently cut, and he's so freshly shaven his
face looks naked. I think of Jedd—the funky hair, the wiseass smile,
the incredible way we used to fuck for hours—then shake it off.

"This could be a great opportunity for me," I tell Perry, who
nods a little too hard. "But it's not like I've decided to go or anything. Life's gotten, I don't know, complicated."

His hand slides out from under mine. "I don't want to be a complication."

"That's not what I meant. God." I stop, try to think. "Okay,
maybe you are a complication, but you're not the only one. I have a
shitload of reasons not to go."

"But . . ."

"But it's almost too good to be true. We'd be on the road only a
couple months at a time, and I'd have weeks with you before we
went out again. Except if we got a recording contract, of course."

"Of course," he says, expressionless.

"And we already have a warm-up gig with John Hiatt in Philly."

"We," he says.

"Come on, Perry." I try not to sound irritated.

"What about his girlfriend?"

I asked Jedd the same question last night. He shrugged, which is what I do now. "I don't know the details of Jedd's personal life," I say. "This is business."

"*Business,*" he says, raising his eyebrows. He's heard enough of my stories about Jedd by now to have formed his own opinions. I know Jedd is vermin when it comes to issues of trust, but somehow it pisses me off, this new side of Perry that is judgmental and stodgy.

"I haven't said I'm going, for crying out loud." It feels odd to speak so harshly to him, but exhilarating at the same time. I feel righteous, entitled.

"You haven't said you aren't." Perry looks at me with dull eyes, then says, "I need to get back to work." He stands and looks at me for a moment. When I don't respond, just sit there with my arms crossed, he pushes through the glass door and walks past the windows. He doesn't look at me again.

Although Perry doesn't believe it, I really don't know if I'm going or not. There are warning signs, just as I'd suspect with anything to do with Jedd. When I asked him if he'd like to hear the song I'm writing, he waffled.

"Well, the material's not a problem," he said. "We've got plenty of songs."

And the band's going to be called, what else, the Jedd Maxfield Band. "Maybe with a tag line," he said. "You know, 'featuring Tallie Beck' or something." Jedd's maybes don't convince me like they used to. But he does have clout in the industry, contacts, a following from the old days. It could turn into something big.

"Something big for him," Sal's voice says. She hasn't been appearing lately. She just talks to me, a voice coming from some shimmery but unseeable presence. "You've got your own path to follow, girl. Let that snake slither on down his."

Yeah, yeah. But where's my path going? I'm a singer in a piano bar, and even though I'm a damned good one, where could it possibly lead?

"Well, if you would just stick to it, you might find out," the Big Gal says. Her honeysuckle scent is faint, but I could swear I feel her brush by me as she makes one of her illustrious exits.

"All right, already," I say. "Your opinion is duly registered."

"Who are you talking to?" Damian asks as he carries a tray past my table.

"Nobody," I say. "Just myself."

I wasn't going to tell Mom or Jane, not just yet, but Audra told Mom about Jedd coming to the bar.

"Please," Mom says, standing in the bathroom doorway as I get ready for work, "tell me you're not seeing that boy again." She's called him "that boy" since the night at the hospital seventeen years ago. Considering her condition at the time, it's surprising she'd remember Jedd at all, but for the few months I was home before I hit the road with him, that's what she'd say—"that boy"—as if he were the poison in my life, not her.

"Of course I'm not seeing him."

"Does he want something from you, now that you're doing so well?" She sounds suspicious, protective.

"Yeah, actually. He wants me to sing with his new band, which has tours lined up, a possible recording contract, you name it. They're probably going big-time. Much bigger than a crappy piano bar in Denver." I sound more vehement about this whole stupid thing than I feel, but I keep ranting. "What's so wrong with me having success anyway? I've worked my ass off all my life. I deserve a break."

"I stuck my neck out, asking Audra to hire you," she says, pissy now. She retreats to her bedroom, saying, "I sincerely hope you're not thinking of deserting her—"

If I hadn't slammed the bathroom door, I'm almost certain there would have been a "too" at the end of that sentence.

It's the last family dinner before Thanksgiving. I called Perry to ask if he'd come, but he said he was busy. I haven't seen him since our discussion at Beelzebub's. When I asked if he was breaking up with me, embarrassed by the adolescent ring to it, he sounded flat, repeating that he was just busy. I might have screamed at him in the old days to get a reaction out of him, but instead I said okay and hung up, then bawled like a five-year-old.

So tonight it's just the four of us—Mom, Jane, Emma, me. The core of our family. We are intricately connected by blood and time and something else more complicated, but much less tangible. I don't know if I'd call it love. It's stickier, messier, more exasperating than I've always thought love should be.

Mom's still mad at me, but she's acting like she's not. "Wine, dear?" she says.

"Absolutely." I shove my glass toward her, and she fills it nearly to the rim.

"So Mom says you might be leaving us again." Jane ladles black bean soup into white earthenware bowls, but I catch the quick glance at my wineglass.

Emma, who is chowing down heartily on fresh baked bread, stops in midchew. "What?" she says, turning to me with a full mouth and wide eyes.

"Jesus, Mom." I give her a look but she pretends not to notice. "Wine?" she asks Jane.

I hit the table with my palm harder than I mean to. "Okay, in the first place, I've been offered a job in Jedd's band but I haven't accepted it. B, if I took it, I wouldn't be gone permanently, just for a few months at a time. And three, I'm a singer, for God's sake. This is what I do! Why are you all acting like it's such a fucking crime?"

They all look at me, stunned. Mom holds the wine bottle aloft. Jane lets the ladle drip black liquid on the tabletop. Emma still hasn't swallowed.

"Bud ah you weaving?" she asks.

"Emma, don't talk with your mouth open," Jane says, then shakes her head. "I mean full. Don't talk with your mouth full."

Emma snickers, blowing small blobs of moist bread on the table before she slaps her hand over her mouth. Then I'm laughing, too— I can't help it. It's something Mom mistakenly said to us all the time when we were kids, "Don't talk with your mouth open" or

"Don't chew with your mouth full," and Jane and I would try not to snort. I look at Jane now, and her nostrils twitch before she breaks into laughter. Pretty soon we've all lost it, even Mom. I laugh so hard I feel an uncomfortable urge to cry. I look at my sister, my mother, tears glistening in their eyes as they laugh, and I let go, burying my face in my hands as my shoulders shake with sobbing laughter.

A small hand presses between my shoulder blades. I peek between my fingers to see Emma standing next to my chair, her bread finally swallowed and her face serious. She wraps a skinny arm around my neck and whispers in my ear, "Don't go, Aunt Tallie. We need you here."

Later, Jane and I clear the table while Mom listens to Emma's latest conquest on guitar, some current pop-diva song that is all of three chords played in endless repetition. I smile, remembering the first song I could actually play all the way through: "Helpless" by Neil Young, three chords over and over and over. I remember the rush of playing a complete song for the first time, feeling like a real musician at last.

"She's getting pretty good," I say to Jane, rinsing bowls and handing them to her to stack in the dishwasher.

"Mm." She sounds distant.

"Hey, listen, I'm sorry I blew up and said 'fuck' in front of Emma. I can usually control my mouth around her, but, I don't know. I'm so pissed that everyone's making such a big deal of this Jedd thing."

"It's not a big deal?" Jane closes the dishwasher door with a bang. She turns and looks at me, one hand on the counter, the other on her hip, back to the persnickety old Jane that drives me crazy.

"I knew you were still mad at me," I say. "God, Jane. When the hell are you going to get over it?"

"How do you expect me to get over it when you're about to do the exact same thing?" she says. "You have no respect for other people's feelings. You don't even realize that what you do affects us."

She chokes on "us," like she didn't really mean to say it, and the hurt look on her face reminds me of the face at the window all those years ago. I know it was there.

"Janie, I'm sorry I dumped you with Mom, I'm sorry I never—"

"Forget about me," she says, eyes tearing. "Forget about back then. That was a horrible thing to do, but I'm talking about now. Emma. You come here, get her to fall in love with you, and now you're just going to waltz off at the first opportunity."

"I didn't say I was going anywhere, did I?"

"Well, then, go tell her right now that you're not. Go tell my daughter you're not running out on her."

"But, what if . . ." I know I shouldn't say it, but there are so many ifs here, goddamn it. Why can't anyone see that?

"Jesus, Tallie." Jane spits the words like she's eaten something rancid. "You haven't changed at all."

We're uncomfortably silent for a long moment, and then another. It's as if all those years have never passed and we're right back where we were seventeen years ago. How can you explain survival? How can you abandon the one person who really needs you?

"I'm not going," I say loudly, then I yell, "Does everyone hear me? I'm. Not. Going!"

"Hurray!" calls Emma from the living room. Jane shakes her head and turns away.

"Why on earth are you girls yelling?" Mom says, poking her head in the kitchen door to give us a relieved smile, then retreating. "You make sure you learn your manners from me, Miss Emma, hear?"

The phone rings just before I leave for the bar. It's Jedd.

"Hey, Tal. Rehearsal tomorrow at one. My place. The guys are itching to meet you."

"Yeah?" I say, trying not to grin.

"You are coming, right?"

"Um . . ."

Jane glances at me, but continues her conversation with Mom. I feel like a criminal.

"Well, I'm still working that out," I say, trying to be cryptic.

"Come on, now," Jedd says. "You aren't going to blow this, are you? This is your shot, Tallulah Jean. There may never be another."

Impatience is creeping into his voice, so I blurt, "Count me in."

"Who was that?" Jane says when I hang up.

"Just Perry. He's going to meet me after work." I haven't told them we're on the outs.

I swing on my coat, throw my bag over my shoulder, say, "Catch you guys later." When I hit the street, I let out the breath I've been holding.

31

♪ The next morning Mom and Audra are drinking coffee and reading the Sunday paper on the couch like an old married couple. Apparently, they've decided it's okay to be "themselves" in front of me.

I'm watching a VH1 *Behind the Music* rerun, the classic episode about Leif Garrett. Leif is crying about hurting his buddy in the car crash when the phone rings. I pick up the cordless sitting on the coffee table.

"We should talk," Perry says, sounding more like himself, like he might still give a damn about me.

"Yeah, we should."

Mom looks up and I mouth, "Perry," and she nods, goes back to her paper.

"Let's spend the day together," he says and all I want to do is lie next to him for hours, talking. I want to kiss and make up. I want to get back the feeling, the certainty that we were going to be something wonderful together.

"I . . . God, I can't."

Mom and Audra exchange glances.

"Hold on a sec," I say and take the phone into my bedroom, close the door. "Today's the day I go to Jedd's," I tell him. "I'll be gone all afternoon."

"I'll go with you," he says, and I feel a rush of relief until I pic-

ture it: Perry dressed in his new khakis, looking like an accoun-
tant, me introducing him to Jedd as my boyfriend. Jedd's smirk, his
caustic remarks.

"I think I need to go alone."

"Oh."

"Just because it's a business thing, you know? I'd love to have
you come, but I don't think it would look, you know, professional."
I feel as transparent as I sound. "How about tomorrow?"

"I'm working." Something in his voice tells me he's rethinking
this whole thing, wondering why he called in the first place.

"Then, I'll come by tonight, afterward. It probably won't be until
after eight or so, but I'll be there. We can order a pizza."

Perry softens and agrees. After I hang up, I slip back into the living room and pretend to be absorbed in Leif's tragic life. I can feel
Mom staring at me.

"What?" I turn and ask.

"Is everything all right, dear?"

Audra hides behind her paper.

"Of course it is," I say. "That was Perry. We're going up to the
mountains for the day."

She nods and pretends to smile, but her lips pull too tight and
she turns quickly back to the paper.

I rummage through my old stage clothes hanging at the back of
the closet. I haven't looked at them in months. Everything seems
over the top, out of date. I've become one of those monochromatic,
neutral-wearing artistic types, but what would I wear if I did go
out on the road with Jedd? What should I wear today? What will
the guys be expecting me to look like?

I pull on my normal clothes, black jeans, tight T-shirt, but I take
extra pains with my makeup. I wear less these days, but I still need a
little spackle job to look my best, to camouflage the deepening
grooves, to add definition to my eyes, my cheekbones, lips. And I slip
Emma's fancy bobby pins into my hair. They worked for me once.

"See you later," I say to Mom and Audra, grabbing a sweater,
trying to get out of the house as quickly as I can.

"Tell Perry hello."

"Okey-doke," I say and pull the front door closed.

Winding along Upper Bear Creek Road I remember my first trip up here, how stupidly naive and impressed I was. As I turn onto Jedd's long dirt driveway, the satellite dish looks bigger, the fleet of cars even more outrageous. My car is still the little scrap heap it was then, but I don't care so much anymore.

"My, my," Sal says, "next thing you know you'll be feeding the hungry. Oh, that's right, you *are* feeding the hungry." Her earthy chortle sounds far away. I look in the backseat but it's empty.

"If you have something smartass to say, the least you could do is show up."

"You just pay attention to the situation at hand," she says, voice fading. "Mind you don't do anything stupid, hear? I can't always be bailing you out."

I sit in the car for a moment longer, smoking another cigarette, trying to feel prepared for whatever I'm about to do and all that will come with it. The wildflowers and greenery from summer are gone, but the place still has a stark beauty. Gray rocks jut from the brushy scrabble along the drive and evergreens tower overhead. When I finally open the car door, the air is icy fresh and smells of pine and dirt. It reminds me of being at the hot springs with Perry and my chest twists for a moment, the pain physical and surprising. I take a deep breath and swing my legs out of the car before I can change my mind.

"You're late," Jedd says, walking up from behind the house.

"Shit, you scared me." I fumble for my bag in the backseat. "I'm not that late. What is it . . ." I look at my wrist. I forgot my watch.

"Twenty after. The guys are all here already."

I can't tell how annoyed he is so I mumble, "Sorry," as we walk toward the house. Inside, the absence of Indian artifacts is a testament to the retreat of Little White Deer and an explanation for his mood.

He walks to the kitchen and grabs himself a beer.

"Aren't you going to offer a girl a drink?" I say. When he reaches for another beer I add, "Got anything stronger?"

"Well, well," he says, a smile teasing his lips. "You still like to party, do you? That's good to know." He winks and reaches into a high cabinet. "Vodka, right?"

"Just a smidge, to take the edge off."

"I've got a surprise for you," he says, pouring half a tumbler full.

"What?"

"If I told you, it wouldn't be a surprise, now would it." He takes my hand and leads me to his studio.

As much as I want to look cool, I am absurdly excited at the prospect of playing with a band again, the possibility of finally having a stab at making it. I've got this itch that hasn't been scratched for too long. I can't explain it to people who aren't musicians, or artists, or someone striving to be heard by masses larger than a packed bar. I can't explain it to Perry, whose main ambition in life is simply to help others. A fine ambition, a gallant one, in fact, but so different from anything I can relate to that I feel unworthy in his presence.

We push through the soundproofed studio door, stepping from quiet to blasting live country blues. Four guys hunker down over drums, bass, accordion, and keyboards, forming a loose circle in the middle of the room. Their heads are lowered; they don't notice we've entered. They have the look of studio musicians, not road musicians, with their pressed clothes, cool haircuts, expensive instruments. No stage presence to speak of, even if it is just a rehearsal. We stand and watch them, Jedd nodding vigorously and air-drumming, me just tapping my foot along to the music. They do have a bodacious groove-thang going, I have to admit.

The keyboard player finally looks up, right at me, his face dissolving from concentration into a wide grin. He quits playing and waves his hand at the other guys to stop. "Tallie Beck!" he yells across the room.

And here I thought these guys would be too cool to recognize me. I nod and smile at him, at all the guys.

"Don't you know who that is, Tallulah?" Jedd asks. "I guess he does look different, but then don't we all. It's been a lot of years."

I squint at the guy. He has a familiar smile.

He shakes his head, laughing. "It's me, Tallie. Pat."

I'm still not quite getting it, until he says, "Here we are, together at last. The last three survivors of the Holy Smokes."

It is him. My old buddy Pat, the California computer genius. God, he looks so . . . grown up or something. His once woolly head is close-cropped where not balding, and the face that always sported at least a mustache is clean-shaven. He walks from behind his keyboards and I go over and give him a hug. If I hadn't ever seen him again, I wouldn't have known how much I missed him.

Jedd introduces me to the other guys, then straps on his fire-engine red Strat. "So," he says, "how about we play something?" We all nod and I walk toward the mike stand in the middle of the circle.

"I happen to know Tallulah here belts the shit out of the blues, so why don't we try 'Crossroads.'" Jedd stakes out his territory as leader; he's not suggesting, he's telling, but anything by Robert Johnson is fine with me.

"Key of E work for everybody?" I ask, and they all nod.

Jedd tunes for a few seconds, then counts us in, blasting into the Clapton intro. Cool, I'm thinking. I can do it Clapton-style.

These guys are good, so tight I'd swear they'd been playing together all their lives. The drummer is clean and precise, no sloppy overplaying like a lot of drummers are prone to. He and the bass player are so dialed in they stare at each other as they lay down the rhythm. The accordion player whips out a harmonica, slaps it against his leg, blows a few test blasts, then steps up to the mike and makes it wail. Pat's punched up a Hammond B-3 sample on his synthesizer, the retro organ sound perfect for the song.

I let the intro go around a few times, because Jedd is clearly loving playing the lead riff. His face has that misty faraway look he only gets when playing guitar or having sex, as I recall. He catches me looking at him and a slow, sultry, almost indecent smile spreads across his face. That smile means only one thing, and I haven't seen it since before we broke up. All of a sudden I realize why I'm here. He assumes he's getting me back and in more than just the musical sense. Half of me is repulsed, but the other half gets a little worked up thinking about it.

I move to the mike, press my lips against the cold metal screen, close my eyes, and let her rip. The words leap up from my gut like a fireball, exploding from my lips in flames and sparks, heating the microphone to burning. I open my eyes, and Pat and the guys are looking at me, their faces a mix of surprise and approval. "Yeah!" Pat yells and rocks back and forth like Stevie Wonder. We go round and round, playing the song for a good ten minutes before we finally bring her to a close with a whimper of surrender.

"Whoa, baby," says the accordion player.

"Shit, girl," the bassist says, shaking his head, "you got some pipes."

Pat nods. "There's more balls in your voice than there was way back when, Tallie, if that's possible."

"What have I been telling you guys?" Jedd asks. "She rocks."

After a few more tunes, Jedd breaks a string like he always used to, he plays so hard, and we take five so he can fix it.

The guys all start talking to one another, about nothing and nobody I know. My glass is empty, but everyone else is still nursing beer. I know Jedd's new studio etiquette—no smoking—so I ask Pat if I can noodle around on his keyboard.

"Sure," he says, moving back to sit on his amp. I play the chord progression from my new song. "That's nice," he says, and I'd like to hug him, but we just start chatting about this and that. Pretty soon, we're rattling on about old times.

"Remember those drunken creeps crawling up your legs at that funky place in Nebraska?" he asks, grinning. "What was it called . . ."

"The Skunk Hole."

"The Skunk Hole, yeah. We had to form a human shield around you."

"You always protected me," I say, feeling a lump in my throat. He did, didn't he. I'd forgotten.

"And how about the time that soundman, Eric—"

"Earache, we called him," I interrupt, laughing.

"Yeah, Earache. He had that phenomenally loud feedback loop going at that frat party, and kids' ears were practically bleeding, and—"

"And we were standing in three inches of beer, waiting to be electrocuted—"

"And it was just about the most fun a body could ever have." Pat looks wistful. "Sometimes I really miss those days."

"Yeah. Me, too."

"But, hey, we get to play together again," he says, perking up. "I paid the devil my due in the business world, made my killing, and here I am. Back in the music biz, thanks to the old Jeddster."

Jedd has his back to us, winding an E string onto his guitar, but turns to give Pat a thumbs-up. "No problemo, bro. At least you had a life. I had to rescue Tallulah here from a freaking piano bar." He snorts a mean laugh, turns back around.

My heart stops dead for a beat, then two, until I draw a deep breath like I've been drowning. Pat looks at me, concern in his eyes, and his kindness reminds me of Perry. I turn away, study some sheet music lying on the floor, blinking hard. For God's sake, I pray, don't cry. It takes all my concentration not to let my nose run—I sniff snot into cavities I never knew I had. I'm relieved when Jedd's ready to play again. He twangs his strings a few more times to make sure he's in tune, then maps out a G on the fretboard. To the untrained eye, it looks like he's flipping the bird.

"How about one of those new ones we've been working up?" he asks the guys, and they all nod. "Let's do 'Long Time Ago.' Tallulah, give a listen and see if you can come up with any background harmonies."

They break into a song that sounds just like fifty billion other songs on the radio, with lyrics about some girl who I can tell from the first verse isn't me. Roots rock, my ass. I wander to the outside of the circle, pick my glass up, and hold it against my chest, then return to the kitchen for a refill. I think of all the things I could have said to Jedd, if only I was a little quicker, if I hadn't destroyed so many brain cells along the way.

When I get back, I take a seat against the wall. Pat looks over at me and I wink and smile. After he's turned away, I take a long pull of searing vodka, then wipe my mouth on the back of my hand. "I'm okay," I say aloud, the sound of it obliterated by the din of Jedd's wailing about someone he loved a long time ago.

The guys have all left and I'd leave, too, but I truly doubt my ability to drive. The vodka bottle is mostly empty and I'm sitting in Jedd's living room toking on a fat joint he twisted up. "Let's celebrate our little reunion, Tallulah Jean," he says, sliding in next to me on his fancy leather couch. "It's been too damn long since we made music together."

I look at him, a trick since the world has shifted forty-five degrees out of kilter and he keeps floating off to my left. "That's not a double . . . shit." I giggle. "I forget the word. That's not a double-meaning thing you're saying, is it? Making music? Because you can forget that shit, buster."

I laugh and lean back, feeling good, the dark moments of the day reduced to pinpricks in the back of my brain. It's been surprisingly easy to wash them there with Jedd's expensive vodka. I take a slug and *whoosh*, out goes Jedd's nasty comment. I take another, and the whispers between the guys at the end of the session evaporate. The exasperated looks cast my way fade, along with the sound of the harmonica player saying a little too loudly as he walked out the door, "No way I'm going out on the road with a drunk."

I focus on the good stuff: When I sang that first song, the guys freaked. They gazed upon me like they'd found hidden treasure. And my good old buddy Pat—how could I have forgotten about him? About those times, when we were all so young and naive and happy?

"I've missed you, baby," Jedd whispers in my ear, the fog of his breath warm. I don't pull away.

"Why do you always have to be such an asshole?" I say. "Why can't you just be nice to me?"

"Come on, Tallulah, you know how I feel about you," he says, reaching up to turn my face toward his. "You know what you mean to me." His eyes loom close to mine, too close, and I think of Perry for a moment, then he fades like everything else.

I try to bring Jedd's face into focus. "What about the band? Am I in or what?"

"Now, Tallulah, you know I can't make that decision by myself."

"Bullshit. It's your band."

"Shh, come on now, darlin'," he says. "It's late. Time to quit talking business." His long fingers stroke my cheek, my neck, my shoulder, and he looks at me the way he always used to. Before I know it I'm leaning into him, putting my mouth on his, sucking his lower lip, caressing his tongue with mine.

It's not that I think I won't regret this. I just decide not to care. I want his hands, his mouth, his excitement for me, again, now, after all these years. I need someone to want me that badly again.

A bloodred glow burns through my eyelids, waking me gradually from a thick mottled sleep. "Turn out the light," I groan, rolling over to hide from it, but it won't leave me alone. "Fuck," I sigh and open my eyes.

I don't know where I am. Worse, I'm *naked* and I don't know where I am.

"Fuck," I say again, sitting up, still drunk, and look around the room. A bright veil of weirdly ethereal light shines from the window. I'm in a bedroom, a huge bedroom with tall ceilings and hulking masculine furniture. Jedd's. That explains the snoring lump to my right. We're in a bed made of what looks like logs, with some god-awful furry thing over us. I throw it off, then climb from the bed.

Holding a pillow against myself, I lurch toward the window like I've just ridden a Tilt-A-Whirl, glad I'm not walking a line for a cop. I'm expecting a huge streetlight outside, a helicopter with a searchlight, but there's nothing like that, not even a full moon. There's only the silvery light, shining down and in, bathing me in pure white. I drop the pillow and look down at my pale nakedness— the white clay mounds of my breasts, the slight slope of my stomach, the dark shadow between my thighs. There is a rough ache between my legs from having fucked too hard, too long, too drunkenly. Without knowing I'm going to, I raise a hand and slap my thigh, hard, and watch red rise to the surface. I slap my stomach, bang a fist on my chest, grab my face, feeling it twist with muted sobbing.

The light blinks out and sensation sweeps over me, a smooth loving hand. A faint scent of honeysuckle. I stare into the blank darkness, breathing heavy and gaining my bearings. I have to get out of here. As my eyes adjust, I peer into the shadows, looking for clothes. A dark lump at the foot of the bed catches my eye and I stumble toward it. There, my jeans and underwear lie twisted together, apparently removed in one impatient swoop. I try to disentangle them, lose my balance, and fall heavily against the bed. Jedd grunts and rolls over, but doesn't wake.

I lean my back against the bed frame and bend my knees, slide to a sitting position on the floor. Swallowing back an ugly queasiness, I lie on the floor and pull on my pants, wad the underwear and stuff it in a pocket, then roll over and crawl across the floor to another lump that looks like clothing. In a jumble of Jedd's clothes I find my T-shirt, my sweater, and from this position I can see my shoes under a chair nearby.

I dress while lying down, breathing deeply when the nausea overpowers me. Then I struggle to my feet, steady myself on the chair, and fight to focus my eyes on just one thing. Through a door is a glint of porcelain, a bathroom. Carefully, I step across the floor toward it and, once inside, ease the door closed. I don't turn on the light, just feel my way across cabinets, counter, sink to the toilet, lift the lid, position myself. Then I am throwing up, wave after wave, bile searing my throat, my mouth, even my nose. If nothing else, I'm glad for the dark so I don't have to bear witness to the certain male filth of Jedd's commode.

When it's over I lie on the cool tile floor, listening for any sound from him, but there's only the rhythm of comatose snoring. The spins have subsided and I'm guessing I won't have to puke again for a while, so I get up and turn on the faucet as hot as it will go to scrub my hands, my face, fiercely. The water scalds my skin but I keep scouring. I grope around until I fumble upon a towel, then wet it with hot water and rub my arms, lift my shirt and scrub my breasts. What the hell, I think, and pull down my pants. I wash every trace of Jedd from me and leave the wet musky lump of towel in the sink for him to find in the morning. Then I spit on it, his last evidence of me.

I pull up in front of Perry's apartment block, relieved to have survived the dizzy drive down the mountain without heaving or wrecking the car, then cut the engine and light a Salem. The sky is turning grayish-purple. It must be nearly dawn. I take a deep drag off the cigarette and try to shake off the last vestiges of vodka. The smoke nauseates me, though, and I have to lean back against the seat, grip the armrest to steady myself.

I did this, I realize. I did all of this to myself. I made myself physically ill. I lost control and fucked the wrong man. I blew what was probably my last chance at making it big. And I probably made Perry hate me forever.

"So, Sal," I say, "I don't suppose there's any chance you're going to help me through this one, is there?" Not that I expect an answer. She warned me.

I've only been here a few times since Perry moved in a month ago. He's embarrassed by it, but it's not that bad. The buildings are newer, neat rows of brick two-stories, and a twiggy sapling stands like a stick figure in front of his window. I remember telling him how pretty it would be to look at in the spring, imagining the two of us doing just that. I could see the pink and white blossoms and the tender young leaves, I could feel Perry's hand at the curve of my hip.

The cigarette has burned out between my fingers. I sit up straight, test the conditions. Then, feeling fairly sober, I get out, flick the butt into the street, and walk up to Perry's door. I'd like to think I'm accompanied by Sal and her supernatural forces of good, truth, and honesty, but it's just me here, and I have no idea what to do.

I rap lightly on the door, listening for any sound of him, but my heart is beating too insistently to hear footsteps. I knock louder, wondering if maybe I shouldn't just be sneaking back to the car, escaping into the daybreak before he even knows I was here. My head whirls again and I shift my gaze to the street. The shit trap sits at the curb like a rusted chariot. Salvation. Then Perry's door creaks open.

Perry stands shirtless in old-man pajama bottoms, hair tufted like an '80s punk rocker. His eyes are swollen.

"I've been trying to find you all night," he says, tired, annoyed. He makes no move to let me in.

"God, Perry, I'm so—"

"Are you all right?"

"Yeah, yeah, I'm—"

"Where were you? Did you ever even leave Jedd's?"

His tone has sharpened, his mouth has tightened, and I don't know how to make this better. My stomach sinks, then roils, and I begin to cry. I clutch my arms over my middle, trying to hold on to something that is evaporating. "Please, don't," I say, and then, suddenly, I am puking on his front step, the smell of bile and vodka and whatever the hell I ate in the last day or so rotted and festering like poison between us.

"Oh, God," he says, backing up. "You're drunk."

"I'm sorry," I wail, trying to wipe at the mess on my face with my sleeve. "I fucked up, I know I did, but I'm sorry, Perry. Please."

He shakes his head and closes the door.

PART FOUR

They say the truth hurts, but they don't know:
The truth, it frees your very soul.

—"Turn It Around," Big Gal Sal

32

♪ "Honey?" Mom says as soon as I walk through the door. She looks like she hasn't slept either. "I was just about to call the state patrol. We've been worried sick. Perry called looking for you last night. He was beside himself. Are you all right?"

I nod, taking off my sweater. "I'm fine," I say.

Mom starts toward me. "But where were you all night, Tallie? You weren't with Perry."

"I was up at Jedd's, checking out the band." I rub at the ache forming behind my eyeballs. "Don't worry. They don't want me."

"At this point I don't give a damn," she says, one eyebrow shooting up, arms crossing in front of her. "You had us worried half to death all night, and now you drag yourself in here looking like . . . this. And what on earth is that smell?" Her face wrinkles and she makes one of her exasperated sounds. "Jesus, Tallie, that boy always did make you do stupid things."

I feel drained, empty. I look at my mother and she looks back at me, really looks at me for once before she turns away. I call in sick to work and spend the rest of the day in a hungover haze.

Tuesday night after work I half expect to see Perry leaning against the lamppost outside, but of course he isn't. He hasn't called either, not that I expect him to.

At home I walk into the kitchen for a glass of water. Grocery bags line the counters. Lots of them. I look inside: potatoes, sweet potatoes, onions, large cans of pumpkin filling, bags of stuffing. Flour, sugar, nuts. Enough to feed an army. Thanksgiving. I'd almost forgotten.

Once in bed, I toss and turn for more than an hour until it hits me: It's too much food. Just like in the old days, Mom bought too much goddamned food.

My chest thunks and I can't breathe. I feel as though I am shrinking into myself, the sensation so frightening that sweat soaks the T-shirt I put on for bed. This must be what it feels like, I think, growing more panicked by the moment. This must be what my mother feels when she's losing it, spiraling inward, going deeper into the dark, and deeper still. I quickly get up and turn on the light. I look into the mirror, not quite knowing what to expect, but it's just me staring back, a little wide-eyed and tired-looking. Fuck, I think, fuck, fuck. I'm losing my mind.

I pull on jeans and a sweater, slip my feet into shoes, and grab my bag, then creep into the hallway, through the living room and out the door. I head to the bar, slip the key in the lock, open the door. I've slept here before. It will feel a damned sight safer than sleeping under the same roof as my mother.

Years ago, Bonnie Raitt sang that love has no pride, and when it comes right down to it, neither do I. I'm a mess without Perry. I have to call him. I sneak back home before the sun rises and stay in my room until I hear my mother get up, dress, and leave.

Settled on the couch with coffee, I dial the shelter, heart pounding.

Someone else answers the phone, which is unusual. Perry almost always answers. A gruff male voice tells me Perry isn't at work today. In fact, he says, sounding irritated, Perry hasn't been in all week.

I hang up and dial Perry's house, but there's no answer. He has no machine—he could barely afford the phone—so I quickly get dressed, my hands fumbling on zippers and buttons. Something's wrong, I can feel it. Perry's in trouble.

And I thought I could only do that to my mother.

*   *   *

I drive slowly by his house a few times, looking for clues in the blank windows. Nothing. I park in front and walk up to the door, ring the bell. I hear it echo inside against mostly empty walls, but there's no answer. Perry's either in there ignoring me or he's gone.

I crunch over dead grass to the living room window and cup my hands against the dusty glass, but I see only his secondhand sofa and the crates he uses for end tables, all neat and tidy. I walk around to the side to peer in his bedroom window, but it's too high. First I try jumping, then I look around for something to stand on. Nothing. I resort to throwing pebbles at the window, hoping if Perry's in there, he'll be curious enough to look out.

If Perry's in there. Images come to me like some sick slide show—Perry comatose on the bed. Bleeding from the wrists maybe? Knocked out by too many pills? No, they say only women do that. Men resort to more violent methods. I can't imagine Perry doing any of this, in actual fact, but I'm so used to imagining the worst.

There's nothing more I can do, except scribble a note to tuck inside his door:

> I can't find you and I'm worried. You don't have
> to call me, but would you let my mother know
> you're okay?

I fold the paper twice and slide it between the door and the frame, then walk slowly to my car. There I turn and stare back at his place, wondering where the hell he could be.

It's an excruciatingly slow night at the bar. Everyone's home cooking, getting ready for the big festivities tomorrow. Mom's been in the kitchen all day long, peeling potatoes, baking pies. Not one pie, or two, enough for a normal family. Four pies—she made four freaking pies. As she was transferring them from the oven to the counter, I couldn't stand it any longer.

"Why did you make four?" I asked, hearing the alarm in my voice. "That's practically a pie a person."

"You know I like to have two pumpkin, an apple, and a mince-meat," she said in a matter-of-fact way that let me know she was still pissed off. "I've always made four pies." She wiped her hands on an old apron tied around her waist, one she had to have worn in the '70s.

"Exactly," I said.

She looked at me and sighed. "What does that mean? 'Exactly'?"

"It seems like too much food, too much trouble."

"For God's sake, Tallie," she said, "it's Thanksgiving. What did you expect? TV dinners?"

"I hate Thanksgiving," I said and left for work.

Now Domingo and I are trying to get a rise out of this measly crowd. Audra isn't here tonight. She's apparently responsible for some fancy kind of bread tomorrow. I imagine her and my mother, in their side-by-side apartments, cooking and baking like homo Betty Crockers. I can't believe Audra even knows how to bake. And I can't believe she'd fuel my mother's holiday delusions like this.

After work, I don't bother going home. I wait for everyone to leave, telling them that Audra asked me to lock up. She actually did, so I'm not even lying. Then I gather the shirts from the back room, arrange them under my piano. I'm hoping Sal will hum me to sleep. I'm hoping tomorrow comes and goes and nothing happens. I'm hoping Perry's okay and that I'll see him at the shelter tomorrow when I go do the volunteer thing. If he's not there, I don't know what I'll do. That will mean he's really gone, either physically or mentally. It will mean all kinds of things I don't want to contemplate.

I thought I'd have a chance at a few hours of sleep if I stayed here, but eventually I realize there's no hope. I get up and wander through the cavernous dark room to the bar. I look at the bottles in the half-light, just stare at them for a few moments, the different colors, shapes, and sizes. I wonder if I should have a drink. I start to reach for a glass until I remember the night at Jedd's. I remember all the other nights like it, the start of them anyway, because all too often I can't remember the end. But mostly I remember

Perry's grimace as he said, "You're drunk." I shudder and light a cigarette instead.

I could call Jedd. I could sweet-talk my way back into his bed and
probably even the band. I could have the rock-and-roll lifestyle
back, but even better. I could sing with an up-and-coming band
that has a shot at making it, party, stay up until all hours, travel,
live out of nice hotel rooms and tour buses. It's everything I've always wanted. Until now.

I walk back to Audra's office and turn on the light, shielding
myself from the sudden brightness and fluorescent buzz. I pick up
the phone and dial Perry's number, looking nervously at the clock.
It's nearly three a.m. No answer. My stomach twists like a mop in
a bucket.

I stub out my cigarette, grab my bag, and head out into the darkness.

As I drive to Perry's house, it strikes me that I've become the
stalker in this relationship. Only I'm not such a good one—I haven't
caught even a glimpse of him since I fucked up everything three
nights ago. If he is sick, having a nervous breakdown or whatever
they call it these days, I want to help. When I've thought about this
very scenario before, about what I'd do if Perry ever wigged out
on me, I thought I'd run away at the first sign of trouble. But here
I am, not running.

The front sidewalk has glazed over with a slick sheen of ice
since earlier today and I almost slip as I walk to the door. I knock
this time—it sounds nicer, gentler than the bell. No answer. I turn
and look at the shadowy rows of apartment buildings around me.
The projects. Why do they call them that? I wonder. These aren't
projects. They're people's homes.

Even though he seemed embarrassed to be living here, I know
Perry was relieved to have a place to call his own, four walls, a bed,
a beginning. Like when I first got to Mom's and fell in love with
my bedroom, even though at times I was surprised to find that I
yearned for the inside of the van, my old cocoon. It had been home
for so long.

That must be it, I think, suddenly terrified. Perry's sleeping out in the open. Didn't he say something about that, way back when he gave me a tour of the shelter: "Some people need more freedom"? What if he's gone back to the streets, the bridges? What if he's somewhere right now shivering inside his old wool coat and trying to get comfortable on a piece of cardboard?

It would be stupid to think I could find him. It would be crazy not to try.

Perry told me once that during Denver's deadly cold snaps, he goes out into the city's dark nether regions, looking for the "unreachables"—the career addicts and drunks and incurably mentally ill who refuse to go to shelters even at the risk of freezing to death. Not that he gets many of them to change their minds, but he takes blankets, hot coffee, hats and gloves if he can rustle some up. "Where do you find these people?" I asked, and he said, "Anywhere I can."

I know some of the places where homeless hang out from listening to his stories and from talking to people at the shelter, so I drive toward a long stretch of abandoned road beneath a crumbling, seldom-used viaduct a few blocks northwest of the shelter. From a block away, I see the glow of waste-barrel fires dotting the dark like a line of porch lights. As I draw closer, they turn into community campfires, each one surrounded by a huddle of dark figures, mummies unraveling in scraps of clothing and dirty blankets. Farther beneath the ramparts lie humps of sleeping people, cardboard-box shelters, shopping carts parked beside them like suburban SUVs. When I pull up and kill the lights, too many edgy eyes turn toward me. I roll down the window, chickenshit now, and call out into the frigid dark, "Perry?" It's freezing out there.

"Perry ain't here," someone yells back. The crowd erupts in snickers and guffaws, punctuated by a few hacking coughs. "I'll be your sweet Perry man," another voice croons. "Come out where we can get a look at you, girlfriend."

I reach to lock both doors and roll the window up three-quarters of the way. "I'm serious," I call through the top of the window. "Has anyone seen him?"

"Ooh, she's serious," the crooner says. Again, laughter.

A large figure ambles toward me, stopping just short of the car door. He leans down to look inside and I flinch.

"Why you here, looking for Perry?" He wears a faded orange Broncos knit cap and a gold medallion flops from inside his army jacket. "You got a cigarette?" he asks. It looks as if he hasn't washed his face or brushed his teeth in years—I breathe through my mouth to avoid the smell.

"You know him?" I ask, sure most of these people must. I shake a cigarette from my pack, hand it through the crack in the window.

He takes it with bare fingers, fingernails broken and dirty, and nods. "Yeah. I know him." He makes a gesture with the cigarette, like "Light?"

I push matches through the window and draw my hand back quickly. "Have you seen him around?"

He takes his sweet time putting the cigarette to his lips, opening the matchbook, tearing one free, striking it, and cupping the blue-orange flame to the cigarette. Exhaling a plume of smoke, he shakes the match to the ground and looks me over. "You got smokes for my friends?"

I push my pack through the window. "Please, have you seen him?"

He grabs the cigarettes, laughs. "You barking up the wrong damn tree, man. Perry don't do this shit no more." He turns and saunters back to the fire, shaking his head and pocketing the Salems.

I drive farther north, deeper into the industrial district. No-man's-land, I keep thinking, and definitely no woman's. When I see clusters of figures in doorways, I slow, inch the window down, call out. The answers vary from dull head shakes to surly come-ons—"I got your Perry right here, bitch. Come and get it." Some of them start toward my car and I peel away, looking for the next bunch, heart pounding.

I turn east on a narrow side street and my headlights sweep over a dark-haired man in a large wool coat, hunkered beneath a loading dock. "Jesus," I whisper, pull a quick U-turn, and park. I climb out of the car, leave the engine running, just in case. "Perry?" I say, walking cautiously toward the man.

His body shakes, from shivering or d.t.'s or crying I can't tell.

"Sweetie?" I try again, heart knocking into my throat.

"Go away," he moans and turns his face toward the concrete. "Can't you just leave me alone?" He is crying and his voice is unfamiliar with the sound of it.

"Perry? Is that you? Are you okay?" I have started to shake, too, and I stand paralyzed between him and the car, unsure what to do.

"How could you?" he cries into the wall. "How could you? How could you?"

I fold my arms against my stomach. "Oh, God, baby," I say, starting to cry. "I'm so sorry. I didn't mean to hurt you." I take a step forward, then another. I can almost touch him. "Really, I didn't. I just—"

"You just what?" he says, turning to look at me, voice going mean. Acne scars the whole of his face, and his eyes are dark and vicious beneath a Neanderthal brow. "You just what, whore? Couldn't obey your vows? Couldn't keep my goddamned brother's dick out of your ugly cunt?"

I freeze and his arm reaches for my leg in slow motion, then his dirty baseball-mitt hand wraps around my ankle, fingers digging into the soft spot behind my ankle bone. I cry out and try to wrench my foot away but he is strong, and now he is trying to pull me down, his other hand groping at my leg.

With surprising calm, I quit struggling, put all my weight on the foot he's holding, then draw back and kick him full force in the face with the other foot. He yelps and lets go of me, pawing his nose and mouth while I turn and run to the car. There I throw myself inside and slam into reverse. Squealing backward across pavement, I see him again in the headlights, face bloodied as he pulls himself to a standing position. With shaking hands, I try to jam the car into first but it makes an ugly gnashing sound. I try again and see him, hulking and as brown as leather, advancing stiffly toward the car like King Kong.

"Come on, come on," I whimper, and finally the stick shift slides easily into gear. The car chugs and sputters—I'm in fucking third— but the man is gaining momentum, so I keep pressing the pedal to the floor, picking up speed as I pass him. Then he shrinks in the rearview, screaming every obscenity at me that I deserve.

33

Three blocks away the crying overtakes me. I find a spot beneath a streetlight and pull over, lock the doors, still shaking. I'd light a cigarette if I hadn't let that asshole gyp me out of them.

"What the fuck am I doing?" I yell, wiping my face with the palms of my hands, then I hit the steering wheel with my fist. "Why won't you just let me find you?"

A light rap at the passenger window jolts me like jumper cables. I scramble wildly for the key in the ignition, then look over. A tiny Asian woman who looks older than God bends over to beam toothlessly through the window. Harmless.

I exhale and shake my head, lean over to roll down the window. "I don't have any spare change. Or cigarettes. Sorry."

"No change, cigarette," she says. Her white hair falls in wisps around her crinkled tissue-paper face and she clutches a thin plaid flannel shirt at her neck. She must be freezing. "You have crying," she says, running ancient crooked fingers from her eyes to her chin. "You okay, *ah lui?*"

I nod, then shake my head. The tears return and suddenly I feel hot, even in this cold. Sweat dampens the back of my neck and I shiver. "No, I'm not okay," I say. "I'm a mess." I take a deep quivering breath. She makes a clownlike frown and nods at me to go on.

"I drink too much, and I do stupid things. I lie. I make a fool of myself. I drive everyone who cares about me away."

Her eyes are dark and kind. She seems to want to hear my confession and I want to explain it to her, to send these ugly things out into the night, let them crumble and dissolve like dirt in the gutter.

"All I want is to be someone who deserves to be loved"—I explain, my voice catching—"but I make it so *fucking* impossible." I bend over then, gut convulsing, crying into my hands.

When I get a hold of myself and sit back up, she is smiling and nodding and still bent over in a way that looks painful. I could be telling her the weather report—she doesn't understand a word I'm saying.

"Oh, God, you don't have to . . . I'm fine, really. Please. Go to . . . wherever you go."

She nods again but doesn't move.

"I'm o-kay," I say slowly, and she looks doubtful. "Really," I say, drying my eyes, sitting up straighter. "You can go home."

She doesn't leave.

"Do you have a—a home?"

She smiles. God knows what she thinks I'm saying. I put up a finger, then grab my bag, dig through it, and pull out a half roll of Wint-O-Green Life Savers, three crumpled dollars, and a mostly used Chap Stick. I get out of the car and walk around it to her. "Here," I say. "Take these."

She doesn't straighten up, just looks up at me sideways. She takes the things I have offered and pockets the money. Then she examines the Life Savers and Chap Stick in her gnarled hand.

"These are pretty tasty," I say, touching the mints and, inadvertently, her hand. It is so cold it could be dead flesh. "Do you want one?"

She nods, so I take the roll and tear the paper, extract a candy and hand it to her. She pops it into her mouth, then smiles and motions for me to eat one, so I do. "Mmm," I say, making a big display of how good it is, wondering if it is the only food she has eaten today, wishing I had something more nutritious to give her.

I hand her back the Life Savers, then take the Chap Stick, uncap it, pantomime rolling it on my lips. When I hand it to her she smooths it on her thin hard lips and smacks them together.

"Okay, then," I say and start back toward the driver's side. She turns to walk down the street, hobbling in that painful L shape. "Wait," I say, and she turns. I jog toward her and pull off my sweater. "This is really warm." I wrap it around her frail frigid body and she lets go of her shirt to clutch it, petting it with the other hand and smiling. "Warm," I say again, immediately starting to shiver.

"Warm," she agrees. "Thank you, *ah lui*."

"What is that, 'ah louie'?" My teeth chatter.

She brings her arms to her bosom and pretends to rock a baby, dropping the sweater. "Daughter," she says.

Tears sting my eyes as I pick up the sweater and wrap it back around her.

She smiles up at me, then turns to go. I watch her struggle down the street, until, half a block away, she steps into a side alley and is gone.

I stand there, watching the empty space where she was and wishing she'd come back. My body trembles against the cold, but for a very long time, I don't move.

I'm back at home in bed with the quilt pulled to my chin, my heart tap-dancing restlessly in my chest. I couldn't find him. I know I tried my best, but the thought that I gave up on Perry tastes like rusted metal in the back of my throat.

It is Thanksgiving Day. The clock on my bedside table reads five a.m. It's still dark outside, ink dark. I don't want this day to begin. I don't want the clock to read 5:09, then 5:18, then 5:37, numbers changing too rapidly. I feel as if I'm sliding out of control, hydroplaning across four lanes of highway, careening toward something large and dark and unknowable.

I get up and turn on the bedside lamp. Packed away with my sheet music in the closet is an old staff book. I dig it out, pull a pen from my bag, and sit on the bed, staring at the white wall. Eventually I write, the words flowing onto the paper with such increasing intensity that I can barely keep up and my handwriting takes on a hard keening slant. When I look up again, it's more morning than night, the world finally beginning to lighten. I sign my name, rip the paper from the book, fold it to tuck it into my bag, and lie down again, spent.

He'll probably never even see the letter. He'll never whisper in my ear again, stroke my forehead, rub the knots I get in my shoulders. I'll never burrow into him in the middle of the night again, lose myself in his sweet smell and sleepy flesh. He won't be around to get me through this or any other day.

Just like every other Thanksgiving I've ever been home, I'm on my own.

My first Thanksgiving away from home was my happiest. I was still enjoying my newfound freedom, being grown-up and making decisions for myself. The Holy Rollers hadn't yet lit out for California; we were still playing the local bar circuit, making occasional trips into mountain towns for short stints at roughneck bars. It was a good time in my life. Everything hopeful, all possibility, stretched out in front of me, like a road full of promise. I was in love, I was a working musician, and I thought I would be somebody someday. Everyone told me so.

That week we were booked in Oak Creek, a small mining town just outside one of the big ski resorts. The bar was called the Broken Shaft, and we were staying in the owner's house next door, sleeping on a scattering of mattresses and smelly old sofas in his basement apartment.

The bar was closed Thanksgiving Day and the owner and his hippie girlfriend invited us to eat with them. We played acoustic guitars and sang old Crosby, Stills and Nash songs, and ate tofu and tabbouleh and things I didn't recognize from cheap paper plates while sitting cross-legged on their dirty brown shag carpeting. It was heaven. I'd never known a holiday could be so easy, so free of any sense of drama.

The owner pulled out his stash after dinner, laying out thick lines of coke on the glass coffee table, lighting joints to pass around. I asked if there was anything to drink. He said to run on over to the bar and grab anything I wanted. I grabbed the Cuervo Gold, Southern Comfort, and a bottle of vodka, so the others could have some, too, and we numbed ourselves into oblivion. When I woke up the next day I was slightly worse for wear, but I felt happier than I ever had. I'd made it through my first pain-free holiday.

I think about the soothing dull sensation of alcohol, the tingling that gives way to such comforting heaviness that I don't care about anything anymore. Then I make myself think about the next-day feeling, the shame, the nausea, the headache. The power alcohol has over me. All I can do today is put one foot in front of the other until the day is done, I tell myself, just get through it and it will be over. Maybe my mother will go crazy, maybe not. Maybe I'll see Perry. Probably not. Whatever is going to happen will just have to happen. There are some things no one has any control over.

"Amen, sister," Sal whispers, the first time I've heard her in days, and finally, I relax.

When I open my eyes again it's bright in the room. There's banging in the kitchen and the smell of something cooking. I drag myself out of bed, pull on my robe, rub the crumbly sleep out of my eyes. I need coffee.

"Good morning," Mom says with forced cheerfulness, even though she looks dead-tired. I push through the kitchen door and head for the coffeepot. She and Audra mill around the stove, drink coffee, stir pots. There are cans of food, bowls, and utensils everywhere, dishes in every possible state of preparation. I wish we'd just order a pizza or something and break the Thanksgiving voodoo spell.

"Busy, busy, busy," I grumble, pouring a mug.

Audra gives me one of her sideways looks.

"Honey, I know you're upset about Perry," Mom says. "But maybe it's for the best."

"What does that mean?" I jam the pot back into the machine.

"Must you speak to your mother that way?" Audra says, testy and tensed like a protective bulldog.

"Must you poke your nose into our business?"

"Your mother is going through a lot of trouble to make your first Thanksgiving home a good one," she says, "and I for one don't want you to spoil it."

Mom reaches out to grab her arm. "Don't," she says; then she turns to me. "Tallie, all I'm trying to say is maybe it's best this way. Maybe you should find someone without so many problems."

"What?" I bang my cup on the counter. "Of all people . . . How can you—how the fuck can you say that? You will never be anywhere near as sane as Perry is."

"Tallie!" Audra protests, but Mom just stands there looking surprised and innocent.

"What?" I say, voice too loud and steely for the cozy kitchen, for their cozy little lesbian lives, but I'm giddy with it. "I'm not supposed to say anything that might upset dear old Mom? I'm not allowed to tell the truth?" My head buzzes and my eyes sting, focused with painful clarity on my wide-eyed mother who has turned as white as porcelain. As pure as goddamned Mother Teresa.

"Well, here's a news flash: I'm an adult now and I can say and do anything I want to. I don't have to follow the fucking rules anymore, and it doesn't make me a horrible person. You have some nerve acting like such a goddamned saint all the time, like you and your craziness didn't fuck up everything in our lives." I'm the one who sounds crazy now, standing here yelling, but I can't stop. I don't want to stop. It's like finally throwing up after a lifetime of nausea.

"You're the one who fucked up the holidays," I shout. "You're the one who made me hate everything about normal life. You never let us *have* a normal life, with your fucking crazy spells, your pills. And it was never your fault. You could be as sick and mean as you wanted to be, and we just had to take it."

Audra wraps her arm around Mom, who seems to have stopped breathing. Neither of them tries to stop me, though, which pisses me off even more.

"Do you hear what I'm saying?" I yell, almost screeching now.

"Say something! Tell me why I had to have such a fucked-up mother. Explain why I couldn't have a normal family, just be a normal kid. Why you couldn't figure it out then, like you did later, when . . ." I stop, overwhelmed by the one thing that chokes me up whenever I think about it. "Like you did when Emma was born."

Mom squeezes her eyes tight, crying. Audra rubs her back, looking more upset than angry now, and says, "Tallie, couldn't you just—"

"No, I couldn't," I say, then to Mom, sternly: "So, are you going to be okay today or what?"

She nods, eyes red and pleading, one hand holding Audra's, the other pressed against her chest.

"Good," I say and leave the room.

On my way to the shelter, I feel spent, and guilty about the blowup, of course, but okay. Not exactly hopeful about anything—I'm not that stupid—just resigned to whatever the day will hold. I walk quietly through a gray landscape: gray skies, gray concrete, gray leafless trees. The sky looks heavy, like it could snow, and the air has that peculiar stockyard smell Denver gets on wintry days, even though there haven't been stockyards here for who knows how many years. For all its growth and boom and bustle, Denver is still just a cow town after all.

I round the final corner and see a crowd milling around outside the shelter. As I get closer, the crowd becomes people: black and Hispanic women with clusters of children, some with men, many without. A few white families, their kids pale and rubbing runny noses. Scruffy-looking men with stubbly faces, ragged clothing, dirty hands, worn-out shoes. Packs of teenagers with shoe-polish black hair, crazy piercings, torn black clothing, dull eyes. I look for the Neanderthal man from last night but don't see him.

A young woman, a girl really, stands by herself, ashen and whisper-thin. Her bleached hair has at least a month's worth of dark roots and the messy look of having just woken up. She wears only a light sweater, torn black tights, and black socks with platform sandals. She rubs her slender arms, a cigarette smoldering between her fingers.

I stop in my tracks and say aloud, "That could be me." Why is she standing here, waiting to eat, while I trot in like I'm any better, serving these people their turkey slices and instant mashed potatoes, then go home to a real Thanksgiving meal? Who am I to help the homeless, the needy, when I could be standing in their shoes if not for a few lucky turns?

"You're an angel of mercy, a good-hearted woman, a friend of mankind." I can tell Sal is smiling even though I can't see her face.

"Got any more clichés to make me feel better?" I ask, not even trying to look for her.

"Nope. Fresh out."

"Where the hell have you been? It's been a rough few days."

"But just look at you, Tallulah Jean," she says. "Look how far you've come. You don't even need me anymore."

"You call this is an improvement?" I snort and start walking again. "I hate to think what you'd consider backsliding."

As I near the shelter door, everyone looks at me, probably trying to figure out if I'm one of them or not, but after just a second they look away, go back to their conversations, their cigarettes, their lives. Something about their demeanor surprises me, but I can't put my finger on it.

"Life force," Sal's voice says. "Dignity. The miraculous power of the human spirit."

"Amen, sister." I take a deep breath and open the door.

My job in the production line is to say, "Corn?" as each of the hundreds of people passes by with a tray. If they nod with more than usual enthusiasm, I place a heaping spoonful of canned corn on their plate, more than I was instructed to. If they stare at me wordlessly, as many of the more scraggly ones do, I give them the normal-size serving. Most of the kids wrinkle their noses, so I look at their mothers with raised eyebrows, waiting for their decision. Most say, "Yes, you will have corn. Tell the lady thank you."

I'm here for half an hour before I finally see Perry across the room, crouched down to talk to the tiny old woman from last night. She turns to me and smiles that toothless smile, and I gasp, spill corn on my shoes. Tears spring to my eyes at the sight of him. He looks fine, healthy, capable in his role here as manager. When he sees me he looks at me for a long moment before turning back to her. I wipe my nose on my sleeve and get back to work, keeping an eye on him whenever I can.

He runs around, helping with problems, finding more plastic forks, carrying heavy pans to refill our empties, consoling temporarily lost children, performing first aid on a volunteer who cuts her finger on an industrial-size can of gravy. All this he does with a sense of calm, an easy smile. He knows every volunteer by name and most of the customers. He takes time to chat with anyone who approaches him, even though there are fifty other things he should be doing. He listens attentively, laughs appreciatively, shakes his head consolingly. Then he mops up where a drunk vomited in the corner, all with the grace of someone who loves what he does.

When he stands in front of the only large window in the place, I notice the sun has finally come out, illuminating Perry with unearthly light.

He is the angel, not me. He always was. I am simply the queen of corn.

34

It seems impossible that hundreds of people could be fed in just a few hours, but the exhilaration of helping to pull off this feat is like a drug. A truly satisfying drug, like no real drug I've ever tried. I am bone-tired, messy with food stains and sweat, and my feet throb from standing on hard tile floors (and I hope I never have to smell corn again), but I'm strangely happy.

Perry is still at it, making his rounds to ensure everything's set for the evening rush of overnighters. I thought we might connect sometime during the day, but it's clearly not going to happen.

Then, as I'm pulling on my coat to leave, he walks over, helps tug it onto my shoulders without a word. My pulse accelerates, and I'm pretty sure a goofy grin spreads across my face as I turn around to look at him.

He looks tired. Dried stuffing clings to the elbow of his sleeve and grease-ringed gravy spots form a constellation on his shirt-front. He's rubbed a grubby hand over his head so many times, in the same exact spot, that a swath of dark lank hair runs the opposite way from the rest of his orderly haircut.

"I was worried about you," I say, feeling shy. "I didn't know what happened to you."

"I took the bus to Grand Junction, to see my sister," he says. "I knew I wasn't going to get a break around here until after the holidays, and I felt like getting away." He clears his throat and looks around the room. "Got back early this morning."

Oh. I nod, consider this. Then, working up what little courage I can muster, I say, "I'm really sorry, Perry. I'm so, so . . ." I break off, swallow hard.

"I know you are."

I dig through my bag, through cigarette wrappers and lipstick cases for the folded piece of paper. I hand it to him and he slips it into his pants pocket without a glance. Even so, I find myself saying, ever so casually, "I don't suppose there's any way you'd want to come to Mom's for dinner."

He shakes his head, eyes down. "I still have work to do. Besides, I'm beat."

"Of course you are," I say carefully. "I know what it's like, trying to sleep on a bus."

He nods.

"And, hey, you really worked your ass off here today. You were great."

"Yeah? Thanks." He shifts from one foot to the other, then says, "Well . . ."

"Yeah, I gotta go, too. Everybody's waiting for me at home." I hitch my bag up on my shoulder, take a step toward the door. He doesn't stop me, so I keep going and before I know it, I'm out in the dark chill of the city, alone. The sky looks heavy overhead, low-lying clouds pinkened by city lights. No one is out; everyone is home with their families. I pull my coat tightly around me and walk quickly toward home.

As the elevator chugs and lurches upward, I feel childishly expectant, almost happy, like I did at the shelter. I picture Jane in the kitchen, complaining about something or other as she helps Mom spoon food into serving dishes. I imagine the fanfare, Emma's high-voltage energy level. I turn the key in the lock, steeling myself for the noise, the smells of cooking food, the exuberant hugs and greetings. Maybe I can sneak off for a quick shower, change my clothes.

I push open the door to black silence.

"Where is everybody?" I call out, my voice dying in the stillness of the dark loft. Even without light, I can see the living room is in disarray. My heart pounds with a painful ferocity. I back up a step. My throat closes, my eyes go funny. I can't breathe.

She did it to me again.

I switch on the light. White couch cushions lie haphazardly crosswise on the floor, one next to Mom's favorite chenille throw blanket, the one she wraps herself in when watching TV. Magazines from the coffee table lie scattered across the floor like stepping-stones; a large paisley-shaped stain is still wet on the rug. Knives, I remember suddenly. Maybe she finally followed through on the bloody threat she implied on those long-ago late nights.

I force myself to walk through the living room, averting my eyes from the mess. I especially don't want to see the kitchen, but I push through the door into the faded smell of things cooking and close my eyes, a reflex.

When I open them, I see that the counters are stacked neatly with good china, cloth napkins, wineglasses, rows of silverware. There's no evidence of violence or mayhem. Although a few dirty pots and pans are stacked precariously next to the sink, everything is orderly, ready for a party.

I go to the fridge and pull open the heavy door. A foil-wrapped turkey in its roasting pan consumes the bottom shelf. Bowls of things are stacked on the other shelves, next to wine bottles lying side by side. As I close the door, I see the note:

> Tallie,
> Mom in hospital, come to Denver General.

Jane's usually neat cursive is jagged and heavy.

The drive to the hospital is short, but I circle the old brick building several times trying to figure out where to go. "Should I go to emergency?" I ask aloud, passing the ambulance entrance. "Where the hell is a parking lot? Why don't they have any goddamned signs?"

Finally, I find a parking spot on the street and slip neatly against the curb, kill the engine.

I keep my grip on the steering wheel, not wanting to move. The old houses that line this street have lighted windows, extra cars in their driveways and more filling the street. Most people do not have dark creepy Thanksgivings. It's a pleasant holiday, an excuse to eat and drink too much, to laugh and tell stupid jokes and hang out. A day that passes easily save for trivial family bickerings or resentments, a day that leads to even bigger and brighter holidays. A reason to give thanks. I remember the glimmer of happiness I felt at the shelter. Maybe I should leave, find someplace new and far away where I can try again. I was always going to leave, anyway. Why the hell have I stayed so long?

Finally, I will myself out of the car and across the street toward a sign I didn't see before. It says ENTRANCE.

35

The light inside the hospital lobby is bright and unrelenting, and I squint against it, trying to adjust. My shoes thud dully as I walk toward the information desk. Except for me, it is dead-quiet.

"I'm here to see Lee Jackson," I say to a tiny, egg-shaped old man in a red volunteer's vest sitting behind the desk.

He runs a crooked finger down his clipboard and breathes heavily, as if the simple act of drawing air is an effort. I'm wondering if maybe he should be checking in himself when he looks up, his eyes a surprisingly clear gray. "Family?" he asks. The way he says it and the way he looks at me, wise old owl behind the decaying, drooping mask, makes me think he knows everything about me, my mother, our twisted lives.

I nod. "My mom."

He nods with me for a moment, then looks back at his clipboard. "You'll need to take the elevator to the seventh floor, young lady, then turn right and inquire at the nurses' station."

"Thank you . . . sir," I say, the formality awkward. He gives me a sympathetic smile.

In the elevator I scan the directory, certain I'm heading for the psych unit. You can never be too prepared to walk into one of those.

SEVENTH floor, I read. ICU. Intensive care unit. What the hell did she do to herself? I shudder with images of knife-gashed flesh, the wet stain on the rug, the certain palpable terror of anyone in that room. What Emma must be going through, let alone Jane and Audra.

The door shushes open and I walk out, turn right. My head has gone tingly and I try to breathe deeper, but I can't because a lump of something, dread, anger, fear, has taken over my throat.

"I'm here to see Lee Jackson," I say to a large black woman at the nurses' station. She's wearing a multicolored top, the kind they wear in operating rooms, only this one has pictures of crazy-looking cats all over it. Her nails are bright pink to match, and when I look into her face I almost faint. She looks so much like Sal I'd bet my life it was, but she doesn't seem to recognize me.

"Are you a family member?" she asks.

I nod dumbly, then say, "Daughter."

"Your mother's still down having some tests," she says, her voice kind. "We don't know anything about her condition just yet, but they'll be bringing her up in a little while."

"Do you know what happened?"

"Sorry." She shakes her head. "But the doctor will be able to talk with you after they get her up here."

"Do you know if my sister's here? My niece?"

"They might be in the waiting room, or maybe down in the cafeteria." She gathers a large stack of files, clutches them to her bosom, and heads around the desk, sticking a pen topped with one of those Koosh balls on top of it behind her ear. It looks like she's wearing a flower.

"What's your name?" I ask as she walks away.

She turns around, smiling quizzically. "Sarah."

"You ever heard of Cheluga, Georgia?"

"No, I don't think so. Why?"

"Nothing," I say, drawing a breath. "You just look like someone."

"You know, people tell me that all the time," she says, flashes a classic Big Gal grin, and sashays down the hall.

I'm the only person in the ICU waiting room, which, I have to admit, is a hell of a lot nicer than most waiting rooms. The couches and chairs are deep and comforting, all in shades of tan and blue, and sets of tables and chairs line the far wall, a place where families can sit and talk, I suppose. A TV stands dark and silent in one corner and a bookshelf contains piles of tattered magazines, a few board games, and a silk plant in a white wicker basket. Across the room there's a counter with a microwave, coffeemaker, kitcheny stuff.

The cafeteria was almost as empty as this room when I went to check it out, except for a janitor on break and a woman who looked like a hooker doing her nails. No Audra, no Jane. No Emma. Figuring they'll eventually come here, I camp out on the blue plaid sofa closest to the door. I pick through the magazines and find an old *People* with Ray Charles on the front. His dark glasses and familiar smile make me feel better, and I hold the magazine to my chest as I sink into the sofa.

I picked the perfect spot to sit, because half an hour later when a group of light blue–clad people hurry a gurney past the door, I look dead into my mother's eyes. Her head is turned toward me and for the half second she's passing, our eyes lock together like a bolt clicking into a latch. I jump up to follow the gurney down the hall.

"Tallie!" Jane calls from behind me, and I turn to see the three of them, Audra, Jane, and sleepy-looking Emma, emerge from the elevator.

And then everyone's talking at once:

"Where have you . . . ?"

"Oh, my God, what hap . . . ?"

"It's okay, just calm . . ."

"Shouldn't we . . . ?"

". . . have to wait for the . . ."

"Is she . . . ?"

". . . won't know anything until . . ."

I'm crying, and everyone's pretty red-eyed, and Audra's handing out tissues, and Emma's looking up at me wide-eyed and looking back at her mother, who's crying now, too.

"It's all my fault," I say to Jane and we clutch each other, pulling into a hug, much more emotional about all this than we ever were as kids. It feels good to hold on to someone, though, and I wish I would have known that then.

"How could it be your fault?" Jane pulls back and looks at me.

"I . . . I just lost it," I say, feeling queasy, not wanting to tell her, but I have to. "I yelled at her, Janie, so bad. I was really mean."

Jane looks confused. "But—"

"Tallie, honey," Audra interrupts. "Your mother had a heart attack."

36

Nurse Sarah lets us all enter Mom's room together, even though the rules are only one at a time and only for ten minutes. "I know you all want to see her, and since I just gave her a sedative, this will be your only chance for a while," she says, busying herself around the bed, pushing buttons on machines, adjusting tubes. "But keep it short and keep it quiet."

Sarah raises her voice to speak to Mom. "Ms. Jackson? I'm letting your family stay with you awhile, but the shot I gave you is going to make you very sleepy. That's a good thing, okay? You get some rest."

Although Sarah looks like Sal, she's plainly not. Her efficient nurse movements are nothing like the Big Gal's slow saunter, and Sarah has no honey-smooth Southern lilt to her voice. And frankly, she's nowhere near as big. But she smiles at me, pats my arm as she's passing by, and I feel my shoulders relax just at the sight of her.

After she's done settling Mom in, Sarah talks to us while she makes notes on a clipboard. "Encourage her to rest. We're giving her morphine, which should help with the anxiety."

"Anxiety?" I ask stupidly. I thought she had a heart attack.

"It's pretty scary having all these people rushing around you and hooking you up to machines and shouting orders," she explains. She glances over at Mom, then back to her chart. "Not to mention having a heart attack."

She continues to talk to the others in a quiet, matter-of-fact way as I move away from them, away from the talk of when the doctor will be here and cath labs and surgery and diagnoses and prognoses, toward the motionless shape on the bed that is my mother. Her skin is pale but her cheeks are flushed, and her eyes droop though she battles to keep them open. A light green oxygen tube snakes across her face, up into each nostril, then down the other side, denting the soft papery skin of her face. This isn't how she really looks, I tell myself, this old and helpless. It's like a preview of an awful day in the distant future. Not now. This can't happen now. I touch her shoulder, the warmth of it a relief.

She struggles her eyes open and I see her fear in them, in the effort she exerts to focus on me through the drug fog.

"It's okay," I tell her. "You're okay. The nurse says you need to sleep."

She looks at me intently. "I thought you wouldn't come," she says, half whisper, half croak.

"Oh, Mom." I look away. What do I say? This might be the last time I talk to her. I look back down and tears have pooled in her eyes.

"Tallie," she says thickly. "I'm . . . so . . . sorry."

I sigh, shake my head. "It's not your fault," I finally tell her. "Don't be sorry." She looks so horrible I have to let her off the hook, but then it occurs to me that it might be true. Why would the damage in her brain be any different than the damage in her heart?

She gives in to the drug and closes her eyes, the lids crisscrossed with blue and purple. They look like something she'd paint.

Behind us, Jane is telling Emma it's time she called her father to pick her up. A hospital room is no place for a kid.

"No," Emma says obstinately, and a little too loudly for the circumstances. "I want to be here with my family."

Mom's eyes flutter. "That's my girl," she murmurs.

Audra comes over and I move to let her stand where I was. She holds Mom's fingers in hers, lightly, as if they were made of glass, and Mom finally drifts into a drug-induced sleep.

And so, amid the hospital smells and incessant beeping of monitors, all of us sitting or standing in close proximity to Mom and one another and talking quietly of surprisingly ordinary things, after so many years and miles and calamities and misunderstandings, my family spends Thanksgiving together after all.

The sun sneaks in through half-opened blinds across the room and lines up directly with my eyes. My head is propped at a wicked angle against the arm of the waiting room couch and my mouth feels dry and salty, like I've been out partying all night. I look around and see Emma curled up on another sofa nearby, snoring softly. No one else is in the room.

I sit up, take stock. The microwave clock across the room says 7:07. My shoes are under the coffee table, and I can tell my hair is smashed flat against the side of my head. It has that bent-at-the-roots feeling, like it will never again flow in the right direction.

Jane appears in the doorway. "Good, you're up. The doctor finally came at five thirty."

"Shit. I missed him?" I rub my eyes. Whatever makeup I was wearing yesterday has to have been cried or slept off by now, but I still check for mascara smears on my fingers.

"It's okay. Between Audra and me, we got more details out of the guy than he was planning to share." She sits next to me, props her feet on the coffee table. Somehow, she looks pretty at this ungodly hour, her hair shiny, her face calm.

"How the hell are you maintaining so well?"

"God, I'm not. I'm a mess." Emma gives a loud snort and rolls over, and Jane smiles at her. "I guess motherhood makes you able to appear invincible."

"And where's Audra?"

"Where do you think?"

"In with Mom."

She nods. "I never realized how . . . close they were. Did you?"

I shrug. "They're happy," I say.

She looks at me, considering this, then continues. "Anyway, the bad news is the doctor says Mom needs a triple bypass. The surgery is supposed to be this afternoon; they don't know exactly when yet, but they're trying to fit her in as early as possible. She's still in danger but at least she's here, getting medication, with doctors nearby."

"But, how did this happen to her? A heart attack?" I picture fat old men puffing cigars, eating steaks and French fries.

"Who knows? The doctor says it could be genetic. She eats pretty well and she's not a smoker—not anymore, anyway. So it probably runs in her family. God, *our* family." She sighs and looks around the room.

I haven't eaten since the day before yesterday—all of a sudden I realize I need food. "Is the cafeteria open?"

"Probably," she says. "Go ahead. I'm going to stay here and watch my daughter sleep." She settles back, one arm behind her head, and gazes lovingly at gape-mouthed Emma, who is snoring her skinny little heart out.

Late in the day, after intermittent short visits in Mom's room, Audra, Jane, and I sit in the waiting room hoping to hear some news. Her surgery still hasn't been scheduled. Our best ally, Sarah, has gone home for the day, and no one else seems to know what's going on around here.

"I think she's looking better," Jane says unconvincingly. "Maybe." Her calmness from this morning has given way to fits of nervous pacing punctuated by nail biting and sighing. It's been twenty-four hours for her and Audra. Emma was finally convinced that it would be okay if she went to Andrew's for a while. This time yesterday I was dishing up food. It feels like weeks ago. It seems like years since I saw Perry.

"So what exactly happened yesterday?" I ask.

"Oh, God." Jane tears up, rubs the heel of her hand over her brow.

Audra coughs, shakes her head, then taps her square red fingernails on the tabletop. "It was a nightmare. She just . . . fell."

"Fell?"

Jane nods, fishing for a tissue in her pocket. "She was done with most of the cooking. It must have been about four—"

"More like five," Audra interrupts.

"Whatever," I say. "She was done cooking . . ."

"She had everything ready," Jane continues. "The linens and china and silver were all sitting on the counters. The food was either in the oven or out and cooling. She was just going to take a break, she said, until it was time to set the table. So she was walking over to the couch to sit with Emma. They were talking about a book Emma's reading in school. *Island of the Blue Dolphins*, I think. She had her glass of chardonnay, of course. All of a sudden, she got this funny look on her face and stopped dead in her tracks. I laughed." Jane has gone hypnotized, staring into space as she talks. "I thought she'd forgotten some stupid little thing, like the relish tray or the dessert spoons, and I was about to tell her to chill out when she dropped her wine."

"I was in the bathroom," Audra says, sounding apologetic. "I heard this *clunk* and I knew something was wrong. Hell, I ran out with my pants halfway down my legs."

"Mom clutched her arms to her chest." Jane presses her forearms into her breasts, her hands heart level, the tissue a white flag. "She just crumpled up." She leans forward in her chair, crumpling herself. "Poor Emma was so upset. She went running over to her." Jane sits back up, looks at me blankly. "But I didn't."

"Honey," Audra says carefully, "you were in shock."

"So? We all were." Jane wipes her nose. "I didn't know what to do. I mean, I took CPR when Emma was born and everything, and all I could do was stand there."

Jane, who always knew what to do in emergencies in the old days, who always calmly called 911, who made sure to clean Mom up before the paramedics arrived so they wouldn't see her with vomit on her face or in some partial state of ragged undress—Jane finally panicked.

Audra made the call to 911, and even though Mom was out cold, Emma tried to make Mom comfortable on the floor by grabbing her chenille blanket and cushions from the couch.

"It was so sweet. She sat with her the whole time," Jane says, half proud, half guilty. "You know what I did? I put food away. Can you believe it? And after the paramedics took her away, I tried to clean the wine off the rug. I didn't get to the hospital until half an hour later."

"Honey, I had the situation under control," Audra says. "There was nothing you could have done." She pauses, like she doesn't know how intimate she can be with Jane yet, and it reminds me of the morning she woke me in the bar. She proceeds cautiously: "You don't always have to be the one to take care of everything, you know."

"Yes, I do," Jane says, finally sounding like herself again. Relieved, we both laugh and wipe our noses. "I most certainly do," she says again.

"She's right," I tell Audra. "That's her job." Jane and I laugh again, an edgy, weird kind of laugh.

"You girls have been through a lot," Audra says, looking sympathetic, which makes us laugh harder. "It's okay," she says a couple of times, trying to comfort us, or to get us to cut it out, but it doesn't happen. We're dancing on the slippery edge of control, but we're dancing together. We're dealing with being our mother's daughters, her caretakers, her genetic material, her next of kin, and no one else on the planet can know what any of that means.

Later, when we've calmed down and Audra's picked up a *Glamour* magazine out of boredom (the sight of it about as ludicrous as me reading the tattered *Scientific American* next to her on the table), I watch Jane standing at the window, staring out at the brick building across the way. I clear my throat nervously, thinking of Perry's definition of courage.

"So, anyway," I say, as if we never quit talking. Jane turns.

"We have this little secret we've been keeping from you, don't we, Audra?"

"What?" Jane says, looking from me to Audra. "What's the secret?"

Audra lifts her head from her magazine. She sighs as it occurs to her what I'm about to say and looks at me the way she did yesterday in the kitchen. "Why on earth—" she starts, but I interrupt.

"No, I need to tell her. She should know." I stop, take a deep breath. My stomach muscles tense and I sit up straighter in the hard chair. "A couple of months ago, Mom had one of her episodes. And she's had other ones, too, that you don't know about."

Jane's face goes blank.

"Like the old days," I explain. "She quit taking her medication. She wigged out. You know. Kablooie."

She quickly absorbs this and the old anger flashes across her face. She opens her mouth to speak, but I don't let her.

"I didn't tell you when it happened. I thought you'd be mad at me. I thought you'd say it was my fault. But here's the deal, Janie. She's just sick and it's not anybody's fault."

"But I had the right to know." Her cheeks flush, her jaw goes taut.

"Yes," I agree.

Jane crosses her arms over her chest. Her chin juts at that angle I see in the mirror sometimes, or in Emma when she's pouting. I want to reach inside my sister and pull the other one out, the one who just laughed with me until she cried, the one who finally seemed like she accepted me. The person who, if Mom dies, is all that's left of my family.

"I'm not an ogre, you know." She bites her lip and looks out the window. "Everyone thinks I'm such a bitch."

"Only when you're mad at me," I say to make her laugh, to get a rise out of her, but she doesn't respond. We sit silently for a few moments, then I try again. "You could just forgive me."

"I could," she says, still looking away.

37

The last vestiges of daylight filter in through the waiting room windows—the sky outside is quickly darkening. I look at the clock on the microwave. It's almost five. It's Friday.

"Holy shit!" I look at Audra. "I forgot—I work tonight!"

"No, you don't," she says. "I made some calls."

"Oh, okay. Thanks," I say, embarrassed at her thoughtfulness. "I mean—"

"It's no problem, Tallie." Audra shifts her large frame uncomfortably in her seat. "So what's for dinner? I don't think I can eat that cafeteria food again. Should we order a pizza?"

"There's that place over on Colfax that makes those huge burritos," I suggest. "I could go pick up something." And get the hell out of here, I'm thinking.

Audra says, "Well, it sure doesn't look like they're going to be making any big decisions around here anytime soon. Maybe you should go."

Jane shrugs. "I wouldn't mind a burrito," she says. "And maybe some guacamole."

As I step from the antiseptic smell of the hospital into the deepening twilight, I rummage through my bag for my Salems, tuck one between my lips. Its paper-tobacco smell calms me even before I light it. I fire up, draw a long hot pull into my lungs, then expel it like a sigh into the cold night air. I feel like a bird escaping a cage. For the briefest of moments I am so happy to be out of there I could weep, until a gnawing twinge of reality snaps me out of it.

Halfway back from the restaurant, it hits me again. As unreal as this all feels, it really is happening.

"I think she's going to die," I say aloud, tightening my grip on the steering wheel and trying to raise the spirit of Sal.

The sky has gone purple-black. The sun is gone.

"Can I tell you a secret?" I say, pretending she's there. "I don't remember ever telling my mother I love her."

I stride purposefully down the hospital corridor, carrying a warm, heavy, salsa-scented bag. I feel as if I'm late, like I've missed an appointment. By the time I round the corner to the ICU, I know something's happened. I run to the waiting room, where Jane is staring out the window. Another family has taken over our table so I set the food on the floor. Audra is nowhere in sight.

"Jane," I call across the room, and she turns. She's crying.

"She crashed," she's saying as I reach her, and I think of twisted metal, spewing radiators, smoke, and steam.

"Is she okay?" I ask. She shrugs and relief surges through me. She's not dead.

"They rushed her to surgery. They said it could be hours before we know anything."

"Where's Audra?"

"Throwing up," Jane says, nodding toward the bathroom door. "She was there when it happened. She's pretty upset."

I shudder, thinking of what it must look like to see the light dim in the eyes of someone you love, to watch them struggle to survive. As selfish as it feels in the middle of all this, all I can think of is Perry.

"Thank God you're here," Audra says, coming through the door. She is the color of paste, walking like her legs are boneless. "I'm so sorry I told you to go—"

"You didn't tell me to go, Audra." I'm afraid she'll faint, and I doubt any of us could lift her off the floor, so I walk to her side, take her substantial arm, and guide her to a chair. "It was my idea."

We settle in for another long wait, burritos going cold in their foil wrappers. No one speaks.

"I forgot to tell her something," I say finally.

"Honey, whatever it is," Audra says, "your mother knows."

"And if anyone would know what your mother thinks," a distinct voice says, "it would be the one who loves her most." I look around for Sal. Her voice was so clear I'd swear she's in the room again, like she used to be, but it's only us and the other worried family. My head goes woozy and I realize I've stopped breathing, waiting to hear what she'll say next.

"I have to pee," I say, standing and trying not to run to the bathroom.

After I've made sure I'm alone and locked myself in a stall, I take a deep breath and say, "Come on, Sal. You could at least show yourself. Where the hell are you when I need you?"

Silence.

"Fine. Dump me." I sit on the toilet, put my head in my hands. "Everyone else has."

"Okay, Miss Dramatic," Sal says from the other side of the stall door. I quickly stand and swing it open. She's floating in midair, beautiful, radiant. Shimmering like something not really there.

"Sal, where have you been?" I'm so relieved to actually see her again. "I need you."

She shakes her ghostly head. "No, child, you don't. You have everything you need right inside that thick head of yours, that beating heart. All you really need is to believe that."

"But, you always helped me," I say, remembering when I was little.

"No, you were the one doing the singing, remember?"

I do. I remember sitting next to my yellow record player, singing along with the scratchy recording as loudly as I could, howling sometimes, drowning out whatever noises were coming from outside the bedroom door. I see the album cover, plain as day. Sal must have been a kid when it was put out—she had the fresh laughing face of a schoolgirl.

"I was nineteen years old," she says, looking wistful. "I'd always thought I'd end up a cleaning woman or a waitress. It was like a dream come true." She's growing more translucent by the moment. "Your dreams just might come true someday, too, if you let them."

"But I can't do this by myself," I say, arguing to keep her from disappearing. "I need you to help me."

"Do you?" she asks, raising an eyebrow. "Really?"

"Well, I *want* you to help me."

"I know you do, honey," Sal says, voice fading, "but you have to get used to using your own wings."

I cover my face with my hands, fall back against the metal stall, sobbing. Everything is happening too fast. Everyone is leaving all at once.

I already know that when I look back up she'll be gone forever.

PART FIVE

When life wrings you out stone cold dry,
Soar those busted-up wings into the sky.

—"Little Bird," Big Gal Sal

38

Mom is finally home, pale and propped against a sea of pillows in her own bed. She looks like she's been beaten up,
her arms and torso bruised, her face drawn and wary. Even though
she's been through the torture of too many disgusting procedures
to count, not to mention open-heart surgery, she keeps saying how
happy she is to be here, in her own room, with everyone she loves
near her. How happy she is to be alive.

The first few days with her here have been frightening. I steal
around like a burglar, trying not to make any noise, and I'm always
half-listening for her to cry out or moan. I'm afraid it will happen
again when I'm the only one around, but, really, Audra's always
here. She and Mom are officially a couple now. Since Mom's heart
attack, they don't care who sees them holding hands or making
goo-goo eyes at each other.

Audra ordained me assistant manager at the bar, so I'm the one
who goes to work every night, overseeing the joint when I'm not
onstage, bringing Audra the books and receipts and money bag so
she can do the paperwork while Mom sleeps.

Jane and Emma come almost every afternoon and we take turns
sitting in Mom's room, keeping her company, making tea, plump-
ing pillows. She has a long, angry-red incision down the front of
her chest, stapled together like a cardboard box, and three lingering, unstitched drainage holes in her torso. Another incision

snakes down her leg, from groin to foot, where they scavenged her new arteries during the six-hour surgery. Emma thinks it's all very cool, this blood-and-guts stuff, and begs Mom to show her either or both incisions, and the holes, please. Especially the holes.

She says she's going to be a doctor someday. Then she reconsiders, adding, for my sake, "Well, and a musician."

Mom is slowly becoming stronger, more alive-looking than dead. Today she admits she hadn't been feeling well for quite some time, but she didn't think it was anything to worry about. "Just this feeling sometimes, like I didn't have the gumption to do anything," she explains when Jane grills her.

"And . . ." Audra prompts, sitting in the rocker she's brought over from her apartment and placed at my mother's bedside.

"Yes, dear, and the shortness of breath. Pressure in my chest. All the classic symptoms." She smiles helplessly. "But who'd have thought I could have a heart attack?"

Who'd have thought any of this, I want to say, but I just watch the dust floating in ribbons of late-afternoon sunlight.

Later, after Jane and Emma leave, Mom closes her eyes to rest and Audra dozes beside her in the rocker. In sleep, Audra is almost sweet-looking, cherubic if she wasn't really too old to be. Her hair looks like rusty steel wool, though, sticking up here and there, like she hasn't fixed it since Mom went to the hospital, and the skin beneath her eyes has the look of bruised fruit. I walk over to her, jiggle her shoulder.

"Huh?" She wakes with a start, eyes wild.

"Audra, go home and get some sleep. It's Sunday. I'll be here."

"Like hell I will," she says, glancing over at my mother.

Mom opens her eyes and says, "Please, dear. Go home. You'll like me much better if you don't have to take care of me every single moment."

Grudgingly, Audra rises from her chair, giving me more instructions and reminders than I can possibly remember, but I finally close the door behind her.

I wander around the loft, opening the refrigerator door, closing it, looking out a window at the quiet street below, the streetlights blinking on. I click on the TV in the living room, but even at low volume it seems too loud, so I turn it off and walk back into Mom's room. She's fallen asleep. I sit in Audra's chair in the dim gray light, rocking to the slow rhythm of her breathing. After a while, I nod off, too.

I'm dreaming about eating peaches with Perry on a red plaid blanket in a big green meadow when I wake to her crying.

I fly out of the chair. I should have paid better attention to Audra's instructions. "Mom? Are you okay?"

"Tallie," she says, weeping. As my eyes adjust, I can see her bluish form in the moonlight.

"What? Are you in pain? Should I call 911?"

"No, no, honey," she says weakly. "I just got scared."

"It's okay. Everything's going to be okay." My words sound false, nervous. I sit next to her on the bed. "Do you want something? Water? Is it time for a pill?"

"Would you hold my hand?"

"Would I . . . oh," I say. "Okay." She still can't move much, so I maneuver to a better angle and grope in the folds of the blankets for her hand. It's warm and softer than I would have imagined, and I shudder at touching her this way. It feels perverse, holding my mother's hand, more intimate than any encounter I can remember.

"I just felt all of a sudden like I might vanish in the dark," she says, sounding small and afraid. "Like I might die if I didn't have something to hold me here."

"I'm here," I say, sounding more confident than I feel.

"Yes," she says, and we sit quietly in the dark, the damp warmth between our hands slowly growing more comfortable. It occurs to me how easy it is to do what she never could for me, how simple it is to comfort someone who is frightened. I could be resentful. I could refuse to sit here with her, tell her she's fine and go to my own room.

I could. Instead, I sit with her until she begins to breathe rhythmically again. Slowly, I release her hand, wiping my own on the blanket, ashamed for doing it. I sit and watch her for a while, my damaged mother, marveling at her wounds, physical and otherwise.

It's been the longest couple of weeks of my life and I don't know if I've ever felt this tired. I'd like to slip off to my room to get some sleep, but I think about the fear in my mother's voice when she woke, the way her hand clutched mine. Finally, I lift the blankets and fit myself into the space beside her, lie down and draw the covers up over us.

In the time it takes for a heart to malfunction—one moment it's fine, chugging along like a trooper, the next it's gone completely haywire—all kinds of things can change. In those moments after my mother dropped her wine, when Jane became paralyzed and Audra waddled in with her pants around her knees, when I was off feeding the hungry and Emma stepped up to bat, our family, as it has always been, fell to pieces right along with my mother, like so many tiny specks of matter after an explosion. Now those pieces are being swept into some new shape, rearranged into an uncomfortable, unrecognizable new whole.

Audra copes by being in charge, being Mom's primary caretaker. She helps with her rehab, making her lean forward and cough while Mom holds the little pillow they gave her at the hospital against her chest incision. Audra knows every medication Mom needs to take and when, what each is for. She tries to explain each pill's importance as she doles them out, but Mom sighs and says, "Please, dear, just give me the damn thing."

Jane is thrashing through the idea that her role in the world has changed, and she has no idea what she should be now. She's not Mom's caretaker and she's no longer a wife, except maybe legally until she and Andrew file papers. She's still a mother, of course, but even that is changing.

Emma is a wild, kicking colt, pulling away from Jane while at the same time needing her more than ever. Ten-year-olds are more like teenagers than we ever were. I know for a fact, and I tell Emma this whenever she'll listen, that I still had Barbies when I was ten.

Mom, of course, has changed the most of all of us. Her emotions have the snap of dry tinder; anything will set her off. Joy, sadness, anger can all make her cry at any given moment. She prays out loud, late at night and first thing in the morning. She is anything but the placid medicated mother I came home to. She is more like the mother from my childhood, but not so much the scary one. It's like rediscovering the other mother I'd forgotten about. The dancing, singing one, the storytelling one who had a playful glint in her eyes. The mother not like other moms, the one who seemed like my own precious thing and who made me want to grow up to be something just as special. The brighter side of an ever-changing moon.

I try not to worry so much about my mother's state of mind. *Que sera, sera,* I think. Whatever will be will just have to fucking be. It's like one of Sal's songs I listened to as a kid, the lyrics a mystery to me back then: *When you are worried, child, turn it over.* I'd picture flipping something upside down, never quite getting what that might be and how it would help, but I realize now she was talking about handing over your worries to God, or Jesus, her chosen sources of comfort. I've decided to release my worries to the sky, to some unknowable something out there. To the Big Gal, maybe. She's my Jesus.

I miss Sal, her full-bodied presence, her honeysuckle perfume, her wisdom. I never even hear her voice these days, but I know what she'd say in any given situation anyway. And I suppose it's an indicator of better mental health not to communicate with a dead blues singer.

I still worry sometimes that I caused my mother's heart to lose its steady beat, to dance so crazily out of sync, but if I did, so be it. Maybe it was the best thing that could have happened after all.

Rebecca is finally getting her ass out of Dodge. Some small-time record producer thinks she's the next Faith Hill and she's on her way to Nashville. Tomorrow. I hear about it as soon as I get to the bar Wednesday evening. Chuck follows me into the office, talking a mile a minute.

"She's leaving us high and dry, and this guy doesn't really seem like much of a producer to me," he says. "I mean, Faith Hill? Has he actually seen Rebecca? Heard her sing?" He picks up the cash drawers for me and follows me back out to the bar.

Normally I'd jump right on the let's-bash-Rebecca bandwagon, but I say, "Hey, at least she's getting a shot. Who knows? Maybe she'll hit the big time."

"Yeah," Chuck snorts, setting the drawers down to draw himself a beer. "And maybe she'll tank." He takes a sip, looks at me hard. "You know she doesn't have what it takes."

"What do you mean? She's got a great voice. She's a knockout. What else does it take?" I brush past him to the next register and he follows me.

"Moxie. And her voice is mediocre, no passion. Not like yours."

"Gee, Chuck, I didn't know you were such a fan."

"And anybody can be a knockout these days, with the right, let's just say, surgical help." He takes a long noisy slurp and smiles.

"Really?" I stop and ponder. "What, boobs? Nose?"

"You name it," he says and pushes through the swinging bar gate, heading for the stage. Then he stops, turns around. "I mean it about you, though, Tal. You really oughta be doing something with that talent of yours."

"Yeah, yeah." I wave him off. "Anyway, I am. I'm here, right? And now I'm a headliner."

"You know what I mean," he says, walking off again. "Don't get stuck here."

Later, when I take the stage for my set, I'm in a strange mood. What Chuck said haunts me, like a hazy dream that I can't quite remember. I realize I'm tired of playing other people's music. And the good news is, without Audra around, I'm the one in charge.

As the crowd chants their usual cacophony of requests, I lean across the pianos. "Let's do something different," I say to the Flamingo.

"And what, pray tell, do you have in mind?" Domingo is so accustomed to me changing things all the time he just leans his slender face into his palm, elbow sliding across his piano.

"Follow me." I play the intro for the song I've been working on.

It's a simple melody with an easy-enough chord progression, and when he's gotten the hang of it, I sing the first verse. *"Times they were dark and I was alone, and I never knew what would become of me."* The crowd settles, grows still, sensing that something different is happening. *"I never knew where I stood in this world 'cause I'd pulled every root just to get myself free."*

It's pretty low-key for this place, certainly not a party song, but the audience is swaying back and forth, and when we hit the chorus, I feel a shiver, like champagne bubbles up my spine, and I sing loud and strong, imagining gospel-choir background vocals and swelling strings. *"Now it's almost daylight. I can see you, baby, coming out of the night. I've been sinking, too much drinking, but now I'm almost home again."*

At the end of the song there is a round of applause, but not the usual rowdy scream and whistle kind. It swells nicely, lasts a bit longer than feels normal, and dies to quiet expectation. It's like playing a concert, where the audience actually wants to hear what you're about to perform.

I look at Domingo. "Got another?" he asks.

"Always," I say and launch into my favorite Holy Smokes song, one of the few I wrote without Jedd, "Little Girl Lost." Then we do a few more I've been working on, even though they're rough around the edges, and, finally, I tell the crowd, "Enough of this stuff you've never heard before. Who's got a request?"

"Do that first one again," a young woman with a bachelorette party says, and everyone claps.

I look at Domingo, shrugging, and he begins the song. He's already memorized it, and when we get to the chorus, he lays down awesome background vocals and plays an embellishing riff that almost sounds like the string section part I always imagine. I nearly stop playing, I'm so surprised, but he keeps playing, covering my stumble, and I pick it back up, our voices commingling and rising into the smoky blue air, dancing together like an old married couple.

The next morning I'm making coffee when Audra comes into the kitchen to get Mom some tea.

"So Chuck told me about Rebecca," I say nonchalantly, scooping coffee into the filter.

"Holy mother of God, it completely slipped my mind yesterday," she says, stopping in her tracks. "I'm sorry, Tallie."

"He says she's leaving today."

"You know, I just assumed you'd slip into her spot, and between you and Eileen and the guys, we'd make it work out."

"Yeah, I kind of assumed that, too." I'm acting calm, but I can barely contain a long looping "Woo hoo!"

"I'm relieved, to be honest," she says, lighting the burner under the kettle, then leaning against the counter. "She was always such a pain in the ass. I mean, if ever there was a prima donna . . ." She trails off, shaking her head. "You know, Tallie, I do realize you're doing a lot of extra—"

"That's okay," I say quickly, before she can change her mind. Then I remember last night. "Actually, I should probably tell you something."

"About . . ."

"I kind of messed with the set list last night." I take a seat at the table and grab a banana from the fruit bowl, peeling it and watching for her reaction.

She raises an eyebrow. "What's new? You're always messing with my carefully planned systems."

"I mean big-time. I did a whole set—well, Domingo and I did a whole set—of originals."

"Really." She looks at me for a long moment. I take a bite of banana, chew, and wait. Then she says, "And are you planning a mutiny? Is everyone going to start doing their own songs now?" She leans farther back, grabbing the edges of the counter, her fingernails playing a little drum solo on the tile.

I can't tell if she's kidding or angry. As close as we've grown recently, when it comes to work I still feel like I'm in the principal's office with her. "No, of course not," I assure her. "It was just a whim."

She's quiet for a moment; then she asks, "So how'd it go?"

"Pretty good. People liked the songs." Relieved, I get up and stick my head in the fridge, looking for the OJ. "They were even requesting them by the end of the set." I take a long swig from the carton and fish a glass from the cupboard. When I sit back down and look at her, it's obvious her brain is whirring.

"So why wouldn't you do it again?" she asks.

"I just thought . . ."

"Not every night, mind you," she says.

"Of course not."

"Maybe on Thursdays."

"Sure."

"We'll call it 'Artist Showcase' night or something."

"Great."

She gives me a look. "Not 'Tallie Beck' night. Everyone gets to participate."

"Of course," I say, grinning. "Cool."

"I'm not opposed to new ideas," she says, pouring steaming water into Mom's teacup. "You can just ask, you know." She walks past me on her way to help Mom get ready for the day. In the doorway she turns. "I trust you, Tallie. You've got a good head on your shoulders. That's why you're running the place."

I have a mouthful of banana, so I just nod. She pushes through the door and then there's the murmur of voices in Mom's room. I sit there, chewing, trying on this new feeling. I'm not sure anyone's ever trusted me before.

39

♪ It's been only a few weeks since Mom's surgery, and the crazy woman is already hosting a Sunday-night gathering. "I have to have a holiday party," she insisted. No one else argued with her, not Audra or even Jane, so neither did I. And, after I'd dropped more than a few hints, Mom finally realized that maybe she should invite Jane.

Now, Mom looks radiant, holding a wineglass full of ginger ale, settled into the overstuffed chair with strict orders from Audra not to move without her assistance. Her flowing, multicolored caftan covers her scars and drapes a much thinner body, but with her up-swept hair in a messy knot and lipstick, she looks the best she has since Thanksgiving.

The place is jammed. Everyone wants to talk to her, lining up to have their moment with her as she holds court. The usual noisy din and clatter is much more restrained and no one puts their clunky shoes on the furniture. It's like a celebration instead of a schmooze-fest. Everyone I've ever met at these things, and some I haven't, comes up and tells me how glad they are that Mom is going to be okay.

"It would have been an unimaginable loss to our little community," says the raisin, the perpetually turbaned Miranda. She takes my hand in her clawlike one, squeezes with her arthritic fingers. Deep within her wrinkled face her eyes are welling. Suddenly mine are, too, and we laugh and turn away in embarrassment.

Jane arrives by herself, standing in the doorway and staring wide-eyed into the crowd. She looks the way she did when Domingo cajoled her on stage at Sing Out!

I walk over to take her coat and she smiles gratefully at the sight of me.

"Boy, this is a lot of people," she says, and I look around at the strange collection of Mom's compadres. I remember all too clearly being at one of these things for the first time. After a moment, she sighs. "So, why do you suppose she finally invited me?"

"I don't know," I say carefully. "But she did."

The lines in her forehead relax and she nods, rubbing her arms like she's cold, even though it's a million degrees in here with all these people.

I point into the crowd. "See that throng of worshippers? Mom's in the middle of it somewhere."

"Yeah, I see Audra's hair," she says, but she makes no move to enter the fray. We stand there for a while, taking it all in. Behind us, the door opens and I turn to see Damian and Mia.

"Hey, you guys," I say, relieved. "Meet my sister, Jane."

Damian goes into his Lee Jackson-worship routine, and I leave my baby sister there to learn how to fend for herself in Mom's world. She's in polite mode, nodding and saying, "Mmm," in the appropriate places, but I wonder how she's taking the nose ring.

I inch along the wall toward my room so I can put her coat on my bed and stand there for a while in the dark, looking out the window at random snowflakes flitting downward toward the street. I am surrounded by people, by my family, even, and still, I can't shake that same old lonely feeling. Finally, I take a deep breath and head back into the party.

Perry is standing near the front door, holding daisies and looking nervous. My first thought is to turn right back around and hide out in my room, but then we make eye contact. He nods, pulls his lips into a quick tight smile that looks more like a grimace. He's here to see my mother. Seeing me just comes with the package, but I want him to really see me, to know I still exist, so I push through bodies until I'm in front of him.

"Hi," he says, looking at me, then past me.

"Hi, yourself," I say, cool, calm.

"I wanted to, uh, come see Lee." The collar on his shirt is too tight and I want to reach over and unbutton it for him, but instead I take his coat.

"I know," I say. "She'll be thrilled. She's right over there." I turn to walk away, holding his coat against me until I'm safely in my room again. There I lift it to my face, breathe in the smell of him lodged in its fibers, rub the scratchy wool across my face.

When I come out again, I know my eyes are red, but I figure people will chalk it up to all the emotion surrounding my mother. Perry is sitting back on his heels next to her chair, the flowers lying across her lap. I am so jealous I could throw up. After a while, he stands and leans over to kiss the top of her head, and she takes his hand between hers. They look at each other for a long moment, smiling, then Perry looks up and catches me watching them. His smile doesn't waver, but he turns back to Mom and tells her something that makes her laugh.

I feel my face flush and busy myself picking up empties and taking orders for refills, then head for the kitchen. I pray he'll be gone when I come back out.

The usual array of wine bottles lines the counter, plus the new addition of plastic liters of ginger ale and seltzer. I stand and study the wine bottles, trying to figure out what the old tweed couple meant by "that nice Merlot."

"I remember the first time I saw you, standing right there."

I turn, and Perry's in the doorway. He's wearing his vintage shirt, something I didn't notice before, and he fills it out better than he used to. "You scared me," I say.

He nods at the bottles. "You were trying to figure out which wine you should have. You stood there for the longest time, studying, like there was going to be a test."

"I had no idea which was which," I say, picking up one of the bottles. "Hell, I still don't. Fumé Blanc. Why would you drink something with fumes?"

"You thought I was a wino." He says it evenly.

"Maybe," I say, putting the bottle back. "But it was me who turned out to be the drunk."

He nods and looks down. I follow his gaze. He's wearing the cool two-tone shoes he wore to the bar that first time.

"I didn't come here just to see your mother," he says to the floor. Then, looking back up, he says, "You walked away too fast for me to tell you that."

"Oh." I take this in for a moment, then say again, "Oh."

He sighs and slumps inside the door frame. "I wanted to hate you, Tallie, but I couldn't. How could I blame you for choosing a rock star over a . . . over me?"

"But I didn't choo—"

"And I know I had some part in your doing, you know, what you did."

"No," I say. "I got drunk and fucked my ex." I bite my lip and tears come to my eyes. "My fault, not yours."

He walks over to stand just in front of me, so close I can smell soap and clean laundry, something recently cooked for dinner. "It's not like we were engaged, Tallie, or even going steady," he says. "We were just getting to know each other."

He closes his eyes and sighs, then opens them. "But here's the main thing I wanted to tell you." He looks at me intently. "I know you weren't getting what you needed from me, and I wasn't doing anything about it. I could have gone to the shrink, asked him to adjust my meds, or change them or something. But, I don't know. Maybe I wasn't ready for a relationship, maybe I just sabotaged it, you know?" His brow furrows, and he looks at his shoes again.

Tears fall down my face and I sniff a loud, embarrassing, wet snort. He looks up, eyes red now and moist, and smiles. Then, serious again, he says, "But, if it makes you feel better, I'll give you the drunk part. That's definitely your fault. You need to do something about that."

I nod. "I know."

After a long moment, I take a deep breath and ask, "So, what now?"

"I don't know." He shakes his head. "We can't just go back to what we were. It wouldn't be the same."

I pull away to wipe my face, my nose, on my sleeve. "I know."

"I'm just saying—"

"I know," I say again quickly. "I was kind of on the road to getting over you, too, believe it or not."

He swallows hard and nods. "Oh," he says, shifting his weight, putting his hands in his pockets, then withdrawing them and crossing his arms. He nods again, says, "Okay," and starts toward the door.

"Perry," I say quietly, so quietly I'm afraid he won't hear.

He stops in front of the door. "What?" He doesn't turn around.

"Maybe we could start over, sometime, try again. Maybe we could just take things a little more . . . I don't know. Slowly."

He turns around and gives me a long look. I have never seen eyes so blue.

"Maybe," he says.

40

The evening sky is rosy purple, puffy dark clouds edged in black with a pink glow rimming the mountains from the last remnants of sun. It's only April, but already warm enough at night that I wear just a thin sweater over my stage clothes, tonight a slinky top made from some sparkly synthetic and a long, tight but stretchy skirt. Audra removed the "assistant" part of my title a month or so ago and my first official act was to eighty-six the polo shirts.

I push my growing-out hair behind my ears as I walk along, but it pops stubbornly back out. I've come to accept my natural brown color, but occasionally I study the Miss Clairol boxes at the drugstore, still convinced in some perverse way that blondes really might have more fun.

My walk to the bar is longer now, all the way from the apartment I rent from Audra in her newest investment property north of downtown. The building will eventually be rehabbed into lofts and I'll have to move out, but for now it's a place of my own—my own kitchen, my own bathroom, my own combination living room/bedroom with a comfortable old chair from Goodwill, a futon and the quilt from my bed at Mom's house. She said my grandmother made it some fifty years ago, and she put it inside one of my boxes when I wasn't looking.

It makes my mother nervous that I walk through such dicey

parts of town to work, but it's my best thinking time, before I hit the raucous commotion of the bar. This is the last night I'll ever be thirty-four, the year I began again, so I walk slowly, taking long lazy pulls off a Salem, "reflecting" as the Big Gal would have said.

Rows of boarded-up windows and security-barred storefronts, bars, and Mexican restaurants eventually give way to architects' offices and sports bars. The top of the massive new baseball stadium dominates the skyline a few blocks over. Since its construction a few years ago, the homeless problem has grown worse than ever, according to Perry. This neighborhood used to house poor people in its run-down apartments and street people in its alleys and doorways. Who knows where they've all gone. Most of the shelters were operating at capacity as it was.

I turn right at Eighteenth, walk a short block then round the corner to Wyanee. As I walk past Beelzebub's, I wave at Damian inside. He motions for me to come in and I push through the door into a burnt-coffee haze.

"I gotta go easy on the caffeine, D.," I say. Then I notice what he's trying to show me. Mom has replaced the painting above the espresso maker with a nighttime scene of our block, the neon Sing Out! sign blazing orange-red over shiny wet streets. I look closely, and through her painted window there is a piano and someone playing it, barely an inch tall. It's a girl with short dark hair and a skimpy black dress. You see from the turn of her head and the rise of her shoulders that she loves singing more than anything else.

"I like your mom's new style," Damian says. "It's, like, a return to the traditionalists' search for meaning in the mundane."

I nod and smile, but I realize that he's missed the entire point.

Back outside, I walk past Mom's building feeling only slightly guilty for not stopping. I'm still required to attend family dinner night once a month, which is plenty of familial interaction for me, thank you very much. Mom and I are still careful around each other, still smarting from a lifetime of blows, but there are times when we forget ourselves and the dark horrible things between us disappear for a little while. We could be any mother and daughter, chatting aimlessly while we chop onions, or reminiscing about some pleasant moment from our past I'd forgotten about. My mother's memory is amazing and selective—even though she rarely claims to remember the bad stuff, she remembers every single good moment our family ever had.

The lights from the bar are warm and welcoming, and I feel instantly at home in the friendly hubbub of bar chatter. It's quiet for a Friday night, but then again it's the day after tax day. I hang out behind the bar, watching the door like I'm expecting someone, but I don't know who it could be. I hear Jedd hit the road with his new band, which does not include Pat on keyboards but does include some nineteen-year-old girl singer named Destiny, of all things. Jason works at a trendy new bar in the restaurant district of Uptown. Not surprisingly, the girls who used to occupy his end of the bar have disappeared, too.

When it's time for my set, I notice a nice-enough-looking man in the front row of tables. He seems out of place, unaccompanied and dressed in a suit. He smiles and watches me intently, so I play to him, just to give him a thrill. He's probably on a business trip, missing the wife and kids at home.

About halfway through the set, he stands and pushes a cocktail napkin across my piano. "Play one of yours" it reads.

I lean away from the mike and ask, "Which one?"

"Whichever one you like best," he says and sits back down.

I don't know what kind of game we're playing here, but I go along, play the intro for "Almost Daylight." It's become my signature song on Artist Showcase nights. When we reach the chorus, the audience sings along. The man pulls a little notebook from his coat pocket and writes in it.

Chuck raises his eyebrows at me. I shrug back. Probably some lonely weirdo, an occupational hazard. Luckily, he leaves before the end of the set, or I'd feel obligated to talk to him.

At the end of the night, I'm closing out the drawers while Eileen washes glasses. "Hey, I almost forgot," she says, wiping a hand on her apron and digging into her back pocket. "Some guy said to give this to you." She hands me a business card, bent at one corner and rounded from her rear end.

"Oh, God. I bet I know which guy it was, too," I say, taking the card. "Did you see that lonely businessman up front?" I make a face, then read it. "Holy shit, Eileen, who gave you this?" I look around quickly, but all the customers are gone.

"Some guy in a suit." She shrugs. "He said to tell you Lyle sent him."

"Look!" I shove it at her. "Cool Town Records! He's from fucking Cool Town Records, the best damned blues label there is!"

"Oh, my God," she says, turning it over. "And he wrote on the back: 'Let's talk. Call collect, anytime.'" She looks up at me, eyes shining, then waves everyone over, saying, "You guys! Check it out—a record guy wants to talk to Tallie!" And then everyone's standing around me, congratulating me, and I'm saying, "For what? For getting a business card?" but it's pretty much the most exciting thing that's ever happened in my whole goddamned life.

I am flying down the highway, headed east into a rising fireball of sun. I suppose I'm in a car. I can't really tell. I'm just flying over miles and miles of road, black and snakelike ahead of me, dotted white line blipping past like Morse code. Blipping a message: Go, go, go. The world around me cracks wide apart like an egg, revealing the potential of life inside. Rolling hills sprout green growth, crisscrossed with blue lines of creeks and rivers, all going somewhere. The sky spans over and around me, open to all possibility.

I hear a high girlish voice in the distance, singing, *"I got them traveling blues, but my man wants me to stay. You know I'd like to ride, but maybe I should wait. Traveling blues, Lord, they got me down today . . ."*

Reluctantly, I wake enough to realize it's Emma. She spent the night and she's sitting out in the kitchen, strumming my Strat. There's an empty dent next to me on the futon, and I smell coffee brewing, hear cooking noises. I open my eyes and see Emma's makeshift bed on the floor—the chair cushion, an assortment of pillows, a wadded-up blanket. I stretch and roll over.

Emma's doing her best to growl out the Big Gal Sal song I've been teaching her. I figure if she's going to be a musician, she might as well start with the basics, the Delta blues, and who better to learn from than the Queen? I hum along with her, eyes closed, then sing loudly on the last line: *"So what's a poor gal to do when she's got them traveling blues, anyway?"*

She giggles when we've finished. "Aunt Tallie, are you awake?"

"Well, now I am," I say with mock exasperation.

"Perry's trying to make French toast and he's making a mess," she singsongs in her tattletale voice.

As much as I love my scrawny niece, I'm looking forward to tonight when she's back at home and Perry and I are alone. His new medication is just what the doctor ordered, if you get my drift.

Emma's getting impatient. "Aunt Tallie, we need you."

"I know, Miss Thing, I know," I say and get up to begin the day.

RIDING WITH THE QUEEN

♪

Jennie Shortridge

This Conversation Guide is intended to enrich the
individual reading experience, as well as encourage us
to explore these topics together—because books,
and life, are meant for sharing.

A CONVERSATION WITH JENNIE SHORTRIDGE

❖

Q. What inspired you to start writing Riding with the Queen?

A. Like Tallie's mother, Lee, my mother struggled with bipolar disorder. Unlike Lee, however, my mom grew progressively worse over the years and died a very early death in 1990 at the age of 57. I've been writing about my mother for most of my adult life, but this time I wanted to write a fairy tale—I suppose to try to console myself. What if Mom had found a way to get better? I realized through writing the book, of course, that the real issues of mental illness had to prevail. Dealing with it is a constant struggle, one that some people are better equipped to handle than others.

Q. Have you experienced Tallie's trying life on the road?

A. Although I've been a working musician on and off since I was sixteen years old, I've never been nearly as successful as Tallie. In the mid-1980s, my band, The Untouchables, played nearly every week, but we all worked day jobs in Denver, so we really couldn't travel too far afield. If our gigs were out of town, we shared crummy motel rooms, but more often, we were driving home at three or four in the morning so that we could get to our respective day jobs by eight, then make the two- or three-hour drive back to the gig that evening.

Q. Who are your literary influences?

A. My three sisters and I were voracious readers from an early age, inspired by our mother. As a kid, I sought out books about characters overcoming obstacles and social injustices: *Berries Goodman* by Emily Cheney Neville, *Adventures of Huckleberry Finn* by Mark Twain, and *To Kill a Mockingbird* by Harper Lee. In my young adulthood, it became Alice Walker, Barbara Kingsolver, Julia Alvarez, Louise Erdrich, Rita Mae Brown, John Irving, and Tom Robbins for good depraved fun. Michael Dorris's *A Yellow Raft in Blue Water* deeply affected me. Recent favorites include Nick Hornby, Sarah Waters, Charles Baxter, Manil Suri, but I find I can't read while writing, so my intake is pretty limited these days.

Q. Does your music somehow inform your writing, and vice versa?

A. I wrote poetry from a young age and it was always set to music in my mind, so that's how I became a songwriter. Once I began to seriously write for magazines and develop my fiction, the songs stopped coming, but I find that rhythm and cadence are still very important to me. I can't stand a sentence without the right rhythm!

Q. Did you ever have an old blues singer for a conscience? Who are your musical role models?

A. I've never had a guardian angel or ghost, but I think as a child I always wished there was someone there who could take care of my sisters and me when times got bad. When Big Gal Sal popped into the story, it surprised me but comforted me, too. I've loved old blues music since being introduced to it by Bonnie Raitt's records in the early 1970s, and I think of those old blues performers as musical elders, our rock-and-roll ancestors.

As a writer, I've been very influenced by brilliant storytelling songwriters like Elvis Costello, Shawn Colvin, and early Jackson Brown. If I could do in print what they do in song, I'd be thrilled.

Q. You capture the range of human emotion so well in Riding with the Queen. *Did you learn something about yourself while writing this book? Do you see yourself in Tallie?*

A. Tallie is willing to do and say things that I sometimes wished I'd been able to, but she's not based on me. I didn't act out as a kid—I was always the quintessential good girl, a little bit like Jane. I think that was the fun of writing Tallie, living vicariously through her.

I set out to write this palliative fairy tale, to make sense of growing up with a mentally ill mother, and ended up relearning old lessons as Tallie learned them for the first time. Mental illness is a disease like any disease of the body. Those who suffer from it are not trying to be sick and can't simply change themselves by trying harder, just as someone with cancer or heart disease can't. All we as friends or family members can do is change our perspective and try to be as understanding and caring as possible while making sure we take good care of ourselves.

Q. Jedd is a great foil to Tallie—he seems to be written with a lot of attention and animosity. Do you know musicians like Jedd?

A. I think Jedd is an amalgam of men and musicians I have known, certainly, but no one I was ever personally involved with, thank God!

Q. Has it been difficult to be a female musician in a largely male-dominated industry?

A. Not in my infinitesimally small experience of being a musician, but then again, I was always a singer in a band of guys—a very acceptable format.

Q. Would you like to say something about singing in a band with your husband?

A. I met my husband, Matt, in a band that never got off the ground. When it fell apart, we became an acoustic duo (he's a guitarist) because we had no equipment. But it was a godsend. I was turning thirty and had no desire to hang out in smoky bars and sing for five hours a night anymore. We played in coffeehouses and at outdoor festivals, doing one- or two-hour shows. My ears stopped ringing. My voice softened. I got some sleep. And I found my wonderful life partner.

Q. Your book is ultimately about redemption and forgiveness. Did you know how it was going to end when you started writing?

A. I knew the basic story line from beginning to end but very few of the details. I didn't know how the characters would act and react under the weight of the situations, and I didn't know at what points they would break or bend or rise above. For me, the fun of writing is experiencing what happens as it happens.

Q. What do you consider important secondary themes?

A. My mission at this point in life seems to be to try to express themes of tolerance and acceptance. From Lee and Audra's relationship to Perry's homelessness, I wanted to show that people are widely diverse, sometimes suffering, sometimes surviving, and sometimes thriving because of their choices, but always, I believe, doing the best they can.

I used a lot of religious imagery and wording in the book to express my views of spirituality. I understand that organized religion works well for some people, but some of us find our spirituality in the everyday, in the small quiet moments of life, in the love we give and receive. I think it's as valid a religion as any other.

Q. *Describe your writing process. Do you have any strange peccadilloes or work habits when you write?*

A. Every morning after breakfast, I trundle off to my little home office with my second cup of coffee, still in my pajamas with my hair sticking out and my teeth unbrushed. I write until I get hungry again, about noon, then go get dressed for the day, take a break, and move on to editing or other tasks. If I try to write in the afternoon, it's like going into a coma or something. I get blocked, frustrated, and write stiff uninspired crap. Mornings are my creative time.

Q. *How long did it take you to write* Riding with the Queen?

A. It took me a little less than a year to write the first draft. Because I was in this huge learning curve, trying to figure out how to write a novel, my revisions and rewrites seemed endless, about another two years.

Q. *What are you working on now?*

A. I'm writing a novel about a freelance food writer with big-time food issues. She's losing someone she dearly loves to cancer, dealing with an emotionally distant mother, and trying to unravel the mysteries of her family's secrets while at the same time trying not to eat herself into blimplike proportions. Like Tallie, like many of us I suppose, she's on a mission to understand her past so she can move on with her life.

QUESTIONS FOR DISCUSSION

❖

1. In the beginning of the book, Jane tells Tallie that their mother's mental illness is no longer a problem. Tallie discovers that this isn't always the case, however, and carries the secret with her for some time. How does she learn to cope with, and finally to accept, her mother's illness?

2. How does Lee's artwork change throughout the story and what do you think this means? How do these changes relate to her tumultuous relationship with Tallie?

3. On page 250, Tallie, Lee, Emma, and Jane are having dinner together. Tallie describes the group as: "The core of our family . . . intricately connected by blood and time and something else more complicated but much less tangible." How is this statement general to all families? How is it specific to this one?

4. In the book, almost every character has a coping mechanism—Lee paints, Perry seeks solace by helping people on the streets, and Tallie channels Big Gal Sal when she's anxious. How does Jane deal with the pressures in her life? How is this different from how the others cope? How is it the same?

5. What prompts Jane to begin to forgive Tallie for running away? Do you think Jane owes Tallie an apology as well?

6. Many of Tallie's problems—including her alcoholism and emotionally destructive one-night stands—stem from her inability to control the circumstances of her life. What do you think is the turning point in the novel when Tallie is finally able to take charge of her own behavior? When does she finally start accepting responsibility for her actions? Why?

7. What role does Emma play in the family dynamics? Why do she and Tallie develop such a close relationship?

8. Roots are a significant symbol in this novel. In chapter four, Tallie ruins her hair by trying to touch up her roots. Later, Jedd manipulates her with his promise that she will sing in his roots rock revival band. What is the author trying to tell us about Tallie's attempts to embrace her roots? What do you think Tallie learns from her attempts to reconnect with her family? Is Tallie's return a failure or a success? Why?

9. What is Perry's definition of courage?

10. How do the themes of homelessness echo throughout the book?

11. In what ways does Tallie mature by the end of the novel? In what ways does she still need to grow?